Rebuilding a Dream

America's new urban crisis, the housing cost explosion, and how we can reinvent the American dream for all

By Andre F. Shashaty

Rebuilding a Dream

Partnership for Sustainable Communities
914 Mission Ave., Suite 4A
San Rafael, CA 94901

Ordering Information:
Quantity sales. Special discounts are available on quantity purchases by
corporations, associations, and others. For details, contact the publisher at the
address above or by email: carol@p4sc.org.
Orders by U.S. trade bookstores and wholesalers. Please contact Carol Fung at
415-453-2100 x 302.

Printed in the United States of America

Publisher's Cataloging-In-Publication Data
Shashaty, Andre.

Rebuilding a Dream: America's new urban crisis, the housing cost explosion,
and how we can reinvent the American dream for all/Andre Shashaty.

ISBN 978-0-9905187-0-9

1. urban policy—housing – United States
2. U.S. Department of Housing and Urban Development.
3. urban development – urban planning
4. affordable housing
5. sustainability – sustainable communities

First Edition
14 13 12 11 10 / 10 9 8 7 6 5 4 3 2 1

Printed in U.S.
Printed on recycled paper with soy based ink

Tell your colleagues about this book!

Thanks for purchasing my book on housing. If you like what you read, please tell your friends and colleagues about it.

The Partnership for Sustainable Communities is a small nonprofit without any government or foundation support. I have worked as a volunteer since starting it in 2010.

We depend entirely on word of mouth to help market this book and get out its pro-housing message. Proceeds from sale of the book and donations from individuals like you are critical to our survival.

Help us get this book out to policymakers and opinion leaders, and continue educating them about how to make American communities more socially, economically and environmentally sustainable.

• Tell your colleagues to buy "Rebuilding a Dream." It's on sale at Amazon, and from http://www.sustainabilitystore.org/

• Make a donation here at the conference, or later by going to www.p4sc.org (click on the "Donate Now" button in the green bar at the very top of the home page)

* Become a corporate member of PSC for $500 for for-profit firms and $400 for nonprofits (per year).

• Buy multiple copies of the book and give some out to policymakers, opinion leaders and colleagues. Call 415-453-2100, ext 302 for special pricing.

Sincerely,

Andre Shashaty, President
Partnership for Sustainable Communities
Visit us at: www.P4SC.org

On the Cover

Cottonwood Creek Apartments is a 94-apartment affordable family development in Suisun City, Calif., by BRIDGE Housing Corp., using federal housing tax credits. It consists of four garden-style walk-up apartment buildings in the Craftsman style. Amenities at the property include a community building plus open spaces featuring a pool, a pool building, tot lot, a play area, a playing field, and a picnic area. The property was designed with many environmentally friendly features, such as landscaping that minimizes the buildings' solar gain in the summer, rooftop solar panels that supply all the electricity for the common areas, and energy- and water-efficient fixtures and appliances throughout.

Architect: KTGY Group
General Contractor: Segue Construction
Financial Partners: Suisun City Redevelopment Agency, state of
California, Silicon Valley Bank, Union Bank

Photo Credit: Keith Baker
http://www.keithbakerphotography.com/

Dedication

This book is dedicated to the people who are homeless in America. We see them every single day, but in a sense they are invisible, an unpleasant part of the scenery, like potholes. Our government has committed to keeping our military veterans from being homeless, but, for most other groups, homelessness at some level has become an accepted fact of life.

Some of us try to help, from the staff at housing providers and shelter operators to the volunteers at free dining rooms. But for many Americans, the homeless are like the lepers of olden times. They are shunned and viewed with disgust.

It's true, there is sickness here, but it's in our body politic, not in the homeless. Making progress to reduce this shameful condition is the strongest argument there is for governments at all levels to get their acts together on housing, and to do it soon.

To any homeless person who sees this book, I dedicate it to you in the hope that it might make some small difference in your ability to eventually find a place to call home.

Andre F. Shashaty

Acknowledgements

For their good work in helping prepare this book for publication, many thanks go to Jennifer Downey and Christine Serlin for editing and Kay Marshall for design and typesetting. I received important help with research from Wesley Palmer. For general assistance, inspiration, and moral support, I want to thank Kevin Collins, Betty Pagett, Todd Sears, and Patrick Sheridan.

For administrative support, my appreciation goes to Carol Fung.

Organizations that provided important support include Low Income Investment Fund (LIIF), Mercy Housing, Pacific Companies, Retirement Housing Foundation, Volunteers of America, Herman & Kittle, and the John Stewart Company.

I want to thank the people who have worked in government agencies and nonprofit groups to provide affordable housing and revitalize our cities. I've met many of them, and I know how hard they work, often at lower pay than they could get in other careers. I admire their dedication and public spirit.

Recognition must also go to people at for-profit development companies who choose to do the very hard work of affordable housing construction and rehab. Many of them could have made far more money doing other things, but they kept fighting the odds to provide housing for lower-income Americans.

Table of Contents

Table of Contents vii

Preface viii

About This Book xv

SECTION I • Housing & Cities in Distress

Chapter 1   Urban Decay Returns...3

Chapter 2   The New American Slums 13

Chapter 3   The Many Victims of Homelessness...............................27

Chapter 4   Struggling to Find Affordable Housing..........................41

Chapter 5   The Bounce-Back Kids 55

Chapter 6   The High Cost of Neglect..63

SECTION II • The Seeds of Hope & Change

Chapter 7   Unleashing the Power of Revitalization..........................77

Chapter 8   America's Housing Success Story....................................91

Chapter 9   Transforming Neighborhoods & Lives...........................103

Chapter 10   Reinvesting in Communities 115

Chapter 11   Restoring the Potential of Homeownership..................125

Chapter 12   Toward a Strategic Vision 135

SECTION III • Retreat from Success

Chapter 13   The Not So Great Society 153

Chapter 14   Shrinking Housing Safety Net 163

Chapter 15   Leaving Grandma Out In the Cold................................177

Chapter 16   The Disinvestment Dilemma...185

Chapter 17   The Anti-Affordability Conspiracy 193

Chapter 18   Why We Hate Housing 207

Chapter 19   Slamming The Door on America's Dream.....................221

SECTION IV • Conclusion

Chapter 20   Where We Go From Here...237

Appendices & Bibliography

Appendix A

Housing & Race: The Issue That Won't Go Away 249

Appendix B

A Citizen's Guide to Improving Housing & Communities 255

End Notes..263

Bibliography 275

Index...286

Preface

It must have seemed like all hell was breaking loose in 1965. The United States sent more troops to Vietnam. In the American South, violent clashes erupted over civil rights. Malcolm X was murdered on the streets of upper Manhattan.

The Beatles performed at New York's Shea Stadium, and Jefferson Airplane debuted in San Francisco. The Rolling Stones captured the mood of the nation best, rocketing to the top of the charts with "(I Can't Get No) Satisfaction."

Then, on a hot afternoon in August, a traffic arrest on the streets of South Central Los Angeles lit the fuse on one of the most devastating civil upheavals in American history. The black residents of Watts rebelled against a mayor and a police force many considered to be racist. The fires and the violence raged for six days, resulting in 34 deaths and the destruction, damage, or looting of 1,000 buildings.

The riot was a fiery exclamation point on a long debate about what should be done to fix America's cities. National politicians and urban leaders had argued for years that slum conditions and racial segregation in our major cities had to be addressed.

Galvanized by the destruction in LA, the federal government accelerated implementation of new housing and urban programs enacted that year. President Lyndon B. Johnson signed a law creating a new Cabinet agency dedicated to creating more affordable housing and revitalizing our cities. In early 1966, the U.S. Department of Housing and Urban Development (HUD) opened for business. It was headed by Robert Weaver, the first black Cabinet secretary in America's history.

It was the hopeful beginning of a series of new federal programs and tax incentives intended to revitalize decaying inner cities and provide affordable housing. It inspired similar initiatives by state governments and launched a whole new industry of nonprofit housing and community development organizations.

But instead of celebrating the 50th anniversary of this historic federal commitment to cities, we are facing a new crisis in our handling of housing and urban development.

After five decades of progress, older cities are slipping back into decay, and the blight is spreading to suburban locations and Sunbelt towns previously thought immune to "urban problems."

The shortage of affordable housing is reaching crisis proportions, especially for poor residents of our cities, but also for moderate-income people in suburban and rural areas. The failure of the government to get the mortgage markets back in order has put the American dream of homeownership out of reach for more and more families.

City streets, parks, and highway underpasses have become the living rooms, bedrooms, and bathrooms for many thousands of homeless people, including young adults, the elderly, and veterans returning from war, many with chronic mental and physical health issues.

There were 1.17 million homeless children of school age during the 2011-2012 school year, according the Department of Education.

Well more than 8 million additional Americans are just one missed paycheck or unexpected expense from being homeless as they struggle to pay rents that eat up half of their household incomes. Others trade low rents for the pitfalls of overcrowding, substandard conditions, or neighborhoods riddled by violent crime.

The halting recovery

You may have heard about a housing market recovery, but it has not reversed the damage done by the foreclosure crisis. The rate at which banks started foreclosure actions declined in 2013. But years of elevated foreclosures have done long-lasting damage to hundreds of neighborhoods and sent some cities tumbling into bankruptcy, and others hovering on the brink.

The foreclosure crisis has turned many fledgling middle-class areas into the new American slums. Since 2007, there have been roughly 4.5 million completed foreclosures in the country. More than 900,000 homes in the United States were in some stage of foreclosure and about 2 million owners were seriously delinquent on their mortgages as of August 2013.

The rash of foreclosures affects entire neighborhoods, as lenders take control of homes but don't always maintain them or resell them. These vacant homes deteriorate, creating blight and inducing crime. They put added demands on city services while reducing overall property tax revenues, the mainstay of municipal finances.

But instead of redoubling efforts to help cities and address housing quality and affordability, the federal government and many states are doing the exact opposite: They are rolling back a 50-year record of government programs aimed at improving lower-income communities and helping minorities move up the economic ladder.

Right-wing extremists and think tanks have mounted a full-scale attack on federal programs that benefit urban areas and create affordable housing.

They contend that the government does too much to help cities, and that this comes at the cost of suburban areas. It is a politically expedient but dangerously misguided characterization of the challenges we face to create and maintain stable, equitable communities.

Funding for programs that help low-income and minority communities and individuals have been cut repeatedly. For example, elderly Americans who are dependent on meager Social Security checks for survival and cannot afford market-rate housing recently learned the government would no longer finance construction of specially designed housing where they can live out their years in safety and economic security.

For cities struggling to find money for basic services, including police and fire protection, the cuts in housing and community development programs hit hard. Most could not even think about making up for cuts in federal programs out of local revenues.

• • •

After Martin Luther King Jr. was killed in 1968, Congress passed the Fair Housing Act to ban discrimination in housing. Later that year, it passed a law intended to create more housing for poor people and give them the ability to move out of inner cities to communities with more opportunity.

The Housing and Urban Development Act of 1968 created a wide array of new government programs intended to eliminate slum conditions in America's cities.

President Johnson called this law "the Magna Carta to liberate our cities." He said it would enable his government to "win a new right for every American in every city and on every country road. That new right is the fundamental and the very precious American right to a roof over your head—a decent home."

I was only 14 at the time. I did not begin to comprehend the importance of what King and Johnson had set in motion until 11 years later, when I left my Ohio home for Washington, D.C. I landed a job as a reporter covering HUD, which was still relatively new at the time.

Jimmy Carter was in his last year as president, and many of the young HUD staffers I met still believed in Johnson's vision of a Great Society. They worked long hours to prove that government could solve our nation's worst social problems. They believed that racial equality was an achievable goal and that decades of discrimination in housing could be eliminated.

After 33 years as a reporter, editor, and publisher on the housing and urban policy beat, I have seen firsthand the progress that's been made under the programs Johnson put in place and the many others that followed.

> *We know that investing in housing and urban vitality pays many dividends.*

I have interviewed hundreds of mayors, housing agency executives, lenders, investors, and developers. I've talked to people who live in government-assisted housing and those who wish they could. I have written about the big picture of government policy and the details of how housing is financed, designed, developed, and managed.

My reporting has taken me to affordable housing developments from townhouses in Southeast Washington, D.C., to supportive single-room occupancy properties on Skid Row in Los Angeles.

I have chronicled the work of visionaries like James Rouse, the real estate developer who defied the naysayers by turning rundown parts of Baltimore, Boston, and New York into thriving retail marketplaces and later founded one of the biggest nonprofit financiers of affordable housing. I've seen the transformation of rundown blocks into vibrant neighborhoods in city after city.

I have seen how decent housing changes the lives of troubled and impoverished people. I have documented over and over how the benefits extend beyond the people who live in those properties to the larger communities in which they are located.

Today, after years of economic difficulty and budget cuts, we risk losing much of the ground we have gained. There's a widespread belief that we can no longer afford to devote federal resources to cities and to affordable housing.

There's an increasing willingness to tolerate the post-foreclosure wave of urban decay and the increase in homelessness, as if they are inevitable facts of life in the new millennium.

Finally, even though we elected a black man to be president twice, racial segregation in housing has made an ignominious comeback, and divisions between Americans of different incomes and races are growing.

• • •

The problems of lower-income communities, both inner cities and the new suburban slums, are complex and difficult to solve. Long-term progress requires a multifaceted effort that encompasses job training, job creation, education, and much more.

But the most fundamental requirement is the availability of decent housing in safe neighborhoods with access to jobs and services like public transit.

With all the recent discussions about income inequality, it's time to recognize that housing affordability and the mobility of lower-income households are crucial factors in their ability to move up economically and narrow the income gap.

Lyndon Johnson recognized that areas with concentrated poverty were the factories of inequality in America. Sen. Robert Kennedy knew it. A long list of prominent Republicans also understood that dynamic, including George Romney, President Richard Nixon's housing secretary. More recently, the late Rep. Jack Kemp campaigned for the same goals of breaking the cycle of poverty with federal investments in housing and urban economic development.

George W. Bush made a very strong case for government and private lenders to work together to increase the percentage of minority households who owned their homes.

Until recently, concern for housing and urban development was bipartisan. I think it still is among our citizens, if not our elected officials in Washington. Americans of all political stripes know our system has failed in a fundamental way as they see more and more people camped out on their streets and under bridges because they can't afford a place to live. They know that it's tragic for children to grow up in overcrowded apartments in crime-plagued neighborhoods because there is no affordable housing in a safer part of town or in the suburbs where most new jobs are being created.

Americans understand that good homes are essential for the

success of our families and communities. They know they are critical infrastructure for our communities and the foundation for children to get a good education and a fair shot at economic opportunity.

Few people would argue with the ideals articulated by Martin Luther King Jr. when he spoke about his dream of racial equality. Few would disagree with Lyndon Johnson's desire to see that every American family could have a decent place to call home and, at some point, the potential to own their own home in a good neighborhood.

The 50th anniversary of the founding of HUD and the start of the modern era of investment in cities gives us an incredible opportunity to start over again. It is the perfect time to ask what we, as a nation, are willing to do to realize King's dream and the dreams of millions of less affluent Americans for a decent safe place to raise a family or to grow old.

Revitalizing our inner cities was not easy then, and it is an ongoing struggle today. But we have 50 years of experience and hundreds of great examples, from new mixed-income, mixed-use communities to the complete redevelopment of the worst of the old public housing high-rises.

We have paid our dues, and we know what works and what doesn't. We have built an infrastructure of developers, financiers, and effective government agencies that can all work together to get good results.

We know that investing in housing and urban vitality pays many dividends. It makes people and families more productive and self-sufficient; it strengthens our economy; it builds social cohesion; and it saves money on the construction of new developments on greenfields while we let existing neighborhoods rot.

I believe it comes down to two choices.

We can renew the commitments of the 1960s and invest once again in proven housing and community development programs to revitalize low-income urban areas and create opportunities for greater self-sufficiency.

Or we can write off the inner cities, keep cutting federal and state aid, let federally subsidized housing and infrastructure crumble, direct all job creation to the suburbs, and watch our bills for food stamps, Medicaid, and prisons grow.

In medieval times, people built walls around their towns to keep barbarian invaders from getting in. If current trends continue, it might not be long before we start constructing walls around inner cities to keep their residents from getting out.

I look back at the vision and compassion of people like Lyndon Johnson, Robert Kennedy, Martin Luther King Jr., Jack Kemp, and, yes, George W. Bush, and I say we are better than that.

I wrote this book to explain why we must renew our commitment to revitalize troubled communities and increase the availability of affordable housing. If enough of us recognize the importance of the problems I talk about in this book, there's no doubt whatsoever we can solve them.

About This Book

This book explains why the popular consensus that housing is now "recovering" from the crisis of the late 2000s is dangerously deceptive. It documents the shortage of housing that is affordable to many Americans, the market and political forces that are making it worse, and why our government's responses have been inadequate at best and counterproductive at worst. It looks at the social and economic impact of the affordability crisis and the growing gap between the housing haves and the housing have-nots. Finally, it examines the challenges of meeting future demand and talks about ways that we can still save the American dream, in the broadest sense of the term—that is, the opportunity for all Americans to have a decent, affordable place to live in a safe, sustainable community.

This book is not intended to take sides in the clash between advocates for big government, massive federal spending, and intensive regulation as opposed to those who favor an unfettered free market that allows builders to construct whatever they want wherever they want. Those extreme ideological positions are not useful, in the author's view.

Rather, this book calls for new awareness among people of all political parties of the nature of housing and urban problems and their consequences. It attempts to inspire a new desire to find consensus on how to address them with a full range of tools, from investing in government programs that work to breaking down barriers to private-market production of housing that is affordable to working-class people.

It is not intended to be an endorsement of any political party's positions or policies or to be partisan. However, it does reflect the author's experience as a journalist who observed six presidents and 16 Congresses in action on housing and urban issues.

At times, both parties have joined forces to solve housing and urban problems. At other times, both have been guilty of bad management and ineffective policies. This book attempts to show that both parties must take responsibility to tackle the toughest fundamental policy issues and adopt long-term strategies or be held accountable for the consequences to our national well-being. Make no mistake, there is a cost for inaction, and this book attempts to illuminate it to some degree.

Finally, this book recognizes the amazing progress we have made in solving problems and the potential for us to build on that success to do even better in the future.

Rebuilding a Dream is organized into four sections:

- What the housing and urban crisis means to our communities and our country and how it contributes to increasing economic inequality;
- Stories of hope and progress, and what works, with insight on how to bring promising efforts to scale to increase housing affordability and make communities more environmentally, economically, and socially sustainable;
- Where we have failed, primarily in terms of federal policies and budget actions; and
- A look at the challenges ahead and what concerned Americans can do to influence government policy.

Issues not covered in this book include rural housing and community development, Indian housing, special-needs housing for the disabled, and housing for migrant workers. These are all important issues.

The people described in this book are real, but, in some cases, names have been changed to protect people's privacy. I wanted to name the real estate developers interviewed for this book, but some refused to allow that. Because they talked about how local governments delay and drive up the costs of their developments, they were afraid they'd be penalized for their candor the next time they apply for a building permit.

Housing & Cities in Distress

CHAPTER ONE

Urban Decay Returns

When the mayors of America's largest cities convened in Las Vegas in 2013, there was not a lot to celebrate, not even in Sin City. Things were looking up from the darkest days of the recession, but conditions were still far from cheery for many places.

In cities where job growth had bounced back, demand for housing was heating up and home prices as well as rents were heading up quickly. Wealthy executives were bidding up home prices in a way that echoed the early 2000s. Meanwhile, workers earning modest salaries struggled to find places to live as rents resumed their upward trajectory.

In areas that continued to struggle economically, housing was cheaper in absolute terms, but not relative to incomes and certainly not relative to the condition of the housing or the neighborhoods in which it was located. Urban decay and economic decline had come close to reversing all the gains cities and their lower-income households had made during the strong economy of the 1990s.

The foreclosure crisis devastated many areas with mostly low-income and minority residents, leaving thousands of vacant, abandoned, and vandalized buildings as stark warnings to others against investing in those areas, and dooming them to continued decline.

Homeownership rates had dropped for all Americans, but especially for minorities, long after prices had started to move up again and record-low interest rates were a fading memory. This was partly a reflection of changing lifestyles and a still sluggish economy, but it also reflected political gridlock over the future of the American mortgage market.

Meanwhile, the brief surge in federal spending in 2010-2011 to help keep a recession from becoming a depression was long gone.

Budget deficit reduction became the single, overriding concern of
Congress. Housing and urban programs were, once again, in the
crosshairs, forcing mayors to fight just to stay even at a time when
their need for assistance was increasing.

• • •

The media has fueled the idea that cities are making an economic comeback, but this is only true for certain geographic and demographic parts of a handful of cities like Boston and San Francisco,
and for thriving boomtowns like Austin, Texas.

Many cities have suffered from years of declining property tax
revenues and chronically high unemployment, especially among minorities. This is compounded by rising costs, including pension li-
abilities. Their citizens are increasingly poor and in need of services,
as affluent people continue a long-term trend of moving out.

"Although the Great Recession officially ended in June 2009,
the fiscal impacts of the recession and the collapse of the housing
market have lingered," according to an analysis of 2011 data by the
Lincoln Institute of Land Policy.

From 2007 through 2009, the average real per capita revenue of
the cities in the institute's database remained largely unchanged,
in part because increases in property taxes and user fees offset declines in revenue from state aid and other local taxes. In 2010 however, average real per capita general revenues fell by three percent
from their 2007 level. This decline continued in 2011, with per capita real revenues nearly five percent below where they were in 2007,
according to the institute's database, which provides a full picture
of revenues raised from city residents and businesses and spending
on their behalf.

The decline in real per capita revenues between 2009 and 2011,
and especially between 2010 and 2011, is attributable to a decline
during those years of the two most important sources of revenue for
cities — the property tax and state aid. On average, for 112 cities in
the sample, the property tax accounted for one-quarter of general
revenue. Revenues from states and the federal government average
nearly 40 percent of total revenue.

Reflecting the decline in property values in most parts of the
country, real per capita property tax revenues declined by 1.6 percent
between 2009 and 2010, and by 4.8 percent between 2010 and 2011.

Following the passage of the federal stimulus legislation, federal aid increased by 6.1 percent between 2009 and 2011. "But during this same period, state aid, a much more important source of intergovernmental revenue for most cities, declined by nearly four percent," the institute stated.

In larger cities, there are pockets of economic vitality, but prosperity usually bypasses lower-income and minority areas. Sometimes it swallows them, and young professionals drive up housing costs to the point that they are out of reach for the people who previously lived there.

In Houston, housing advocates decry the "hollowing out" of their city, as growth and jobs bypass large swaths of the inner city and the inner suburbs. In what they describe as "lost neighborhoods" hit by foreclosures, many lots are empty, and houses are either overcrowded or vacant. In Stockton, Calif., the top city planner said foreclosures had "sucked the air out of our sense of community."

As of 2013, over two-thirds of the 383 metro areas in the United States had not recovered the jobs lost following the 2008 economic downturn, according to data from the U.S. Conference of Mayors.

Cities face financial woes

Most cities experienced some degree of financial difficulty, and many were in deep trouble, teetering on the brink of joining Detroit, San Bernardino and Stockton, Calif., and other cities that had taken the very drastic step of entering bankruptcy.

In 2009 and 2010, over 85 percent of American cities reported that they were less able to meet their financial needs than in the prior year, according to the National League of Cities. The immediate outlook improved in 2011, 2012, and 2013, but not for every city. In 2013, a full 28 percent of cities were still less able to meet their financial needs than they had been in 2012. That's after several years of national economic recovery.

"In comparison to previous periods, the past 12 years have been marked primarily by challenging city fiscal conditions. Recessions in 2001 and 2008-2009 were followed by lackluster economic recoveries. While conditions are no longer deteriorating, the capacity of city budgets remains weakened coming out of the Great Recession," according to the League.

As a nation, our policies and programs were not sufficient to address housing and urban problems in the best of times. But after the foreclosure crisis and the prolonged economic woes that now affect us, those policies are completely inadequate. What's worse, there is a strong political movement to do even LESS to help cities and provide affordable housing.

Congress has already eliminated a number of programs that have been critical to the health of cities. Republican presidents and Republicans in Congress have repeatedly taken aim at the most important remaining grant program, Community Development Block Grants. If they take control of the Senate or White House, they may finally succeed in eliminating it.

• • •

American cities began to face new challenges after World War II, when new highways and federal mortgage insurance made it easy for more affluent residents to live in the suburbs, leaving cities with fewer taxpayers and a higher proportion of poor and minority residents.

Jobs and people moved farther and farther out, past the contiguous suburbs and into what are called the exurbs. This process of sprawl continues, posing a huge challenge for the combined affordability of housing and transportation, as well as contributing to carbon emissions and air pollution.

Between 2000 and 2010, the total U.S. population grew about 10 percent, from 281 million to 309 million. Over that same time, the exurban population grew by more than 60 percent, from about 16 million to almost 26 million people, according to an analysis by the Urban Institute.

Some metro areas continued to see their exurban populations grow even after the recession began. From 2007 to 2010, metropolitan areas grew about 2.4 percent, while exurban areas grew by 13 percent. "In 22 of the largest 100 metros, the average annual growth rate in the exurbs from 2007 to 2010 was higher than that of the previous seven years," the researchers wrote.

The problems posed by older central cities struggling to survive while the exurbs continue to grow are summarized very well in a report by the Northeast Ohio Sustainable Communities Consortium, which is working on long-term planning for that region.

To illustrate the problem of inner-city blight and decay, it said that cities in the region's 12 counties will lose an average of 18 houses a day to abandonment between 2013 and 2040. That's about 177,000 homes that should be demolished over that time period, if there was money to do so—a very big if.

One can see this firsthand in Youngstown, Ohio. Modern urban archeologists have photographed some of the thousands of decrepit, crumbling houses and commercial buildings that stand like gravestones memorializing a bygone era. Inside some of the homes, they still find family photos that were left behind.

Across the region, cities are emptying out while residents flock to more thinly developed areas on the fringes, requiring new roads, sewers, power lines, and other infrastructure, the consortium said.

"The net result, with the region's total population predicted to grow by just 94,000 people in the next 27 years, is more infrastructure and fewer people to pay for it. And that means higher taxes," the report concluded.

The consortium summed up the situation clearly: "Suburban growth can't pay for itself without a bigger hit to taxpayers. And cities will have to pay for the cost of removing unwanted houses rendered surplus by an epidemic of decay and abandonment launched by the foreclosure crisis and the Great Recession."

"Those of us who are doing better have to ask ourselves [whether] we are on the top deck of the Titanic. We may not like to admit it, but as they [the poorer counties] go, so do we," said Steven Hambley, a commissioner in fast-growing Medina County, Ohio.

Hambley may be looking ahead for his constituents, but the spread of poverty and blight from the inner city of Youngstown to the nearby suburbs actually started quite a few years ago. That's part of the reason governments throughout the region are finally talking seriously about how to work together for a better regional future.

• • •

The concentrated poverty that worried President Lyndon Johnson so much in the 1960s was a problem once again in 2014.

After substantial progress to reduce concentrations of poverty during the booming economy of the 1990s, the economically turbulent 2000s saw those gains largely erased, according to a study by the Brookings Institution. The report, "The Re-Emergence of Concentrated Poverty: Metropolitan Trends in the 2000s," analyzes data on neighborhood poverty from the 2005-2009 American Community Surveys and Census 2000.

It found that about 75 percent of the nation's largest 100 metro areas saw an increase in the number of "extreme-poverty neighborhoods" within their borders, along with an increase in the number of poor living in them. Only 16 metro areas experienced decreases in the number of such neighborhoods.

Midwestern metro areas registered a 79 percent increase in extreme-poverty neighborhoods in the 2000s.

An extreme poverty neighborhood is one where at least 40 percent of individuals live below the poverty line.

While concentrations of poverty have persisted or increased in cities, the overall poverty rate is increasing fastest in the suburbs. Between 2000 and 2011, the poor population in suburbs grew by 64 percent—more than twice the rate of growth in cities (29 percent), according to "Confronting Suburban Poverty in America," a 2013 book. However, the percentage of the population in poverty remained higher in urban areas. The urban poverty rate was 10 percentage points higher than the suburban rate on average (22 percent versus 12 percent, respectively).

"Our big challenge now is that many pockets in urban areas are just full of desperately poor people, poorly functioning institutions, and families that are broken".

The foreclosure crisis added to the problems of concentrated poverty by leaving a wake of abandoned and vandalized homes in lower-income and minority areas, not to mention the financial damage it did to homeowners who lost their homes.

Based on the Zillow Home Value Index, home prices dropped 26 percent between 2006 and 2013 in neighborhoods that were predominantly minority—more than three times the decline in neighborhoods that were predominantly white, according to Harvard University's Joint Center for Housing Studies (Harvard JCHS). The Joint Center puts out an annual report titled "State of the Nation's Housing," which is widely considered the most comprehensive analysis of U.S. housing conditions. [For a complete list of Harvard

JCHS reports with titles and full citations, see bibliography]

The share of homeowners in minority and poor areas with mortgages that exceeded their home values was 27 percent in 2013, nearly double the share in white and low-poverty areas, Harvard said.

• • •

But as bad as urban problems were becoming (again) in the wake of the foreclosure fiasco and recession, the problem of housing affordability affected more Americans overall, up to and including the children of the middle class.

Among lower-income households, including those working minimum-wage jobs, a startling percentage has had to pay more than half their income for rent. In Miami, for example, the 2012 data showed that 35 percent of all renters paid more than half their income for rent, according to "The State of the Nation's Housing 2014" report from Harvard JCHS.

Nationwide, more than 1 in 4 renters (27 percent) paid more than 50 percent of their income for rent and utilities in 2012.

From 2001 to 2007, median monthly rental costs rose 4 percent while renter incomes fell by 8 percent. The slide in renter incomes continued through 2011 with another 8 percent decline. Although conditions improved somewhat in 2011-2012, the changes were not nearly enough to make up for lost ground.

As a result, median renter incomes were 13 percent lower in 2012 than in 2001, falling from $36,000 to only $31,500. Meanwhile, the median rent paid, at $880, was up about 4 percent over this period, Harvard JCHS reported.

Lower-income Americans were competing for an extremely limited and dwindling supply of housing with low rents. "Given the cost of land, building materials, financing, and operations, the private sector is simply unable to provide additional low-cost housing without subsidies," Harvard JCHS said.

It was unclear if federal and state governments could continue to help the same number of households pay for housing in future years as they did in 2013, let alone increase those numbers.

Recent history was not reassuring.

Between 2007 and 2011, the number of Americans eligible for federal rental assistance rose by 3.3 million, while the number of assisted housing units was essentially unchanged. In 2013, there was

---

Massachusetts Cities Still Struggling

In the 1800s, Fall River, Mass., became a prosperous center for the manufacturing of textiles. In more recent years, after its textile mills had long been closed, it has been one of 26 old industrial cities in the state battling for economic viability.

While Boston boomed with new jobs in medical and high-tech sectors, these cities, designated "gateway cities" by the state, were not fully participating in the state's economic reinvention and may actually have fallen further behind.

A study of 11 gateway cities showed that from 1970 to 2006, they had lost more than 11,000 jobs or 3 percent of their job base.

"Gateway cities are home to 30 percent of all Massachusetts residents living below the poverty line, even though they account for only 15 percent of the state's population. Educational attainment levels remain low with just 16.5 percent of gateway city residents possessing a four-year college degree," according to "Reconnecting Massachusetts Gateway Cities," by Benjamin Forman et al.

---

a decline in the number of people the federal government helped with housing vouchers to cover the gap between their rent and what they could afford to pay.

Less than 25 percent of the people eligible for housing assistance received such help in 2012. For many others in cities around the country, it was not even possible to have one's name added to the waiting lists of people seeking assistance: They were too long and were closed to new applicants.

• • •

The problem of affordability extended to people earning at or around the median income for their area as well as the young adult children of more affluent families, who are generally not eligible for any housing subsidies.

But the worst tragedy of the housing crisis is readily apparent on the streets of any town of any size in America. It is the scourge of homelessness.

There is controversy about how to count this group of people. But the most reliable and consistent data shows that about 1.2 million schoolchildren were homeless in the 2011-2012 school year. That's according to the U.S. Department of Education, which requires school districts to know who is homeless among their students so they can provide them with an education.

When one adds to that total the siblings of those children who are too young for school, as well as their parents, around 2 million people in families were homeless for some period of time during that school

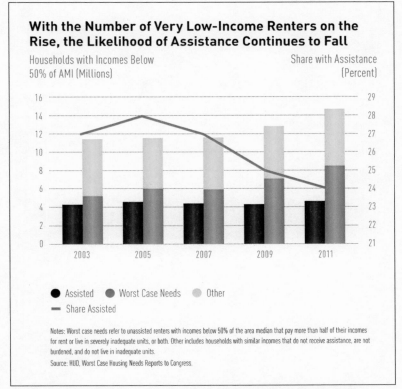

With the Number of Very Low-Income Renters on the Rise, the Likelihood of Assistance Continues to Fall

Households with Incomes Below 50% of AMI (Millions)

Share with Assistance (Percent)

● Assisted   ● Worst Case Needs   ○ Other
— Share Assisted

Notes: Worst case needs refer to unassisted renters with incomes below 50% of the area median that pay more than half of their incomes for rent or live in severely inadequate units, or both. Other includes households with similar incomes that do not receive assistance, are not burdened, and do not live in inadequate units.
Source: HUD, Worst Case Housing Needs Reports to Congress.

Source: Harvard Joint Center for Housing Studies, "The State of the Nation's Housing 2014".

year, the most recent for which data was available at press time.

That doesn't include the large numbers of single people and unaccompanied youths who are homeless. Estimates for these groups vary, but probably total anywhere from 500,000 to 1 million.

Most Americans don't see the homeless families, and they've learned to ignore the individuals sleeping on benches, in doorways, and in parks. But cities know they are there because of the damage they do to municipal vitality.

The costs come in direct expenditures for police, fire, health services, and sanitation, as well as the indirect costs from retail business that is lost to suburban locations and malls where shoppers don't have to see the folks who got left behind by the American housing market and a shrinking housing safety net.

CHAPTER TWO

New American Slums

Normally, visitors to the Bank of America Corporate Center in Charlotte, N.C., wear business suits and don't have blood on their faces. But, on one morning not long ago, many of the people in the plaza looked like they'd crawled out of their own graves.

A group of community activists and homeowners facing foreclosure by BofA played the part of zombies to draw attention to the neglected condition and deterioration of the properties the bank controlled.

BofA became one of the nation's largest owners of bad loans and foreclosed properties when it took over the failing Countrywide Financial in 2009. Countrywide financed as much as 20 percent of all U.S. mortgages in some of the years prior to the foreclosure crisis, and many of those had gone bad.

"In lower-income areas around the country, BofA and other banks are letting their properties rot," said Peter Skillern, who led the zombies in his capacity as executive director of Reinvestment Partners, an advocacy group. Such was the case with 519 Park Ave. in the eastern part of Durham, N.C., a vacant, BofA-owned four-unit property that had been "vandalized from top to bottom," he said.

A property becomes a zombie when a mortgage servicer files for foreclosure but does not complete the process. Instead of taking ownership or resolving the foreclosure by other means, like rewriting the mortgage so a troubled borrower can remain current, lenders let properties go idle indefinitely. They often do this in lower-income areas, adding to an already growing problem. That's why housing advocates are raising the alarm about so-called zombie properties.

In Cook County, Ill., in 2013, there were more than 11,700 zombie properties where a foreclosure proceeding had not been resolved for more than three years, according to The Woodstock Institute.

"Because neither the borrower nor servicer has clear control of the property, neither has a strong incentive to assume responsibility for the property. Zombie properties, therefore, are likely to be poorly maintained or blighted, which threatens the stability of surrounding communities," Woodstock said.

Properties in foreclosure or subject to loans that are in default are often abandoned or neglected.

In 2012, there were some 4,700 neighborhoods across the country where more than 1 in 5 homes were vacant. This ratio translates to a significant blighting influence on these communities, according to Harvard JCHS. The average vacancy rate in these communities was 26 percent, more than three times the U.S. average.

• • •

In the most distressed neighborhoods of Baltimore, Chicago, Cleveland, and Detroit, about 60 percent of vacant units have been held off market, indicating they are in poor condition and likely a source of blight, JCHS added.

In Pittsburgh, 27 percent of single-family homes were vacant in 2013. The city had 35,000 real estate parcels that were delinquent on property taxes.

Property abandonment and neglect create a downward spiral that is hard to stop. Even solvent homeowners think twice about keeping up their property or paying their tax and mortgage payments if their neighborhood is going downhill.

"On average, families affected by nearby foreclosures have already lost or will lose $21,077 in household wealth, representing 7.2 percent of their home value, by virtue of being in close proximity to foreclosures," according to the Center for Responsible Lending (CRL) in Durham.

Lower-income areas have little prospect for home prices to recover soon. That means their problems will continue for years because there's not much potential for any lender to recoup the cost of completing foreclosures, and fixing up and selling properties in these areas.

"In some communities with many foreclosed properties, the crisis threatens to doom the entire neighborhood to a cycle of disinvestment and decay. A cluster of vacant properties can destabilize a block. A cluster of troubled blocks can destabilize a neighborhood. The costs are substantial," according to Chicago's Business and Professional People for the Public Interest.

Cities affected the most by foreclosures can't pick up the slack left by negligent owners and lenders. Wrestling with budget shortfalls themselves, city governments can't afford to fix up properties or clean up trash left by vagrants and vandals. In Maryland's Prince George's

The Areas Hardest Hit by Foreclosure

Rust belt cities were hit especially hard by foreclosures and had little prospect for a quick rebound because they also faced long-term economic decline. Illinois communities included three of the top 10 hardest-hit neighborhoods and 24 of the top 100. In Carpentersville, Ill., nearly 9 percent of all the homes went into foreclosure. Michigan, Ohio, and Pennsylvania also had high foreclosure rates.

But the disaster also had a powerful impact on Southern communities, which grew in recent decades while Northern cities declined. Florida and Georgia were home to the largest number of ZIP codes with the highest foreclosure rates of 2012.

Florida had 33 ZIP codes among the 100 hardest hit, more than any other state, according to RealtyTrac. In that state, 1 in every 32 households received a notice of default, auction, or repossession in 2012, more than double the national average.

In Homestead, Fla., south of Miami, the foreclosure rate hit nearly 10 percent in 2012, up from 5.4 percent in 2011.

Georgia homeowners were also hit hard. Statewide, 42.1 percent of Georgia homeowners with mortgages were underwater in 2013, according to The Atlanta Journal-Constitution. Nationally, the rate was 27.5 percent.

In 101 of the state's ZIP codes, at least half of mortgage holders were underwater. In metro Atlanta, there were a dozen counties where at least half of mortgages were underwater: Barrow, Bartow, Carroll, Clayton, DeKalb, Douglas, Gwinnett, Henry, Jackson, Newton, Paulding, and Rockdale.

In Lawrenceville, Ga., nearly 13 percent of homes—1 out of every 8—received some kind of foreclosure notice in 2013, making it the hardest-hit ZIP code in the country. This suburb of Atlanta had seen home prices plunge by more than 40 percent from the early 2006 peak, according to real estate database Zillow.

County, for example, the county could not even manage to board up the windows and doors of one house before squatters set it on fire.

Obviously, boarding up vacant houses is no more than a temporary fix. The long-term solution would be for cities to buy, repair, and resell or rent foreclosed homes—if only they had the money.

To help cities do this, Congress provided $6.9 billion at the height of the recession. The money funded three rounds of the Neighborhood Stabilization Program (NSP), which was created in 2008, to help cash-strapped cities fix up and resell abandoned properties.

The program helped many cities address the problem. However, the funding was sufficient to deal with only a small percentage of the homes left vacant or abandoned by the housing market collapse, and additional appropriations have not been made for this purpose.

Minorities targeted for bad loans

The foreclosure crisis hit predominantly black and Hispanic areas especially hard. Data shows that unscrupulous lenders targeted these areas for the highest-risk, highest cost types of mortgage loans, such as adjustable-rate mortgages and loans with high prepayment penalties.

This led to higher-than-average default rates within the Hispanic and African-American communities, according to the Housing Commission established by the Bipartisan Policy Center, which consists of equal numbers of Republican and Democratic housing experts.

The commission said many of the families had good credit, decent incomes, and everything else necessary to qualify for traditional long-term, fixed-rate loans. Despite that fact, they were not offered those kinds of loans. They were "steered into exotic and costly mortgages they did not fully understand and could not afford," the commission said.

This "deliberate targeting of minority areas for the sale of risky and expensive loans," as the commission described it, continued to have an impact every day in inner cities and lower-income towns across America long after the press declared the housing crisis to be over.

African-American and Latino borrowers were almost twice as likely to have lost their homes to foreclosure as non-Hispanic whites, according to Center for Responsible Lending (CRL).

Differences in income and credit history did not explain why communities of color were harder hit, CRL said.

For example, the foreclosure rate for low- and moderate-income African-Americans was about 80 percent higher than that for comparable white households. Foreclosure rates for higher-income Latinos were more than three times that of higher-income whites.

African-Americans and Latinos with good credit received high-cost loans more than three times as often as white borrowers, CRL said.

"Communities of color got the worst of everything. They were given the highest-risk, most expensive mortgages, they received the worst servicing from their mortgage lenders, and they have suffered the most damage from the nation's long economic slump," said Liz Ryan Murray, policy director for National People's Action, a Chicago-based group that has been fighting against discriminatory home lending practices since the 1970s.

These combined effects can be seen in the plummeting rate of minority homeownership.

The homeownership rate for African-American households peaked at 49 percent in 2004, according to Harvard's JCHS. It fell to 43.9 percent in 2012, the same year that Hispanic homeownership dropped to 46 percent. The homeownership rate among white households declined during that time too but remained at 73.5 percent.

• • •

"The black-white gap [in homeownership rates] has reached historic proportions," Harvard's JCHS said in its 2013 report.

There has also been a powerfully negative ripple effect on other property owners who never had a problem making their mortgage payments but owned property near people who did default or lose their homes. The losses in household wealth that resulted from the impact of foreclosures and abandonment of nearby properties have disproportionately hurt communities of color, according to many sources that have studied the issue.

Families in minority neighborhoods that are affected by nearby foreclosures have lost or will lose on average $40,297, or 16 percent, of their home value, CRL said. This is almost double the national average.

The decline in African-American homeownership will have intergenerational consequences because "black wealth is more concentrated in homeownership than any other asset," said U.S. Rep. Gregory Meeks (D-N.Y.).

The impact on cities

Gayle McLaughlin doesn't look or sound very intimidating. She is petite and soft-spoken. But she scared the daylights out of real estate brokers and some of the nation's biggest banks in 2013.

McLaughlin was mayor of Richmond, Calif., which is 17 miles from San Francisco but worlds away economically.

During World War II, the city's shipyard built 747 ships and employed many thousands of people, mostly women and African-Americans. In 2013, it had a population of 106,000 residents with a median household income that was about 60 percent of San Francisco's.

Elected mayor in 2006, McLaughlin watched foreclosures hit the working-class town like a tsunami. Many of the town's roughly 16,000 homeowners inherited their properties from parents who worked in the defense industry. But job losses coupled with predatory lending practices took a heavy toll. In 2012, about one-half of the city's homeowners were "underwater," meaning the outstanding loan amount secured by the property was higher than the property's estimated market value.

Despite repeated pleas from McLaughlin, lenders on most of those homes refused to modify loan terms or reduce the principal amount owed on the loans. That meant there was no end in sight for the homeowners' struggle to make their payments and stay in their homes.

"Whole neighborhoods are affected in terms of reduced property values and increased crime rates," McLaughlin said. "We find ourselves with lower property tax revenue and higher costs for dealing with crime and trying to enforce building codes on vacant homes."

In 2014, she said, home values citywide had declined 66 percent since before the crisis. "Wages are not going up. Even those holding on to their homes are skimping on other necessities. People email me all the time saying they are holding on by their fingernails," she said.

To stop that downward spiral, she proposed to use the city's power of eminent domain to compel lenders to sell 600-some loans to the city. This would give the city, as opposed to lenders, the power to modify those loans to help the troubled homeowners make their payments.

The Richmond city council agreed to the plan, but McLaughlin and her allies faced an uphill struggle to see it through to completion. Bankers and real estate interests were determined to kill the plan or tie it up in court for years. They also campaigned to get the officials behind the plan voted out of office.

• • •

Richmond was not alone among California cities hurt by foreclosures.

From 2008 to 2012, California localities lost an estimated $3.8 billion in property tax revenue, or $2,058 for every foreclosure, according to the Alliance of Californians for Community Empowerment.

California cities and counties ran up a total of $17.4 billion in costs—or $19,229 for every foreclosure—for maintenance of blighted properties, sheriff evictions, building inspections, trash removal, and other related costs.

The cities of San Bernardino and Stockton both declared bankruptcy due in large part to the fiscal impact of foreclosures.

In Stockton, 3.98 percent of housing units had a foreclosure filing during 2012, nearly three times the national average. In the Riverside-San Bernardino-Ontario metro area, 3.86 percent of housing units had a foreclosure filing that year.

Although these cities had other fiscal problems, including high pension obligations, the decline in property values and tax revenue from so many foreclosures tipped the scales against them.

What hit us

With typical bravado, President George W. Bush sounded the charge to make homeownership the focus of America's housing and economic policy.

"In order to change America and to make sure the great American dream shines in every community, we must unleash the compassion and kindness of the greatest nation on the face of the earth," he said in 2002. To encourage homeownership, he said, "We must use the mighty muscle of the federal government in combination with state and local governments."

Bush focused on increasing homeownership among minority families, who had much lower ownership rates than whites, saying it was the best way for them to build wealth. He won enactment of the American Dream Downpayment Program, which made grants available to cover downpayments. He encouraged Fannie Mae and Freddie Mac, the government-sponsored buyers of home mortgages, to stretch their underwriting as far as possible down the income scale.

The Bush administration also worked to prevent state attorneys

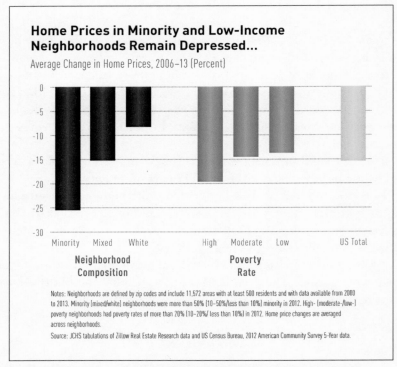

Home Prices in Minority and Low-Income Neighborhoods Remain Depressed...

Average Change in Home Prices, 2006–13 (Percent)

Notes: Neighborhoods are defined by zip codes and include 11,572 areas with at least 500 residents and with data available from 2000 to 2013. Minority (mixed/white) neighborhoods were more than 50% (10–50%/less than 10%) minority in 2012. High- (moderate-/low-) poverty neighborhoods had poverty rates of more than 20% (10–20%/ less than 10%) in 2012. Home price changes are averaged across neighborhoods.

Source: JCHS tabulations of Zillow Real Estate Research data and US Census Bureau, 2012 American Community Survey 5-Year data.

Source: Harvard Joint Center for Housing Studies, "The State of the Nation's Housing 2014".

general from curtailing high-risk types of mortgage lending, as reported by Eliot Spitzer, then governor of New York in a Washington Post op-ed on February 14, 2008.

Bush was right: Homeownership is a great way for people to build wealth, gain control over their living situation, and put down roots in a community. But he was dead wrong to be so single-minded in his approach.

Bush was the lead player in a cast of thousands determined to put as many people as possible into homes. Although his actions were ostensibly for the greater good, he helped create a perfect storm of lender greed, political opportunism, government incompetence, and borrower ignorance.

The rush to expand homeownership using high-risk lending led directly to a wave of foreclosures and loan defaults that has devastated thousands of communities. It was the financial and social

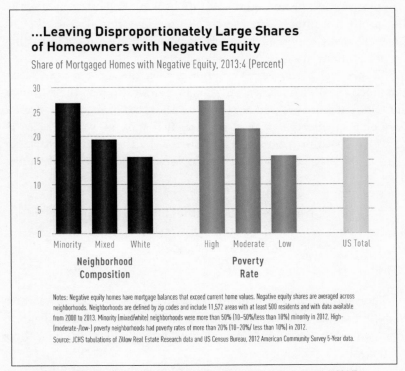

...Leaving Disproportionately Large Shares of Homeowners with Negative Equity

Share of Mortgaged Homes with Negative Equity, 2013:4 (Percent)

Notes: Negative equity homes have mortgage balances that exceed current home values. Negative equity shares are averaged across neighborhoods. Neighborhoods are defined by zip codes and include 11,572 areas with at least 500 residents and with data available from 2000 to 2013. Minority (mixed/white) neighborhoods were more than 50% (10–50%/less than 10%) minority in 2012. High- (moderate-/low-) poverty neighborhoods had poverty rates of more than 20% (10–20%/ less than 10%) in 2012.

Source: JCHS tabulations of Zillow Real Estate Research data and US Census Bureau, 2012 American Community Survey 5-Year data.

Source: Harvard Joint Center for Housing Studies, "The State of the Nation's Housing 2014".

equivalent of Hurricane Katrina, but unlike that Gulf Coast storm, this one has lasted for years and spared no part of our country.

Five years after Bush's 2002 directive to increase homeownership, a housing market collapse began that would cause 8.4 million households, or about 21.1 million people, to lose their homes by mid-2012.

From the beginning of the financial crisis in September 2008 through 2013, there were approximately 4.9 million completed foreclosures across the country, according to CoreLogic. Between 2010 and 2013, another 1.3 million families lost their homes to short sales.

In 2013, the tide of new foreclosure filings finally began to recede. The foreclosure process was started for 1.36 million U.S. properties, less than half the absurdly high level of 2.9 million in 2010.

• • •

The decline in new foreclosure filings, plus the rise in home prices in many cities, prompted real estate brokers and other businesses that profit from home sales to crank up a new round of marketing that heralded the end of the crisis. It wasn't quite true, at least not for less affluent areas and households.

"Depressed home prices combined with the most severe recession since the 1930s caused millions of families to lose their homes, and millions more are still at risk of foreclosure because they owe far more on their mortgages than what their homes are worth," according to Underwater America, a 2014 report by the Haas Institute for a Fair and Inclusive Society at the University of California, Berkeley.

More than 9.8 million American households were still underwater on their mortgages as of December 31, 2013

The report added that many homeowners were still locked into predatory adjustable rate loans with interest rates that will jump up, meaning they remained at risk of eventually defaulting on their mortgages.

As 2014 began, the monthly rate of new foreclosure filings was still more than twice as high as it was from 2000 to 2006. In 10 states the rate of new foreclosures actually increased in 2013, including Maryland (up 117 percent), New Jersey (up 44 percent), New York (up 34 percent), Connecticut (up 20 percent), Washington (up 13 percent), and Pennsylvania (up 13 percent), according to RealtyTrac.

Crisis not over

"It is clearly too early to declare an end to the crisis given the substantial backlog of homes in the foreclosure pipeline," said "The

State of the Nation's Housing 2013" report from Harvard's JCHS.

The foreclosure process can be extremely slow, so there's no telling how long it will take for the rate to normalize in every state. Banks can hang on to foreclosed properties or draw out the process for years. Where banks have gone bankrupt, the federal government gives them five years to get their affairs in order, including dealing with troubled home loans. In some states, like Nevada, new legal safeguards intended to protect people living in foreclosed homes have made the process slower than ever.

For households that did lose their homes to foreclosure, the financial impact has been devastating. A large proportion of them had refinanced homes they had owned for some time. For them, an otherwise stable financial situation turned upside down overnight. Most of the victims lost all their savings and had to move into much smaller apartment rentals. Some former homeowners even became homeless.

More than 9.8 million American households were still underwater on their mortgages as of December 31, 2013, According to Zillow, the on-line real estate information service. That's close to one-fifth of all mortgaged homes in America.

All those households were stuck on a financial treadmill. There was little prospect that they could sell their homes for enough to pay off their mortgages, so they had little incentive to repair or even maintain their properties. In many cases, they had trouble making their mortgage payments, causing ongoing uncertainty about whether they would eventually lose their homes.

The ripple effects of the crisis extended to entire neighborhoods and even whole towns. Property owners facing foreclosure often just walked away, seeing no benefit in continuing to keep up their homes. As foreclosures increased, the number of vacant, crumbling homes steadily increased.

Overall, the number of vacant properties across the country increased 51 percent, from nearly 7 million in 2000 to 10 million in April 2010. Ten states saw increases of 70 percent or more, according to the Census Bureau. Analysts believe this is due primarily to the foreclosure crisis.

Vacant homes often deteriorate drastically. In hard-hit areas, they can become havens for squatters, prostitutes, or drug dealers. These areas are the new American slums—blocks, neighborhoods, and even entire towns full of shattered dreams, broken windows, weed-choked yards, caving roofs, and pervasive crime.

Absentee landlords take over

The drop in home prices after the recession might have created a great opportunity for less affluent people to buy homes. The decline in mortgage interest rates also promised greater affordability.

However, the hoped-for silver lining of the crisis never materialized.

After the foreclosure crisis, the mortgage lending industry underwent a dramatic realignment. Mortgage banking companies went bankrupt. Fannie Mae and Freddie Mac, the two giant buyers of mortgage loans, were taken over by the federal government. Among the institutions still solvent enough to make loans, underwriting standards suddenly swung from very lax to extremely conservative.

A suddenly constricted credit market meant "the evaporation of loans to borrowers with weaker credit histories," said Harvard's JCHS.

Local people often could not get loans to buy homes at the lower prices that prevailed after the crisis. Investors that were able to pay the entire price in cash swooped in. Well-heeled entrepreneurs started buying up homes, making some cosmetic repairs, and "flipping" them for a quick profit. Some preferred to play the role of slumlord, making few if any repairs to beat-up properties, then leasing them at rents that few families could afford on their own. They would then look the other way as families sublet bedrooms to other families to make each group's rent manageable.

After the dust settled, bigger companies got involved, some of them backed by Wall Street equity and debt firms.

The situation turned out to be a golden opportunity for others with large sums of capital. For example, rental housing investment companies had already bought 200,000 single-family homes by 2013, according to the Center for American Progress.

Invitation Homes, a branch of The Blackstone Group, spent $7.5 billion acquiring 40,000 houses from 2011 to 2013 to create the largest single-family rental business in the United States.

The big unknown is what the larger investors will do with the properties. They say they intend to keep the homes as rentals for the long term and manage them well.

Some housing advocates think the investors are more likely to aim at making a quick profit by flipping the houses as soon as the local markets have recovered enough. The fear is that the investor-owners will try to control entire neighborhoods, drive up prices, and then sell the homes to their tenants at inflated prices.

This could lead to a new cycle of price inflation, the bursting of the price bubble, price collapses and a new round of foreclosures.

Those fears were speculative, but they are based on a fundamental dynamic of real estate markets: When control of homes is handed over to financial interests far removed from the neighbor-

Anatomy of a Predator

Wall Street investment bankers and large mortgage banking firms took much of the blame for the foreclosure crisis.

But the executives of those firms did not talk the African-American and Hispanic homeowners of Richmond, Calif., suburban Atlanta, or the South Side of Chicago into taking out toxic mortgages. Individuals in the mortgage brokerage business did.

They were smooth-talking salesmen who did not care about the communities in which their customers lived. They were the kind of salespeople who have preyed on people with lower incomes and very little financial sophistication for many years.

They were the shock troops that laid the groundwork for the mortgage disaster. If someone did not yet own a home, they talked those people into getting in on the growth of home values by stretching to buy with high-risk loans.

It was easy to play on the hopes of lower-income homeowners, many of whom had inherited their homes free and clear or had safe, long-term, fixed-rate loans in place.

"Take out some of the built-up equity tied up in this house and use it to pay off your other bills," they advised.

They offered to make it possible for inner-city residents to finally stop worrying about money and to help struggling family members get out of debt, start businesses, or save for college.

Did the borrowers have the income or the ability to repay? In many cases, the brokers did not care. So-called "no-documentation" loans made it easy to lend to anyone, regardless of their income. Sales commissions did not depend on whether the borrower stayed current. It only mattered if the loan closed.

Federal law has long required many disclosures about loan terms and risks to be stated in the mortgage documents. Most borrowers probably never read them.

hoods involved, short-term profits almost always trump the long-term stability of the neighborhoods involved.

CHAPTER THREE

The Many Victims of Homelessness

Julianna Martinez had tolerated her husband's periodic physical abuse, but the day that he became violent toward their 14-year-old son, she fled the house with nothing, not even shoes on her feet, and very little money to her name.

That night, the U.S. Army veteran and her four children left their home in Arizona and entered the world of homelessness in America.

They joined the ranks of a growing number of homeless families, most of them headed by women. She quickly learned what other homeless mothers already knew: Few shelter spaces are available for a family of any kind, much less those with a teenage son.

Julianna, her son, and her three other children (ages 9 to 12 at the time) had no family members to support them. They prevailed on friends to put them up, despite the crowding that five more people would cause and notwithstanding the risk of a visit from her violent husband.

They arranged to stay with friends, each for a few weeks, spending as much time outside the house as possible before moving on to someone else's couch and floor.

Barbara Garfield is a personable, nicely dressed 53-year-old. She does odd jobs and attends community college classes in an affluent California town. She helps the local street preacher counsel the many other homeless people in the area.

Barbara has not had a full-time job for years, but even if she found one, it would not solve her housing problem. The cheapest studio apartment would eat up 50 percent or more of the net income from a minimum-wage job. But with no recent rental history, credit references, or a security deposit, she could not expect any landlord to rent to her. In her town, the few apartments that become vacant are rented within days to people with all those things.

So she hauls her possessions around in a grocery cart until evening, when she and others like her retreat to makeshift plywood and cardboard shacks under a freeway overpass. She does not go to a government-funded homeless shelter because, even when there's a bed available, she feels unsafe. There is no facility for single women or families anywhere near her.

One morning as the eastern sky turns pink, she hears trucks rumbling nearby. With two cops in the lead, workers from the state transportation department dismantle the camp. A sanitation crew hauls plywood and cardboard shelters, along with abandoned personal belongings, to the dump.

Barbara and her neighbors move to another overpass about a mile away. It isn't as dry or as sheltered from the wind, but it would do.

Luther Hill was a Vietnam veteran who lived on the streets of Washington, D.C. One October morning, his body was found slumped in his wheelchair in the doorway of the old Hecht's warehouse on New York Avenue, according to an article in *Street Sense*, a newspaper in Washington, D.C., often distributed by the homeless.

No one knows for sure if he had sought a bed in a homeless shelter the previous night. One story says he'd been turned away because he would not give up his alcohol.

There are many thousands of stories like those of Julianna, Barbara, and Luther across America these days. Some of them end well, and the lack of housing turns out to be temporary. But many people remain without a stable home for years. Their health declines, and they became less and less capable of finding a job or taking on the responsibilities of keeping up a household.

In almost every major city, in any given year, some of them end up dead. In 2011, it's estimated that at least 1,963 people died homeless in 44 states.

When homelessness first emerged as a national concern under the Reagan administration, the president and others said most of the homeless had mental health or substance abuse problems, seeming to suggest they had made the choice to live outdoors.

Today, homelessness can't be explained away as a matter of personal choice or even the lack of mental health care in our country, although that's part of it. It is primarily an economic problem that's been growing since the 1980s, surging again after the recession started.

It is the inevitable result of some very simple math: For many Americans, incomes have been stagnant or declining for years. However, housing costs have continued to rise briskly in many places. Sooner or later, for people on the margins, this gap becomes unmanageable. For increasing numbers of very low-income people, finding an apartment they can afford—any apartment—is impossible, even if they are working.

Families in despair

In Washington, D.C., just two miles from the U.S. Capitol, a drama plays out every autumn as the temperatures fall and homeless families with nowhere else to go try to cram into the city's only shelter for families.

During one recent October, 190 families (242 adults and 390 children) managed to squeeze into space meant for 135 at the rickety old building that used to be D.C. General Hospital. Families bunked together in common rooms and slept on cots along the hallways.

The fact that so many families competed for tiny rooms in an ancient building in terrible condition illustrates the growth of homelessness among families in our country, and our lack of preparation to address it.

The most thorough tabulation of homeless families comes from the U.S. Department of Education (DE). A total of 1,168,354 public and charter school students were homeless during the 2011-2012 school year, according to the DE.

While many estimates of numbers of homeless involve a fair bit of guesswork and extrapolation, there are very specific data on homeless children in public schools. Their numbers increased 72 percent since the beginning of the recession, according to the DE.

The 2011-2012 data reflects a 10 percent increase from the 2010-2011 school year. Forty-three states reported increases in the total number of homeless children and youths enrolled in public and charter schools in the 2011-2012 school year.

There were increases of 20 percent or more in Idaho, Maine, Michigan, Missouri, North Carolina, North Dakota, Oklahoma, South Dakota, Vermont, and Wyoming.

• • •

In Michigan, one of the states hardest hit by economic problems, the number of homeless children enrolled in public schools almost tripled from 2008 to 2011. In New York City, the number of homeless children enrolled in public schools nearly doubled from 2006 to 2011. There were close to 70,000 of them.

In Dallas, about 54 percent of the homeless identified in 2012 were families with children, a 36 percent increase since 2010. "Services and housing for homeless children have really been neglected," said Mike Faenza, president of the Metro Dallas Homeless Alliance.

The DE's numbers are "devastating, but sadly, entirely predictable," said Ruth White, executive director of the National Center for Housing and Child Welfare. "This data simply provides more evidence that the federal government has abandoned its commitment to fill yawning gaps in affordable housing options for low-income families."

The total number of children who were homeless for some period over 2010, including those too young to be enrolled in school, was at least 1.6 million, according to the National Center on Family Homelessness. That was a 33 percent increase from 2007, the center said.

A tale of two counts

While the Department of Education sounded a wake-up call about the future health and well-being of more than a million homeless children, the federal department in charge of housing took a much different approach.

The Department of Housing and Urban Development (HUD) provides funding to local agencies to help house or shelter the homelessness. In 2014, Congress appropriated about $2.1 billion for what the agency calls its "continuum of care."

HUD also counts the homeless once a year, on a single night in January. Based on those annual counts, HUD says homelessness has been steadily declining.

When the recession began in 2007, there were 671,888 homeless Americans, according to HUD. In January 2013, HUD said there were 610,042.

Housing advocates and homeless services providers have expressed skepticism about HUD's data, partly because of the techniques it uses, and partly because of its highly positive results: HUD has shown steady declines in homelessness even as foreclosures skyrocketed and employment and incomes tanked.

"The point-in-time numbers chosen by HUD run counter to what service providers and advocates witness in their communities," according to the Institute for Children, Poverty & Homelessness.

Others put it more bluntly. "The HUD count is an absolutely shameful fraud," said Diane Nilan, founder and president of HEAR US a national nonprofit organization in Naperville, Ill., that is dedicated to bringing attention to the fate of homeless children and youth.

HUD's method of counting relies mainly on lightly trained or untrained volunteers who, armed with clipboards and pens, fan out on a single night in January each year, often one of the coldest nights of the year. They ask people who happen to be visible on the night of the count to voluntarily answer questions about their housing status and use that data to determine how many of the respondents were homeless.

HUD claims this is the best way to measure changes in homeless numbers from year to year. However, the agency offers no evidence of the statistical validity of year-to-year comparisons using this approach.

Advocates are particularly critical of how HUD determines the number of homeless families.

HUD reported there were 222,197 homeless people in 70,960 families in 2013, a decline of 8 percent from 2010.

The number of children who are homeless was the subject of HUD's count for the first time in 2013. The volunteers who do the HUD count started asking about the age of people they found and deemed homeless, and from that, HUD estimated that about one-quarter of all homeless people (23 percent or 138,149) were homeless children under the age of 18.

Assuming that two-thirds of those were of school age, HUD's data suggests there were about 92,000 school-age children who were homeless at roughly the same time during which the DE reported 1.17 million of them.

What explains the wildly different numbers from two different federal agencies? Simple. The agency that governs education counts the homeless using a broad definition of the term. The one that provides housing, and works at ending homelessness, uses a very narrow definition of who is homeless, and only measures their numbers on a single night each year, not over a period of time.

The DE counts homeless students very carefully because it is required by law to provide every child with a good education. This includes children with no stable place to call home. Every school district has a staff member who uses detailed procedures to calculate numbers of homeless kids each year.

School districts count a student as homeless if he or she is "sharing the housing of other persons due to loss of housing, economic hardship, or a similar reason; are living in motels, hotels, trailer parks, or camping grounds; are living in emergency or transitional shelters; are abandoned in hospitals; or are awaiting foster care placement," as per the DE's official definition.

HUD defines people as homeless if they were located in emergency shelters on the single night of its count, or if they were "unsheltered," meaning they slept on the streets, in parks, in cars, or under freeways (and are visible and willing to talk to HUD's counters.)

HUD does not count people as homeless if they are sharing someone else's living quarters or living in a motel that is not paid for by a government agency. Nor does it admit such people to the network of homeless shelters it operates unless they can prove their living situation is temporary.

This methodology ends up omitting large numbers of families with children. They are the least likely to sleep in the open, where volunteers in HUD's annual count can find them. They are not likely to be found in shelters, since there are so few shelters designed to serve families. On the contrary, they are the most likely to find a friend to put them up or to get a motel room. This means they would be excluded from HUD's count, even if the volunteers doing the counting happened to encounter them.

Some defenders of HUD's definition of homelessness say that "sharing the housing of others" is not the same as being homeless. They describe it with innocuous terms like "doubling up" or "couch surfing."

Obviously, the legislators who wrote the DE's definition know the truth about "sharing housing." For most people, it is not like moving into the guest room in a friend's suburban ranch house.

Doubling up usually involves a poor family living with people who are almost as poor but have a lease. Shared living quarters often don't offer use of a kitchen or easy access to a bathroom. They lack any shred of security or stability, making it hard for children to stay safe, let alone have success in school.

Privacy is nonexistent. It puts enormous strains on everyone involved, especially children.

For the host family, there's the risk that the landlord will object to the over-occupancy and kick everyone out of the building. Less scrupulous landlords overlook overcrowding but ignore the wear and tear the crowding puts on a building.

It's hard for the most motivated child to study if there is no privacy or quiet, or if they never know for sure when they may have to move again and start attending a new school. That's why Congress passed the law that requires schools to make special efforts to help these children get a good education, including transporting them to their "school of origin."

Homeless kids tell their stories

Members of Congress got a better picture of the problem at a recent committee hearing, which featured testimony from a number of children who had experienced homelessness. A boy from Colorado testified about his experience living in a cheap motel. He said the yelling and cursing of neighbors kept him up at night. "I was afraid they might just come in and rip off my books. This is why I always carry all of my important belongings and schoolbooks with me everywhere I go. I had a very hard time to actually focus on my studies, because somewhere in my mind, a worry of my mom being beaten or myself being kicked out again unexpectedly is always present," he said.

Homeless families are typically comprised of a mother in her late 20s with two children. More than half of all homeless mothers do not have a high school diploma, according to the National Center on Family Homelessness. More than 92 percent have experienced physical and/or sexual abuse during their lifetimes. About 50 percent have experienced a major depressive episode since becoming homeless. More than one-third have a chronic physical health condition.

The center said children experiencing homelessness are sick four times more often than other children; go hungry at twice the rate of other children; and have three times the rate of emotional and behavioral problems compared with non-homeless children. It states that by age 12, 83 percent have been exposed to at least one serious violent event.

Children who are homeless are twice as likely to have learning disabilities as non-homeless children, according to the center.

Only recently have researchers begun to look at the impact of homelessness on the educational success of children. "Homeless students have the lowest graduation rates and the highest dropout rates even compared to other poor kids," said Barbara Duffield, policy director of the National Association for the Education of Homeless Children and Youth.

States and localities, with help from HUD and the Department of Veterans Affairs (VA), have had notable success in reducing homelessness among veterans.

No one has calculated the cost for the services that will be required over a person's lifetime because he or she was homeless as a child or because of family disintegration caused by homelessness. Nor has anyone measured the loss of productivity that will result from the health and educational deficits homeless children have in such high proportions compared with the general population.

These impacts are hard to quantify, and that's part of the reason they don't rank more highly in the congressional budgeting process.

While the kids of homeless families have it bad, unaccompanied youths have it even worse. Debby Shore works with such youths. She directs Sasha Bruce Youthwork in Northeast Washington, D.C., which helps children and youths reconnect with families and provides short-term housing and support services for 70 young people at a time.

In the past, children became separated from their families largely because of conflicts at home, such as domestic abuse or parental disapproval of their life choices. Now, Shore says, the housing problems of the parents lead directly to the homelessness of their children. "We've seen a lot of kids whose families have had to double up. The older kid has felt or been told that they have to get out on their own," she said.

Most of these youths can't expect any help from the U.S. government. HUD-funded emergency shelters have a total of 111,351 beds for people in families but only 2,212 for unaccompanied children nationwide.

Federally funded transitional housing facilities offer only 1,130 beds for unaccompanied children. Those are pitifully low numbers given the need among children who have left home, who have become disconnected from their families, or who have grown up in foster care.

Reliable data on the number of unaccompanied youths who are homeless is hard to find. However, about 30,000 young people "age out" of the U.S. foster care system each year after turning 18. Even if all the federally funded beds available for unaccompanied youths became vacant tomorrow, they would not house more than 10 percent of those who leave foster care each year.

Veterans get help

There's better news for other subsets of the homeless population. States and localities, with help from HUD and the Department of Veterans Affairs (VA), have had notable success in reducing homelessness among veterans and those referred to as the "chronically homeless."

The number of individuals experiencing chronic homelessness declined by 16 percent, or 17,219 people, between 2010 and 2013, according to HUD.

The chronically homeless are defined as 1) having health and/or substance abuse problems, and 2) having been homeless for a year or more or had at least four episodes of homelessness in the previous three years. They require enormous amounts of costly public services for long periods.

One of the only programs that offers the homeless both housing and supportive services is HUD's Supportive Housing program. Another major contributor to progress is the increasing willingness of states and cities to invest in their own versions of the supportive housing program. Cities are starting to understand that providing the homeless with supportive housing reduces costly impacts to their social services later on.

• • •

In Salt Lake City, for example, Mayor Ralph Becker anticipated putting every chronically homeless person in housing and providing them with intensive social services by the end of 2014.

Veterans are beneficiaries of increased congressional appropriations to help keep them from becoming homeless after the withdrawal of our troops from Afghanistan, and previously, from Iraq.

The VA has reported steady declines in homelessness among vets, down to 107,000 in 2009, according to the federal Interagency Council on Homelessness.

In more recent years, HUD and the VA have issued joint press releases that rely on HUD's data. Based on the HUD count conducted on one night in January, 2013, there were 57,849 homeless vets in 2013, down from 76,329 people in 2010. However, the interagency council flatly dismisses HUD's data, saying: "That count is believed to undercount Veterans who are unsheltered."

VA says it is committed to ending veteran homelessness by the end of 2015. It has received increased appropriations to do so, and has focused on preventing vets from becoming homeless or remaining homeless for more than a few weeks.

But again, the question of what constitutes homelessness will remain for vets as well as others. In addition to the vets counted

---

Two who risked their lives for the homeless

In the early 1980s, affordable housing construction programs were being ended, and austerity was the rule for social programs. There was not much to suggest that Congress would enact a brand new, billion dollar program to help deal with the problem of homelessness.

In the winters, commuters to jobs in Washington's federal office buildings were seeing increasing numbers of people sleeping on heating grates outside their buildings. But the government had no programs to help the homeless.

The attitude in the nation's capital changed dramatically, thanks to the dedication of two men who risked their lives to help the homeless.

On the evening of March 3, 1987, a group of homeless advocates, Congressmen, and celebrities convened on the sidewalks near Capitol Hill. They slept outside to dramatize the need to pass pending legislation to create the first federal program to help address homelessness.

Rep. Stewart McKinney, a moderate from Connecticut, was the first Republican to get involved. He did not just argue for creation of a program in the halls of the Capitol, he slept outside that day in early

as homeless, "many other veterans, according to the VA, are considered near homeless or at risk because of their poverty, lack of support from family and friends, and dismal living conditions in cheap hotels or in overcrowded or substandard housing." That's according to The Substance Abuse and Mental Health Services Administration's Homelessness Resource Center, which is funded by the U.S. Department of Health and Human Services.

The cost to cities

For all but a handful of the 535 members of Congress, homelessness is a nonissue. They know there is no political price to pay for ignoring it. However, for mayors and city councils across America, homelessness is an enormous political and budgetary problem.

Every day, they hear complaints from business owners in downtown areas who say they lose customers because of the increasing presence of the homeless. Most of the homeless may be harmless, they say, but if a customer is panhandled or sees rowdy or dirty

---

March. This was despite the fact that he was suffering from AIDS, making him vulnerable to infections like pneumonia.

Two months later, in May, 1987, McKinney died at the age of 56 from AIDS-related pneumonia.

After the sleep-out, the homeless assistance legislative passed both chambers of Congress with veto-proof majorities. The law was later renamed the McKinney-Vento Homeless Assistance Act, to also acknowledge Bruce Vento, a democratic member of Congress from Minnesota, and his efforts on the issue

Mitch Snyder was another man willing to put his own health on the line to raise awareness of the homeless. He was a leader of the Community for Creative Non-Violence, one of the organizers of the sleep-out. Snyder put his body on the line time and again to get media attention, sleeping on the sidewalk in a box multiple times, and nearly starving himself to death three times. Snyder died in 1990.

Snyder and McKinney were willing to risk their lives at a time when there were "only" 250,000 to 350,000 homeless people, according to a May 1984 government estimate. In 2013, there were at least twice as many homeless people, by the most conservative estimate.

people loitering on the sidewalk in front of a business, they may go elsewhere and never come back.

Most homeless people maintain a fairly low profile, but there are those who dig through garbage cans, do drugs on the sidewalk, panhandle, litter, and relieve themselves in public. Merchants who must constantly deal with this implore city leadership to do something to "clean up the streets."

City leaders recognize that homeless people are an economic and public safety problem. They negatively impact the sales of goods and services, which mean less sales tax revenue. And their presence around the city increases commercial real estate vacancies, leading to lower property values and property tax revenue for the city.

From Atlanta to Dallas to Santa Monica, Calif., cities have tried to limit this economic damage by banning panhandling, prohibiting sitting or lying on sidewalks, and even curtailing the outreach done by charities to feed the homeless. However, even the strictest measures rarely work for the simple reason that the homeless have nowhere else to go and charities refuse to stop helping them.

Cities and counties must find dollars in their already stretched budgets each year to clean up after the homeless, put out their campfires when they get out of control, treat them in local hospitals, or house them in local jails.

The cost of the public services in Los Angeles County was recently estimated to be about $60,000 a year for a chronically homeless person and $36,000 a year for a less troubled homeless person. This includes costs for hospital care, police services, jail time, general relief, paramedics, and other programs.

It does not include any costs for shelter (other than jail or the hospital) or for police or other personnel who regularly remove people from parks and highway underpasses.

The LA study found that if the people consuming all those services could be placed in permanent housing, they'd need fewer services and cost taxpayers 19 percent to 79 percent less, depending on the kind of person and the type of housing they obtained. In addition, police, park, and highway staff would spend a lot less time patrolling and removing them.

Cleaning up homeless camps and trying to prevent them from reappearing later is very costly. In one example, the California Department of Transportation said it would spend $200,000 or more to fence off a single overpass along Interstate 280 in San Francisco to keep homeless people from returning there after being rousted in police sweeps.

In San Jose, to clean up just five of the estimated 70 homeless encampments, the city invested $632,000 in 2011, or more than $100,000 per camp.

The chronic homeless cost a fortune in medical care and incarceration. In San Diego County, the chronically homeless represent 14 percent of the overall homeless population, but they use 50 percent of available public resources, including shelters, emergency medical and law enforcement services, mental health support, and detox services. One local study found that 15 homeless San Diegans consumed $1.5 million in medical services alone over a year and a half.

In theory, it would cost much less to build and operate shelters or apartments to accommodate people without homes. But this is rarely the course that cities take. Voters in most jurisdictions would rather pay increased costs for police, fire, sanitation, and medical services than to have tax money used to house the homeless. No one wants to do anything that would give the homeless a reason to be in their neighborhoods.

• • •

The majority of federal funding for the homeless goes to emergency shelters. These are usually barrack-style facilities designed to provide only temporary respite from very cold weather. But because shelter users have nowhere else to go, these overcrowded facilities often end up housing people for long periods of time.

HUD has moved away from funding transitional housing intended to help homeless people get back on their feet. Now, the priority is for local agencies to use federal grants to prevent people from becoming homeless in the first place.

While that's a promising concept for areas with a good supply of low-cost housing, it won't work on any scale in the many areas with rapidly rising rents—that is, in almost any city with positive job growth.

In 2002, President George W. Bush announced his plan to end chronic homelessness in 10 years. President Barack Obama picked up where Bush left off. He said he would end chronic homelessness and homelessness among veterans by 2015 and family homelessness by 2020.

The current plan includes a long list of bureaucratic platitudes about better coordination between various programs and government agencies, and other similar adjustments.

The plan acknowledges the need for government subsidies to increase the supply of affordable housing, including places with supportive services.

That's the essence of the "housing first" approach that more and more mayors and advocates are pursuing. They know that emergency shelters are a costly stopgap solution that masks the extent of the problem but does little to end it. They understand that the only sustainable solution is to provide affordable, permanent housing to the very poor, and to link many of those units with social and health services. Unfortunately, the U.S. Congress shows no interest in doing that for the general population.

Meanwhile, millions more Americans are just one missed paycheck or unexpected expense from joining the ranks of the homeless as rents rise and incomes stagnate.

CHAPTER FOUR

Struggling to Find Affordable Housing

When Rosalinda Garcia was interviewed on camera about the terrible living conditions she and her family endured before getting a government-subsidized apartment, she cried so hard the camera operator had to stop taping.

The memory of the bitter year her family of four spent living in a single room in a commercial building was too fresh. They had no kitchen, no heat, no bathroom, and only a single sofa bed for all four of them. Not only was the living situation dangerous and uncomfortable, it was so embarrassing to the family's teenage daughter that she attempted suicide.

The Northern California town where they lived had lots of jobs paying low to moderate wages, but no rental housing of any kind had been built for at least 50 years. When a real estate developer finally managed to overcome all the obstacles and open new, government-subsidized apartments, the Garcia family finally got a decent apartment they could afford.

Their daughter had a room of her own and a place she could be proud to call home. There was a kitchen, a bathroom, central heating, and plenty of space. The building was energy efficient.

The Garcia family is just one of millions of households who have had to endure awful conditions while still paying as much as 50 percent or even 60 percent of their incomes for housing.

The shortage of affordable housing affects all types of communities, albeit in different ways. In rural areas, there is often little construction of housing for decades at a time, which means very little housing is available at any cost.

In suburban areas with employment growth, it's common to pay over $1,200 for a small studio apartment.

In major cities, the problem is more complex. In the fashionable parts of town, a studio apartment might go for $2,500 or more per month. In lower-income districts, costs are not as high, but neither are incomes, and low-rent units are in the worst neighborhoods and in the worst condition.

Housing costs have been rising faster than incomes for most Americans for a long time, and, after a brief pause during the recession, this "affordability gap" has been growing even wider.

The decline in home values from 2008 to 2011 has created the impression that housing is becoming more affordable. But that's a very misleading impression. In most places, prices started rising again in 2012 or 2013. For the most part, they are back on an upward trajectory that could last for decades.

• • •

Rents for apartments remained stable briefly during the recession but then quickly resumed their long upward trend.

Demographic trends point to far higher demand for housing in the near future. This comes at a time when environmental constraints and rising development costs mean that new housing construction will be insufficient to meet our needs, especially for units affordable to low- and moderate-income people.

The standard financial wisdom is that a household should budget 30 percent of its income for housing costs. By that measure, about 50 percent of all American households who rent their homes were paying more than was considered affordable in 2012, according to Harvard's JCHS.

That represented an increase of 100 percent from 1960. In that year, when Sen. John F. Kennedy was running for president, only 24 percent of Americans paid more than 30 percent of their incomes for rent. High rents relative to incomes were primarily a "big city" problem.

The data shows that the range of people and areas affected by the affordability problem has increased. But the problem is most serious for people who have less income to start with, and who are on fixed incomes such as Social Security or other forms of assistance, or a small pension.

The steady increases in the "affordability gap" are likely to continue unless something changes in how and at what cost we deliver housing, or how much state and federal governments are willing to spend on subsidies to help bridge that gap.

April 2013 marked the 34th consecutive month of growth in rents as measured by the Consumer Price Index, according to JCHS. In its "The State of the Nation's Housing 2014" report, JCHS said rents were up 2.8 percent nationwide for 2013, about the same increase as in 2012.

Rents have jumped dramatically in many places. In Portland, Ore., for example, from late 2011 to late 2013, rents increased 7.1 percent, according to the Oregon Office of Economic Analysis. In cities like Boston and San Francisco, where employment has been strong, demand for housing is driving up rents even more quickly.

The affordability gap for tenants has been getting worse for one simple reason. While rents were rising, incomes were declining, on average.

Rents rising, incomes stuck

Compared to January 2000, the median annual household income was 7.2 percent lower in June 2013, according to an analysis of Census Bureau data by Sentier Research. As of June 2013, median household income was $52,098. It had dropped 4.4 percent after the economic recovery officially began in 2009, the researchers said.

It has been an "unprecedented period of economic stagnation," said Gordon Green of Sentier Research. The data shows that almost every demographic group was worse off in 2013 than it was in 2009, with the exception of households with householders 65 to 74 years old. The declines in income have been larger than average for some groups, including black households, men living alone, young and upper-middle age brackets, part-time workers, the unemployed, females with children present, and those with only a high school degree or some college but no degree.

The problem of poverty is especially damaging to children. In 2011, more than one-third of black children (38.8 percent) and Hispanic children (34.1 percent) were living in poverty. The poverty rate for families with children headed by single mothers hit 40.9 percent in 2011.

The media has reported extensively on the financial challenges facing employees of Wal-Mart Stores, which owns Walmart and

Sam's Club and is the largest private employer in the United States. Their plight was similar to that of the roughly 5 million Americans who worked as retail salespeople in 2014.

Their median pay was $21,410 per year in 2012, or $1,784 per month, according to the Bureau of Labor Statistics. The median gross rent for an apartment in America was $861 in 2012, almost half of that gross annual wage, according to Harvard's JCHS.

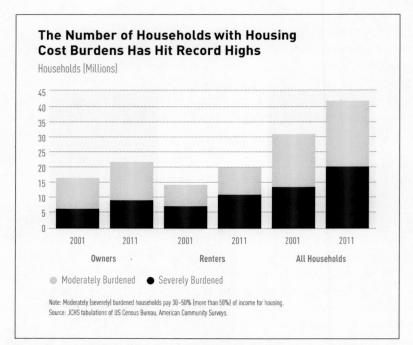

Source: Harvard Joint Center for Housing Studies, "The State of the Nation's Housing 2013".

Housing economists have coined the term "extreme rent burden" to describe paying more than half one's income for rent. In 2011, 28 percent of renter households at all income levels paid more than 50 percent of their incomes for housing, according to JCHS.

That amounts to 11.3 million households, 2.5 million more than in 2007.

Among households earning less than $15,000 per year, an astounding 70 percent paid more than half their incomes for rent. That meant they had only $7,500 left for every other household expense—for a full year.

By three separate measurements applied by Harvard's JCHS, median rents have gone up as a percentage of income in most years since 1986, with the notable exception of years when the economy was in a recession.

In its report "America's Rental Housing," Harvard's JCHS said the number of very low-income renters is increasing while the supply of housing available to them is decreasing. In 2013, 16.3 million very low-income renters competed for 12 million rental units that were both affordable and in adequate condition.

By 2009, the number of very low-income renters rose to 18 million while the number of affordable, adequate, and available units dipped to 11.6 million, pushing the supply gap to 6.4 million units. For purposes of this analysis, Harvard's JCHS excluded units occupied by higher-income households since they were not part of the universe of housing available to the very low-income group.

The affordability gap is worst for those who have no ability to increase their incomes. Seniors and the disabled rely on fixed government assistance that may not keep up with rising housing and living costs. They depend heavily on government housing subsidies, and the level of funding for that assistance has not kept up with demand.

Similarly, single parents and low-wage earners are caught in a cycle of ever increasing housing-to-income cost ratios with no chance to get ahead.

Of all Americans who are eligible for government housing assistance because they have low incomes, about 24 percent receive it. The other 76 percent must find other ways to stay sheltered.

Coping with high costs

For those paying more than 50 percent of their incomes for rent, the first of the month looms large with stress, anxiety, and uncertainty. A rent increase or an unexpected expense can mean not making the rent. They must choose whether to keep a roof over their heads in a safe neighborhood or pay for education, health care, or basic necessities.

If they fall short and their landlords don't give them a break, they face eviction, but most move voluntarily before that happens.

Half of families that spend more than 50 percent of their incomes on rent had moved within the previous 24 months, according to American Housing Survey data from 2010. A substantial number of such households move every year.

In case there is any misconception, these families generally do not move to a nicer place or neighborhood. They generally choose from among the following options:

- Move to a cheaper, smaller place or to a worse neighborhood;
- "Couch-surf" with friends or relatives;
- Split rent and share space with one or two other households;
- Move to an outlying area where housing is less expensive but commute time and costs are higher; or
- Leave the area where they were raised and have connection for somewhere cheaper

All of those adaptations help reduce the direct cost of housing, but they take a toll in other ways.

A common strategy to make rent affordable is for two or even three families to crowd into a place meant for one family.

Visit almost any lower-income area, whether multifamily apartments or single-family rentals, and you'll see the telltale signs of overcrowding. The first is the deteriorated condition of the housing. Landlords who allow over-occupancy generally don't keep up with maintenance, even though crowding creates more wear and tear.

At detached homes, you will see more cars than one family would have, some of them parked on the lawn. Inside, you will see three or four mattresses on each bedroom floor and maybe one in the living room.

Imagine what it's like to live in such a place. Waiting one's turn for the bathroom and the kitchen is just the beginning. For children, there's no place to study in peace and no way to avoid engaging with people who have no interest in helping advance the cause of education (to put it mildly).

High rent burdens require families to cut back on other expenses.

"In order to pay their monthly housing costs, low-income households with severe housing cost burdens cut back most heavily on their spending for food, transportation, health care, and retirement savings," according to the JCHS. "The lowest-income households spend about $130 less on food each month—a reduction of nearly 40 percent relative to those without housing cost burdens."

Apartment owners and managers repeatedly hear the same stories of hardship from people who beg them to overlook late rent so they can stay in their homes: The tenant lost their job or had their hours cut, their child needed medical care not covered by insurance, or their car broke down.

Many families in this situation are headed by single mothers who must decide on a daily basis what expenses can be paid and what must be neglected. As one housing assistance caseworker said, "These folks have no disposable income, they have no access to credit. They eat a lot of beans and rice and pray that there are no surprise expenses, but of course there always are."

When all other options fail, these families face the grim reality of homelessness, or living in a single motel room and trying to get by however they can. Once they have hit this point, climbing back up is nearly impossible unless they get lucky enough to find government-assisted housing.

Variations by region

Miami is popular for many reasons, but housing affordability is not one of them. In 2012, 35 percent of renter households paid more than 50 percent of their incomes for rent and utilities there, according to Harvard JCHS. That's up from 26 percent in 2000. It is among the most expensive major cities in the nation.

The share of severely cost-burdened renter households rose in every one of the top 100 metro areas in the United States from 2000 to 2009, according to data Harvard JCHS drew from the 2000 Decennial Census and the 2009 American Community Survey.

The only metro that even came close to staying level was El Paso, Texas, where the percentage only increased from 19.8 percent to 21.8 percent.

In 12 metros, the proportion with severe rent burdens rose by 10 percentage points or more, according to Harvard JCHS.

The problem of high rents as a percentage of income affects relatively affluent cities as well as relatively poor ones since it is based on rents relative to incomes. In Boston, 24.8 percent of renters had severe rent burdens in 2009. In Youngstown, Ohio, a city that has struggled with very high unemployment for decades, 24.3 percent had high rent burdens.

The good news is that severely dilapidated housing is no longer the problem it once was. Government data shows the percentage of households living in severely dilapidated housing has been decreasing steadily.

However, the improving conditions refer only to the structures involved, not the neighborhoods in which they are located. The government does not count how many Americans live in neighborhoods that are severely troubled by blight and crime.

It's a major gap in the data, since the trade-offs involved in finding something affordable to a low-wage worker are extreme. Sometimes, it's as simple as taking a place near a noisy freeway or

---

Where renters have highest cost burdens

According to 2012 data from the Census Bureau, there were 128 metro and micro areas in the U.S. in which 30 percent or more of renter households paid more than 50 percent of household income for rent and utilities. There were 11 areas where 40 percent or more of renter households had severe rent burdens, including:

- Auburn-Opelika, AL Metro Area
- Ithaca, NY Metro Area
- Alma, MI Micro Area
- Mount Pleasant, MI Micro Area
- Lawrence, KS Metro Area
- Gainesville, FL Metro Area
- College Station-Bryan, TX Metro Area
- Albany, OR Metro Area
- Corvallis, OR Metro Area
- Bloomington, IN Metro Area
- Boone, NC Micro Area

Source: the Harvard Joint Center for Housing Studies, "The State of the Nation's Housing 2014."

---

next to a vacant lot or an oil refinery.

In many cases, it's much more dangerous. The worst compromise is to move to a rundown neighborhood with a high crime rate in order to get an affordable rent. The price of this compromise can be enormous, especially for families with children.

In many inner-city neighborhoods, random gunfire is not uncommon. Stray bullets killed at least 22 children younger than 10 in 2012, according to The Washington Post. The analysis was done by a search of news databases, federal crime statistics, and websites that track violence against children. It does not include shootings that went unreported by local media.

Why would parents choose to live in such dangerous places? The answer is simple: It's the best housing they could afford.

Why the gap will widen

John Stewart builds apartments in Northern California. But like every other builder, he faces increasing obstacles every year. The San Francisco area attracts scores of jobs and young professionals, and they all need places to live. But the city usually does more to prevent housing development than to encourage it.

In 2011 and 2012, about 36,000 jobs were created in San Francisco. In the same two years, 538 residential rental units were added to the housing stock. The situation has improved more recently, but construction still falls far short of need, partly because of the elimination of all the redevelopment agencies in California, which had been a major source of housing finance. "It is just pathetic. We need a major infusion of political will to get any housing built, not to mention new financing tools," Stewart said.

With new housing construction so badly constrained prior to 2013, rents rose dramatically. This prompted calls for new restrictions on the rights of property owners to evict tenants in order to take occupancy of their own buildings or sell them.

The imbalance between housing supply and demand in San Francisco is just an extreme example of a problem that affects almost every community: It is very hard to deliver enough housing at costs that average working people can afford.

• • •

The outlook for change was not encouraging. "What does seem certain is that—absent a dramatic expansion of federal assistance to help defray the costs of renting, or a shift in state and local land use and building regulations to allow expansion of modest, high-density rental developments—affordability problems will remain at staggeringly high levels, if not worsen," according to Harvard JCHS.

As the economy started to improve, the number of U.S. households hit 117 million in 2010, up 12 percent from 2000. The number of households will rise again by about 12 million or so from 2010 to 2020, depending on assumptions about immigration, according to Harvard JCHS.

New households will drive a surge in demand for housing, but it will fall increasingly on the side of renting rather than owning, thanks to dwindling access to mortgage loans, stalled job prospects, and changes in lifestyles.

Homeownership rates have steadily declined from a historical high of 69.2 percent in 2004 to 64.8 percent in the first quarter of 2014, a decline of more than 4 percentage points.

For each percentage point decrease in the rate of homeownership, there is a shift of approximately 1.1 million households to the rental market, according to "The Trillion Dollar Apartment Industry," an analysis of Census Bureau data from the National Multifamily Housing Council (NMHC) and the National Apartment Association.

The prediction is that 400,000 or so households will enter the rental market each year through 2020. That's in addition to those who are already in the market and those who are homeless or living with friends but would love to have their own apartment if they could afford it.

In the coming years, there are many ways that housing could be made even more expensive and harder to build—and very few possible ways production could be increased and costs per unit reduced.

Incomes for most Americans will not rise nearly as fast as the costs of housing in the coming years. In fact, demographic projections indicate they will rise only marginally or even stagnate or decline for many people.

Changing demographics will accelerate the shift from ownership to rentals. "By 2030, nearly three-quarters of our households will be childless," said Douglas Bibby, head of the NMHC. "In fact, between 2000 and 2040, fully 86 percent of our household growth will be households without children."

"Our future society will be dominated by single people, unrelated people living together, couples without children, and empty nesters, and these households are much more likely to choose the flexibility, convenience, and superior locations offered by rental housing," he added.

Minority groups with their lower incomes and savings, on average, will also make up a very large percentage of new households, and those new households will be mostly renters.

The course of future demand for rental housing is pretty clear.

The big unknown is whether production of new rental housing can come anywhere close to meeting that demand, especially after subtracting the number of older units lost each year to obsolescence and demolition.

On Wall Street, stock traders focus on the real estate companies that build for solidly middle-class and affluent Americans, so you may hear them say there's a good supply of housing in the construction pipeline.

But for the "other" housing market, that is, the people with modest incomes in most parts of the country, the private market simply can't deliver large amounts of affordable housing anymore.

The rate of new apartment construction had risen from the sluggish pace of the recession years. But it would have to increase a lot more to make a dent in affordability on a national level.

New construction typically adds residences at the upper end of the rent distribution; the median monthly gross rent for units built between 2007 and 2010 was $1,052—affordable only for households earning at least $42,200 a year, according to Harvard JCHS.

"Capital sources today are investing mostly in the acquisition and development of higher-end apartment product and apartment properties in first-tier, core markets, such as New York and Los Angeles," according to a report by the NMHC.

Less affluent households have to rely on the diminishing stock of older, poorly located, or substandard housing, which is shrinking due to obsolescence and demolition.

It's almost impossible to provide new housing affordable to low- and moderate-income people in most parts of our country without the help of a state or federal government subsidy. Even in states that have a free-market orientation that involves light regulation of construction, there are considerable barriers.

"I'm a big-time free-market guy. But over the past nearly 40 years, I've come to realize that the free market can't solve this problem," said R. Lee Harris, president and CEO of Cohen-Esrey Real Estate Services in Overland Park, Kan.

For example, he said, to cover the cost of a new development in his state, a building owner would have to charge $1,300 in rent per month, assuming no government subsidy was involved.

To afford that apartment, a household would need to have $53,289 in annual salary assuming 30 percent of monthly income would go toward rent. That translates to an hourly wage of $25.62.

Unfortunately, that's about 50 percent higher than the average hourly wage of $17.02 for people working in production occupations, like factories, according to the Kansas Department of Labor.

• • •

Obviously, there's nothing to prevent people from paying more than 30 percent of their incomes for rent, but the math still doesn't work for developers. Builders will not undertake development if rents are so far out of reach of the average tenant. To help make new development appealing to investors and developers, government must offer incentives and assistance, Harris said.

The problem of future supply will also be affected by the availability of debt financing to developers and owners of apartments. The same uncertainty that gripped the single-family home mortgage market also affected multifamily housing finance after the recession. Fannie Mae and Freddie Mac played a critical role in financing apartments. As long as there was still active effort in Washington to terminate their existence, availability of an adequate supply of loans for apartments was not assured.

Many existing properties have short-term loans, and those loans have to be refinanced when they mature. There is concern that there may be few refinancing sources available for smaller properties serving a less affluent clientele. That would make it hard for owners of such properties to continue to maintain or repair them, and may accelerate the loss of affordable units.

If interest rates rise, as was widely expected to happen if economic growth accelerated, it would be one more factor driving up rents.

Demand will grow

"As the minority share of the population increases, as more and more young people form households and enter the market, so too will the demand increase for affordable rental housing," said Ron Terwilliger, who ran one of the largest apartment development firms in America for many years and also chaired Habitat for Humanity.

Earnings required to afford housing

The most expensive places to rent an apartment are Hawaii and San Francisco, according to Out of Reach 2014, a report by the National Low Income Housing Coalition.

Each year, the coalition looks at the "fair market rent" for apartments as determined by the U.S. Department of Housing and Urban Development. It then calculates how much a single wage earner needs to earn to pay for an average apartment in metro areas and states across the U.S., assuming 30 percent of income would be spent on rent. It refers to those figures as the "Housing Wage" for the state or area.

In 2014, the national average Housing Wage was $18.92 an hour. At the then-current federal minimum wage of $7.25, Out of Reach 2014 showed that, in the most expensive states, it would take 3 or 4 people working full-time minimum wage jobs to afford a decent two-bedroom rental home.

According to the report, the five most expensive states are:
- Hawaii, with a Two-Bedroom Housing Wage of $31.54.
- District of Columbia, with a Two-Bedroom Housing Wage of $28.25.
- California, with a Two-Bedroom Housing Wage of $26.04.
- Maryland, with a Two-Bedroom Housing Wage of $24.94.
- New Jersey, with a Two-Bedroom Housing Wage of $24.92.

The most expensive metropolitan area in 2014 was San Francisco, where an individual needs to earn $37.62 an hour to afford a decent two-bedroom rental unit at the fair market rent.

Meeting that demand poses a formidable challenge. In the coming years, there are many ways that housing could be made even more expensive and harder to build—and very few possible ways production could be increased and costs per unit reduced.

One of the biggest obstacles to increasing the housing supply is the cost of land. Many cities don't have significant numbers of good building sites left. Of the sites that are available, a large number are in environmentally sensitive areas or are considered brownfields, meaning that they were once the location of activities that involved toxic materials. Building housing on brownfield sites involves very high costs to fix environmental issues.

The most obvious way to cut costs is to put more units of housing on each building site, but this is far harder than it should be.

The political decisions about land use—what can be built where—
are controlled by people who already have housing. In most places
outside our major cities, those people do not approve of higher-density housing construction.

The newcomers who would benefit from new, lower-cost apartments have absolutely nothing to say about whether a locality encourages or prevents such construction.

One way around the increasing cost of land and the rising fees
is to build on green fields farther away from town centers and places
where people work. However, any savings on the costs of housing
would be offset by increased commute times, additional road construction and maintenance, and the damage done by the associated
increases in greenhouse gases.

Until governments at all levels get serous about finding solutions to the growing affordability gap, Americans of modest means,
including growing numbers of elders, face a lifelong struggle keeping a roof over their heads in a halfway decent neighborhood.

CHAPTER FIVE

The Bounce-Back Kids

Many parents expect at least one of their children to come back to live in their family home for a year or two after graduating college. But, with the new economics of housing, many young adults are staying much longer than that. Some people are even coming back to their parents' homes in middle age, after finding they can no longer earn enough to afford their own place.

The affordable housing crisis affects lower-income people the most. But the increasing number of "bounce-back kids" shows that affordability is also a problem for the middle class. And while lower-income people are eligible for government housing assistance, the children of the middle class generally get no such help.

"So far, many young adults prevented by the Great Recession from living on their own have still not formed independent households," Harvard's JCHS reported in 2013.

"As unemployment rates rose during the downturn, the share of young adults living independently dropped significantly even as the population under age 35 climbed," JCHS reported. That means more young people headed home to Mom and Dad's house: 15.3 million adults in their 20s and 3.1 million in their 30s lived in their parents' homes in 2013, JCHS said in its 2014 report.

That's 18 million people, many of whom would be forming households of their own in normal economic times, when housing costs and incomes were more in line. That means they are not generating the economic activity that comes from buying furniture, household utilities, and other home-related purchases. They are also far less likely to start families and buy the things that young parents need (and that create jobs).

The problem is partly about income. The young adults who lived with their parents had an official poverty rate of only 8.4 percent, since the statistic is based on the incomes of their entire family. However, if their rankings were determined by their own incomes, 45.3 percent would have had income falling below the poverty threshold for a single person 65 and younger, the Census Bureau stated.

Young workers have endured several years of high unemployment. Things have improved slightly, but in April 2014 the official unemployment rate was 10.6 percent for 20- to 24-year-olds, according to the Bureau of Labor Statistics.

• • •

However, this statistic understates the problem, according to liberal think tank Economic Policy Institute (EPI). There are nearly 1 million "missing" young workers—those who are neither employed nor actively seeking work because job opportunities remain so scarce, according to EPI.

Their absence from the official unemployment count gives a skewed reflection of what job-hunting is like for young adults. If these missing workers were in the labor market looking for work, the unemployment rate of all workers younger than 25 would have been 18.1 percent instead of 14.5 percent.

Among college graduates, unemployment rates are better, but not great. For young college grads, the unemployment rate was 8.5 percent in mid-2014 (compared with 5.5 percent in 2007), and the underemployment rate was 16.8 percent (compared with 9.6 percent in 2007).

Finally, the institute said that the long-run wage trends for young graduates are bleak. Since 2000, the inflation-adjusted wages of young high school graduates have dropped 10.8 percent, and those of young college graduates have dropped 7.7 percent.

The prospects for young black men and women to start their own households are much worse than those of white young adults, since they generally have a higher rate of unemployment. The unemployment rate of young black college graduates was 8.1 percent in 2007 and rose to 20 percent by 2010. It declined back to around 13 percent by mid-2014.

The unemployment rate for black young adults aged 16 to 24 as a whole, with or without college degrees, was 28.2 percent as of mid-2013, according to the Bureau of Labor Statistics.

The burden of paying for college has had a big impact on the fi-

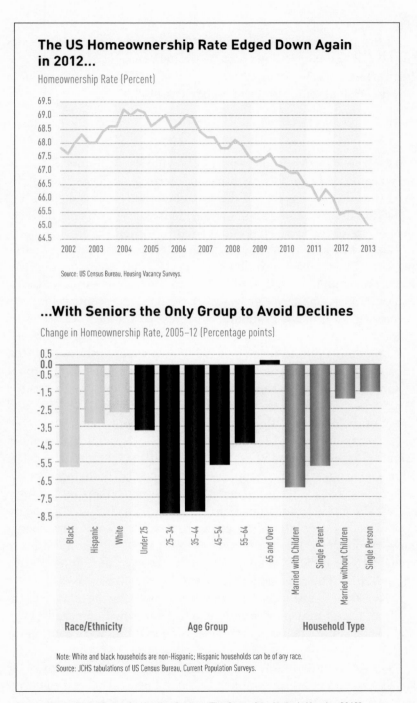

The US Homeownership Rate Edged Down Again in 2012...

Homeownership Rate (Percent)

Source: US Census Bureau, Housing Vacancy Surveys.

...With Seniors the Only Group to Avoid Declines

Change in Homeownership Rate, 2005–12 (Percentage points)

Race/Ethnicity   Age Group   Household Type

Note: White and black households are non-Hispanic; Hispanic households can be of any race.
Source: JCHS tabulations of US Census Bureau, Current Population Surveys.

Source: Harvard Joint Center for Housing Studies, "The State of the Nation's Housing 2013".

nances of young graduates, including their ability to pay for housing.

Education loans have fueled the surge in consumer debt, jumping 50 percent from the end of 2009 through the end of 2013, according to Harvard's JCHS. In 2010, 39 percent of households aged 25 to 34 had student loans, up from 26 percent in 2001.

• • •

On the waterfront just south of downtown Boston, a 21st century economic boom has been taking place. A neglected industrial area that was once considered a wasteland has become a sparkling collection of office towers full of ambitious young medical and technology entrepreneurs. They call it the Innovation District.

But while jobs are abundant and real estate is booming, the area perfectly illustrates the trouble recent college grads are having finding an apartment they can afford. In Boston, like San Jose, Calif., Austin, Texas, and other growing job centers, high rents relative to incomes pose a major economic challenge to young workers, their employers, and the cities trying to maintain economic growth.

Boston is notable because it is home to many universities that turn out the kind of graduates technology businesses want. About a third of Bostonians are between the ages of 20 and 34. That is the largest percentage of so-called "millennials" in any U.S. city, and many of them cannot afford the typical apartment rent.

A study of the local housing market in 2013 found that rents in Greater Boston averaged $1,800 compared with $1,300 a decade earlier. That's an average for the entire area. When you drill down to where the bulk of new jobs are being created, the story is much more disturbing.

In the city's Innovation District, job growth is spurring an influx of young people needing places to live. Real estate developers have responded. One of the newest apartment rental buildings is called 315 on A. The cheapest one-bedroom was renting for $3,019 in mid-2014. The most expensive went for $5,000 per month.

To reduce costs and rents, the city allowed the developer to include a large number of studio apartments, which generally have 400 to 600 square feet of space. Most of these units were renting for $2,500 to $2,900.

Only the most highly paid young adults could expect to cover those rents and still save money to buy a house. The vast majority will struggle to make ends meet, and some, if their salaries don't increase fast enough, may very well have to move back home.

In 2011, the median earnings for young adults aged 25 to 34 with a bachelor's degree was $45,000, according to the National Center for Education Statistics. After federal income taxes, a single person would be taking home about $40,000. If they have student loan debt, they'd take home less. So, to rent a studio apartment in a new building such as 315 on A, they would have to pay well over half their income for rent.

• • •

The traditional path for a college grad has been to get a job, rent an apartment, work a few years, save some money, get married, and buy a house. In theory, buying a home should have been easier than ever in recent years, with home prices below pre-2007 highs and interest rates still relatively low.

But it's gotten harder, not easier, to buy a home. Student loans and high rents eat up savings that would have gone toward down-payments. Plus, mortgages are much harder to get for young adults looking to buy their first homes.

New home prices dipped immediately after the foreclosure crisis, but this hiatus in their long upward climb did not last long. In March 2014, the national median price of a new home had recouped every bit of the mid-2000s' loss and then some, hitting an all-time high of $290,000.

From 2004 to 2014, the median price increased 30 percent, or $70,000. Over the two decades from 1994 to 2014, the median price rose by 100 percent, an increase of $126,000.

The upturn in house prices occurred across much of the country. CoreLogic reported that home prices in all but two states were on the rise as of April 2013. Prices were rising in 94 of the top 100 metropolitan areas. The pace of appreciation in 2012 ranged widely, with the largest gains in Phoenix (up 23.1 percent) and San Jose (up 18 percent).

Prior to the 2008 recession, 40 percent of households headed by individuals aged 18 to 34 owned their homes.

By the first quarter of 2014, only 36.2 percent of Americans younger than 35 were homeowners. This is the lowest percentage on record since the Census Bureau's Housing Vacancy Survey began tabulating homeownership by age in 1982. The rate of homeownership for all age groups dropped to 64.8 percent.

"Clearly, reduced access to mortgage credit, the weak economy, and uncertainty about the path of the housing market have decreased the likelihood that young heads of household will live in owner-occupied housing today," the Federal Reserve Bank of Cleveland reported.

• • •

Debbie Rohr lives with her husband and twin teenage sons in a three-bedroom home in Salinas, Calif. "The ranch-style house has a spacious kitchen that looks out on a yard filled with rosebushes. It's a modest but comfortable house, the type that Rohr, 52, pictured for herself at this stage of life. She just never imagined that it would be her childhood home."

The account of this 52-year-old woman and her family moving back into her 77-year-old mother's house appeared in the Los Angeles Times in 2014.

The newspaper reported that Rohr has been chronically unemployed and her husband lost his job in 2013, forcing them to sleep in their vehicle or live with Rohr's mother. They chose the latter option, and they are definitely not unusual.

For seven years through 2012, the number of Californians aged 50 to 64 who lived in their parents' homes swelled 67.6 percent to about 194,000, according to the UCLA Center for Health Policy Research and the Insight Center for Community Economic Development.

Looking at all adults who live with their parents, the numbers are staggering. More than 2.3 million adult children in California were living with their parents in 2011, 63 percent more than in pre-recession 2006, according to UCLA.

"A college degree is no guarantee of a job today, and an unprecedented number of families have been forced to return to a multi-generational household," said Steven P. Wallace, associate director at the UCLA Center for Health Policy Research and a co-author of the study. "Until the economy provides the kinds of jobs that allow all adults to be self-sufficient, families will need help."

The burden of making these forced extended family living situations work often falls on people who can't afford the extra stress and cost.

For one thing, it's not just affecting middle-class parents. Low-income parents account for almost one-quarter of the total number of

The Homeownership Tax Credit

What is being done to make homeownership more affordable for young adults trying to buy their first home? Not very much, at least not lately. At the height of the recession, there was a federal program of tax credits that could save eligible first-time buyers up to about $8,000 on the cost of their first home purchase. But the credit expired and was not renewed.

There is a long-established tax deduction for the cost of interest on mortgages used to buy homes, but it does "little to achieve the goal of expanding homeownership," according to the Center for Budget and Policy Priorities. "The main reason is that the bulk of its benefits go to higher-income households who generally could afford a home without assistance: In 2012, 77 percent of the benefits went to homeowners with incomes above $100,000."

The center said, "close to half of homeowners with mortgages—most of them middle- and lower-income families—receive no benefit from the deduction."

That's why a number of bipartisan groups have proposed to convert the deduction to a tax credit, which can be taken dollar for dollar against tax liability regardless of income or whether a taxpayer itemizes their deductions. This would make it much more useful to less affluent people.

The idea of enacting a permanent tax credit to reduce the cost of homeownership keeps resurfacing in Washington, but it's unclear if it will ever become law.

older parents supporting an adult child, UCLA reported. Despite having incomes that make it difficult to survive at a basic level in high-cost California, many do not qualify for state and federal assistance.

• • •

Most middle-class parents can tolerate taking their children back into the fold long after they should have formed their own stable households. But the fact that so many young people who earn modest incomes cannot go out on their own hurts our economy. The shortage of housing these young workers can afford is an economic problem, whether it's because they are just starting their careers or because they work in a low-wage field, like retail, food service, or even public service. The problem is centered among people just entering the job market, but it's part of the bigger problem of housing for the people in the workforce who earn at or near the area median income. They are not poor enough to get housing assistance, but they don't make enough to afford market-rate housing in many places.

In Austin, one of the nation's fastest growing cities, rising rents have been a big concern. "Along with other business owners and managers, I hear the concerns of employees who wonder if they will still be able to afford to live in the city where they work," said Buddy Nicoson, a vice president of Samsung Austin Semiconductor. "When hourly wage workers cannot find affordable housing, it puts at risk the ability of businesses to grow," he added.

Among people under age 35, the rate of homeownership is the lowest on record since the Census Bureau began tabulating homeownership by age in 1982

The cost of housing poses a major obstacle for companies seeking to hire and retain good employees in many large cities.

There is general agreement among politicians and policy analysts that we need affordable workforce housing.

Housing for workers should be treated like infrastructure, the same as public transit, schools, and hospitals, said Barry Zigas, director of housing policy for the Consumer Federation of America and a member of the Housing Commission of the Bipartisan Policy Center, a Washington-based organization that includes leaders from both parties.

However, there's little political agreement on what government can do to make housing more available for this group.

There are state and local programs intended to help moderate-income people buy homes, including the mortgage interest deduction. They are limited in scope and effectiveness, but at least they are of some value.

Young adults earning at or near the median income who wish to rent a home or apartment will not find much if any help from the federal government. Only a few state governments and large cities, like New York City, make any effort to address the problem of workforce housing.

CHAPTER SIX

The High Cost of Neglect

Homelessness, neighborhoods ravaged by foreclosure, cities on the verge of bankruptcy, the struggle millions of Americans face to find a nest for their families: It is hard to take it all in. There is a temptation to dismiss these problems as facts of life, things that can't be helped.

Americans who live in comfortable homes in nice neighborhoods may not see how housing and urban problems affect them. But if we take a careful look at the human and economic impact, it becomes clear that these problems affect all of us.

"A community is nothing more than a patchwork quilt, and if somewhere in a city a neighborhood is beginning to decay, the entire quilt is in jeopardy," said Jerry Abramson, lieutenant governor of Kentucky and former mayor of Louisville. He won broad support from business and political leaders as well as the voters who elected him five times partly because he built a political consensus that it was in everyone's interest to provide housing for people of all incomes.

To citizens who did not believe it was their concern if lower-income people were homeless, poorly housed, or living in blighted neighborhoods, Abramson explained that no neighborhood is an island that can hold itself aloof from the forces of urban decline.

"You better get engaged today because the patchwork quilt is fraying, and your neighborhood may be next," Abramson would tell the skeptics.

The shortage of quality affordable housing and the decay of neighborhoods from foreclosures and disinvestment are inextricably linked. The idea some people have that "good" locations can be held apart from problems in other parts of their metropolitan areas was never completely valid, and it is even less so now, given the widespread blight left by foreclosures and the sluggish pace of our economic recovery.

Look no further than the foreclosure crisis for evidence of this simple truth. It devastated lower-income communities and dashed the hopes of millions of families for increasing their wealth. But even people who were not in default on loans or living in one of the neighborhoods riddled with vacant homes have been indirectly damaged. Consider the cases of Detroit and Stockton and San Bernardino, Calif., all of were in bankruptcy in 2014, and the many other cities teetering on the brink, at least partly because of foreclosures.

> *"Public expenditures for decent housing for the nation's poor are not so much expenditures as they are essential investments in the future of American society."* —Kaiser Commission.

Our country pays multiple times for the failures to address the true nature of the housing problem.

First, there is the economic impact of housing markets that do not work for increasing numbers of our citizens. "Housing will not help lead the U.S. economy out of this recession, as it has done many times in past recessions," housing economist Anthony Downs predicted in 2011. In April 2014, construction starts were at an annual rate of just less than 1.1 million, a full 1 million units below the total for 2005. That represents a huge loss of economic activity from construction.

Then there is the social impact of severe housing problems. Housing providers and mayors know what paying more than half one's income for rent or living in horrid conditions does to people, and what it does to a neighborhood. It saps the energy and optimism of young people, leaving them vulnerable to bad influences of all kinds. Research shows it hurts the health and educational achievement of children, greatly affecting their chances to become productive, self-sufficient members of society.

We pay again as foreclosure and disinvestment causes neighborhoods to deteriorate, sometimes dragging entire cities into bankruptcy, forcing taxpayers to pay more in taxes for fewer services, and damaging property values for everyone.

Finally, even well housed city dwellers are affected by declines in property values and local tax revenue due to the declining physical and financial condition of older cities, especially those that were already in economic trouble before the recession.

Economic impact

"Beyond its benefits to families and communities, housing is an engine of the national economy and crucial to its strength. The residential housing stock itself represents more than one-third of the nation's tangible assets. The housing sector—including residential investment, housing consumption, and related spending—consistently generates more than 20 percent of the nation's gross domestic product (GDP)," according to the Millennial Housing Commission, which was appointed by the U.S. Congress in 2000.

The contribution of housing to U.S. GDP dropped to 15 percent in 2013, the Bipartisan Policy Center reported.

"This decline is a major reason why the recession and its damaging effects have lingered for so long. According to some estimates, if residential investment reflected its historical average, the current rate of economic growth could double," the center concluded.

Economists figured that, as in past recessions, there would be "pent up" demand for housing after the latest downturn ended. With mortgage rates still fairly low, that should have resulted in big increases in home sales. But in March 2014, existing home sales were down by 7.5 percent from the same period the prior year. New housing starts were down by 5.9 percent for the same period.

"The recent flattening out in housing activity could prove more protracted than currently expected rather than resuming its earlier pace of recovery," said Federal Reserve Chair Janet Yellen.

Downs and other economists pointed to the obvious answer: There is demand, but it's not "effective" demand, in economic lingo. People definitely want to buy homes. They just can't afford them.

Everyone from Yellen down to your local building contractor knows what that means: One of the most important engines of economic growth and job creation is sputtering badly.

Whether they are renters or buyers, all the people who cannot afford to form households of their own do not buy the things one needs to furnish a house or an apartment. They don't spend money on furniture, cable television, utilities, or appliances.

Families with high housing cost burdens for rent, or who lost their only sizeable asset to foreclosure, are less likely to have money for educating their children, or themselves. They are likely to be heavy users of public services and less likely to be productive taxpayers.

Housing means jobs

The National Association of Home Builders says that building an average single-family home created 2.97 jobs and generated $110,957 in taxes in 2014. Building an average rental apartment created 1.13 jobs, and generated $42,383 in taxes. (The jobs are given in full-time equivalents. A full-time equivalent is enough work to keep one worker employed for a full year based on average hours worked per week in the relevant industry). Taxes include money paid to all levels of governments, including fees and charges, such as residential permit and impact fees.

For every 100 apartment homes that are constructed, on average, $8 million is spent and 176 jobs are supported, according to "The Trillion Dollar Apartment Industry," an analysis of Census Bureau data from the National Multifamily Housing Council and the National Apartment Association.

Apartment development also creates permanent jobs for people to manage the rental and management process. The direct expense of managing 100 apartments is $352,000 per year and supports 8.5 jobs, the study reported.

Construction and renovation also generate tax revenue for states and localities, helping to support the provision of essential public services.

Government spending on subsidized housing has an added benefit: It is countercyclical. When the economy slows, development of market-rate housing decreases dramatically, but affordable housing construction generally continues. Those subsidies helped lessen the depth of the recession.

New housing also brings secondary economic activity generated by the spending of people employed in new construction and management jobs, as well as the long-term increase in spending by the people who will live in the new housing. One of the greatest unexamined costs of the decision some communities make to exclude new housing is its impact on retail sales and job creation and retention. In simple terms, if no one new is allowed to move in, growth in sales, jobs, incomes and tax revenues is not going to happen.

• • •

In New York State, the construction and rehabilitation of affordable housing generates an average annual total of 18,490 affordable housing units. This creates 31,800 jobs during construction and sustains 5,650 permanent jobs. That results in $1.8 billion in compensation during construction and $230 million in compensation annually thereafter. That level of job creation remains fairly consistent in good economic times and bad.

In addition to its direct economic contribution, construction and rehabilitation of housing plays a key role in allowing all kinds of business to recruit and keep employees.

In larger cities, like Boston and San Francisco/San Jose, business owners know it's very hard to recruit workers to fill entry-level and even mid-level jobs because of the high cost of housing.

But this is not a big-city problem. It affects small and medium-sized communities, too. In Kansas, for example, the struggle for economic progress is hampered by a lack of housing.

"Labor availability is the highest-priority long-term economic development issue in small and medium Kansas communities. An adequate supply of affordable housing is the common solution across Kansas," said Dennis Lauver, president and CEO of the Salina Area Chamber of Commerce.

In New Hampshire, the shortage of affordable workforce housing is expected to reduce employment in the state by 1,300 to 2,800 jobs annually, resulting in $21 million to $33 million less in state and local revenues.

Social benefits

Not long ago, school district officials in Glastonbury, Conn., a town with a median income of $80,660 near Hartford, kicked 48 students out of classes in their town. The children lived in nearby Hartford, and their parents lied about residency in order to get them into the high-quality schools in the affluent suburb.

The situation illustrates the lack of access to affordable housing in most of Connecticut's cities, according to David Fink, policy director for the Partnership for Strong Communities, a statewide housing policy organization, writing in the Hartford Courant.

If lower-income parents could find affordable housing in

Glastonbury, they would have been entitled to send their children to those high-quality schools, but they cannot find such housing.

Noting that Connecticut is the nation's richest state, Fink said only 31 of the state's 169 municipalities have any "appreciable" affordable housing.

"Low-income families are trapped in the 31 municipalities that,

Housing at the Heart of Financial Crisis

The official government report on the financial crisis puts much of the blame for it on foreclosures and the failure of government to prevent them. Describing the growth of high-risk lending that lead up to the crisis, it said:

"These trends were not secret. As irresponsible lending, including predatory and fraudulent practices, became more prevalent, the Federal Reserve and other regulators and authorities heard warnings from many quarters. Yet the Federal Reserve neglected its mission to ensure the safety and soundness of the nation's banking and financial system and to protect the credit rights of consumers. The Office of the Comptroller of the Currency and the Office of Thrift Supervision, caught up in turf wars, preempted state regulators from reining in abuses." – The Financial Crisis Inquiry Commission.

The report refers to the bipartisan political desire to increase home-ownership even as prices inflated into a fairly obvious bubble:

"As a nation, we set aggressive homeownership goals with the desire to extend credit to families previously denied access to the financial markets. Yet the government failed to ensure that the philosophy of op-portunity was being matched by the practical realities on the ground."

What did the government's failures in regard to housing cost us? There does not appear to be any cumulative, national estimate through 2013. However, the Joint Economic Committee of Congress estimated the following costs for the foreclosure crisis from 2007 through 2009:

- About $71 billion in housing wealth destroyed directly by foreclosures;
- More than $32 billion in housing wealth indirectly destroyed by the spillover effect of foreclosures, which reduce the value of neighboring properties; and
- State and local government losses of more than $917 million in property tax revenue as a result of the destruction of housing wealth caused by foreclosure

not coincidentally, have overburdened schools, fewer enrichment classes, and even fewer resources—parks, children's programs, sports, library branches—that foster school success," he stated.

Beyond just providing shelter, one of the goals of housing policy has been to reduce segregation of housing by income and race. There is sound social and economic basis for this. One of the most compelling benefits is to give lower-income children access to higher-quality schools, where they can obtain a good education.

Housing and zoning policies determine where people with lower incomes can afford to obtain housing. In most cases, the location of one's home determines what school they may attend.

A recent national study confirms that so-called exclusionary zoning (i.e., zoning laws that allow only low-density housing) increases the likelihood that low-income households are priced out of homes located in neighborhoods with schools that are ranked highly on the basis of standardized tests, according to research by RAND Corp.

Approximately half of students in "high-poverty schools" fail the National Assessment of Educational Progress assessments, compared with fewer than 1 in 5 students in low-poverty schools, the study said.

There is a growing gap between the academic performance of children from the wealthiest households and those from the poorest families. The gap has doubled over the last 55 years, which poses a daunting challenge for schools trying to raise low-income student achievement, according to RAND.

A concentration of low-income children within a school adds layers of challenges since it is harder to attract and retain well-prepared teachers and administrators, and also to maintain high rates of parental involvement, RAND found.

Access to good schools makes a huge difference in a child's chance for becoming a productive citizen rather than a chronic user of public services, with all the cost that entails. But it is just one of the ways in which affordable housing in good neighborhoods affects the success of our communities, our states, and our nation.

In addition to getting stuck with lower-quality schools, poor inner-city children have to contend with crime and other impacts of high housing costs, like moving every year or living in crowded conditions.

"Decent, affordable, and accessible housing fosters self-sufficiency, brings stability to families and new vitality to distressed communities, and supports overall economic growth. It improves life outcomes for children. In the process, it reduces a host of costly social and economic problems that place enormous strains on the nation's education, public health, social service, law enforcement, criminal justice, and welfare system," according to the Millennial Housing Commission.

"The failure to achieve adequate housing leads to significant societal costs," said the chairs of the commission in their cover letter to Congress.

A study released by The Pew Charitable Trust found that the economic segregation of neighborhoods is linked to a person's prospects for moving up or down the economic ladder, or what's known as economic mobility. In an analysis of 96 U.S. metropolitan areas, Pew found that those with distinct pockets of concentrated wealth and concentrated poverty have lower economic mobility than places where residents are more economically integrated.

• • •

"Where you live matters to economic mobility," said Erin Currier, who directs Pew's economic mobility research. "Neighborhoods play an important role in determining a family's prospects of moving up the economic ladder, which is especially important since a majority of metro areas have become more economically segregated over time."

None of this should come as a surprise to any policymaker or member of Congress who actually bothers to read the history of urban policy. The social benefits of providing housing assistance for low-income people was clearly described in the mid-1960s by the President's Committee on Urban Housing. The panel was better known as the Kaiser Commission after its chair, Edgar Kaiser, whose company produced hundreds of ships to help us win World War II.

"Public expenditures for decent housing for the nation's poor, like public expenditures for education and job training, are not so much expenditures as they are essential investments in the future of American society," the commission report said.

More recently, the Bipartisan Policy Center, which includes leaders from both parties, seconded that conclusion. "Affordable housing strategies that help low-income families access low-poverty neighborhoods or communities with high-performing schools can contribute to positive educational outcomes. Better educational performance, in turn, may lead to greater employment opportunities, higher incomes, and a boost to national wealth and productivity."

Another well-established benefit of new affordable housing is to improve the health of the people lucky enough to live in it, especially children, the homeless, and frail elders.

"Quality, affordable housing helps improve the health of children, older adults, and others. It can be a platform for more effective delivery of health care services. Housing that combines the attributes of stability and good quality promotes positive physical and mental health outcomes for children and adults alike," according to the Bipartisan Policy Center's Housing Commission.

Some housing providers are working in partnership with hospitals and other health care systems. Mercy Housing, for one, has formed partnerships with health care institutions. Nearly one-third of people who are low-income or homeless have a chronic health condition, according to Mercy. The nonprofit group works with several major health care systems to provide enhanced services to contribute to the well being and health of thousands of residents in the communities it serves, with a strong focus on preventive care.

Improving health

"Public health professionals say community developers have a better chance of positively impacting community health in the broad sense than the epidemiologists do, or the many acute care settings do," said Sister Lillian Murphy, former CEO of Mercy in an interview in Shelterforce, a magazine for people in the affordable-housing and neighborhood revitalization movements published by the National Housing Institute.

"Only 10 percent of a person's health can be attributed to medical care. The rest is environmental factors and lifestyle choices that either have positive or negative effects on people's broad overall health," Murphy said in the Shelterforce interview.

Chronically homeless individuals use an enormous amount of health care at public expense. Cities recognize that supportive housing would reduce their need for emergency services.

Children living in substandard housing with lead-based paint, mold, and other toxic conditions can enjoy far healthier conditions in new affordable housing.

For elders, the rate of hospitalization for people living in new affordable housing is substantially lower than for the aging population in general. Residents of seniors housing also tend to avoid the need to move to nursing care longer than other elders.

Given the enormous expenditures of federal and state governments on Medicare and Medicaid, it is certainly worth exploring the potential for affordable housing to reduce those costs. There have been limited experiments along those lines, but for the most part, Congress has not considered the potential savings in health care costs when it looks at housing program appropriations.

· · ·

The idea that we should be compassionate for those less fortunate than ourselves gets no traction in American politics today. But demographic and economic trends should give everyone a healthy concern about the economic ripple effects of the housing affordability crisis and the new wave of urban decline.

Even suburban mayors and city council members increasingly understand that the economic fate of their communities is tied to the fate of the central city in their region. That is one of the reasons they have put their political necks on the line to draw up regional plans for future development that encourage cooperation in meeting regional needs for housing. That's also the reason they have supported new taxes for regional transit systems.

Central cities are still critical to regional economic strength. Jobs may be locating in the outer areas, but regional economic strength still depends on the history, culture, arts, and tourist appeal of central cities. Even in old industrial cities without a lot of obvious tourist appeal, downtowns are still central gathering places where people can hear music, see a play, catch a sporting event, or get a good meal.

Some suburban communities have learned the hard way that ignoring the problems of inner cities simply does not work. "You cannot contain those problems. You cannot put a wall around the urban core and keep these problems from creeping out into the suburbs. You can't just keep moving farther and farther out to try to escape," said one former top federal housing and urban development official who declined to be named.

If Congress looked at the whole picture of costs and benefits, they might not be so quick to see housing and urban programs as easy targets for budget cuts. They might even begin to understand that the cuts they make today will turn into costs later—very high costs.

When neighborhoods have been allowed to deteriorate for decades, it gets harder to make them vital or self-sufficient again. They could swallow millions of dollars in spending on redevelopment with very little improvement, as several states have learned when they tried belatedly to save nearly bankrupt cities.

The damage done to young people and their prospects in life is incalculable.

But then again, the members of Congress who like to cut funding for urban and housing programs, as well as things like food stamps, almost never have to see the consequences of their actions. Local government officials are the ones who have to deal with the repercussions.

The Seeds of Hope & Change

CHAPTER SEVEN

Unleashing the Power of Revitalization

O n May 5, 1959, a real estate developer named James Rouse spoke about the urbanization of America, warning that something had to be done to help millions of Americans living in slum conditions.

He said it was the paramount purpose of architecture, urban development, and housing construction to create communities offering people of all races and incomes the chance to realize their full potential. As a nation, he said, we were making a grave mistake by failing to do that and needed to change our ways.

"We must hold fast to the realization that our cities are for people, and unless they work well for people, they are not working well at all," the Baltimore businessman told a conference in Newark, N.J.

He insisted that we could do far better and asked his audience to go forward "with a clear understanding of how to build such cities, a rich awareness that it can be done, and a fierce determination to do it."

In the half-century since, tens of thousands of Americans—from corporate CEOs, bank presidents, and real estate firms right down to municipal housing departments, ministers, and small nonprofit groups—have pulled together to do exactly that.

Empowered by the upsurge in federal, state, and local spending on housing and urban development that began in the 1960s, they have helped millions of adults improve their lives and their prospects—and given their children new opportunities. They have transformed entire neighborhoods from places of hopelessness and crime into havens of hope and opportunity.

Every politician knows they can get more votes by attacking

government programs than by celebrating success stories. They know they can raise more money by stirring up fear than betting on people's potential. This kind of negativity is everywhere in today's politics. It is particularly popular to find fault with housing and urban programs.

But politically opportunistic attacks cannot hide the truth about housing and urban programs: Over the past 50 years, they have yielded very good results.

There have been mistakes. Some programs had good intentions but flawed designs. We have seen bureaucratic delay, waste, and corruption in federal program administration at times.

Even allowing for mistakes and waste, and the setbacks caused by constant attacks from opponents of housing and urban programs, that spending has yielded a very good return on investment. It has increased our capacity to renew our built environment, strengthen the social fabric of our communities, and provide affordable housing.

"People in affordable housing want the same thing more affluent Americans want: a safe secure place to live," – Rev. Betty Pagett

---

We have shown that we know how to create communities of opportunity for people of all races and incomes. The programs have evolved and improved, and today there is an amazing amount of sophistication and a steady flow of innovation and new ideas.

The first part of this book painted a picture of urban decay and described the shortage of affordable housing. Those problems are serious and hard to solve, but the fact is, we KNOW how to solve them, if we can muster the political will to do so. This section celebrates what has worked, what has been accomplished, and new ideas for cost-effective solutions—all of which form a foundation on which to build and keep moving forward.

To start to tell that story, let's go back to James Rouse, for he, more than any other private citizen, dedicated himself to creating the communities that would help people and families thrive. He inspired thousands of people to follow in his footsteps and commit themselves to creating communities of hope for all kinds of people.

In 1967, at the height of the debate over fair housing and racial unrest, Rouse's company built a completely new town that embodied the ideals of mixed-income and racially integrated housing. Columbia, Md., is today a city of over 100,000 people. The Rouse Co. gave new life to aging cities by attracting tourists and suburban shoppers through adaptive-reuse of old industrial buildings for uses as retail markets.

Presidents and members of Congress called on Rouse to advise on housing and urban issues, starting during the Eisenhower administration. He took every chance to lobby other developers and civic leaders to care as much about the urban poor as he did. Later in life, as a philanthropist, Rouse helped create a new system of producing housing and revitalizing communities all over America. He and his wife, Patty, started The Enterprise Foundation in 1982.

As the founding chairman, he helped to establish the brand-new low-income housing tax credit (LIHTC) program, which set out to bring private corporations into key roles as investors in affordable housing construction and rehabilitation. Enacted in 1986, this new tax incentive would end up attracting billions of dollars in private equity to create roughly 100,000 apartments per year for lower-income Americans.

The foundation, now known as Enterprise Community Partners, became a major provider of housing, mortgage loans, grants, technical assistance to local nonprofit groups, and equity investments—all aimed at helping low-income families and neighborhoods.

From its inception through the end of 2013, Enterprise had done the following:

- Invested approximately $16 billion in affordable housing, health care and educational facilities, as well as commercial development in disadvantaged areas. This included $10.9 billion in equity for 2,000 affordable housing communities using the federal Low-Income Housing Tax Credit program.
- With its equity investments, grants and loans, leveraged development of real estate with a total value of $43 billion.
- Created or preserved 318,996 homes for low income families across 49 states, Washington, D.C., and Puerto Rico
- Created 13.8 million square feet of ground floor retail or community rooms in housing projects and commercial real estate in lower-income areas.

The Local Initiatives Support Corp. (LISC) has played a similar function. It got rolling in 1980 with a $10 million capital pool from the Ford Foundation, Aetna Life & Casualty, Atlantic Richfield,

Continental Illinois Bank, International Harvester, Levi Strauss & Co., and Prudential Insurance Co.

From 1980 to 2013, LISC has been instrumental in helping to create $41 billion worth of housing, community facilities, schools, and child care facilities. This includes the following accomplishments:

- 313,400 affordable homes and apartments;
- 51 million square feet of retail and community space;
- 193 schools for 77,200 students; and
- 190 child care facilities for 20,270 children.

LISC and Enterprise have devoted much of their efforts to helping local nonprofit organizations develop real estate that changes lives and improves communities.

Thanks largely to their work since 1980, there has been substantial growth in capacity of the local nonprofit groups working on the front lines of housing and community development. They know the players and the problems in their neighborhoods and towns, and they know how to work the local political angles.

Many of them have moved from serving little more than a community relations role for larger for-profit development firms to working on their own, without a for-profit partner. These community development corporations have won the trust of local lenders and investors. They have mastered the art of putting together resources from dozens of different sources to improve neighborhoods and provide housing.

A mother's new hope for her children

When Wilmina Augustin was offered a lease on a brand-new affordable apartment at Broadcreek Renaissance in Norfolk, Va., she was overjoyed. "I felt like God was right there with me," she said.

She and her two young children had been living in an emergency shelter and transitional housing after she moved out of her home to get away from an abusive relationship.

She had been earning about $20,000 a year working for a credit union, but that was not enough to rent an apartment and cover all her family's expenses. At the peak of the recession, she was laid off. With no income and nearing the end of the time limit for staying in the transitional housing, the 32-year-old faced the grim prospect of being out on the streets with her children.

Wilmina applied for assisted housing in Norfolk and other communities. All the existing affordable properties were full. It would have taken two or three years or longer to get to the top of their waiting lists. But The Community Builders, a Boston-based nonprofit developer, had just completed Broadcreek, thanks to substantial funding through the federal HOPE VI program. She was able to land an apartment there just before her stay in transitional housing was scheduled to end.

She knows she is very lucky to have an apartment with a bedroom for each member of her family at a rent she can afford. She says the property gives her and other single mothers an opportunity to build a better life for themselves and their children.

She is attending classes toward obtaining a bachelor's degree in human services. Her goal is to move back into the private housing market. "I cannot wait to see what the future brings. I want to be fully self-sufficient and give my space in the property to someone else," she said.

If it wasn't for Broadcreek, she added, she would probably have very little chance to make that happen.

When she talked about how Broadcreek had changed her life, she kept coming back to one simple fact: She knew that her children were safe at the property.

Wilmina is one of the tens of thousands of parents who trade a life of fear and uncertainty for a new start in life when they get to live in affordable housing. They go from scraping by in survival mode to being able to look for work or better work and begin saving money. The parents can get more education, and the children do better in school.

In many cases, people in affordable housing increase their incomes and their ability to pay taxes, and reduce their reliance on public services. Some families manage to do well enough to move to private, market-rate housing or save sufficient cash for a downpayment to buy a home.

Such is the power of the affordable housing being developed today. That's why housing advocates, civic leaders, elected officials, and business owners all over America are increasingly vocal in supporting it.

• • •

Slowly but surely, they are getting out in front of arguments against affordable housing development, or what is known as NIMBY, which is short for "not in my backyard." This refers to the fact that, when new affordable housing construction is proposed, many property owners say they do not want it in their backyard. These so-called NIMBYs often lobby local officials very aggressively to prevent issuance of building permits for affordable housing.

One of the first steps toward greater understanding and acceptance of affordable housing is to explain that the federal government uses two very different approaches to helping the poor afford shelter.

The Housing Choice Voucher Program gives low-income families a housing voucher they can use for any privately owned apartment that meets basic federal standards. This has the advantage of giving people mobility. However, a substantial percentage of voucher recipients end up living in single-family homes or older apartment buildings owned by individuals or small companies with little capability for providing professional management, rule enforcement, or security.

Depending on the landlord's capacity for management and need for immediate income, they may or may not do much to screen out potential tenants who have criminal records or substance abuse issues, or to evict people who cause a nuisance.

The housing tax credit program takes a completely different approach. It is used to create apartments, either through new construction or rehabilitation of older buildings. They are carefully planned and designed. They are professionally managed and often include structured social and educational programs. Family-oriented projects often have after-school programs for children. Potential tenants must go through an extensive application process and may be screened out for a variety of reasons. The properties usually have good security and do not let people who break the house rules remain in occupancy.

The resulting properties are almost always an asset to the communities in which they are built, said Rev. Betty Pagett, who worked in affordable housing development and is a minister and housing advocate in California.

"People in affordable housing want the same thing more affluent Americans want: a safe secure place to live," she said. "New affordable housing gives that to them."

When a family lives in a dangerous, overcrowded, or substandard space and has to struggle to make its rent or move regularly to avoid eviction, it creates the kind of instability and insecurity that can make a young person vulnerable to bad influences, she added.

Affordable housing offers a safe, calm, stable living situation. After-school programs at affordable housing properties add structure to a young person's life. There is also usually good security at new properties, which reduces the insecurity and fear that is a fact of daily life for people living in inner cities.

New rental housing properties usually have less crime than low-cost housing on the private market, whether detached single-family homes or a multifamily structure, she said. "New, high-quality, affordable housing doesn't bring crime, it helps reduce it," Pagett added.

Housing advocates are also increasingly winning over people who fear that construction of a new affordable housing development might reduce the values of their home.

They cite study after study that found no negative impact on property values from affordable housing construction.

Mayors and other elected officials are spreading the word that affordable housing is to be welcomed, not feared. They make three key points:

- We can create social and economic mobility without jeopardizing anyone's quality of life or safety;
- We can create more sustainable communities and help connect housing and jobs by linking housing and public transit; and
- Density does not mean concrete towers that ruin the local ambience. Good design is the norm for today's developments, and it goes a long way to making higher-density more appealing.

• • •

Jerry E. Abramson had a smile on his face when he emerged from a state helicopter in Frankfort, Ky., in the spring of 2014. The lieutenant governor of Kentucky, he had just come back from giving a small town a grant from the state's pot of federal Community Development Block Grant funds.

The money would allow the town to tear down an abandoned school and build affordable housing. Abramson did not need to present the check in person, but he was glad he did because a large number of the town's 435 residents turned out to thank him profusely. The project would never have moved forward without that check.

Abramson has been one of the most outspoken advocates for affordable housing, first as mayor of Louisville for 20 years and then as lieutenant governor.

Along with mayors like Boston's Thomas Menino (who left office in 2014), Abramson was willing to work very hard to bring disparate business and political interests together to make housing a priority for his city.

As mayor of Louisville, Abramson was a persuasive advocate for mixed-income housing and helped engineer the redevelopment of one of the city's oldest and most decrepit public housing projects. It's now called Park Duvalle and has been a great asset to the city, thanks to the federal HOPE VI program.

Abramson persuaded banks to put up the money to create the Louisville Housing Development Corp. to build affordable housing. It evolved into The Housing Partnership, Inc., and serves the entire region.

He even managed to get the suburban communities surrounding Louisville to join the effort to provide housing. In 2006, he laid the groundwork for the creation of the Louisville Affordable Housing Trust Fund, Inc.

The trust fund provides financial assistance to organizations dedicated to addressing affordable housing needs of low-income individuals and families in Jefferson County.

The city has enjoyed continuity of leadership on housing. Greg Fischer continued to support housing after taking office as mayor in 2011.

In smaller towns, elected officials also are taking the lead in meeting housing needs with the goal of increasing diversity and solving shortages of workforce housing.

Cary, N.C., is an affluent town that encourages affordable housing development. Located in the area known as the Research Triangle, which has a strong employment base, it had 135,000 residents and a median household income of $110,609 in 2011.

Many similar towns work to prevent affordable housing development. But Cary has a tradition of trying to encourage such construction. It explains why right on its website:

"Cary leaders have sought increases in the amount of affordable housing to promote economic, racial and ethnic diversity while also enlarging the pool of workers for local employers, including town government."

The city actively encourages affordable housing, sometimes providing grants, loans, and education programs aimed at preventing NIMBY responses, according to Tracy Stone-Dino, the planner for the town.

In 2010, the town consulted with citizens to create the 2020 Affordable Housing Plan, which included a range of very specific mechanisms for achieving affordable housing goals.

One of the properties the city helped to bring about is The Grove at Cary Park, a development of 120 units for families and individuals of all ages in a well-landscaped setting.

Community opposition to development of such housing has faded away to a large extent, according to DHIC, Inc., the area's oldest and largest nonprofit housing organization.

"The face of affordable housing has changed. These are not affordable homes; these are just homes that people can afford. They

Affordable apartments save energy, emissions

Affordable apartments help save energy and reduce carbon emissions even as they help address homelessness and housing cost burdens.

New housing developed with government subsidies is setting new standards for energy efficiency and reduced carbon emissions. Most developments using federal housing tax credits have high levels of efficiency, and many use alternative energy sources, like wind and solar power.

A great deal of effort is also going in to retrofitting older multifamily housing to be more energy efficient. However, even without retrofitting with modern technology, multifamily housing is inherently more energy efficient than single-family housing due to size per unit, reduced exterior exposure, and other structural differences.

On average, a household living in a building with five or more apartments consumed 24 million BTUs (British thermal units) in 2009, according to the 2009 Residential Energy Consumption Survey by the Energy Information Administration.

That is substantially less than the average consumption for a household in a single family detached dwelling units, which was 38 million BTUs in 2009. In terms of dollar costs per household, the apartment dweller would have spent about half of what the detached home dweller paid for energy in 2009.

Apartments that are occupied by lower-income families save energy in another way. The combination of higher density housing and lower average incomes means less private car trips. On average, residents of multifamily housing own fewer cars than residents of single-family housing.

are safe, stable, and clean," said DHIC President Gregg Warren.

"I can understand some of the fear because of perceptions people have had [of unattractive structures], but now it's completely different," he said. Many of the DHIC low-income communities are more attractive than surrounding market-rate apartments, he added.

Leaders in Boston, Cary, Louisville, and dozens of other cities are stepping up to the task of promoting affordable housing for two reasons: First, the programs in place today have worked very well, producing quality housing and strengthening communities. Second, the need for affordable housing is growing everywhere, and that need is affecting the economic stability and the quality of life for all portions of those communities.

Changing negative expectations

One conservative think tank used to say it was okay if lower-income people had to live in dilapidated buildings in crime-infested areas. Bad living conditions would motivate them to work harder to improve their economic status so they could move to a nicer area.

Many housing developments have discredited that theory. But no one has been more eloquent in explaining why than Bill Strickland, an inspirational leader who came from the mean streets of the Manchester area of Pittsburgh.

As a young man, Strickland watched his neighborhood go into decline. He saw black teens there fall into bad habits and drop out of school in large numbers every year. To help turn things around, he founded the Manchester Craftsmen's Guild and Bidwell Training Center. His goal was to help give young people marketable skills and a purpose in life.

From the beginning, he set out to create the highest-quality educational facility he possibly could. He filled it with the best equipment and artwork. He created a world-class facility. Critics asked him if it was wise to trust inner-city youths to treat a high-quality facility with respect.

Strickland was very clear in his response. He said that if he set high expectations for the youths and if he trusted them to meet those expectations, they would respond. He believed they would change their own expectations of themselves, and they did.

"We greet them all with the same basic recipe for success," Strickland said, "high standards, stiff challenges, a chance to develop unexplored talents, and a message many of them haven't heard before—that no matter how difficult the circumstances of their lives may be, no matter how many bad assumptions they've made about their chances in life, no matter how well they've been taught to rein in their dreams and narrow their aspirations, they have the right, and the potential, to expect to live rich and satisfying lives."

Ninety percent of the youths who come to Strickland's program get their high school diplomas and 85 percent enroll in college or some form of higher education.

Strickland now oversees a three-building campus, including a music performance and recording facility that attracts the best jazz musicians in the world. He is focused on providing education, but he knows the starting point is to give young people a positive environment that brings out the best in them.

No one explains it better than Strickland. But the exact same principle underlies everything that mayors, housing sponsors, and community development groups do every day in America.

Affordable housing providers offer families safe, high-quality homes in which they can take pride. Many go beyond that, offering tenants opportunities for social, educational, and vocational advancement.

The range of efforts being made at the state and local level is impressive. Despite many obstacles, nonprofit groups, for-profit developers, bankers, and government agencies are still finding ways to:

- Provide supportive housing for elders, the homeless, and the disabled, including veterans;
- Create affordable homes for farm laborers and rural workers;
- Repair the damage foreclosures did to the social and physical fabric of communities;
- Keep millions of people who still have mortgage problems from losing their homes;
- Redevelop blighted blocks and attract job-creating private business; and
- Better link housing development to public transit to help people get to jobs without having the cost of owning a car (or the greenhouse gas emissions).

Other groups are hard at work trying to save millions of units of existing low-rent housing from decay and demolition, including publicly owned housing and market-rate buildings.

It's hard to change entire neighborhoods and reverse years of physical and economic decline. But the combination of physical improvements, social programs, and educational efforts is making a difference. It is helping break the cycle of poverty, underachievement, and crime in America's inner cities.

• • •

When Lyndon Johnson started his War on Poverty and pushed Congress to create the Department of Housing and Urban Development, he assumed government would have to do almost all the heavy lifting to save the cities and provide affordable housing. If he were still alive, he would be amazed at what's been accomplished since then to bring private-sector financial resources and expertise into the ongoing effort to achieve his vision.

First, the Community Reinvestment Act of 1977 brought commercial banks into the business of lending and investing in low-income areas. Later, the low-income housing and New Markets tax credit programs became important tools for attracting private corporate capital.

Meanwhile, the Treasury Department worked quietly behind the scenes to create community development financial institutions (CDFIs) to provide financial resources for the nation's underserved people and communities. They handle money just like big banks and real estate investment firms do, but they are more like gardeners than traditional financiers: They see their work as nurturing the growth of communities.

They are an entirely new type of institution in America. Like charities, they aim to help people, but like businesses, they have a responsibility to give their investors a return on investment.

Many CDFIs started with housing and then expanded to provide community facilities, like charter schools and day care centers. Some of them get involved in creating commercial ventures that help create jobs in low-income areas.

This growing community capital sector offers an important path forward in an era of cynicism about the big banks and political opposition to high-cost government programs.

They have prospered as investors have realized the importance of the "double bottom line," that is, the ability to earn a reasonable investment return while achieving something for the public good.

Because CDFIs are intermediaries between people with money

and people who need it, they have to be accountable to investors, and their ability to deliver the results they promise is obvious for all to see.

Government program administrators, on the other hand, are judged by how well they follow detailed rules and procedures, and how thoroughly they fill out the paperwork to prove they complied with all those processes.

One of the CDFIs leading the charge for new ways to get things done is the Low Income Investment Fund (LIIF).

The housing and community development business is in the midst of a "knowledge revolution" that will facilitate the integration of people-oriented and "place-based" investments, said Nancy Andrews, president and CEO. In other words, the place-based work of fixing decaying neighborhoods and building housing will increasingly merge with traditional people-oriented things like child care and early childhood development, mental and physical health care, and education.

With hundreds of CDFIs at work on multiple fronts, including some for-profit organizations, there is enormous potential for bringing in double or triple the amount of capital now flowing into housing and community development. Of course, that depends on the U.S. Congress having the good sense to maintain regulatory and tax incentives and to keep providing grants for "patient money," as developers like to call investments that don't have tons of strings and time limits attached.

There are enormous challenges ahead as we cope with economic weakness, decaying infrastructure, competition for resources, and runaway housing costs relative to incomes. But when one looks back at all that's been achieved since James Rouse started his campaign to eliminate slum conditions, it's clear that we CAN do great things, if we CHOOSE to do them.

CHAPTER EIGHT

America's Housing Success Story

Despite the nationwide trend of rising rents, thousands of American families are finding housing they can afford and much more thanks to a program that began as an afterthought to Ronald Reagan's overhaul of the U.S. tax code in 1986.

The longest-running success story in public policy on housing is officially known as the Low-Income Housing Tax Credit (LIHTC). It is the only nationwide program for constructing and rehabilitating affordable rental housing in America.

It is the key ingredient in everything from new apartments for low-income elders to the rehabilitation of decaying public housing. It provides critical funding for such diverse things as supportive housing for homeless people and the adaptive reuse of unused school buildings for housing.

Housing finance agencies in all 50 states, plus the District of Columbia, Puerto Rico, and the Virgin Islands, used tax credits to finance more than 2.6 million affordable rental homes from 1987 through 2011, according to the National Council of State Housing Agencies. By the end of 2014, the total was expected to be well more than 3 million units of housing.

The program represents a departure from previous federal programs because it relies on decentralized administration by state housing finance agencies. The state agencies, rather than the federal government, decide which projects should be financed with tax credits based on each state's housing needs and make sure deals are feasible and compliant with the goals and requirements of the statute.

Furthermore, instead of a direct government subsidy, property developers are given the opportunity to sell the tax credit that accrues to eligible properties. It is possible for individuals to invest in a pool of tax credit properties, claim a tax credit on their tax return, and, with that credit, get a dollar for dollar reduction in their tax liability. However, the largest source of investment comes from corporations with substantial levels of tax liability.

In return for the break on their taxes, corporations invest for a period of at least 15 years in housing that serves people earning no more than 60 percent of the area median income.

This puts the responsibility for underwriting the feasibility of each property in the hands of investors like Warren Buffett's Berkshire Hathaway, Chevron, Google, Verizon, and Allstate, to name a few. Banks are very active in the program, providing construction financing, permanent loans, and equity investments.

The most amazing thing about the program is the bipartisan support it enjoys in Washington. Legislation to increase the amount of tax credit authority available under the program received co-sponsorship by 456 of the 535 members of Congress in 2000. In 2005, in the wake of Hurricane Katrina, Congress gave the program still another vote of confidence, creating a special pot of tax credit authority to help build housing in the areas most impacted by the hurricane.

The positive results are evident in the program's track record, according to the Bipartisan Policy Center's Housing Commission. "Over the first 24 years of the LIHTC program's existence, it financed more than 16,000 properties. During that period only 98 properties experienced foreclosure, an aggregate foreclosure rate of just 0.62 percent. This record is unmatched by any other real estate class, including residential and nonresidential real estate," the commission reports.

But that only describes the program from a statistical point of view. The true legacy of the program is its power to improve the lives of Americans and create supportive, safe communities. There is powerful testimony from many people who say their lives were changed or even saved thanks to housing produced by the tax credit.

"Once I found out I would be able to get an apartment [at a tax credit property in Michigan], it seemed to be a dream come true, like a terrible weight had been lifted from my shoulders," said Deborah

Helbig. Prior to finding that housing, the U.S. Army veteran was homeless and could not find a job. "I was really without any hope of where or how I would be able to find or afford to have a home. I was praying that I would be accepted (at the property)."

The tax credit is the lynchpin in a complex but highly effective public-private partnership. It has encouraged private developers and city and state governments to work together in hundreds of creative ways.

They joined forces to combine funding from multiple sources, from foundations and social service organizations to state mental health departments. They acquired land for construction from the surplus supply held by school districts or city departments.

The program always provides good quality rental housing, but, in most cases, it goes far beyond that. Many developments for families provide services like job training, social services, youth programs, and more. Properties designed for the elderly usually incorporate basic social services.

The program also provides a critical building block for developments that combine the provision of housing with the delivery of social and health services. These developments serve people with all kinds of special needs, including veterans, the elderly, and the chronically homeless.

Tax credit developments often address the conditions of the neighborhoods where they are to be located, such as reducing the blight from large numbers of foreclosed homes and vacant lots, or the adaptive-reuse of historic buildings for new use as housing.

Recycling real estate

In June 2014, St. Paul, Minn., got back a piece of its heritage—along with 260 units of top-quality housing – thanks to the LIHTC.

It had been 20 years since the lights went out on the iconic "Schmidt" sign over the brewery that made beer under that brand name. In 2014, the sign was restored and relit in a public ceremony, but this time it was calling attention to a new residential community rather than a manufacturing plant.

The project was the work of Dominium, a Minnesota-based real estate developer specializing in renovating older buildings that were built to last longer than their original owners or uses lasted. The firm is one of many in America that use the housing tax credit along with a tax credit for historic preservation to practice the art of "adaptive reuse."

Over the years, that has involved a wide range of transformations in cities across the nation. Empty office buildings, old hotels, surplus schools, and old industrial buildings have been renovated and adapted to serve as housing.

Partly because many of our solid but functionally obsolete buildings are industrial facilities with high ceilings, they have lent themselves to conversion into loft-style apartments that have a special appeal to artists.

Cities like this type of housing for several reasons. First, it takes care of the problems that come with having a giant, derelict building in the middle of town, bringing activity and jobs where once there was just a decaying hulk of a building. They also like the idea of providing housing for low-income artists.

Artists are the pioneers of urban revitalization. They are the ones who happily take on the challenge of living in areas undergoing redevelopment. What's more, they bring vitality and creativity to these areas, making and displaying art that helps attract visitors.

The new Schmidt Artist Lofts offers 247 residential units and 13 new townhouses in a St. Paul landmark dating back to 1855.

• • •

In America's Rust Belt, many communities were hit hard by the foreclosure crisis, compounding a long struggle with economic woes. On Milwaukee's north side, a local real estate developer used the housing tax credit to help address the scars left by foreclosures there.

Gorman & Co., Inc., took a bite out of two prevailing problems in its Milwaukee neighborhood—foreclosures and unemployment. Focusing within a two-mile area, Gorman purchased vacant lots from the city to build 40 single-family homes for rent to lower-income families. This infill development helped restore the vitality and stability of the area.

But the firm did not stop there. It also substantially rehabilitated a series of duplexes that were in dilapidated condition to provide another 40 affordable units and preserve the neighborhood's character.

"It has stabilized the neighborhood," said Ted Matkom, Wisconsin market president for the firm. "It has eliminated blight. When you drive down the street it looks like a new subdivision."

Known as the Northside Housing Initiative, the project also helped address unemployment, which stood at 50 percent for African-Americans. Gorman partnered with the Northcott Neighborhood House to train youths and adults with troubled backgrounds to work in construction. More than 50 full-time jobs were created for graduates of the program during construction, giving them valuable experience on top of their training.

Residents of the single-family homes will have an opportunity to buy their houses at the end of the federally mandated 15-year rental period.

The new homes are part of a forward-looking decision by the city at the height of the foreclosure crisis. City leaders recognized that homes could be acquired inexpensively, giving the city the ability to take control of not just individual homes but entire blocks and neighborhoods. This control would be essential to helping stabilize areas with high rates of foreclosure.

The $16.4 million Northside Housing Initiative is made up of two low-income housing tax credit projects that target families earning no more than 50 percent to 60 percent of the area median income.

It is a prime example of how private developers and corporations looking to reduce their tax liability are working with cities to address local housing and community revitalization goals.

• • •

In a park-like setting in San Antonio, a building financed with housing tax credits is helping pregnant teens and teenage mothers to improve their lives and become contributing members of society. More importantly, it is giving their babies the chance to avoid the neglect, poverty, and educational failure that many of their moms endured.

Seton Home is named in honor of St. Elizabeth Ann Seton, the first American-born saint. A mother of five children, she raised them on her own after losing her husband. She is a model for single mothers in her commitment to improving her community, founding St. Joseph's Academy and Free School, the first free school for girls in the United States.

Using the tax credit, Seton Home and DMA Development Co.

created a campus with 24 efficiency apartments of about 500 square feet each. Each unit has a kitchen, a bathroom, a built-in kitchen table, and living and sleeping areas. There are several common areas, including a teaching kitchen and dining area, as well as a seperate childcare center for the babies while the teen mothers attend school.

The facility helps desperate young mothers progress from crisis to self-sufficiency through a model of care that interrupts the recurring pattern of teen pregnancy, child abuse, and neglect. Most of the

Struggling to the Finish Line

The process of creating new affordable housing is incredibly complicated. While it usually produces a very good-quality product, getting to completion involves intense effort to put together financing, since no single source of capital is sufficient to cover all costs. The cost of all this effort is substantial, not just in labor and time spent, but also in terms of fees and interest payments, not to mention legal fees.

These costs are in addition to the cost of getting entitlements and a building permit, as well as hard construction costs. An article in Hawaii Business by Dennis Hollier described the challenges for one developer very well:

"Building affordable housing is complicated," says Makani Maeva. She should know. As Hawaii director for Vitus Group, an affordable housing developer, she recently completed the Lokahi Apartments with 307 units in Kona. Between January 2007, when another developer laid the project in her lap, and July 2010, when the apartments first were offered for rent, almost all the financial and technical details of the deal changed dramatically: The permanent loan went from $16.4 million to $19.2 million; the original equity investors—GMAC, Wachovia, and others—had to be replaced; $7.8 million in housing tax credits from the County of Hawaii became unavailable, replaced by a soft mortgage of $11.75 million from the state's rental housing trust fund; and the cost of construction rose from $53 million to $60.6 million, largely due to interest costs."

"The complexity of Lokahi's financial arrangements is hardly unique. In fact, the average affordable housing project in Hawaii is funded by at least seven financial instruments—industry insiders say some projects require as many as 14—each of which comes with its own rules. That's just the financing. The truth is everything about affordable housing is complicated and constantly changing—the money, politics, regulations, ethics".

young mothers and mothers-to-be are 12 to 17 when they come to the facility and have no income or savings.

They typically come from homes where there is drug and alcohol use or domestic violence. Many have suffered physical and/or sexual abuse by someone in their own homes. They often do poorly in school or drop out altogether. Some of the girls come to the facility from the streets, having already fled the terrible conditions in their homes.

If they had remained on their own, few of the girls would finish school, but Seton Home helps them get an education. The staff provides day care for their babies and transports the mothers to schools. It also teaches some courses on-site at the property. A key goal is to make sure every girl gets a high school diploma or passes the General Educational Development exam. Psychotherapy and counseling are also offered.

Without Seton Home, many of the teens would have ended up repeating the cycle of domestic abuse. The goal of the facility is to break the cycle, said Margret Bamford, executive director. "We believe that we can end that cycle, and we can give those children a chance at a decent life", Bamford said.

Residents are permitted to stay in the housing until they turn 22. During their stay, the staff at Seton Home works hard to help them become self-sufficient. "It has helped so many teenage mothers get onto the right path and have a productive life," said Bamford.

Most tax credit properties involve a lot of "creative financing." Funding must be cobbled together from a wide range of government and private sources. In this case, even more money was needed since none of the tenants could pay anything out of their own pockets for rent.

The development cost about $5.8 million. Equity investment attracted by the availability of the tax credit covered just over half that cost. Other funds came from the city of San Antonio and Bexar County (from federal HOME funds), the Federal Home Loan Bank of Dallas, foundations and gifts from local corporations, businesses and individuals.

A new start for vets

On Veterans Day, 2013, some of the estimated 2,500 veterans who are homeless in the state of Michigan had reason to celebrate. Using the tax credit program, a private developer opened the doors to 100 one-bedroom apartments designed and managed just for them.

Together with apartments built in an earlier phase, it brought the total number of apartments for homeless vets at the Silver Star Apartments to 176, all of which were quickly leased. In response to the still-unmet demand, a third building was in the planning stages in 2014.

The Battle Creek, Mich., property was developed by Kalamazoo developer Marvin D. Veltkamp on surplus land owned by the U.S. Department of Veterans Affairs (VA) adjacent to its medical facility in the town.

Named after one of the military's highest honors, Silver Star provides much more than just a roof over the heads of vets who were previously homeless.

Many of the first vets to move into the property had no income at all. Many lived a life of despair, according to Veltkamp. They suffered from post-traumatic stress disorder and other after-effects of their military service. Then after discharge, they found themselves unable to afford good housing. Navigating the VA bureaucracy was impossible for most, so they couldn't access the services and financial benefits they needed.

Silver Star provides its residents with counseling, as well as assistance in dealing with the VA to get their benefit entitlements. There is a training program to help tenants learn job skills, such as building maintenance.

The apartments are all one-bedroom units with kitchens. They are furnished, down to shower curtains and bed linens.

Residents of Silver Star can walk to the medical center, or access on-site case management, job training, healthcare, and other supportive services.

Michael Carter was one of the vets who moved in with hopes of making a new start. With a new apartment, he went back to school part-time, studying human services. "I look at it as my chance to give back for all the things that I've been given," said Carter. He also got a paying job at the property providing assistance to other vets.

Michigan State Housing Development Authority gives supportive housing like Silver Star high priority for its limited volume of tax credit authority. It provided tax credits to attract the private capital needed to build the project. It also provided housing vouchers, which were necessary to cover the gap between what the tenants could pay and the actual rents for the units.

Baseball, housing & school

The East Harlem section of Manhattan is packed with apartments and commercial buildings, leaving few outdoor spaces for children to play.

That changed when a group of volunteers transformed an abandoned, garbage-strewn lot into two baseball diamonds that became known as the Field of Dreams. The volunteers who made it happen organized a youth services group called Harlem RBI, which has become an important provider of educational services for local kids, operating a charter school, among other things.

> *"We are doing everything we can to make sure these kids have the opportunity to become the leaders of tomorrow," –Mark Teixeira, New York Yankees first baseman.*

Thanks to the LIHTC, Harlem RBI has now started construction on its first affordable housing project.

This project includes a permanent home for DREAM Charter School, a 450-student, K-8 program, as well as 89 units of affordable housing, headquarters for Harlem RBI, and the renovation of the nearby Blake Hobbs Park.

"These children and families deserve a beautiful, state-of-the-art educational facility where they can learn, a park where they are safe to play, and Harlem RBI and DREAM by their side to help them grow," said Mark Teixeira, Harlem RBI board member and New York Yankees first baseman.

The project was being developed by Jonathan Rose Cos.

"There are five critical elements that help create communities of opportunities, and this development provides them all: safe, green affordable housing, energy efficiency to lower residents' utility bills, easy access to mass transportation, a nearby park, job training, short-term and permanent employment opportunities, and a superb education for the community's children," said Jonathan Rose, president of the firm.

The apartments are for households earning less than 60 percent of the area median income.

"We are doing everything we can to make sure these kids have the opportunity to become the leaders of tomorrow," Teixeira concluded.

• • •

The housing tax credit program started out as an experiment in 1986 and was set to expire after just a few years. But in 1993, it was made a permanent part of the tax code. Many states followed the federal lead and created credits against state tax liability for the same kinds of housing.

The program harnessed the power of public and private sectors working together in partnership.

It gave rise to new capacity on the part of state housing finance agencies and helped create a thriving group of nonprofit developers.

What housing developers liked best was that the program completely bypassed the federal bureaucracy. The up-front process of deciding which properties receive tax credits is handled at the state level by state housing finance agencies, according to the qualified allocation plans they devise to meet their housing needs. There is no approval or application process with the federal government.

What government officials liked was that private developers, lenders, and equity investors bear most of the real estate risk of each property, not the government. If they do screw up on a specific project, the government can get back all the tax credits it authorized for that property.

The only problem with the tax credit program is that the hundreds of thousands of people who find apartments subsidized by the program each year represent only a fraction of the people who need help. When a new property opens, it often has five to 10 times more applicants on opening day than it can accommodate.

The program is also limited by the fact that it is a shallow subsidy, which means it does not provide enough subsidy dollars to produce housing for people who earn much less than 60 percent of the area median income without other government subsidies, which are increasingly scarce. In communities with very low incomes, it doesn't work at all without large amounts of additional funding.

At the same time, federal and state cutbacks in other housing programs put an increasing burden on the program. For example, elimination of the Sec. 202 program for new construction means tax credits are the only source of subsidy for new development of seniors housing.

The tax credit program also bears a heavy burden for financing the rehabilitation of old buildings subsidized under the public housing and Sec. 8 program. In other words, the tax credit has become the catchall program that has survived while other more specialized programs have been reduced or eliminated. It's not an exaggeration to say that almost all our housing eggs are in this one basket.

To make sure it can meet future needs, housing advocates are calling on Congress to double the size of the tax credit program. If Congress agrees to double the amount of tax credit authority, the program can come closer to meeting future needs for new, high-quality rental housing.

CHAPTER NINE

Transforming
Neighborhoods & Lives

In the fall of 2013 as the snow began to fly in Denver, families were settling into brand-new apartments at a community that demonstrates how once-distressed neighborhoods are being transformed across our country.

A bright, mosaic-style painting of a butterfly and a sculpture of a flower blooming greeted people as they started new lives in 93 new apartments at Mariposa, as the development is called. The new residents ranged from those living on public assistance up to downtown office workers earning good salaries.

The Denver Housing Authority's multiyear plan, worked out with extensive input from residents and neighbors, called for six phases of development, replacing rundown, 1950s-vintage, cinder-block public housing on a 17.5-acre site in the Lincoln Park/La Alma area west of downtown with 457 new residences—and much more.

There would be 200 brand-new public housing units, 104 rental units for people earning up to 60 percent of the area median income, 147 apartments at market-rate rents with no income limits, and six for-sale townhomes to be built by Habitat for Humanity.

Besides housing, Mariposa will have public gathering spaces, office and retail space for educational and social service groups, parks, and a large early childhood education center.

Developed by the housing authority with help from the city and a grant from the federal HOPE VI program, Mariposa provides vastly improved housing to the folks who lived in the old South Lincoln Homes. But it does much more than that. It was designed from the ground up to create a new community that would be an asset for the entire neighborhood and a place of security and opportunity for residents.

The design connects the mixed-use structures to a station on the region's new light-rail network, giving residents immediate access to transportation and much less need for a car. Mariposa will generate much of its electrical power and heat from solar panels and geothermal installations. It will feature extensive programs to help residents lead healthy lives, with social services for those who need help and plenty of creative stimulation, from a music studio to several public art installations.

Mariposa is a model for redevelopment of decaying neighborhoods in the 21st century. It is carefully integrated into the overall plan for the city, but it also reflects the concerns and objectives of local residents and businesses, thanks to a lengthy citizen-driven planning process.

> *"Supporting families in mixed-income residential environments is the best anti-poverty strategy the nation can have."*
> –**Patrick Clancy**

The property is particularly innovative in addressing two of the dysfunctions that typically afflict inner-city residents: bad health, particularly obesity, and lack of motivation for youths.

In a unique approach to encourage healthy living, a sculpture was placed in the central stairwell of the five-story building that opened in 2013. But it's no ordinary, static sculpture. It is an interactive sound and light display that reflects the Hispanic culture of many area residents and educates tenants about the history of the Mayans of Central America—all while they are walking up and down five flights of stairs instead of taking elevators.

Young residents are encouraged to get involved in educational and creative activities. "We want to give them the opportunity to break out of the cycle of intergenerational poverty, " said Ismael Guerrero, executive director of the housing authority. The grand plan calls for an extensive array of services and programs, from an early childhood education facility run by Catholic Charities to a recording studio operated by Youth on Record, a nonprofit providing music education to at-risk youths. There will be a computer lab, a cafe that doubles as a culinary training center, and meeting spaces for all kinds of neighborhood groups.

In addition to the HOPE VI grant, the project was funded by equity investment attracted by federal tax credits. The equity investment was provided by The Richman Group and Enterprise Community Partners.

Origins of HOPE VI

HOPE VI is a fitting name for the program that made Mariposa possible. It stands for Housing Opportunities for People Everywhere. When it was first started under President George H.W. Bush, it was intended to address the problems of poverty among residents of public housing by helping them take ownership of their apartments.

In 1993, a new variation on the HOPE theme was launched. Called HOPE VI to distinguish it from previous efforts, it provided large grants to transform the worst public housing in America, much of it dating back to the 1950s, into mixed-income and mixed-use developments. The program encourages tenant self-sufficiency and sometimes includes for-sale housing, but it is about starting over, rather than selling existing apartments to tenants.

HOPE VI got underway under Henry Cisneros, the former mayor of San Antonio and HUD secretary in the first Clinton Administration. It had the monumental goal of turning around the 86,000 units of public housing that were considered "severely distressed".

"We are transforming public housing projects with problems into new mixed-income communities with promise," said Andrew Cuomo, HUD secretary in the second Clinton administration. "We are making public housing a launching pad to opportunity, jobs, and self-sufficiency—instead of a warehouse trapping people in poverty and long-term dependence."

The program's goals have been realized to a large extent. HOPE VI has turned the worst public housing projects into catalysts for revitalization of neighborhoods and the growth of individuals. It has provided distressed areas with exactly what its name suggests: hope.

Over the course of 15 years, 254 HOPE VI grants have been awarded. They went to 132 housing agencies to demolish 96,200 public housing units and produce 107,800 new or renovated housing units, of which 56,800 would be made affordable to the lowest-income households.

In 2009, Atlanta reached a milestone when the walls started coming down at Bowen Homes. The demolition marked the end of Atlanta's large, old-line public housing projects. After being the nation's first to build public housing, Atlanta was the first major city to redevelop all of its large projects and to replace them with mixed-use, mixed-income communities, planned, developed, owned and managed by public/private partnerships, with the private sector developer leading the effort.

As of December 2013, 16 such communities have been developed, leveraging approximately $300 million of public housing development funds with over $3 billion of private funds, other public funds and private investment.

In Chicago, after more than 10 years of steady effort and having received significant HOPE VI funding, the Chicago Housing Authority has demolished all of its old, high-rise public housing and redeveloped most of the project sites.

Millions of Americans have visited Fisherman's Wharf in San Francisco. Before 2005, they would have walked quickly past the public housing project close by the cable car line on Taylor Street. Today, tourists stop in at Trader Joe's or one of the other retail shops on the block while the people who used to endure terrible conditions in the old public housing enjoy modern, comfortable housing, plus a high level of security. Developed by BRIDGE Housing, The John Stewart Co., and E.M. Johnson, North Beach Place, a HOPE VI redevelopment, has 341 units of housing.

It's no wonder that some public housing was in serious trouble. The program was created at the height of the Depression to provide large quantities of housing as cheaply as possible. Over the decades, partly because of housing and job discrimination in the private housing markets, an increasing proportion of the tenants of the "projects" were poor minorities.

By the 1990s, public housing had become the federal program that provided housing for the poorest of the poor in America.

Among households residing in public housing in recent years, 45 percent were black compared with 12.6 percent of the general population, according to HUD. Sixty-seven percent of public housing tenants had incomes below 30 percent of the area median income.

In Atlanta in 1994, over 90% of public housing residents were black and greater than 77% had incomes below $7,000, well below 30% of the area median.

There are dozens of reasons why public housing projects have deteriorated—in some cases to the point of becoming uninhabitable. The first reason can be found in the initial design of the program itself, relying as it did on public housing agencies known more for being part of local political machines than for their ability to manage housing efficiently.

Most public housing agencies have been totally dependent on federal subsidies for survival and did not, until recently, have to bother mastering the normal steps involved in real estate management. With less than competent management and repeated cuts in federal subsidies, many agencies allowed their housing properties to decay badly. There were always exceptions, of course. Some public housing agencies have been well run and effective, such as the New York City Housing Authority. Many others have taken great strides to improve operations in recent years.

"In an era when much is written and said about the widening income gaps between America's affluent and its poor, HOPE VI showed how to turn America's worst neighborhoods from factories of inequality into beacons of opportunity and inspiration".

Some of the worst failures in public housing can be traced to an urban design concept that has proved to be a costly mistake. While some planners of the early projects argued for low-rise buildings or even townhouses, they often lost out to those who wanted high-rise construction. The idea was that by building 10-, 15-, or even 20-story buildings, there would be plenty of room for open space between buildings. This often also involved building on so-called "super blocks," where the normal grid of streets and blocks was interrupted.

The idea was to separate the housing in a park-like setting. However, the concept often failed miserably. The high-rise towers were isolated from the surrounding neighborhoods, and security was hard to maintain. Factor in problems with maintenance and management, and it's easy to see how some poorly maintained properties became hellholes with rampant crime.

One of the leaders in the movement to change the terrible fate of public housing residents was Renee Glover, who took over the Atlanta Housing Authority in 1994. She knew she had to do something to change the very old public housing properties in her city. She saw her chance when Atlanta started planning for the 1996 Olympics.

Tens of thousands of visitors from around the globe would be heading for Olympic venues that were nearly within sight of Techwood Homes and the neighboring Clark Howell Homes, two of the oldest and most decayed public housing projects in America.

Built in the 1930s, they had deteriorated badly over the years. In 1993, over one-third of the 1,195 barrack-style units were vacant and another third occupied by overcrowded households. The units had outdated heating, sewer, and plumbing systems, as well as lead-based paint. In 1992, there were 8,670 calls to police and private security staff about crime at the property. That's almost 24 calls per day.

Glover knew the Olympic Games were the catalyst she needed to deal with the failed property. She marshaled support throughout the city and in Washington for a comprehensive plan to reverse the corrosive effect of concentrated poverty on the buildings' residents and the surrounding neighborhoods.

Glover wanted to do more than just impress visitors to the Olympics with new apartment buildings. She wanted to eliminate the terrible living conditions and severe concentrations of poverty that were commonplace in Atlanta's old public housing projects.

Glover described older properties as "warehouses for the poor" that perpetuated intergenerational poverty.

"In the large public housing family communities, you'll find extreme, multigenerational poverty—average incomes of approximately $7,300 per year and exceedingly high rates of unemployment—with only 15 percent of the able-bodied population working," Glover testified to Congress.

The schools near those properties had very poor test scores, high levels of illiteracy or functional illiteracy at graduation, and high truancy rates, she added. The surrounding areas had high crime rates, no new private investment for decades, and high levels of disinvestment.

In 1993, the Atlanta Housing Authority was awarded a $42.5 million HOPE VI grant to renovate Techwood Homes and one-third of Clark Howell Homes. The authority and its partners used the grant to plan, create and develop a new mixed-use, mixed-income community called Centennial Place. It is considered the prototype for all the HOPE VI developments that followed. It has 738 units spread over 60 acres. There is nearly an even split between its market-rate units (311) and its public housing units (301).

Another 126 apartments are rented to households earning no more than 60 percent of the area median income. The affordable apartments are seamlessly mixed with the market-rate apartments.

Centennial Place has a new high-performing elementary school, Centennial Place Elementary, a new YMCA, which provides early childhood development and after-school programs, a SunTrust bank branch, a Sheltering Arms early childhood development center, and for sale market-rate and affordable townhomes.

In Denver and many other cities, the most important part of the HOPE VI transformation is opening up new opportunities and a new outlook for children and youths. In Denver, there are 26,000 residents of public housing, and about one-third of them are younger than 18.

In Atlanta, this focus on youths has involved construction of completely new schools. Improved educational facilities have been critical to the goal of long-term economic progress for people returning from the demolished public housing projects.

Saving the children

At The Villages of East Lake, another Atlanta mixed-use, mixed-income community that involved redevelopment of old public housing, there is a seamless educational program for infants through high school students. The new Charles R. Drew Charter School was the highest-performing elementary school and the third highest-performing middle school in the Atlanta public school system.

Parents with children as young as 6 weeks old can get much more than day care for their infants and toddlers. The property has a language and literacy program intended to address the early childhood period when inner-city kids often fall behind in intellectual development.

In 2014, East Lake opened a 200,000-square-foot extension of the charter school to offer classes all the way through 12th grade.

The priority on education is part of a new management focus that comes with the new buildings. The sponsors of mixed-use, mixed-income communities work hard to give people a new sense of purpose and to create new possibilities for children.

Property managers and other partners also work with adults to help them gain skills and find jobs.

The new mixed-use, mixed-income communities, represent a new start, not just physically but also socially. Residents of the old public housing buildings that are redeveloped don't get to take a unit at the new housing automatically. They must apply to come back to the rebuilt public housing units, and they may be rejected if they don't agree to new rules and meet a new set of tenant screening criteria. In some places, there is a requirement that at least one member of each household must hold down a job or be in job training. People with criminal records are generally rejected.

The new management attitude, coupled with physical measures to enhance security, has vastly reduced the rampant crime that often afflicted tenants before redevelopment.

For families and the elderly, who make up a large proportion of public housing residents, nothing is more important than being able to come and go from their homes without fear. "Kids feel safe about playing outside and walking to school, and their parents feel secure in letting them do so," said Guerrero of the Denver Housing Authority.

Promoting mixed-income communities

The story of HOPE VI is primarily about replacing obsolete, decaying buildings with new, comfortable, efficient housing. But at its best, the program has been a bold experiment in achieving something the nation's fair housing laws have not accomplished: Bringing people of all races and at all income levels into cohesive, healthy communities.

Denver Housing Authority says it is working to create "vibrant communities," that is, places that appeal to people with moderate to high incomes and give lower-income people a new outlook and new opportunities.

The public housing agencies and private developers that work together on HOPE VI ventures believe diverse, mixed-income communities are the only way to permanently end the concentration of poverty and the crime and social dysfunctions it breeds.

The goal is to mix the residents so that there is no physical dividing line between public housing tenants and higher-income families. Oftentimes, separate buildings for elderly people are part of the overall development.

"We looked at concentrated poverty as the result of what happened when financially successful people who had choices left a neighborhood," said Egbert L.J. Perry, chairman and CEO of Integral of Atlanta. "To change that, you have to reintroduce disposable income, and you can only do that by making the community attractive to affluent people once again," he added.

Integral partnered with McCormack Baron Salazar, Inc., of St. Louis to develop Centennial Place. Since that project, McCormack Baron Salazar has completed 30 HOPE VI projects. As of 2014, it was developing five properties under the new federal Choice Neighborhoods program, making it one of the largest practitioners of neighborhood transformation in America.

• • •

In Denver, mixing incomes is having a very positive effect, said Guerrero. "We are seeing a diversity dividend. We are attracting folks who want to live in a diverse community. It gives our lower-income tenants pride of place to know they are in a nicely designed, desirable location, with people who choose to live there." The Denver Housing Authority believes this is important because the more pride tenants feel, the more effort they will make to take care of the property and advance their own economic condition.

One organization that has studied the complexities of making mixed-income housing work is The Community Builders (TCB), a Boston nonprofit that has completed 15 public housing redevelopment projects.

"The mixed-income model is what many urban neighborhoods were like 75 years ago, but today it means working hard to recreate environments where diverse people live together," said Pat Clancy, TCB's former president and CEO.

TCB works very hard to help public housing residents improve their job skills and find jobs, while offering their children educational opportunities. At TCB, services are provided through a program called Ways & Means.

The program is really more like life coaching than property management; it just happens to be delivered in a residential setting. It requires TCB staff and tenants to work together to meet ambitious and measurable goals. Key goals include doubling tenants' earned incomes and cutting the high school dropout rate for young tenants by 50 percent.

The main areas of focus are:

- Financial coaching and access to financial products and asset building tools;
- Career development; and
- Youth development.

The fourth element of Ways & Means is to build what TCB calls

Deconcentrating Poverty

People used to call Atlanta's East Lake public housing project "little Vietnam," not because of the nationality of the people who lived there, but because it was like a war zone. The East Lake Foundation worked with the Atlanta Housing Authority to transform the area into The Villages of East Lake, a mixed-income apartment community with 542 townhouses, duplexes, and garden apartments, a charter school, a YMCA, a golf course, and more.

"We all knew that tinkering around the edges wasn't going to change anything. We decided we were going to start over. We wanted to create a neighborhood that was a launching pad to help everyone reach their full potential," said Carol R. Naughton, senior vice president of Purpose Built Communities, a nonprofit consulting group that has helped with this project and others like it. The transformation is reflected in these statistics:

Before redevelopment when all tenants were in public housing:
- The average income was $4,500 per year per family;
- The average age of a grandmother was 32;
- The high school graduation rate was 30 percent;
- The percentage of adults employed was 13.5 percent;
- 59 percent of adults relied on welfare; and
- Only 5 percent of fifth-graders met state standards for math.

After redevelopment as a mixed-income community:
- All adults receiving government housing assistance were working or in job training;
- Only 5 percent of adults relied on welfare;
- 98 percent of Drew Charter School students (grades three to eight) met or exceeded state standards for math and reading;
- The crime rate dropped by 70 percent, and the rate of violent crime was down 90 percent; and
- The median income was $15,000 for families in public housing.

"social capital." Clancy defined it as "neighbors connecting with neighbors to get things done or families getting value from each other and becoming part of each other's success."

In a lot of urban settings, where new combinations of people live side by side, the social fabric is pretty thin, Clancy said. "If you maximize diversity, you have got to lay a common foundation. You have to build a spirit of community where people want to support each other. It's a long-term investment," he said.

The payoff comes after years of effort, Clancy added, when youths graduate school instead of dropping out, and think about jobs and higher education instead of being lured by the toxic culture of "the street."

"Supporting families in mixed-income residential environments is the best anti-poverty strategy the nation can have," Clancy said.

In an era when much is written and said about the widening income gaps between America's affluent and its poor, HOPE VI showed how to turn America's worst neighborhoods from factories of inequality into beacons of opportunity and inspiration.

In Denver, 54 percent of the people living in the old South Lincoln Homes were children. The name of the new property is Mariposa, which is Spanish for butterfly. It's a fitting name for a property that will give flight to the dreams of children so that they might have better lives than their parents had.

· · ·

HOPE VI redevelopment cost the government a lot of money, but everyone who works on them and sees the transformation first-hand firmly believes it was worth every penny.

Developers and government agencies consider HOPE VI a great investment because the grants it provided served as a financial foundation, providing the assurance of viability needed to attract large quantities of private debt and equity capital.

"The HOPE VI grant is typically the first money that is committed to a development and is totally catalytic," said John Stewart, chairman of The John Stewart Co, co-developer of North Beach Place. A typical development brings together eight to 12 other sources of funds, with each dollar of federal money leveraging anywhere from $5 to $10 of money from other public and private sources.

Stewart explains why the program has been very popular with

Republicans as well as Democrats: It has privatized many properties that were previously owned and operated by public agencies.

In most cases, private investors put up large amounts of the cost of these developments, attracted by the HOPE VI grant as well as federal low-income housing tax credits for the "workforce housing" included in the new mixed-income buildings.

While the land under the buildings remained federal property, control of the housing, including property management, shifted to the private sector.

But the HOPE VI program did even more to transform publlic housing. It encouraged a large number of public housing authorities to contract with private real estate companies to manage their buildings, enabling delivery of better services at lower costs.

It set a new direction for public housing based on the idea that properties should be operated well enough to compete with private housing for tenants.

The federal government encourages this by allowing some housing authorities to convert federal public housing subsidies into rental assistance that can be used to attract private capital, something not possible with traditional public housing. The Rental Assistance Demonstration was limited in scope in 2014, but had great potential, according to Conrad Egan, chairman of Community Preservation Development Corporation, which is adapting an old school in Richmond VA., for use as affordable housing under this program.

In 2011, the HOPE VI program morphed into a program called Choice Neighborhoods. HOPE VI was focused on making physical improvements, with the requirement that housing agencies also encourage tenants' self-sufficiency. Choice Neighborhoods takes the best parts of the HOPE VI experience and tries to build on them for a larger universe of low-income housing properties, not just public housing.

Choice Neighborhoods makes it a fundamental requirement to do what the best HOPE VI properties did voluntarily: improve education, job training and health services in addition to improving housing, including obtaining funds from other government agencies for those purposes.

The only question was whether Congress would continue to see it as a good investment for the future of tens of thousands of children, seniors and other people living in public housing and provide sufficient funding to continue it on a significant scale.

CHAPTER TEN

Reinvesting in Communities

W hen bankers stopped making loans on homes in Chicago's working-class Austin neighborhood, they did not bargain on the reaction from a housewife named Gale Cincotta.

The bankers said the neighborhood was "in transition," which meant its racial composition was changing. For that reason, they had drawn a red line around the area on the city maps they kept on their walls. That meant they would not lend there for home improvements or home purchases.

A brash, straight-talking woman who knew how to use a megaphone, Cincotta would not sit still for that. By 1972, she and her friend, Shel Trapp, had started a national movement to outlaw the practice known as "redlining."

She and Trapp formed National People's Action (NPA) and sought meetings with everyone from the presidents of banks to Paul Volcker, then chairman of the Federal Reserve Board. If they were told to go away, they would camp out in front of the buildings where the executives worked and try to attract media attention until meetings were arranged.

Forty years later, the community reinvestment movement has advanced dramatically. The people who followed in Cincotta's footsteps have been working in partnership with major banks and Fortune 500 corporations to funnel billions of dollars into lower-income and minority areas and affordable housing. Battles with banks still occurred, but they have been about advancing already substantial progress.

A whole new type of lending and investment company has taken root, offering investors the double bottom line of a reasonable return on investment and a positive impact on society. These community development financial institutions (CDFIs), many of which made no profit, were handling billions of dollars in capital with excellent social results and solid financial performance.

Innovative financial instruments have been created, and new ones are in development to bring the sophistication of Wall Street to bear on solving social and community problems. The Obama Administration has tried to encourage one of the most intriguing, which is the Pay for Success (PFS) financing model. In broad terms, under this technique, government agencies rely on private investors to finance programs with a social service component and pay them back their investment plus a profit if the program delivers the desired results, such as measurable increases in high school graduation rates.

But most promising of all has been the progress toward tapping into hundreds of billions of dollars controlled by individual investors. The goal is to make it as easy for any individual investor to put $1,000 or $5,000 in housing and community development projects as it is for them to buy stock in any publicly traded company through Schwab or E-trade.

The roots of reinvestment

In the 1960s and early 1970s, if one bank decided to stop lending in a certain area, other banks followed suit. It meant that no one in that area could get a loan to fix a house or buy one. The dearth of credit meant homes would deteriorate and lose value. It was a self-fulfilling prophecy: Banks feared they would have too much risk so they stopped lending, and when they stopped lending, they created exactly the kind of decline they feared.

Cincotta and Trapp organized Chicagoans around the need to stop redlining and restart the flow of credit for home purchases and home improvements in neglected areas. Through National People's Action, they, with many others, convinced Congress to enact two landmark laws that ushered in a new era of vigorous bank participation in inner-city and minority areas.

The first was the Home Mortgage Disclosure Act (HMDA), a 1975 law that requires banks to publicly reveal where they make loans, giving activists a way to see what areas had been neglected. In 1977, Congress passed the Community Reinvestment Act (CRA). This requires banks and savings institutions to offer credit throughout their entire market area. After CRA, they could no longer take deposits from people in lower-income areas and then deny credit to the people in those neighborhoods.

CRA regulatory considerations have been a driving force to encourage bank involvement in community and economic development. The law applies only to depository institutions, that is, those that take deposits in checking accounts and savings vehicles, so it leaves out a lot of institutions, including insurance companies. However, it has still had a substantial impact.

In 2011, U.S. financial institutions made $209 billion in CRA-related loans, including $47 billion of community development lending, according to the Federal Financial Institutions Examination Council, which coordinates the work of the federal banking regulatory agencies that enforce CRA.

The CRA also helped convince hundreds of bankers that investing in places they once feared was perfectly good business. It has been instrumental in getting banks to make equity investments and loans for affordable housing developed using the low-income housing tax credit program.

Activists use HMDA to identify lending patterns in their areas. Then, if they see a problem, they can file a challenge based on CRA. The federal banking regulators consider CRA compliance whenever a bank applies for approval for a merger or other action, and if compliance is not good, the application could be denied.

Cincotta passed away in 2001, but the legacy she and Trapp left can be summed up succinctly: Instead of running away from lower-income neighborhoods and their credit needs, banks are having a positive impact in such areas—and bragging about their good works.

Not long ago, Bank of America issued a press release boasting about having received its seventh consecutive "outstanding" rating under CRA. The rating shows that Bank of America had done very well in meeting the need of underserved communities in areas such as affordable housing, small business lending, and financial education during the period covered by the ranking.

"As America's largest bank, we know that our success hinges on the success of the communities we serve," said Andrew D. Plepler, a global corporate social responsibility and consumer policy executive at Bank of America. "Our seventh consecutive 'outstanding' rating reflects Bank of America's continuing leadership and commitment in serving the needs of low- and moderate-income individuals, businesses, and neighborhoods across the United States."

Small business lending generally counts toward compliance with CRA, and many banks focus in this area. For example, in 2014, Wells Fargo announced plans to extend $100 billion in new lending to small businesses by 2018.

Goldman Sachs also received an "outstanding" rating, largely because it made $2 billion in loans and investments in lower-income communities from October 2010 until December 2012, a 32 percent increase from its previous level of CRA activity.

In many cases, the question of whether a bank is doing enough to comply with CRA has been resolved through negotiation.

Community development groups file a challenge to regulatory approval of a bank merger or expansion (or other regulated activity). This gives banks a compelling reason to negotiate commitments to specific investment and lending programs so that the challenge will be withdrawn, eliminating any obstacle to receiving the regulatory approval the bank needs.

These agreements commit banks to specific amounts of loans and investments for affordable housing, small businesses, economic development, and community service facilities in minority and lower-income neighborhoods.

From 1977 through the first part of 2007, lenders and community organizations have negotiated and lenders have committed over $4.56 trillion in reinvestment dollars. That's according to the National Community Reinvestment Coalition, which represents local groups working on increasing credit availability.

• • •

If you have not visited Cincinnati for some time, you might not recognize it. The Ohio River port city had suffered a long period of decline, especially in the area known as Over-the-Rhine, a name that dates to the 1800s when it was settled by German immigrants who referred to the Miami and Erie Canal as their version of the Rhine River.

For decades, the neighborhood had been losing population, and crime had been rising. Now the city and private developers are turning it back into a thriving neighborhood with mixed-income apartments and a variety of retail and entertainment thanks to a program of federal tax credits for economic development.

Making space for charter schools

Although they are public schools, charter schools often do not have the right to use school district buildings or easy access to traditional methods for financing school construction. That's why a number of Community Development Financial Institutions (CDFIs) founded the Charter School Financing Partnership (CSFP).

The CSFP aggregates capital and uses its member's access to secondary market financing for charter schools that serve disadvantaged students and communities.

Since November 2010, CSFP has committed support to ten charter school facilities in New Jersey, New York, Massachusetts, California, Minnesota, Arkansas and Michigan. This represents almost $20 million in credit enhancements from CSFP, which in turn leverages almost $158 million of financing for schools serving over 7,300 disadvantaged students from low-income communities.

According to a 2012 survey by the National Alliance for Public Charter Schools, 56 percent of public charter schools said their current facility would not have adequate space for enrollment in five years. Demand for public charter schools is at an all-time high, as states across the country continue to establish and strengthen charter school laws. More than two million students attend approximately 6,000 charter schools, and tens of thousands more students are on waiting lists nationwide, according to CSFP.

The CSFP was founded by NCB Capital Impact, Low Income Investment Fund, The Reinvestment Fund, Raza Development Fund, the Community Reinvestment Fund and the Housing Partnership Network

One of the ways these CDFIs solve the dual problems of affordability of housing and access to education is to finance development of charter school facilities on the same sites as housing built with low-income housing tax credits.

Local corporations working through a nonprofit known as 3CDC, have spearheaded the revitalization efforts, investing more than $466 million in Cincinnati's Central Business District and Over-The-Rhine area.

Crime has dropped more than 50 percent, about 4,000 construction jobs have been created, and over 30 new businesses have moved into the neighborhood, and that's just for starters.

A key driver of this reinvestment was a federal tax incentive called the New Markets Tax Credit (NMTC) program.

The Community Reinvestment Act works behind the scenes but does not direct capital into any specific investment. Congress created the New Markets Tax Credit to attract capital for bigger, riskier projects that would create jobs. The U.S. Department of the Treasury awards the credit through a competitive application process. The idea is to encourage economic development in places that had been neglected by the regular flow of investment, hence the name "new markets."

This tax credit program offers those willing to invest in economically distressed communities (those with poverty rates over 20 percent) a seven-year, 39 percent federal tax credit. With the capital raised from the tax credit, community development entities finance loans and investments in business and economic development projects that otherwise might not get off the ground.

"Since its inception, the NMTC has generated $60 billion in capital for projects in low-income communities resulting in creation of over 550,000 jobs in traditionally overlooked communities in order to spur economic development, private investment, and create jobs," said Rep. Richard Neal (D-Mass.).

"This is a federal program that works—spurring investment that grows local economies and generates jobs in the most distressed communities across the nation," Neal added.

Between 2003 and 2012, $20 billion in private capital was invested in communities with high poverty rates, low incomes, and high unemployment rates. This $20 billion leveraged an additional $25 billion in capital from other public and private sources, financing everything from health care centers to charter schools, healthy and affordable groceries, community centers, domestic violence shelters, factories, and small business loan funds in distressed urban, suburban, and rural communities.

A Treasury Department analysis found that every $1 of foregone tax revenues under the NMTC program leverages about $12 of private investment in distressed communities.

The NMTC has been used to great effect by CDFIs. However, they do much more than orchestrate these economic development projects. Their creativity and ingenuity in addressing community needs is one of the most exciting untold stories of the 2000s.

They focus a great deal of effort on affordable housing and economic development, but they have branched out to address the need for healthy grocery sources, higher-quality schools, and day care facilities in low-income areas.

Nancy Andrews runs one of the most dynamic CDFIs in America, known as the Low Income Investment Fund (LIIF). It was founded in 1984 with a primary focus on affordable housing but has expanded dramatically since then.

"While the nation faces a recession, the people and places we serve experience a depression. These communities suffer unemployment levels as high as 20 percent, while basic services like health care and child care are stretched to the point of breaking," said Andrews.

LIIF is a critical financial resource for the people working in those places to provide housing and community facilities. "We provide stopgap financing to service providers facing state and local funding shortfalls that threaten their programs; we struggle to keep community projects alive, even as the resources to support them dry up," Andrews said.

LIIF and groups like it raise capital from foundations and other philanthropic organizations, government agencies, and traditional lenders, including the nation's largest banks.

"We build bridges between unconventional borrowers and commercial lenders, providing capital in ways that allow socially important projects to go forward. We provide only that portion of a financial package that will not come from more traditional sources," said Andrews.

Over 30 years, LIIF has invested $1.5 billion in projects that served 1.7 million people. It estimates that this investment has yielded social benefits of $30 billion. This includes, for example, $13 billion in social benefits from early childhood education centers it has made possible, assuming $7 in benefit for each $1 invested, generated by increased family income, educational attainment, and reduced societal costs such as incarceration and special education.

Individual investors

The next frontier in the battle to attract more private investment capital for affordable housing and community development is to get individual investors involved. CDFIs know there are millions of affluent Americans who invest their savings in stocks and bonds but also would invest for social impact if they had an easy, safe way to do so.

The Northern California Community Loan Fund (NCCLF) is one of those CDFIs trying to appeal to socially responsible investors, said Mary A. Rogier, president.

NCCLF already gets a substantial amount of its capital from individuals. These investors can choose the rate of interest they wish to receive, from zero up to 3.25 percent (as of mid-2014 for a ten-year investment). The maximum rate was reasonable, considering the yield on 10-year Treasury notes was only 2.59 percent at that time.

Investors with NCCLF like the idea that their money is used to provide loans and lines of credit to nonprofit groups to build housing, develop community facilities, and provide social services. These are considered risky uses of loaned money, but the organization's cumulative loss rate was very low, and over 26 years of operation, none of its individual investors have lost any money at all.

However, Rogier and other community lenders know they are just standing at the doorway of the individual investor market. There are millions of Americans who like the idea of "socially responsible investments," known as SRI.

The next goal is to get Wall Street to help make the connection between the CDFIs and those individual investors. Stockbrokers and investment advisors are heavily regulated, and generally are not familiar with community development investing. Therefore, this is a complicated and slow process.

There are thousands of mutual funds in America. They offer investors easy ways to invest in everything from Treasury bonds to biotech stocks to commodities. But as of 2014, there was only one publicly offered fund open to any investor that targets community development and affordable housing. The Calvert Foundation's Community Investment Note, and it makes investments worldwide, not just in the United States. Investors working with stock brokers can invest as little as $1,000 and earn up to 3% for a 10-year term. Individuals can invest as little as $20 through on on-line system.

From 1995 to 2013, more than 13,000 people have invested in it, knowing their money would help finance job creation and affordable housing, and promote education, protect the environment, and create numerous other social impacts.

Rogier and many others are working hard to create other options for investors. By the 2020s, it is very likely that Calvert will have multiple competitors and that the number of individual investors will be in the millions.

Meanwhile, other groups are working to expand and update the CRA. In this case, community credit activists are perfectly aligned with the big banks on one of the key goals for change: To expand the scope of the law to include credit unions and financial institutions that do not take deposits such as insurance companies. It's a challenging goal, but, given time, they are very likely to succeed, creating a new flow of credit and equity investment into disadvantaged areas.

Congress gave the growing CDFI industry a very big shot in the arm recently, approving a program of federal guarantees for bonds to be issued for CDFI programs. The Small Business Jobs Act of 2010 authorized federal support for up to $1 billion in bonds. This is in addition to previously enacted programs to support CDFIs.

CHAPTER ELEVEN

Restoring the Potential of Homeownership

The foreclosure crisis left many people, including members of Congress, believing that helping low-and moderate-income families become homeowners only leads to trouble. But every day, government housing agencies and nonprofit groups are proving that assumption is unfair, shortsighted, and just plain wrong.

Their message is as simple as it is hopeful: Homeownership remains a viable option for working people when it is done deliberately and prudently, without using risky kinds of mortgages and without the "get rich quick" hype that drove people to leap before they looked during the early 2000s.

"We've proven over almost 20 years of providing opportunity for low- and moderate-income people that the American dream of sustainable homeownership is alive and well," said Marietta Rodriguez, vice president of homeownership and lending programs at NeighborWorks America. Her organization works with a network of 235 local, community-based nonprofit groups to deliver services and programs that help low-income people buy homes and stay in those homes.

The foreclosure crisis did not deter state housing finance agencies and private nonprofits all across America from helping less affluent families become first-time homeowners. They do that with a wide range of programs, from development of low-cost homes and counseling about household finances and mortgage loan options to the provision of safe, low-cost mortgage financing.

The potential to create equity by becoming a homeowner is a critical step for people to achieve upward economic mobility. It is also important for the creation of stable, mixed-income communities.

That potential is one of the reasons the federal government has funded programs to promote homeownership since 1934. It's also the reason that thousands of people working in housing and community development do the hard work required to help people buy their first homes and keep current on their mortgages.

A key political champion of government efforts to help low-income families become homeowners was a prominent Republican. Jack Kemp, a congressman and former secretary of the Department of Housing and Urban Development, spoke eloquently about the potential benefits of helping people move from public housing to owning their own homes. He died in 2009, but his idea has been implemented on a small scale all over America.

In Louisville, Ky., for example, the housing authority is one of many that allow recipients of housing choice vouchers to use the subsidy toward a mortgage payment instead of rent on an apartment.

Over 12 years, the authority has helped 200 households buy homes in this way. Thanks to intensive counseling before and after the purchase, it has had only two of those low-income households default on their loans, said Tim Barry, the authority's director.

Chris Krehmeyer is another one of the people leading the efforts to encourage homeownership and strengthen lower-income neighborhoods. In 2013, he marked his 20th anniversary with Beyond Housing, a nonprofit based in St. Louis.

"Home is the bedrock for a stronger nation. It is where we are nourished, protected, supported, encouraged to dream, and enabled to thrive," he said.

Krehmeyer knows that making homeownership possible and sustainable for less affluent people is not mysterious. It is just very hard work that requires sustained effort and continuous contact between borrowers and lenders. It also costs money, and that's a primary reason why community-based nonprofits like Beyond Housing can succeed where for-profit lenders might fail.

Beyond Housing and similar groups start by helping potential buyers understand the housing market and mortgage lending process. The next step is counseling buyers on their own finances, goals, and housing needs.

Another step is to help people get their financial affairs in order. This usually means helping them save money for a downpayment, manage other debt, and cut expenses. It's what old-fashioned lenders used to call being "thrifty."

One of the primary tools to help lower-income people save money for downpayments is the Individual Development Account (IDA) matched-savings program. Housing counselors help a family set a goal, map out a savings plan, and begin saving. Every dollar saved by a participant is matched, typically, at a rate of $3 for every $1 saved. The match is funded by the federal government, state governments, and private donations, which are sometimes attracted by state tax credits.

A critical element is direct financial assistance, including grants to help pay the required downpayment. Beyond Housing, like many other groups, uses federal funds under the HOME Investment Partnerships Program for this purpose. It can be used for people earning up to 80 percent of the area median income.

NeighborWorks calls its approach to mortgage lending "full cycle lending." In addition to up-front education and counseling, NeighborWorks groups maintain a financial relationship with their borrowers. They help clients with refinancing their loans or paying for home repairs. They also help borrowers if they have problems staying current on their loans.

The system works, according to a study by outside experts. Borrowers working with NeighborWorks were one-third less likely to become 90-plus days delinquent over the two years after receiving their loans compared with borrowers who did not receive pre-purchase counseling from NeighborWorks organizations.

Housing counseling got a huge boost in 2012 when five major mortgage servicers agreed to pay $26 billion to settle a suit by state and federal governments for abuses in mortgage loan servicing and foreclosures. The agreement provided substantial financial relief to homeowners and established new homeowner protections for the future. About $2.6 billion of the settlement was paid in cash directly to states.

The states have used these funds to assist distressed homeowners in a variety of ways, such as funding state and local foreclosure assistance hotlines, housing counseling services, legal assistance programs, and foreclosure mediation programs.

• • •

Sarah Ferrer knows the value of being able to build wealth by owning a home. She also knows she could not have done it without help. Although she made a decent wage in a professional job, the cost of even a modest house in her South Florida region was just too high. And this was after the foreclosure crisis dampened home prices.

"I have a good job and a college education, but I could not afford anything," said Ferrer, a professional with the Drug Abuse Foundation of Palm Beach County.

Like millions of other would-be buyers, Ferrer's problem wasn't so much about education and counseling as it was about finding ways to bridge the gap between what she could pay and the price of a home.

"I have a good job and a college education, but I could not afford anything (on the housing market.)" –Sarah Ferrer

---

The solution for her was the Delray Beach Community Land Trust, one of a growing number of land trusts that make homeownership affordable for moderate-income households. In this innovative model, a nonprofit organization buys land (or accepts donations of land) and then leases it to an eligible family at a cost far less than what it would be as part of the home purchase price.

The net effect is to "zero out" the cost of the land for the homebuyer.

The trade-off is simple: When the owner wants to move, they can sell the property to another income-qualified land trust client for a price that reflects a limited degree of appreciation. This forestalls the wild inflation in home prices that helped precipitate the foreclosure crisis. The owner shares some of the equity gain with the land trust, helping it expand assistance to more buyers. All parties benefit, including future buyers.

"I tried to find a home for about two years before I got involved with the Delray Beach Community Land Trust," said Ferrer. "If it weren't for the land trust, I wouldn't be a homeowner—that's for sure," she added.

"Working households with normal salaries struggle to afford a home to live in and are unable to use real estate as an investment for their future. It feels good to know that your hard work is an investment in your family's future, not an investor's future. It feels good to come home each day to your own home and have pride in sharing your home with family and friends," she said.

Ferrer purchased a newly built three-bedroom townhome in downtown Delray Beach for $185,000—compared with the $285,000 it would have cost without the land trust. The cost of land would have made the townhouse an impossible dream, but the land trust leased her the site for $40 per month.

There are more than 200 land trusts around the nation running programs similar to the one in Delray Beach. The state of Maryland is one of the jurisdictions that encourages this approach. It passed its Affordable Housing Land Trust Act as part of a multifaceted effort to provide more affordable housing in the state. Gov. Martin O'Malley has prioritized using state resources to support affordable housing and has called on the federal government for support.

Land trusts also help buyers finance home purchases. Loans made by community land trusts were much less likely to go bad compared with loans by conventional lenders, according to a study by Lincoln Institute of Land Policy.

The research concluded that the active involvement of trusts with their borrowers explains the lower rates. "The high prevalence of comprehensive stewardship practices—spanning education, prevention, and intervention activities—may help to explain the low rates of delinquencies and foreclosures and high cure rates in trusts," it found.

State housing agencies step in

The largest and most stable source of mortgage loans for less affluent people after the foreclosure wave hit were the private lenders offering loans insured by the Federal Housing Administration (FHA). The FHA insures repayment of loans for modestly priced homes, giving lenders the confidence to make loans to people who might not qualify without that federal guarantee. In the fourth quarter of fiscal year 2013, FHA insured about 204,000 home loans, a rate of about 800,000 per year.

From 2008 to 2011, FHA made homeownership possible for 2.27 million first-time buyers. The agency supported 56 percent of all first-time buyers in 2009 and 2010, according to annual surveys performed by the National Association of Realtors. The average downpayment on FHA loans has held steady at just 6 percent of the purchase price.

In 2011, FHA reported that it led the market in support for minority homeownership. FHA insurance was used for 46 percent of all mortgage loans made to minority borrowers. That compares to FHA's 37 percent share of the entire mortgage market.

While FHA has continued to provide insurance that enables lenders to make loans, like other federal housing programs, it has been affected by budget cutbacks. The federal Treasury has liability to cover losses in FHA insurance programs. This has led to political pressure to reduce FHA activity.

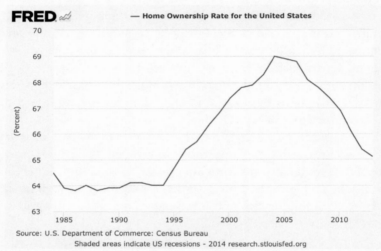

Source: FRED, Federal Reserve Economic Data, from the Federal Reserve Bank of St. Louis.

The overall national rate of homeownership has dropped dramatically in recent years, but it has declined more for blacks and for young adults than for the population as a whole. The rate of homeownership among black households fell to 43.9 percent in 2012.

Where FHA is trying to reduce its lending activity, state housing agencies have stepped up their efforts to help moderate-income households become first-time homeowners.

For many years, these agencies have issued tax-exempt bonds, or mortgage revenue bonds (MRBs), to raise funds for mortgage loans. They issued $8.4 billion in MRBs in 2011, up from $7.4 billion in 2010.

These mortgages have made first-time homeownership possible for almost 3 million lower-income families, approximately 100,000 every year, according to the National Council of State Housing Agencies.

Eligibility is restricted to first-time homebuyers who earn no more than the area median income. In 2011, recipients had an average income of $38,967, just 77 percent of the national median income. The price of a home purchased with a MRB mortgage is limited to 90 percent of the average area purchase price.

One of the most active state homeownership programs was in Massachusetts, where the housing finance agency is known as MassHousing. While many lenders were backing away from lending to moderate-income borrowers, MassHousing, like other state agencies, was stepping up to fill the gap.

The agency worked with Fannie Mae to grow its annual residential mortgage production from just under $200 million in 2005 to $1.1 billion in 2012. That is an increase of more than five times, and much of it came at a time when borrowers had few other places to turn for mortgage financing.

"The program's success thus far has been astounding—and beyond anything MassHousing could have anticipated," the agency reported.

The program was particularly successful in what the agency calls "gateway cities." These are cities identified by the state as having the greatest concentration of low-income residents and the lowest levels of academic achievement.

In addition, MassHousing has expanded its services to include helping borrowers refinance existing mortgages. This saved borrowers an average of $400 in monthly mortgage payments. Those 1,500 borrowers saved a total of $600,000 a month or $7.2 million in mortgage payments that went right back into the Massachusetts economy.

Living free, with ownership

With their state motto "live free or die," the citizens of New Hampshire are not prone to dependency on government programs. However, they are believers in the idea of community-based lending and cooperative ownership of land as a way to help extend homeownership further down the income scale.

In 1983, in the picturesque capital city of Concord, a group of citizens came together to found one of the nation's first community development financial institutions (CDFIs).

They believed that low-income households could achieve greater self-sufficiency if they were not continually rejected by lenders as bad credit risks. The New Hampshire Community Loan Fund set out to prove that such people could advance themselves if given good credit on fair terms.

What's more, they set out to show that affluent local people and organizations would finance those loans by investing in the loan fund. They were right. More than 30 years later, the fund raises most of its capital from private individuals and businesses who want to help their neighbors, even if it means earning a little less than they might in the stock market or with high-yield bonds.

The group does many things, but its claim to fame is helping owners of manufactured housing take cooperative ownership of the land on which their houses rest. In many of the state's 460 manufactured housing parks, the land is owned by corporations and leased to the homeowners.

The lack of control over the land subjects homeowners to a great deal of uncertainty about their long-term costs to stay in their homes. If the landowner sells out to a corporation, the cost to lease a home site could rise dramatically.

New Hampshire's loan fund assists these homeowners to purchase the land from the investor-owners as a means of securing and improving the community. Since the first cooperative purchase in 1984, 70 resident-owned communities have followed. They are home to more than 3,400 homeowners and make up about 15 percent of the state's manufactured housing parks.

Because the co-ops, rather than individuals, own the land under the homes, the risk of a spike in land cost is minimal. This helps ensure that the resale of the manufactured homes to new families will be sold at reasonable costs, giving more families and working people a chance at ownership.

Fixing loan delinquencies

Many of the same groups and agencies that help low- and moderate-income households become owners also work very hard to help them remain owners.

The Home Affordable Modification Program (HAMP), a federal program launched in 2009, has been a very important tool for helping people avoid foreclosure on their home mortgages. More than 1.3 million households obtained permanent mortgage modifications through HAMP as of early 2014.

However, HAMP depends on the participation of the banks and

institutions that own the delinquent loans and the companies that service those loans, which was not always forthcoming.

The biggest sticking point in helping borrowers who can't pay their mortgages is whether lenders should reduce the mortgage amount to a level that is in line with a property's value. Through the middle of 2014, the Federal Housing Finance Agency, which runs Fannie Mae and Freddie Mac, would not permit any degree of "principal reduction."

Some nonprofit groups have tried to take matters into their own hands from lenders who would not modify loans or make principal reductions. They purchase troubled loans from the lenders. Then, as the owner of the loans, they have the freedom to modify the loan in any way they choose. Their goal is to keep people in their homes and stabilize communities, so they typically reduce outstanding loan balances to make the monthly payments affordable.

One of those programs is the Mortgage Resolution Fund. It purchases nonperforming mortgages from banks and loan servicers at a discount, modifies the mortgages to align with the properties' current market values and the families' abilities to pay, provides intensive educational and debt management support, and eventually recapitalizes the mortgages.

Another key in the multifaceted process of cleaning up the foreclosure mess is the purchase of homes from banks after they have gone through foreclosure.

The National Community Stabilization Trust was formed to help communities acquire vacant, foreclosed homes at below-market prices from the nation's largest mortgage servicing companies. To date, this sector-wide collaborative has helped communities and nonprofits take possession of 10,000 foreclosed homes from financial institutions, according to the Housing Partnership Network, which founded the trust.

Housing at less cost

Of all the strategies being used to help lower-income people buy homes, the most important one is to bring down the price of housing. It's also the hardest strategy to execute on a large scale.

Modular and manufactured housing offers excellent potential to deliver housing at lower costs than housing that is built board-by-board and brick-by-brick at the construction site, the traditional method in use for hundreds of years.

The average new manufactured home cost $61,900 in 2012, according to the Manufactured Housing Institute. However, in 2012, only 55,000 new manufactured homes were sold.

The other major source of lower-cost housing is to let existing homeowners build "accessory dwelling units" on their properties. This saves money on the cost of land, allowing construction of small units that can be sold much more cheaply than a larger house on a large piece of land.

The trick is to convince local governments to change building codes and zoning policies to allow wider use of both these solutions to the housing shortage. The availability of financing is also an issue. Progress is slow, but the potential is great for vastly increased delivery of affordable homes.

CHAPTER TWELVE

Toward a Strategic Vision

Detroit invented the mass production of cars affordable to working Americans. Housing may be next. General Motors has teamed with a designer, a developer, and a nonprofit group to create a prototype low-cost home from a steel shipping container and materials recycled from a GM factory.

The 40-by-8-foot "container home" has 320 square feet of living space with two bedrooms, a bathroom, and a kitchen. GM donated many of the building materials from scrap at its Detroit-Hamtramck Assembly plant, which produces the Volt, the firm's electric vehicle.

GM is working on the home with the nonprofit Michigan Urban Farming Initiative, which will use the reclaimed container to demonstrate the effectiveness of repurposed materials on dwellings oriented toward urban agriculture.

Like a number of other Rust Belt cities, Detroit is exploring local food production as a new use for land that is no longer in residential or commercial use after years of declining populations. A university student will live year-round in the home while managing the farm and conducting agricultural research.

This project is exciting because it shows a way to tap corporate backing, create low-cost housing using existing materials, and support the repurposing of surplus urban land for farming to produce healthy food locally. It shows a way forward for dozens of other Rust Belt cities.

This is just one of the intriguing ideas on display in Motown. Since the city filed for bankruptcy, advocates, architects, builders, environmental groups, and social activists have turned the town into a laboratory for new ideas.

Detroit stands out as a hotbed of creativity, but it's not alone.

Good things are happening all over America to address housing and urban development needs. The power of community involvement, fresh ideas, and new collaborations is at work in many places. While these ventures are often little more than prototypes or demonstrations, they are making an impact. If taken to scale, they could achieve a lot more in many more places.

Most Americans have heard of Habitat for Humanity, and many have volunteered to help the nonprofit build houses for lower-income families in the United States as well as worldwide.

However, it's only one organization among many that is addressing the housing affordability crisis. For example, in every major city, churches and nonprofit housing groups labor mightily with few resources to ease the suffering of homeless individuals and families.

There is no lack of ingenuity, imagination, or genuine concern among Americans for their less fortunate neighbors, especially those who struggle to obtain decent affordable housing or to reinvigorate neighborhoods ravaged by foreclosure or decades of economic decline. Sometimes they work through government programs, and sometimes they work with entrepreneurial groups, foundations, corporations, and faith-based groups.

This chapter highlights some of the efforts that have set a particularly high standard for innovation, established exemplary track records of success, or point the way to future advances on important issues.

Housing ideas that work

In Montgomery County, Md., just north of the nation's capital, local officials have found an effective way to keep up with the steadily rising demand for housing. It is called inclusionary zoning.

As discussed earlier in this book, suburban communities often use zoning regulations to exclude housing affordable to lower-income families. Inclusionary zoning is the exact opposite of exclusionary zoning. It rewards developers for including units for less affluent people as part of larger developments serving middle-class and even higher-income buyers or renters.

More than 500 localities in the United States have adopted inclusionary zoning policies in some form, producing approximately 129,000 to 150,000 units nationally over 40 years, according to a 2012 study by RAND Corp.

In essence, Montgomery County's inclusionary zoning program induces private developers who want to tap the booming market for market-rate housing to incorporate small numbers of affordable homes into their development plans. The advantage: It does not necessarily require government subsidies. The incentive for getting developers to do this is the local government's authorization to build more housing units than zoning would otherwise allow. This is referred to as a "density bonus."

In Montgomery County, there is another twist. The county's public housing authority has the right to purchase up to one-third of the affordable homes in any given subdivision. This helps create mixed-income neighborhoods and gives poor children from public housing access to better schools.

Between 1976 and 2011, the Montgomery County program produced more than 13,000 affordable housing units that have been sold or rented to low- and moderate-income households.

• • •

Massachusetts Gov. Deval Patrick is one of the nation's governors who fully understand the need to provide affordable housing. He set a goal of creating 10,000 multifamily units from 2013 to 2020.

There are many different ways the state pursues that goal. One is by encouraging localities to overcome the temptation to block development of higher-density housing.

The Smart Growth Zoning Overlay District Act encourages communities to create dense residential or mixed-use "smart growth zoning districts" near transit stations and in other areas. Twenty percent of the housing in these areas must be deemed affordable.

This program addresses the fact that towns in Massachusetts generally don't zone for such housing as a matter of right, said Eleanor White, one of the authors of the legislation.

More than 50 cities and towns in the commonwealth have either created such districts or were considering doing so as of 2013.

The most impressive part of the Massachusetts effort is its direct approach to getting local governments to participate: The state pays them to do so.

Upon approval of a district, a municipality receives a zoning incentive payment. The amount of the incentive payment is based on the potential number of new housing units that can be constructed in the district. A community will also receive a bonus payment of $3,000 for each unit of new housing unit built in the district which is payable once the building permit has been issued for the housing unit.

Finally, the state removes any concern about the added cost to school districts for students who live in the new housing. Communities are reimbursed for any net cost of educating students living in new housing in a smart growth district.

Revitalizing cities

Most cities try to increase economic activity and employment opportunities by offering financial incentives for businesses to locate within their borders. This is the time-honored concept behind the relatively new idea of "innovation districts," where cities try to build a critical mass of entrepreneurial activity and new business start-ups.

For example, Boston, Cambridge, Mass., and St. Louis, are among those trying to attract high-tech and bioscience companies by providing facilities and infrastructure on attractive financial terms in hopes that new companies will put down roots and grow in their towns. To a large degree, at least in those towns, it seems to be working well and offering a good return on city investments.

Many other cities are relying on recreation and entertainment to bolster economic activity. Coastal cities started transitioning their waterfronts from industrial to entertainment and recreational use decades ago. But other cities are showing that you don't need a bay or an ocean to have an appealing waterfront.

After losing several competitions to attract new business, Oklahoma City leaders realized the city lacked the quality-of-life amenities that separate good cities from great cities, according to Mick Cornett, who took office as mayor in 2004.

The city then began a long process of reinventing itself as a lively, entertaining place that would attract the kind of smart, young people that employers wanted to hire – in addition to generating tourism and economic activity from the recreation itself.

The centerpiece has been transforming the Oklahoma River into a major recreational, entertainment, and economic asset.

The river has been the focal point for a variety of festivals and civic events as well as kayak and canoe competitions, and it has attracted a fair amount of real estate development.

Another project features a 70-acre central park linking the core of downtown with the Oklahoma River; a modern streetcar system; a new convention center; miles of new sidewalks and hike-and-bike trails; and river improvements, including a public whitewater kayaking facility.

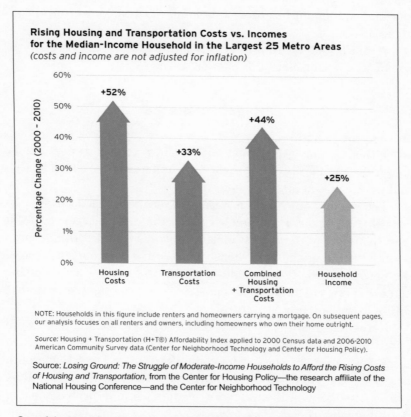

Rising Housing and Transportation Costs vs. Incomes for the Median-Income Household in the Largest 25 Metro Areas
(costs and income are not adjusted for inflation)

NOTE: Households in this figure include renters and homeowners carrying a mortgage. On subsequent pages, our analysis focuses on all renters and owners, including homeowners who own their home outright.

Source: Housing + Transportation (H+T®) Affordability Index applied to 2000 Census data and 2006-2010 American Community Survey data (Center for Neighborhood Technology and Center for Housing Policy).

Source: *Losing Ground: The Struggle of Moderate-Income Households to Afford the Rising Costs of Housing and Transportation*, from the Center for Housing Policy—the research affiliate of the National Housing Conference—and the Center for Neighborhood Technology

One of the ways Americans coped with high housing costs in the last decade was to move farther and farther away from urban centers and job centers to where housing built on virgin land was more affordable than properties that had better locations. The problem was that the cost of commuting offset any savings on housing costs. Overall, the combined cost of housing and transportation increased faster than incomes from 2000 to 2010.

At the same time, the city has been tackling Project 180, a $140 million redesign of 180 acres of downtown streets, sidewalks, parks, and plazas to improve appearances and make the central core more pedestrian friendly.

In the Bricktown area, an entertainment district with historic brick buildings, the city dug a mile-long canal right through the district and lined it with trees to create a water-themed attraction.

Innovative strategies are helping smaller cities, too. In Durham, N.C., several old tobacco company facilities have been converted to entertainment venues. The old water tower advertising Lucky Strike cigarettes still looms over the area, and some of the old industrial equipment has been preserved, tying the downtown firmly to its history.

A short walk away, a relatively new stadium plays host to the minor league Durham Bulls baseball team.

Tying it all together

In some cities and regions, planners figure they know more about what their region needs than voters and property owners do. To Ralph Becker, mayor of Salt Lake City and a planner by trade, that makes no sense at all.

The region known as the Wasatch Front contains about 80 percent of Utah's population and several of the state's largest cities. It is in the midst of the largest urban rail transit project in the country. It is encouraging higher-density, mixed-use development around the new rail lines. It has made excellent progress toward reducing homelessness, cutting vehicle emissions, and saving money on the cost of extending infrastructure.

In the late 1990s, 71 percent of the region's housing units were single-family dwellings with an average lot size of almost a third of an acre. Many of those who couldn't afford a large home on a large lot—like police officers, firefighters, and teachers, as well as those just beginning their careers—couldn't find desirable housing in good neighborhoods close to work.

Since that time, the housing supply has shifted so that most communities now include townhouses, apartments, and homes on smaller lots. Now, the average lot size on the Wasatch Front has declined 22 percent, to a quarter of an acre, and it continues to fall.

In many regions, reaching consensus on how to manage growth is very divisive, but not so in Utah. "What distinguishes our area is that everyone works together. There is true collaboration on these issues," said Becker.

That was not by sheer good luck or strength of character. Becker and hundreds of other civic, business, and political leaders worked very hard for many years to achieve consensus.

Leaders in the state recognized the need for careful planning to balance economic growth and environmental protection. In 1997, a nonprofit called Envision Utah began acting as a neutral facilitator for an extraordinary series of meetings and discussions.

Envision Utah conducted public values research, held over 200 workshops, and listened to more than 20,000 residents between 1997 and 1999.

After digesting all that input, the group created the Quality Growth Strategy, which provides voluntary, locally implemented, market-based solutions. The plan covers Salt Lake City and the Greater Wasatch Area, including 10 counties, 88 cities and towns, and more than 150 special-service districts.

Since facilitating the Quality Growth Strategy, Envision Utah has partnered with more than 100 communities in the state to put the plan into action. One of the key issues is housing.

There are lessons from Utah's experience for other states:
- No matter how detailed a plan may be, it may go nowhere if it does not spring from extensive and legitimate citizen participation;
- Regional collaboration is crucial. The big goals can't be achieved without full participation among localities; and
- Regular citizens can and should be trusted to know what's best in overall strategy, but smart, market-based incentives are key to getting people to follow the plan.

The citizens of Utah have a lot of company in the general thrust of their vision for the future—especially when it comes to housing development.

Many states and regions are working to reverse a process that began in the 1950s, when federally financed highway construction made it possible for middle-class Americans to move to new, suburban subdivisions and easily commute by cars to jobs in the city. Some call the resulting dispersion of households into automobile-dependent "bedroom communities" a great achievement. Others call it suburban sprawl.

Citizens as well as policymakers show a remarkable degree of consensus about the need to refocus on development of housing and commercial real estate together, as opposed to putting them in separate districts. This generally includes higher-density configurations, closer to existing urbanized areas and in proximity to transit.

For the average citizen, it's mostly about reducing road congestion. For environmentalists, it's largely about reducing carbon emissions and preserving open space. And for government budget crunchers, it has much to do with the high cost of highway systems

Boston Mayor Set the Pace on Housing

In one of his last official acts before the end of his 21-year tenure as mayor of Boston in 2014, Thomas Menino did one of his favorite things: He broke ground for the construction of new affordable housing.

He and Cardinal Sean O'Malley struck their shovels into the cold soil of Dorchester, four miles southwest of downtown, to start the redevelopment of a Catholic parish named after Ireland's St. Kevin.

The project would result in 80 units of affordable housing, including 20 units for homeless families.

It was an appropriate location for housing. According to legend, St. Kevin once held out his hand and kept it still for such a long time that a blackbird built a nest in it. The true story of St. Kevin's life is lost, but, to the mayor and cardinal, the need for affordable homes was crystal clear.

"Throughout the archdiocese, we hear about families made homeless when they lost their house to foreclosure; families paying high rents for apartments that are in poor condition or are far from good schools and good jobs; working people who cannot afford to rent an apartment," said the cardinal. "We hear about elderly residents on fixed incomes who have to choose between paying their rent and buying their prescriptions and food."

Menino knew American cities require many things to remain healthy, but affordable housing tops the list. In 2013, set a goal of building 30,000 housing units by 2020. "We don't want to be a city of the rich and poor," he said. "We want to make sure the working-class people have a place to live."

Menino knew city policies that add to the cost of housing should also change, allowing construction of smaller units, streamlining the building permit process, and relaxing parking requirements.

"We have to get building costs down," he said. "Some of those high costs are the government's fault. We have stringent regulations, and we have to look at that. We have to get the developers and the unions to work with us on this." Truer words were never spoken.

and infrastructure. For lower-income folks, it helps cut housing and transportation costs.

The principles are simple:
- Housing should be located close to job centers;
- Mass transit should be more available and more appealing to users;
- Land located near transit stations should be intensively developed since it has access to transit;
- Commercial, residential, and entertainment should be combined in close proximity; and
- Walking and bicycling should be encouraged.

Getting voters involved

Critical to the new wave in regional development is the willingness of voters to tax themselves to build brand-new transit systems. In Los Angeles, for many decades, mass transit other than buses was considered an impossible dream. Not anymore. Taxpayers who were sick of congestion on the roads agreed to new sales taxes, and Metro Rail has been rolling throughout the region for years.

From 2000 to 2012, more than 70 percent of public transit ballot measures have successfully passed, most of which imposed property or sales tax increases to fund mass transit or adapt roadways to encourage more biking and walking, according to the American Public Transportation Association (APTA). In 2012, 46 out of 58 pro-transit measures were approved by voters.

Voters in Arlington County, VA, overwhelmingly approved a nearly $32 million bond that will support a number of public transit projects, including capital projects for the Washington Metropolitan Area Transit Authority. This goes hand-in-hand with the county's effort to transform the Tyson's Corner area from a traffic nightmare into a more transit-oriented community with a mix of uses and housing cost levels.

The Atlanta BeltLine is a $2.8 billion redevelopment project that will shape the way Atlanta grows throughout the next several decades. The project provides a network of public parks, multi-use trails and transit along a historic 22-mile railroad corridor circling downtown and connecting 45 neighborhoods directly to each other.

At the heart of the BeltLine is an integrated approach to land use, transportation, greenspace and sustainable development that will create a framework for future growth in Atlanta. The project attempts to attract and organize some of the region's future growth around parks, transit, and trails to change the pattern of regional sprawl in the coming decades.

BeltLine transit will connect to existing public transit service in up to five locations and to future transit systems, such as the Peachtree Streetcar and commuter rail lines. Affordable housing is a vital component of the project, with 5,000 units of workforce housing expected to be developed.

The process of turning general concepts and goals into the reality of buildings and neighborhoods presents many challenges It requires convincing local mayors and city councils to modify zoning

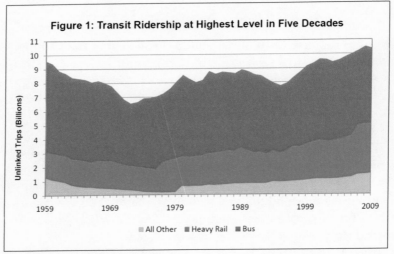

Source: American Public Transit Association

Public transportation use is at its highest since the 1950s, and voters throughout America are making it possible for even greater growth by approving local tax measures to help fund construction of new systems.

and land-use policies to increase the density of housing and commercial development near transit hubs.

A California law that took effect in 2009 requires regional planning agencies throughout the state to coordinate their strategies on transportation and housing development with the goal of reducing greenhouse gas emissions from private car travel. The process of drawing up regional "sustainable communities strategies" was largely complete in 2013. Most of the plans called for changing land-use patterns by increasing the density of housing development, increasing spending on public transit as opposed to highways, and making sure the densest housing was located near mass transit.

The law's authors tried to encourage affordable housing development in several ways. One method is to waive environmental reviews for certain affordable developments located in designated high-density development areas. However, it will be many years before the effectiveness of the law on encouraging higher density, transit-oriented development can be assessed.

The most effective state strategies reward localities that modify zoning to encourage higher-density development around transit, with an emphasis on mixed-use properties and affordable housing. Part of the strategy is to use local money to buy up land near planned transit lines to make affordable housing feasible before commercial interests bid up land prices.

New alliances & collaborations

When it comes to increasing density, the old environmentalist versus builder conflict gets completely turned around. Anti-housing groups no longer find that environmentalists automatically side with them, as previously had been the case.

The Sierra Club joined with the National Multifamily Housing Council and the Urban Land Institute, trade associations representing developers, in a campaign to convince city governments to allow higher-density development.

The Natural Resources Defense Council works with the U.S. Green Building Council to actively encourage sustainable community development, including high-density residential and mixed-use projects that are near transit and connected by bikeways and pedestrian-friendly streets.

The friendly relations between builders and environmentalists reflect the simple fact that housing people in existing built-up areas has far less impact on the planet than building on virgin land, or what is referred to as greenfields. Urbanists strongly support it because it supports city finances and general vitality.

In many cases, this so-called "infill" development is far more difficult than building on open land. Many of the vacant pieces of land available for construction have some degree of contamination, from uses as gas stations or dry cleaning shops, for example. These are called brownfields. Before they can be used for housing, the sites must be remediated. Financial support from federal and state governments is critical to paying for this very costly process.

Connecting the dots

Soon after taking office, President Barack Obama created the Partnership for Sustainable Communities to formally link policymaking at the Department of Transportation (DOT), the Department of Housing and Urban Development (HUD), and the Environmental Protection Agency (EPA).

Until then, these agencies had worked almost entirely independently, despite the obvious connections between transportation, housing, and the environment.

To carry this kind of holistic approach out into the state, regional, and local levels of government, Obama and HUD Secretary Shaun Donovan created a program to encourage regional planning based on the integration of economic development, land use, transportation, and environmental investments.

"While the nation faced a recession,
the people and places we serve experienced
a depression," –Nancy Andrews, LIIF

Donovan used the foreclosure crisis to explain why it was important to look at housing and transportation together.

"During the housing boom, real estate agents suggested to families who couldn't afford to live near job centers that they could find a more affordable home by living farther away. Lenders bought into the 'drive to qualify' myth as well—giving easy credit to homebuyers without accounting for how much it might cost families to live in these areas or the risk they could pose to the market.

"And when these families moved in, they found themselves driving dozens of miles to work, to school, to the movies, to the grocery store, spending hours in traffic and spending nearly as much to fill their gas tank as they were paying on their mortgage—and in some places, more."

"Hidden costs like transportation can put families over the edge into increased financial vulnerability," he added, noting that the highest foreclosure rates were often in the places with high costs for transportation to job centers.

As Donovan pointed out, the federal government's previous efforts to engage in planning local land use and development had not always gone well, largely because the feds tended to try to make the same plans fit every locality, despite their unique concerns and problems. But this new approach held tremendous promise to help local people make their own decisions in an intelligent way.

The leaders of the most successful planning efforts recognize that the highest purpose of planning is to build consensus about where ordinary citizens want to see their city or region in 10 or 20 years.

In Pittsburgh, for example, the city made obtaining citizen input the central goal of a planning process it dubbed PLANPGH. The website (www.planpgh.com) describes it as "an open and inclusive process focused on public participation." According to the site, "PLANPGH is all about finding common threads among people and the places they care about."

The goal is to get citizens to tell planners where new housing should be built, how the identity of neighborhoods should be preserved, and other things.

In Raleigh, N.C., extensive citizen input was sought for a new 20-year comprehensive plan recently. The city of over 400,000 people expected to add 120,000 households by the end of the period, and it had to look ahead at how it would accommodate and transport the new households.

"We realized sprawl was not sustainable," said Mitchell Silver, planning director. "We realized we needed a new way to deal with growth so we had a serious conversation with our residents."

For one thing, projected increases in vehicle traffic would be difficult to accommodate, and most roads would need to be widened if the previous patterns of development continued.

The city also had to consider the fact that by 2050, the overwhelming majority of households would consist of a single person. That kind of demographic trend has huge implications for land-use planning, since it could easily lead to a substantial oversupply of single-family homes. It also happens to be a nationwide trend.

To get the most out of that land, the plan calls for increased density in eight growth centers and 12 growth corridors.

Density is a key method for keeping the tax base stable, Silver said. It would take 600 homes on 150 acres to equal the tax value of one high-rise downtown. A downtown high-rise on three acres generates enough taxes to pay off the required infrastructure in three years, for an annual return on investment of 33 percent.

• • •

The challenges for the future are daunting, as our population continues to increase. In growing areas, planners must keep adjusting their strategies to accommodate more growth. Here's how Envision Utah put the challenge it faces:

"As we add another 2.5 million people by 2050, we will need to figure out how we can ensure there are good housing options for people of a variety of life stages and incomes. And if we can put those homes near work and near public transportation, we can also reduce household transportation costs and improve air quality. That way we can all afford a high quality of life, and our children and grandchildren can afford to raise a family here in Utah."

The problem is the opposite in our fading industrial cities, the places in the Rust Belt (mostly) that still had been suffering from long-term economic decline when the latest recession hit.

They don't need to accommodate growth but to cope with loss, including people, jobs, tax revenue, and, to put it somewhat dramatically, hope.

As the people working on the long-term regional plan for Northeastern Ohio stated so clearly, balancing the needs to manage growth and deal with decay is the challenge of the decade, if not the century. There are lots of people working on the issue at the state and local level, but it remains to be seen how much help will come from Washington. As of 2013, even the modest appropriations to help localities undertake long-term regional planning had been terminated.

Retreat from Success

CHAPTER THIRTEEN

The Not So Great Society

Looking at all the good things that have been achieved, one might think Congress would maintain substantial funding levels for federal housing and community development programs. That is not the case. As the political balance of power in Washington has shifted, these programs have faced a veritable tug of war over funding from year to year. Some have been eliminated.

Housing and urban policy have rarely been the subject of any serious or sustained discussion in Congress since the new millennium began, even after the foreclosure crisis devastated cities and housing markets, and after the recession reversed much of the progress older cities had made in the 1990s and early 2000s.

After Republicans gained control of the House in 2010, the lack of interest in policy was complemented by a distinct lack of interest in funding existing programs. Budget cuts were the order of the day, the month, the year, and probably the entire decade.

Americans twice elected Barack Obama president, but it was unclear what his legacy would be in regard to housing and urban issues. A moderate Democrat and our first black president, he campaigned on the idea of restoring hope, and did some positive and innovative things. However, after the change in control of the House, he had little power to fight the tide of budget cuts in Congress.

This recent political struggle over cities and housing is a continuation of a long running battle that reflects a deep political ambivalence about cities and people in need of housing help, which happens to be an increasingly large proportion of the American population.

The history of the debate is long and involved, but it's worth recounting in broad strokes.

After American troops began returning from World War II looking for places to live, frequently without much success, President Harry Truman convinced Congress to pass a law committing the nation to relieve the housing shortage.

The National Housing Act of 1949 declared it a national goal to provide "a decent home and a suitable living environment for every American family." This was necessary, it said, to ensure "the general welfare and security of the nation and the health and living standards of its people."

Nineteen years later, Congress reaffirmed this promise by passing the Housing and Urban Development Act of 1968. This time, it set a specific numerical goal. It committed the nation to producing 2.6 million units of new and rehabilitated housing each year, including 600,000 annually for low-income families. The law created a comprehensive set of programs designed to meet that goal, help people rent existing housing, revitalize urban communities, and more.

As the 21st century entered its second decade, the national housing goal was still officially on the books. However, the grand plan President Lyndon Johnson laid out had been gradually dismantled.

In the early 1970s, President Richard Nixon took policy in another direction. He instituted the Sec. 8 rental subsidy program to pay rent on behalf of poor tenants for privately owned rental housing that was newly built or rehabilitated. This began a long-term shift from publicly owned housing to reliance on private owners to provide affordable apartments.

The Nixon administration also gave cities more flexibility in how they spent federal funds. It consolidated the old Urban Renewal and Model Cities programs into the Community Development Block Grant (CDBG) program. This gave cities and counties much more authority over how they could spend federal grant money for a wide range of projects, from building and rehabilitating housing to putting in new sidewalks and sewer pipes.

Reagan reverses course

The presidency of Jimmy Carter represented a brief return to the kind of activist and even experimental approach to housing and urban policy that Americans saw under Johnson. He put forth a new urban policy and tested new ways to channel more government help through neighborhood groups as opposed to city halls.

But his most important single act was signing the Community

Reinvestment Act. This law has been the primary motivation for banks to invest hundreds of billions of dollars in community development and affordable housing projects.

During Ronald Reagan's two terms in office, there was a shift from federal funding for construction of new rental housing to reliance on helping families pay rent for existing apartments. The families' rental assistance was paid directly to property owners on behalf of the tenants. The units involved are often owned by small, entrepreneurial landlords instead of professional real estate firms.

Federal spending on the Sec. 8 new construction program and the public housing program, which began in 1937, was sufficient to produce 517,000 new apartments in fiscal year 1976.

At the Reagan administration's request, Congress slashed funding for the Sec. 8 and public housing construction programs in 1982. Construction was shut down completely a year later.

"There is no question that the country can no longer afford the whole production subsidy that existed heretofore," Philip D. Winn, the assistant secretary for the Department of Housing and Urban Development (HUD) and federal housing commissioner said at the time. "The whole attitude that the federal government can solve all the housing problems of this country—those days are over."

However, the legacy of the Reagan administration did not stop at just cutting funding.

There was still an active program of rent subsidies for the rehabilitation of existing rental housing. Some officials at HUD began awarding those subsidy contracts to developers who had paid "consulting" fees to former Republican officials to make sure their applications were successful.

This became known as the Sec. 8 moderate-rehabilitation influence-peddling scandal.

The criminal investigation stayed in the news for months and damaged HUD's reputation quite badly. It seriously undermined the department's ability to run the remaining programs under its control and to manage the apartment buildings it had already built and financed.

Another lasting legacy of the Reagan administration was the foundational shift in how affordable housing development was financed. Four years after the deeply subsidized construction programs were shut down, the government began financing housing for the "working poor" through the U.S. tax code rather than through direct federal spending.

Reagan was the driving force in enacting the 1986 Tax Reform Act. That law created the low-income housing tax credit described earlier in this book.

Under this new tax-based program, it was state housing finance agencies, not HUD, that decided which projects received government assistance. The Internal Revenue Service was tasked with overseeing compliance with program regulations and could recapture allocated tax credits if there were problems.

Under President George H.W. Bush, the HOME Investment Partnership program was enacted. Like the Community Development Block Grant program, it offered a combination of a fixed amount of funding per year (determined by formula) and flexibility in how it could be spent. The primary restriction was that it be used for housing.

However, other programs were ended, including the Sec. 8 moderate-rehab program, which had been the main source of scandal under Reagan.

• • •

In 2000, Congress created the Millennial Housing Commission to undertake a comprehensive review of housing policy for a new century. A bipartisan group of 22 commission members were appointed by the heads of the congressional committees on housing and urban policy.

After holding hearings in six cities at substantial cost to taxpayers, the commission released its policy recommendations on May 30, 2002. The report, "Meeting Our Nation's Housing Challenges," said:

"At the opening of the new millennium, the nation faces a widening gap between the demand for affordable housing and the supply of it. Rural areas and Native American lands present especially difficult environments for affordable housing ... And despite civil-rights and fair housing guarantees, the housing shortage hits minorities hardest of all."

The commission's report set out 13 recommendations for "how our society can produce and preserve more housing for more American families in a more rational, thoughtful, and efficient way in the decade ahead."

The report was dead on arrival. It came out eight months after the terrorist attacks of Sept. 11. National security concerns had quickly drowned out all other domestic issues, and no one on Capitol Hill paid any attention to the report.

The commission was dissolved. Not a single hearing was held. The idea of a proactive effort to update federal programs and policies and stimulate private housing production had been tabled indefinitely.

Bush pushes ownership

When he became president, George W. Bush saw the opportunity to steer housing policy in a new direction that would pay political benefits and, he hoped, empower minority groups.

In June 2002, he announced a plan to increase minority homeownership by 5.5 million families by 2010. Bush directed mortgage lenders to stretch their underwriting to help get more people qualified for home mortgages. He won enactment of the American Dream Downpayment Initiative, which provided grants to low-income homebuyers to cover their downpayments.

High-risk mortgage lending was a symptom of the underlying dysfunction in the housing market, not its cause.

Fast-forward to the fall of 2007. Bankruptcy rumors were swirling around Countrywide Financial, the giant mortgage banking firm, after it suffered its first quarterly loss in years. At the same time, foreclosure filings were piling up and would end up totaling 2,203,295 that year.

By 2008, housing markets, investment banks, and the economy as a whole were in free fall.

A spate of books on the foreclosure crisis placed all the blame on excessive volumes of high-risk mortgage lending. It's an obvious observation but it misses the most important lesson of the crisis: High-risk mortgage lending was a symptom of the underlying dysfunction in the housing market, not its cause.

Our government set the stage for the crisis by ignoring the growing disparity between what Americans could afford to pay for housing and the cost at which housing could be delivered.

From low rates for federal funds to relaxed policies on mortgage lending, our government encouraged the use of financial engineering, including high-risk loans, to obscure the rapidly decreasing affordability of housing.

Boiled down to its essence, the strategy was not unlike putting one's entire nest egg on a single number at the roulette table in Vegas: If everyone could get a mortgage with a low initial rate and if housing prices kept climbing, homebuyers would at least feel wealthy, real estate companies would make money, and politicians could celebrate a booming economy.

In short, reckless lending based on the assumption of ever-increasing home prices was the closest thing to a housing policy that we had at that time.

Housing groups were begging the White House and Congress to take a more complete and balanced approach to housing policy. But like mothers who badger their children to eat healthy foods, they were ignored.

Apartment owners, through the National Multifamily Housing Council and National Apartment Association, argued repeatedly for a "balanced housing policy" that encouraged rental housing development as well as home buying. They were ignored.

Nothing was done to address Americans' need for rental housing. No consideration was given to what would happen when the homeownership bubble burst, forcing millions of households who lost their homes back into the rental market.

Farewell to Fannie and Freddie

Mortgage financing is the lifeblood of homeownership, and the government has had a primary hand in ensuring its availability since 1934, when the Federal Housing Administration (FHA) was created to insure private lenders against most of their losses if a borrower was to default on an FHA-insured loan.

The federal role grew from there.

The newspapers have been full of news about Fannie Mae and Freddie Mac, but few people understand that they were both created by the federal government to serve the public purpose of making mortgage loans widely available. Fannie Mae was created in 1938 and was an agency of the government for years before it was "privatized."

Their mission was to buy home mortgage loans from banks and

mortgage lenders. For many years, they did so without much con-troversy. But they grew larger and larger, partly due to their hybrid nature: They issued stock and were driven to increase market share, but they each continued to enjoy access to the financial backing of the U.S. Treasury, a very powerful advantage for any organization dealing in world capital markets.

They also were exempt from federal, state, and local taxes, an-other huge advantage over other mortgage market players.

In 1992, Congress passed a law that required them to do more to help lenders provide loans to low- and moderate-income borrowers and for properties in underserved areas. The idea was, that since they had so many advantages courtesy of Uncle Sam, they should do a heck of a lot to help less affluent people and areas, even if they were less profitable.

The law worked. Hundreds of thousands of families were able to purchase homes because of these policies, greatly increasing the percentage of minority households who owned their homes in the 1990s. Homeownership among lower-income groups and minorities increased dramatically.

After the foreclosure crisis, when Fannie and Freddie were put under federal conservatorship, these goals were suspended. Since 2008, the two organizations have operated with absolutely no man-date to make loans to lower-income people or in low-income areas, despite the fact that home prices became more affordable than they had been in years.

The surge & sequestration

The recession prompted a massive federal response, including the bailout of many banks and insurance companies. It also prompted Congress to provide a temporary surge in spending under the economic stimulus legislation of 2009 for several housing and urban programs.

The American Recovery and Reinvestment Act of 2009 was en-acted in February 2009. The approximate cost of the economic stim-ulus package was estimated to be $787 billion at the time of passage.

The money was intended to be spent quickly to boost the econo-my, and within a few years, most of the money had been spent.

When Republicans took control of the House of Representatives, a new wave of budget cuts was unleashed on all domestic programs, including housing and urban programs.

Non-defense discretionary (NDD) programs comprise domestic and international programs outside of national defense that Congress funds on an annual basis. They exclude "entitlement" programs such as Social Security, Medicare, and Medicaid.

Spending on NDD programs peaked in the late 1970s at 5 percent of gross domestic product (GDP). It declined to 3 percent in the late 1990s, surged briefly in 2010, and then headed downward again. The Center on Budget and Policy Priorities projects it will drop to 2.5 percent by 2022.

This projected drop is largely due to the future effects of the 2011 Budget Control Act (BCA), which set limits or "caps" on annual discretionary funding through 2021. It imposes separate caps for defense and non-defense funding. In addition, the BCA mandated automatic further reductions—called "sequestration"—after Congress failed to adopt a more comprehensive deficit-reduction plan.

In addition, there has been frequent discussion in Washington of revisions to the tax code, including modification or elimination of provisions that promote urban development and affordable housing development.

Future generations may look back at the Obama presidency and express shock at the extent to which the federal attitude toward housing and community development had shifted.

It had gone from a comprehensive, bipartisan commitment to help our cities and provide housing under Truman and Johnson to a tug of war that favored first one side of the debate and then the other.

Most recently, advocates for housing and urban programs appeared to be destined to play defense for years to come. Any discussion of what policies made sense for housing and cities had been pushed not only off the table but also out of the building.

Amid political gridlock, there was no strategy for dealing with housing problems and urban problems. Even getting the home mortgage market back on its feet was a Herculean task that would probably end up taking a full decade to achieve.

Meanwhile, state and local governments continued to behave like Dr. Jekyll and Mr. Hyde when it comes to housing. Most cities and states have housing departments and agencies that work hard to finance development of apartments for lower-income people and to help first-time buyers purchase a home.

At the same time, other agencies in the same states and city work to increase the cost of housing. They would never describe that as their mission, but it is generally a well-known and widely accepted effect of their work.

In many affluent, suburban communities, direct effort is made to prevent any meaningful reduction in the cost of housing. This usually takes the form of political activism aimed at preventing construction of housing that has rents affordable to people earning less than the median income for the area.

Between the budgetary attacks on housing and urban programs in Washington and the state and local efforts to drive up costs and/or prevent housing construction, the obstacles to continuing the progress made in the half-century since the creation of HUD were formidable.

CHAPTER FOURTEEN

Shrinking Housing Safety Net

In the summer of 2013, something previously unthinkable happened to staffers at the 2,400 public housing agencies that administer the housing voucher program: They had to cut assistance to some of the people who were already receiving it and deny it to others who had finally been offered help after waiting for years.

The Housing Choice Voucher program has been a mainstay of federal housing assistance for decades, helping very poor households pay rent for privately owned apartments. The number of new vouchers that could be issued in any year has fluctuated for budgetary reasons, but the agencies that administer the program were rarely, if ever, required to cut assistance to families already holding vouchers.

That changed in 2013 under the Budget Control Act (BCA). Through an arcane process called "sequestration," there was a net decrease of 70,000 housing vouchers from December 2012 to December 2013.

Much of the cut was achieved by canceling vouchers that were turned in by previous voucher holders who no longer could use them. But in some places, housing authorities had to tell people who had already received vouchers after being on waiting lists for years that they needed to give them back, because they would not be getting rental assistance after all.

In the Minneapolis-St. Paul area, Corinne Lewis had to wait six years to get a rental subsidy under the voucher program, according to the *Star Tribune* newspaper. She was elated to learn that she, her disabled daughter, and her granddaughter finally would receive a subsidy under the program. She began hunting for an apartment. Then a second letter arrived, saying the subsidy was on hold because of the budget cut. "We were devastated". "All our hope got taken away. We were so excited to be moving to a decent place," Lewis was quoted as saying in the *Star Tribune*.

In Jacksonville, Fla., the housing assistance waiting list had reached 10,266 individuals in 2013, with an average of four to five years to start receiving assistance. The budget cuts meant the wait would drag on even longer.

In some cases, public housing agencies reduced the size of the apartments for which voucher holders were eligible. As a result, the people affected would have to move to a smaller place or share bedrooms regardless of age, gender, or relationship.

The affordability restrictions on more than 190,000 units of subsidize housing are set to expire each year on average over the next decade.

Only a portion of that reduction was restored in 2014, and the future budget outlook was not good. The BCA, which requires government agencies to cut spending if Congress fails to do so in the annual appropriation process, was suspended for 2014 and 2015, but it was scheduled to kick back in again in 2016, requiring further reductions in spending.

Federal funding to help poor tenants pay rent on privately owned housing has been around since 1965, and the voucher program is the latest permutation of that effort.

Vouchers help lower-income households by effectively "capping" their monthly rent payments at 30 percent to 40 percent of their incomes. The voucher covers the difference between that amount and the full rental price—up to a standard "fair market rent" set by the Department of Housing and Urban Development (HUD).

Of the roughly 2 million households that receive vouchers, half have children and one third are seniors or have disabilities.

The reduction in voucher funding was only the most visible in a series of cuts over the past two decades to federal programs for affordable housing. As a result, we are falling behind in the quest to help the poorest families obtain and keep decent, safe housing.

"In the aftermath of the Great Recession, the number of very low-income renters that are eligible for federal rental assistance mushroomed from 15.9 million in 2007 to 19.3 million in 2011, but less than a quarter (23.8 percent) actually received housing assistance in 2011, down from 27.4 percent in 2007," according to Harvard University's Joint Center for Housing Studies.

The Center on Budget and Policy Priorities (CBPP) said that spending on low-income housing assistance as a share of non-defense discretionary spending had declined 20 percent from 1995 to 2013.

• • •

Lawrence Williams has managed public housing programs in several California cities for more than 14 years. In the first 10 years of his career, he would jump on a plane to Washington, D.C., every year for the legislative conference sponsored by the trade association for public housing agencies.

Williams and his colleagues would fan out on Capitol Hill to tell members of Congress why their programs' funding should not be cut.

Williams took his last trip to Washington in 2011.

After watching funding get cut over and over, he decided his time would be better spent in his office, trying to stretch the money his agency had left, rather than banging his head against a wall in Washington.

Williams has watched the need for federal housing assistance grow steadily even as the available funding keeps shrinking.

Among the recent major reductions in funding for housing programs have been the following:

- The fiscal 2014 appropriation provided $1 billion for the HOME Investment Partnerships Program. This is $820 million less than the funding level in fiscal year 2010 when the program was funded at $1.82 billion. The program was started in 2003 with funding of close to $2 billion.
- The Sec. 202 program for new construction of housing for the elderly no longer finances any new construction, only renovations and improvements to existing properties.
- The U.S. Department of Agriculture's Sec. 515 Rural Rental Housing program was used to construct 38,700 rural rental units in 1979. In recent years, program funding has only been provided to support preservation of existing units. The federal government no longer finances construction of rentals

in rural areas. Even the program that provides insurance to induce lenders to make private-market loans (the Sec. 538 program) has been cut in recent years.

The nation's primary program for producing and preserving low-cost rentals is the low-income housing tax credit (LIHTC). The program has survived a succession of budget reductions to housing and urban programs largely because it is a tax credit that has a fixed national volume level as part of the Internal Revenue Code. It is not subject to annual appropriations.

To a great extent, the tax credit has become a victim of its own success. As other programs are cut, it is called on to take care of more and more of the nation's housing needs. Some developers say if trends continue, a larger and larger share of the program's available credits will be used to preserve aging units built under older

---

Debunking the Housing Assistance Myth

The biggest myth about government housing assistance is that it's only provided to people who are poor. Along with that belief comes a great deal of resentment. Many taxpayers believe that it's not fair that the poor should get help while middle-income Americans get none.

The underlying assumption is categorically incorrect.

Plenty of middle- to upper class Americans own housing subsidized by the federal and state governments, it's just that the subsidy comes through the tax code. Their benefits come in the form of tax breaks for homeownership. These so-called "tax expenditures" are less visible than direct appropriations for housing subsidies but have the same impact on the budget deficit.

Homeowners who itemize on their tax returns can deduct the interest paid on mortgages on first and second homes up to a total mortgage amount of $1 million. They also get to deduct local property taxes paid. Finally, they get a break on capital gains taxes for any gain on the sales of their primary residences, which basically means that most people receive all their appreciation on their homes completely free of taxes.

The tax expenditure for the home mortgage interest deduction in fiscal year 2010 was $103.7 billion, according to the congressional Joint Committee on Taxation. In that year, the cost of the state

subsidy programs, like public housing and Sec. 8. Since Congress ended funding for Sec. 202 new construction, the LIHTC will be the only way to finance new housing for seniors.

The tax credit is a shallow subsidy and is rarely sufficient on its own to make new construction feasible. Developers always need additional sources of subsidy to make it work for people earning much less than 60 percent of the area median income.

It is intended to create workforce housing for policemen, teachers, civil servants, and others who earn relatively low wages.

Even then, tenants are not promised that they will pay a fixed percentage of their incomes for rent. In many cases, tenants pay 40 percent or 50 percent of their incomes for rent.

In order to make the program useful for lower-income people and in areas with low median incomes—and to offer lower rents—project

---

and local property tax deduction was $16.4 billion. The cost in lost revenue of the reduced tax rates on capital gains on owner-occupied housing was $15.3 billion. That comes to $135.4 billion in foregone federal tax revenue for just one year.

"More than three-quarters of federal housing spending in 2012 (counting both federal outlays and the costs of tax expenditures) went to homeowners. Renters received less than one-fourth of federal housing subsidies despite making up more than a third of households," said Barbara Sard, vice president for housing policy at the Center on Budget and Policy Priorities.

The tax benefits for homeownership have no targeting or income limits. More than three-fourths of the value of the mortgage interest and property tax deductions goes to households with incomes of more than $100,000. Close to a third goes to families with incomes above $200,000. That's according to estimates by the congressional Joint Committee on Taxation.

There is a prohibition against taking the deduction on mortgage amounts over $1.1 million and for more than two homes, but those are the only limitations.

As Cushing Dolbeare, founder of the National Low Income Housing Coalition, put it during a long career of advocacy for rental housing assistance, there is no question that we can find federal resources to make housing more affordable. The only issue is who gets that assistance.

sponsors rely on other direct government subsidies, like grants and low-interest loans.

That's why even though the amount of tax credits had not been reduced, cuts in other programs have curtailed its effectiveness. For example, the Community Development Block Grant program and HOME programs has been widely used as an additional source of subsidy, but both have seen substantial funding reductions.

In 2008, Congress authorized the creation of the National Housing Trust Fund. The purpose was to provide subsidies deep enough to bring rents on housing tax credit projects down to more affordable levels. But this too fell victim to the foreclosure crisis. Fannie Mae and Freddie Mac were supposed to provide funding for the trust fund from their profits. After the Federal Housing Finance Agency took over the two mortgage firms, that plan was suspended. Housing advocates had been working steadily to convince Congress to find another way to capitalize the program.

The end of HOPE

The story earlier in this book about Mariposa, the HOPE VI development that opened its first apartments in Denver in 2013, is not all positive. The property is a great example of neighborhood transformation. It is also a monument to the end of an era.

It was among the last group of housing projects to receive a HOPE VI grant.

Congress did not completely abandon the idea of comprehensive revitalization of distressed areas. HOPE VI was replaced by something called Choice Neighborhoods. It took the best of the HOPE VI program's focus on comprehensive redevelopment to eliminate concentrations of poverty. It then expanded eligibility to include privately-owned properties subsidized by HUD and other public housing funding.

While it covers more eligible properties, it has less funding – only $90 million in 2014. That funding won't go very far, considering that a single comprehensive redevelopment program can easily require $20 or $30 million in federal grant support. The 2014 funding is less than one-sixth the $570 million appropriated for HOPE VI in its first year of operation.

The Bush administration proposed termination of funding for HOPE VI, contending that it had redeveloped most or all severely distressed public housing units. However, The Urban Institute estimated that 47,000 to 82,000 severely distressed units remained in the public housing inventory in a 2005 study.

Those numbers have probably grown since that report was issued, given the advanced age of most public housing buildings, some of which are functionally obsolete and many of which are very energy inefficient.

As every public housing agency director can testify, federal funding cuts are starving them of money for repairs, maintenance and capital improvements. There was room for greater efficiency at many agencies, but in many places, the cuts no longer can be offset by improved operations.

"We have cut to the bone. We don't have anywhere else to go," said one housing agency director. Those agencies that have done a good financial management job are filling gaps in federal appropriations with reserve funds, but that is not a sustainable solution.

Decreased capital funding for replacement of major systems and operating subsidies for maintenance, security, and operations have a long-term cumulative impact: They directly result in the deterioration and loss of public housing units.

In San Francisco, a 2005 study found that the Housing Authority had a backlog of $267 million in repair and renovation needs. "Buildings were failing because of years of reduced investment by the federal government. Funding shortfalls had resulted in significant problems with basic building systems such as plumbing, roofs, and heat. Old, deteriorating buildings were putting thousands of families, seniors, and children at risk," according to an analysis by the city.

San Francisco has substantial local resources, thanks to job creation and a growing tax base, enabling it to try filling the gap in federal funds with local resources. But the majority of cities cannot muster extra financial assistance for their troubled public housing.

• • •

The public housing program was created in the 1930s to provide publicly built and owned apartments. New construction was halted in the 1980s, but public housing agencies continued to rely on federal funding for operating costs, maintenance, and capital improvements.

The nation's 14,000 public housing developments, located in more than 3,500 communities, provide affordable homes to nearly

1.2 million households, nearly two-thirds of which include seniors or people with disabilities.

A HUD-sponsored study in 2010 estimated the need for $26 billion in capital repairs for public housing. However, outlays for these investments were cut 18 percent between 2008 and 2012. There was a slight uptick in 2014 from 2013, but it was not sufficient to make any dent in the backlog of repair needs.

Federal spending for the cost of operating public housing, including maintenance, was cut from $4.7 billion in 2010 to $4.4 billion in 2014. That's enough to cover about 86 percent of costs, based on HUD's established formula for calculating needed funding.

Concern about the impact of these cuts is shared by Democratic and Republican experts. The Bipartisan Policy Center's Housing Commission called it "slow death by attrition" that "wastes valuable federal housing assets and risks the loss of both high-quality and deteriorating units alike. In addition, it penalizes residents."

The supply of public housing is shrinking at a rate of 10,000 units per year, largely for lack of funds to make necessary repairs, according to "The State of the Nation's Housing" report from Harvard's Joint Center for Housing Studies.

• • •

The supply of housing created under some federal programs is shrinking not so much because the buildings are falling apart, but because they are in good shape and located in areas that have become popular.

These programs rely on privately owned housing that is subsidized by the government. They depend on the willing participation of private owners who sign contracts with the federal government to make the housing available to lower-income people for specific periods of time.

Over the past two decades, increasing numbers of owners have decided not to renew those contracts, reducing the supply of affordable units.

That means the housing ceases to be available for poor households. Instead, the owners, when their contracts expire, rent the properties to higher-income households who generally are able to pay more rent than the government program would have allowed.

They call this "opting out" of the programs. The owners may

face some restrictions on how quickly they can raise rents and evict poor tenants. However, eventually, they can do exactly that.

Between 10,000 and 15,000 units of affordable Sec. 8 housing were being lost every year as property owners exited the program, according to a 2013 report by CBPP.

More than 165,000 public housing units have been demolished or otherwise removed from the stock without being replaced, according to CBPP. It said this was "often because the agency administering the units received inadequate funding to operate and occasionally renovate them, and the condition of the units consequently deteriorated."

The future outlook is not promising. "On top of federal funding cuts to rental assistance programs, much of the existing supply of privately owned subsidized housing is at risk," according to Harvard's Joint Center on Housing Studies. The National Housing Preservation Database shows that the contracts or affordability restrictions on more than 190,000 units are set to expire each year on average over the next decade.

There's no accurate way to predict how many of those units will leave the supply of subsidized housing. Owners of properties located in desirable areas with strong rental demand are particularly likely to opt out of the programs, according to Harvard's JCHS. Recent budget cuts to the programs involved probably won't help persuade owners to remain involved with the government since it creates uncertainty about payments under subsidy contracts going forward.

Private market housing

The majority of low-income renters live in private housing that is not subsidized but has low rents due to its location or age. That supply of housing is declining every year.

Of the 34.8 million rentals that existed in 2001, some 1.9 million were demolished by 2011—a loss rate of 5.6 percent, according to Harvard's JCHS.

Smaller and older rental buildings, which account for high shares of affordable units, are especially vulnerable to loss, Harvard's JCHS said.

The losses are certain to continue due to the age of our housing stock. In 2011, the median age of the rental housing buildings in America was 38 years, according to JCHS. "As housing ages, owners must devote an increasing share of rents to maintenance and replacements of aging systems to maintain the structures in adequate condition," JCHS said.

In 2002, the Millennial Housing Commission pointed out the need for changes in federal tax policy to encourage owners to keep up older properties, but Congress took no action on the recommendation. There has been no serious discussion of the issue in Congress since then.

State programs cut

Some states have also made extreme reductions in their programs. One of the most damaging was California's decision to completely eliminate funding for affordable housing that had been provided by local community redevelopment agencies.

Most housing tax credit projects in the state had received low-cost capital from these agencies. However, during the state's budget crunch, citing abuses by some agencies in regard to commercial real estate projects, Gov. Jerry Brown eliminated these agencies.

Another key way for states to finance affordable housing development has been to create trust funds that have stable sources of funding that is removed from the uncertainty of annual budget debates. In Florida and several other states, there are trust funds that get money from a dedicated source of tax revenue.

The usual source of this revenue is real estate transfer fees or fees for recording real estate transactions.

In California, the proposal that went before the legislature in 2012 called for a $75 document recording fee on real estate transactions, which would generate an estimated $525 million annually for the development, acquisition, rehabilitation, and preservation of homes affordable to low- and moderate-income households.

However, while the need for affordable housing increases, so does the difficulty of passing laws to authorize such programs. There is fierce opposition to this funding approach in many states, coming primarily from real estate agents. They say they oppose it because the addition of a fee to help fund affordable housing would discourage people from buying homes.

Running in place

Even if Congress does restore the full amount of the cuts to the Housing Choice Voucher program, which is unlikely, there would still be a gradual erosion in the impact of the program, according to Harvard's JCHS.

"Between 2008 and 2012, the Housing Choice Voucher program received a 15 percent nominal (funding) increase. At the same time, however, rising market rents and utility costs—along with losses

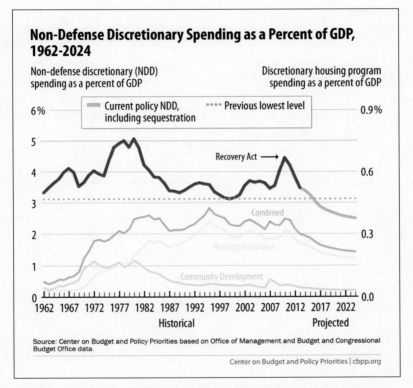

Non-Defense Discretionary Spending as a Percent of GDP, 1962-2024

Non-defense discretionary (NDD) spending as a percent of GDP

Discretionary housing program spending as a percent of GDP

— Current policy NDD, including sequestration   •••• Previous lowest level

Recovery Act →

Combined

Housing Assistance

Community Development

1962 1967 1972 1977 1982 1987 1992 1997 2002 2007 2012 2017 2022

Historical   Projected

Source: Center on Budget and Policy Priorities based on Office of Management and Budget and Congressional Budget Office data.

Center on Budget and Policy Priorities | cbpp.org

In this graph, the Center for Budget and Policy Priorities shows how funding for housing and community development has fallen over the years as a percentage of Gross Domestic Product. It projected future spending by assuming the each subfunction would continue to receive the same share of total NDD spending as it did in 2013.

in household income resulting from recession-induced unemployment—raised the per-household cost of vouchers. As a result, the increase in program funding did nothing to expand the number of families assisted, Harvard's JCHS said."

Because of the increasing cost of private market housing, the federal government has had to pay more for each unit of housing for which it subsidizes the rent.

The same is true for Sec. 8 rental assistance that is attached to designated buildings, as opposed to vouchers that go to tenants to use at any eligible property.

Sec. 8 spending increased by $946 million, or 11 percent, from 2007 to 2010. Over the same period, per-unit assistance costs also increased by 11 percent, Harvard's JCHS noted. Therefore, it appears that all of that increase in Sec. 8 funding went to cover increases in the gap between what tenants could pay and the rents at the properties.

"As in the Housing Choice Voucher program, per-unit assistance costs are determined by the gap between the tenant's contribution and actual housing costs, as determined by each owner's contract with HUD. This suggests that a widening gap between household incomes and housing costs explains the entirety of the increase in program spending from 2007 to 2010," Harvard's JCHS said.

How Congress will respond to continually rising costs is hard to predict, but it is unlikely it will provide funding to increase the number of households receiving assistance. Factor in the ongoing impact of the Budget Control Act, and there is good reason to think the debate in future will be about how many people lose the housing assistance they already receive rather than how many new people start receiving assistance.

• • •

Public housing agencies maintain the official lists of households and individuals waiting for assistance from a variety of government programs.

People in need of housing assistance generally find that there is a long list of people waiting for help in most places, so long that housing authorities are not accepting new applications.

They have to bide their time until the number of people on the list declines enough that more names can be added. Once they are on the list, depending on the conditions in their area, it can take upward of five years to rise to the top of the list.

Many housing agencies find that the best way to handle the high volume of applications is through a lottery to choose the people who will be added to the official waiting list for assistance. Those not chosen have to wait for the list to open again before they can join the numbers of those already in line for help.

It's fairly rare that a new affordable housing complex opens up, but when it does, demand can be overwhelming.

When the Hollywood Community Housing Corp. accepted applications for 56 affordable units in Los Angeles a few years back, 3,000 people lined up and some slept outside the night before, according to the *Los Angeles Times*.

CHAPTER FIFTEEN

Leaving Grandma
Out In the Cold

After Elizabeth Schmidt's husband died, she sold their mobile home to pay off debts and began living out of her car. Even the $309 monthly payment on her 2006 Suzuki Forenza became hard to afford, considering her Social Security check was only $570 per month.

Then Mrs. Schmidt got lucky according to an account in The Post and Courier newspaper. She found an apartment at Marshside Village, a 48-unit multifamily building for low-income elders in North Charleston, S.C. "It was cold out there, I tell you. I got all my stress out when I moved in here," she recalled. "I have a safe, clean apartment for just $118 a month."

The rent is so low because Marshside Village was built using federal funding under a program referred to as Sec. 202 – the number of the section in the Housing Act of 1959 by which it was authorized.

The buildings it has produced for over 50 years offer modest apartments with basic architecture. But those properties, totaling more than 400,000 units, have transformed the lives of many older Americans, most of whom get by on nothing more than Social Security.

There are thousands of stories like Elizabeth Schmidt's. Tenants of Sec. 202 properties are as close to universally happy as any group of people could be. They have a ready community of peers so they're rarely lonely and disconnected, a common problem for elders living on their own. They have well-maintained homes with security and social activities. They receive help connecting with social and health services.

Most importantly, they have economic security. They no longer have to worry that their savings will run out and they'll have to try to rely on Social Security to pay for shelter as well as food, medicine, and other necessities.

The program provides all the capital needed for nonprofit groups and public housing agencies to create housing that gives elders a new lease on life.

"We want to eliminate circumstances in which persons have to make desperate choices about whether to pay the rent, buy sufficient good food, or purchase all their needed prescriptions and take them in the dosages prescribed by doctors," said Dr. Laverne Joseph, CEO of California-based Retirement Housing Foundation, a nonprofit that builds housing for elders in 28 states, Washington, D.C., Puerto Rico and the U.S. Virgin Islands.

Sec. 202 housing is open to households that earn no more than 50 percent of the area median income and that include at least one person who is 62 or older when they move in. Tenants pay just 30 percent of their income for rent. In most places in America, people at those income levels have no decent options in the private, unsubsidized housing market.

Congressional action ends construction

Given the program's profound success, it was a shock when, in 2011, Congress voted to eliminate all new construction under the program. Although more than $380 million was provided in 2014, it was all allocated for modifying and supporting existing buildings, not for constructing new apartments. It was a decrease from $668 million in 2010.

At its peak in the 1970s, the Sec. 202 program produced 20,000 housing units per year. In 2002, the Commission on Affordable Housing and Health Facility Needs for Seniors in the 21st Century reported to Congress that we needed to build 40,000 units per year to house the growing numbers of low-income elders. But instead of ramping up, Congress ramped down, all the way to nothing.

The Sec. 202 program also financed housing for low-income disabled people, but in 1990, the Section 811 Supportive Housing for Persons with Disabilities program was split off and Sec. 202 was limited to housing for elders. In 2010, Sec. 811 was funded at $300 million. In 2013, it was at $156 million.

In Taylor, Mich., Volunteers of America began construction in mid-2014 on what was expected to be the very last apartment community built under the program. The funding came from a pot of money appropriated before Congress decided to end new construction.

Plans called for Heritage Park Senior Village to have 77 one-bedroom apartments of about 540 square feet each, including a small kitchen. The development was set to have a community room, a fitness room, a computer lab/library, laundry, and a beauty/barber shop. Plans also called for a walking trail around the five-acre site for exercise.

Like many sponsors of Sec. 202 properties, Volunteers of America has spiritual roots. It is a national nonprofit organization based in Alexandria, Va. Many other sponsors are locally based subsidiaries of churches and fraternal organizations trying to give elders in their communities a place to call home.

Why did the federal government end the Sec. 202 program at a time when our older population is growing dramatically and their financial resources are shrinking?

People who provide housing for elders see no logic in the decision to kill new construction under the program. They say that members of Congress have generally expressed support for the program. Even in today's vitriolic political climate, it doesn't appear that the program had any enemies on Capitol Hill.

As best as anyone can figure, killing the program was just part of the general rush to cut federal spending and did not involve any cost-benefit analysis.

But while the motive is unclear, the impact will soon be apparent, since the demand for low-cost apartments suited to elders is growing while the supply is set to start shrinking.

"The bottom line is that, with the end of new construction under Sec. 202, we are very close to the point where we will begin losing affordable seniors housing faster than it is being developed," said Thomas Slemmer, president and CEO of Columbus, Ohio–based National Church Residences, one of the nation's largest nonprofit providers of affordable seniors housing.

Slemmer explained that poor elders make up a large proportion of the tenants of housing that was built many years ago by a variety of now-defunct federal housing programs, not just Sec. 202. The programs housing the highest numbers of elders include public housing and Sec. 8 project-based rental assistance.

The supply of this subsidized housing is shrinking. Old, poorly located buildings are being lost to deterioration. Some newer, well-

located units are being converted to market-rate use after legal obligations to serve the poor expire. Either way, if the units are lost, the
tenants have to move, something that can be very hard for elders.

Sec. 202 buildings are also getting old, considering that the program began in 1959, so an increasing number of properties will be
lost to obsolescence each year. With no new construction planned,
they will not be replaced, and over time, the overall supply of subsidized housing for elders will shrink.

A 10-to-1 shot

For every person like Mrs. Schmidt who gets into a government-subsidized apartment, there are 10 more households waiting for one.
Demand is highest relative to supply in urban areas. In places with
large proportions of low-income elders, it's off the charts.

"It is very hard to tell seniors in desperate need of housing that
the wait in most cases is two to three years," said Steve Protulis,
executive director of Elderly Housing Development and Operations
Corp. Depending on their age, some of those who are turned away
might have no choice but to spend their final years living in squalor
and fear.

In testimony before the Commission on Affordable Housing and
Health Facility Needs for Seniors in the 21st Century at a hearing in
Miami, one nonprofit housing developer recalled the crush of people
who showed up to apply for units in a new property in Little Havana.

There were 100 apartments available for rent. A total of 6,897
people showed up to submit applications.

What happens to the 6,797 people who could not get into the
property? The same as happens to elders waiting for Sec. 202 (or
other subsidized apartments) to open up anywhere. The lucky ones
live with relatives, but this has become less of an option in recent
years as people have suffered economic setbacks and families have
become more mobile.

The unlucky ones end up living doubled or tripled up with other
poor elders or take space in whatever filthy rooming house they can
find.

In the center of Little Havana, it's not unusual for a single el-
der to live in "a roach-infested, 10-by-10 room with a hot plate as
a kitchen, paying $350 to $400 a month," said the director of one
housing nonprofit.

The demographic bulge

The gap between supply and demand is about to explode.

In the coming years, demand for affordable housing among elders will skyrocket, said Robin Keller, vice president of real estate development for Volunteers of America, which operates 149 Sec. 202 projects with 7,718 units.

The number of older Americans is quickly increasing, and their financial resources, taken as a group, have declined, she said.

The population 65 and older will grow by 15 million from 2010 to 2020, when it will be 55 million (a 36 percent increase). The 85 and older population will grow by 3 million during the same period to 8.75 million. As the baby boom generation pushes into old age, the number of those older than 85 will hit 14.2 million in 2040, according to Census data compiled by the U.S. Administration on Aging.

The need for assisted-living facilities is increasing rapidly. By 2020 there will be 1.3 million low-income elders who require assistance with activities of daily living. Sec. 202 properties are very adaptable to this purpose.

Households headed by persons 65 and older reported a median income in 2010 of $45,763. But women older than 65 who lived alone had a median income of only $15,000. They are the primary users of Sec. 202 housing, and their numbers are growing.

Among Social Security beneficiaries, the average monthly benefit is $1,269, or about $14,000 per year. Obviously, in almost any metropolitan area in America, those people who rely on Social Security for income cannot afford any housing available on the private market.

In 2011, 35 percent of renter households with a member who was over 65 paid more than 50 percent of their income for rent and utilities. Twenty-six percent of such households paid between 30 percent and 49 percent of their income for rent and utilities. The data is from the American Housing Survey by the Census Bureau.

Many elders have savings that can be tapped to pay rent. But very low interest rates have limited the growth of those savings. Elders are also affected by the drying up of pension coverage, a trend that will only grow as the baby boomers age.

The decline in home values has reduced their ability to raise money from the equity in their homes.

"Many older Americans are heading into their retirement years with little financial cushion and may find it difficult to find suitable housing that fits within their budgets," said "The State of the Nation's Housing" report from Harvard's Joint Center for Housing Studies.

The private market no longer produces housing affordable to people who earn less than 50 percent of the area median income, said Keller. In the past, many cities had large numbers of single-room occupancy (SRO) hotels, which offered inexpensive housing for low-income elders. One estimate says that 1 million SRO units were razed between the mid-1970s and 1990s.

Program saves money

Sec. 202 properties were designed as independent-living facilities intended for residents who cook their own meals and take care of themselves. But they also help people live active, socially rich lives, which allow them to stay healthier longer, reducing or postponing their need for medical care.

Developments under the program are usually located close to transportation and services. Most feature accessible design, so that people can live in them even after losing mobility or other physical capabilities.

Every Sec. 202 property has a system in place for connecting residents with outside services, such as health care, transportation, education, and social activities. Increasingly, they also have a coordinator on staff who works directly with residents to help them access those community services.

The government is converting some of the rental apartments in Sec. 202 properties to assisted living, where frail elders get help with activities of daily living, like bathing and taking medicine. Many more could easily be adapted for that use.

Sponsors of Sec. 202 properties see the housing they provide as a part of the health care system even though they do not provide medical care. However, the buildings do help people stay healthier longer, and that saves the government money.

"Sec. 202 housing is a bargain," said Slemmer. "Stable living environments can lower health care costs on their own, but when you factor in the work our managers do to link tenants with services, it is an even greater savings," he said.

Joseph and Slemmer point out that providing affordable housing under the Sec. 202 program reduces government spending on nursing care. They said people living in their properties do not need nursing care until very late in life compared with people in other living situations.

"If we keep people in affordable housing with social service coordinators connecting them to low-cost or free services, it keeps them out of nursing homes, where the daily cost is much higher," Joseph said.

Without enough Sec. 202 units to meet the needs of a growing poor elderly population, more and more older adults will make their way into nursing homes, whether they really need to or not, since the cost would be covered by Medicaid, an entitlement program.

The residents of Sec. 202 housing are hospitalized at much lower rates than people of the same age living in private market housing. It costs the government $7,000 a year to house a person under the Sec. 202 program, but one trip to a hospital emergency room can cost $15,000 or more, Slemmer said.

But the economic arguments pale in comparison to the enormous positive energy one feels at properties serving elders. The tenants are engaged in living, not waiting to die. The Archives of Internal Medicine published the results of a study involving 1,600 elders that proves what housing property managers know from observation: Lonely people suffer loss of functionality sooner than those who are not lonely. They also tend to die sooner.

Long-term plan

When Congress terminated new construction under Sec. 202, it was about reducing the budget deficit. But the flaw in that rationale is apparent when you consider the projections on the aging of the U.S. population and its increasing cost to taxpayers.

Government spending on long-term care will suck up a larger and larger portion of federal and state budgets in coming years. For example, New York state has the biggest Medicaid budget in the country, spending around $54 billion each year. About 41 percent of that is for long-term care.

Affordable housing can help control that cost in two ways:
- Quality housing that is designed for elders keeps people healthier longer, putting off or eliminating government-funded nursing care.
- Residential settings are cheaper (and better) places to deliver all but the most intensive medical care.

Housing providers lament the fact that Congress ended the Sec. 202 program without giving any thought to the complex, interconnected challenges of housing and caring for our aging population.

As the Commission on Affordable Housing and Health Facility Needs for Seniors in the 21st Century noted, 80 percent of seniors live in homes they own and want to stay in them as long as possible.

The problem is that their homes are not designed to be accessible, unlike Sec. 202 apartments. Plus, the older people get, the harder it becomes for them to stay in their homes, even with modifications.

There are many creative solutions to the multiple problems of housing an aging population. For example, local governments could modify their building codes and zoning to make it easier for homeowners to build "accessory" or "mother-in-law" units in their backyards.

This would make it financially feasible to provide good housing since the family already owns the land. It would also allow elders to enjoy the support of living with family while still preserving their independence.

Unfortunately, Congress has shown no inclination to actively promote anything resembling a comprehensive solution.

The challenge of providing assisted-living services to the increasing numbers of frail elders without bankrupting the Medicaid program is also still waiting for attention. The one thing Congress got right is to continue funding for converting existing Sec. 202 properties to provide assisted living, but the meager level of funding it provided won't go far.

CHAPTER SIXTEEN

The Disinvestment Dilemma

Housing is the crucial building block of vital and stable communities, but there is so much more that goes into keeping our cities healthy. Unfortunately, mayors throughout America spend almost as much time defending federal programs for community and economic development from congressional budget-cutters as they do running their cities.

According to one estimate, federal spending on community development has fallen by 75 percent over the last 30 years measured as a share of gross domestic product.

"At the federal and state level, with funds being systematically eliminated that used to go to cities, where we have the most problems, more and more is being put on the backs of municipal governments," said Ed Pawlowski, mayor of Allentown, Pa.

The attacks have been made year after year on direct federal and state spending as well as on tax policies that have helped attract private capital to cities. There is also a strong lobbying effort in Washington aimed at laws that prohibit banks from ignoring the credit needs of low-income people in their service areas.

Attacks on programs that benefit cities have appeared regularly on the budget proposals of Republican presidents and Republican members of Congress. One recurring target for elimination has been the Community Development Block Grant (CDBG) program, a mainstay of housing and urban development since 1974.

In recent years, as both parties have worked on long-term strategies for reducing the budget deficit, there is increasing talk about ways to reduce tax expenditures that benefit cities. One target that comes up repeatedly is the federal income tax break that goes to investors in tax-exempt bonds issued by city and county governments.

Reductions in housing assistance programs affect communities of every size, as well as rural areas. But cities are especially dependent on state and federal support for basic infrastructure, like streets and bridges, as well as community development activities, like fixing up crumbling buildings and sidewalks, and providing community facilities, like parks and recreation.

Many cities and counties have already increased local taxes to make up for cuts in federal funding for things like roads and mass transit. But in Allentown and other cities without strong economic growth, there is little potential to make up for the cuts in federal and state funding by raising local taxes, Pawlowski added.

Pawlowski and other mayors warn of a downward spiral: The less cities have to spend on keeping their neighborhoods and downtowns in good shape, the harder it is to attract the investment and jobs that help them expand their tax base and maintain economic viability.

Targeting block grants

In 2005, President George W. Bush proposed eliminating the CDBG program. Mayors nationwide campaigned fiercely to keep it alive. They prevented elimination, but they could not prevent a series of steep reductions in funding.

In 2010, the CDBG appropriation was $4.45 billion. In 2011, it was reduced to $3.5 billion. In 2012 through 2014, it had dropped to a little over $3 billion per year.

For fiscal year 2014, the Republican majority in the House of Representatives proposed cutting that to just $1.6 billion. The Senate would not consent to that deep of a cut. However, it is highly likely that opponents of the program will try again to slash it, if not kill it.

The reduction of roughly $1.4 billion in CDBG funding since 2010 has "significantly undermined projects and shuttered services that cities need to create jobs for our residents and that drive economic growth throughout our communities," according to the National League of Cities.

Mayors consider CDBG funds to be indispensable, because the program gives them the flexibility to use the money for a wide variety of programs.

The annual grants can be used for just about everything that cities need to provide housing and improve downtowns and neighborhoods. The most important use is to help make housing development feasible, including production of apartments that utilize the low-income housing tax credit (LIHTC). They are also being used increasingly for economic development projects like helping commercial ventures obtain land or buildings.

Other areas of spending include rehabilitation of single-family homes, creating senior centers, as well as improvements to sidewalks, streets, parks, and water and sewer systems.

CDBG is often used to finance programs operated by nonprofit, community-based organizations. These cover the gamut of purposes, from housing advocacy to youth services. CDBG funds can also be used for operating expenses of local nonprofit community development corporations.

Repeated reductions in CDBG allocations have had "a devastating impact" on nonprofit groups engaged in housing and community development, wrote Rick Cohen in the Nonprofit Quarterly.

In addition to the flexibility it offered, CDBG had been a source of consistent, reliable funding.

For large cities and counties, known as entitlement communities, annual funding is determined by a formula allocation system. The Department of Housing and Urban Development (HUD) crunches a set of specific data from each city, including the average age of a city's housing stock, to arrive at each city's proportional share of the national funding pot.

Budget cuts have undermined that aspect of the program, too. The 2014 funding level is only slightly higher than the funding level in fiscal year 1976, when there were 597 entitlement grantees. The number of entitlement communities has roughly doubled since then.

As a result, the formula in use will leave many communities with grants that are too small to make a difference.

One mayor told a meeting of the U.S. Conference of Mayors he was considering refusing to accept his city's CDBG allocation in 2013. The cost of complying with all the federally mandated reporting requirements would come close to or even exceed the amount of the grant itself, he said.

Working for food

Akron, Ohio, Mayor Donald L. Plusquellic and then U.S. Rep. Betty Sutton (D-Ohio) held a press conference outside Dave's Supermarket in East Akron to talk about the importance of the program for job creation, especially in the wake of a terrible recession.

"The Community Development Block Grant program is essential to help our communities retain small businesses, make critical infrastructure improvements, and promote neighborhood development," Sutton said. "These targeted investments create job opportunities for our people, and recklessly cutting them when local governments need them the most would be a serious mistake."

---

*Repeated reductions in Community
Development Block Grant program
allocations have had "a devastating impact"
on nonprofit groups.*

CDBG funding gives cities the power to attract private employers who would not be comfortable investing without government involvement, said Plusquellic, mayor of this northeastern Ohio city since 1987. "CDBG has been the signature partnership between the federal government and local government to create jobs, increase economic development opportunities, expand homeownership, and maintain neighborhoods," Plusquellic said.

Akron used CDBG funds to convince Dave's Supermarket to locate in East Akron, bringing 180 part- and full-time jobs with it, as well as a source of fresh produce and groceries to an area that had not had such an outlet.

In 2012, many cities began to feel the impact of reductions in congressional appropriations as well as the effects of changes to HUD's formula for allocating funds, according to an article in *Governing* magazine by Ryan Holeywell in 2012.

- New Orleans lost more than $4 million in CDBG funds, or 27 percent of its 2011 total;
- Los Angeles lost $12.5 million, or 19 percent of its 2011 total;
- Hialeah, Fla., received $1.8 million less than it did in 2011; and
- Allentown lost about 22 percent of its 2012 grant amount.

Most local leaders say their cities are so fiscally strained that they cannot find local revenue to help plug the hole left by federal funding reductions.

"It's forcing us and a lot of other communities to start making very hard choices," said Eric Brown, director of housing and community development for Prince George's County, Md.

Ending urban action

CDBG is typically used for relatively small expenditures on housing needs as well as community and economic development. The Urban Development Action Grant (UDAG) program, on the other hand, was a competitive program that awarded large grants for major projects intended to create jobs and revitalize downtown areas.

It was part of a wide range of federal spending on urban development enacted under the Jimmy Carter administration. Over an 11-year period, UDAG provided $5 billion toward the revitalization of distressed urban areas by stimulating private-sector investment. In the late 1970s, cities competed for UDAG funds four times a year, with the best projects receiving funds.

The program was terminated in 1988.

As with many fights against funding cuts, Republican and Democratic mayors were united in asking Congress to spare the program from the budget axe. But the mayors lost that battle. Among the reasons cited in the press for elimination: Members of Congress wanted to spend more money on space exploration than investing in cities.

Cities have been coping with decreases in federal and state support for many years. Mayors who were in office during the 1980s still remember the day Congress eliminated the general revenue sharing program like it was yesterday.

Revenue sharing was started in 1972 under President Richard Nixon. It distributed $4.5 billion to 39,000 municipalities in fiscal year 1986. It was terminated in 1987.

Revenue sharing affected more local governments than any federal program in history. It was the only federal disbursement without restrictions on the use of the money.

The only good news for urban and economic development in recent years was creation of the New Markets Tax Credit (NMTC) program, which offers an attractive tax incentive for private investors to finance job-producing projects in low-income areas. However, that program expired at the end of 2013. As of mid-2014, it was uncertain if Congress would renew the tax incentive.

Program supporters, including Republican mayors and members of Congress, argued that the provision should be made permanent, that is, that it should be extended indefinitely with no pre-established expiration date.

"By creating a permanent NMTC program, Congress would provide stability in the program, leading to increased investor and developer interest in the program, better NMTC equity pricing, greater benefits to low-income communities, and increased leveraging of government funding," according to Enterprise Community Partners, a national nonprofit group that is active in the program.

Permanence is important because a great deal of planning goes into putting together a NMTC project. Sponsors and investors alike must undertake extensive legal and financial work. If there is uncertainty that the tax incentive will remain available, it discourages participation, so there are fewer good projects to choose from.

There is little question that the program has been effective. Since its inception, NMTC investments have been involved in developing or rehabilitating over 109 million square feet of real estate and creating over 500,000 jobs in low-income communities. According to the Treasury Department, for every $1 of tax credit authority from the NMTC program, approximately $8 of private capital is leveraged for investment in distressed communities.

Tax reform threatens

Since 1986, there has been a shift in the federal government's approach to housing and community development. We moved from direct federal outlays to a system of tax incentives intended to attract private capital. State and local governments, as well as community development financial institutions also increase their reliance on issuance of bonds exempt from federal taxation.

It was thought that this approach would make it possible to have some consistency in the level of financial support, since tax incentives are not subject to the annual appropriations process in Congress.

However, the recent political focus on cutting the budget deficit has put them in jeopardy too. There is no telling what Congress may do. However, the National Commission on Fiscal Responsibility and Reform, created in 2010, has called for reduction in use of tax-exempt bonds by cities and counties.

From 2003 to 2012, localities nationwide financed $1.65 trillion in infrastructure projects through the issuance of tax-exempt, municipal bonds. If their ability to continue to do so were reduced, it would be devastating.

"While Washington holds hearings, fights ideological battles about infrastructure funding, and otherwise wrings its hands about our nation's aging infrastructure, state and local governments are busy creating jobs and building, renovating, and maintaining the core infrastructure that are essential to our economy," said Mayor Stephen Benjamin of Columbia, S.C.

Any reduction in local governments' ability to issue bonds would curtail their ability to do all those things. Coupled with further attempts to eliminate things like CDBG or failure to renew the NMTC, it would condemn American cities to a new dark age of decline.

Jerry Abramson served as mayor of Louisville, Ky., for 20 years. He also headed the U.S. Conference of Mayors for a period of time. He said the power over budget priorities in Washington lies with big banks, big pharmaceutical companies, big energy companies, and so on. The mayors of America have always had to fight just to hold on to their small piece of a budgetary pie that is subject to myriad demands from high-powered lobbyists.

"When the private sector comes in with their guns blazing, we are outmatched. We are dodging and weaving just to hold onto our morsels," he said.

CHAPTER SEVENTEEN

The Anti-Affordability Conspiracy

The revitalization of America's inner cities and decaying sub-urbs cannot occur on any significant scale without financial support from state and federal governments. But shouldn't the private market be able to produce housing affordable to most working Americans, greatly reducing the need for government subsidies?

The answer is yes, of course, and our ability to do just that in the 50s and 60s helped drive our economy and enlarge our middle class. In those days, a far smaller percentage of Americans needed government help to afford a place to live.

But those days are over. In most parts of our country, new, un-subsidized housing generally cannot be produced for anyone but the upper middle-class and the affluent.

With the exception of recessionary periods, housing costs have risen consistently, increasing the number of people in need of gov-ernment help as well as the government's costs for helping the sub-set of needy households lucky enough to receive assistance.

"An army of regulators at every level of government is choking off the supply of affordable housing," said the late Congressman Jack Kemp in 1992. He was referring to the fact that local govern-ments add costs to housing by virtue of their control over how land may be used and how buildings should be designed and constructed, as well as their fees to provide basic utilities like water and sewage treatment.

Over the years, housing development has become one of the most heavily regulated industries in America. The web of local, state and federal regulation has grown year by year with remarkably little public discussion of its impact on housing costs.

It may be a bit strong to call it a conspiracy because the many separate decisions that pile on costs are not coordinated to achieve that particular result, at least not consciously or explicitly. But if one looks only at the results, it's easy to impute the intent to drive up costs. Only a handful of jurisdictions, have made any serious effort to balance the legitimate need for regulation against the need to keep housing affordable.

In the case of government-assisted housing, there is another layer of regulations intended to meet social and political goals that drive up costs, like requirements to pay the prevailing local wage on any subsidized construction project.

• • •

The process of getting a proposed housing development from the conceptual stage into actual construction is referred to as the "entitlement" process. The developer of the housing, working with architects and other professionals, must go through a long process that includes reviews by a dozen or more agencies and departments. Some of the steps include review of project plans against zoning codes, design standards, environmental requirements, and many other regulations.

The process theoretically ends with the issuance of a building permit, but there is rarely any assurance that a permit will ultimately be issued or how many units it will allow to be built.

Obtaining a building permit for a housing development with as few as 30 units can easily take three to five years and cost $1 million or more. Larger developments can run up costs of $2 million to $4 million, all of which are incurred with no certainty a permit will ever be issued.

That's only counting the direct costs of working through the entitlement process. During the time that takes, construction costs may rise significantly. Interest expenses on loans continue to add up month after month. The cost of keeping an option on the building site adds up and may increase.

In 1991, President George H.W. Bush tried to deal with this problem by appointing the bipartisan Advisory Commission on Regulatory Barriers to Affordable Housing.

The panel estimated that excessive fees and regulations were jacking up housing costs by around 25 percent. Anthony Downs, a housing economist on the panel, said it was more like 50 percent, and possibly even more. A fellow at the Brookings Institution, Downs was a veteran of the very first federal commission on housing and urban issues, which was convened 23 years earlier.

Despite intense lobbying by Kemp, who was secretary of the Department of Housing and Urban Development at the time, Congress showed very little interest in the issue. The commission made 31 recommendations for action, but the most important of them were not implemented.

The problems cited by the commission are worse today. The gauntlet of costs and regulations has increased exponentially. So have the costs imposed on housing of all kinds, including everything from starter homes to working-class apartments all the way up to large single-family homes.

This added layer of costs is a serious problem for the apartments that taxpayers subsidize through government housing programs. This is a primary reason government agencies have to spend more each year just to continue to assist the same number of households as in previous years.

Twenty-one years after the Bush commission report, the same concerns were echoed by the Bipartisan Policy Center's Housing Commission. It said that excessive regulation and fees were preventing development of "rental housing that could help meet the needs of moderate-income households and allow older developments to filter down to rent levels affordable to low-income households."

In addition, both federal and local regulations "often discourage or inhibit the development of economically diverse, mixed-use neighborhoods that can help support educational achievement and economic mobility for low-income families," the bipartisan report added.

All the regulations and fees the localities impose on affordable housing have legitimate or well-established rationales. But these myriad regulations and fees are piled on one after the other with no cost-benefit analysis. Very few local agencies stop to analyze how they will affect housing affordability.

In Washington, no one adds up how much regulation and fees add to the cost of housing or weighs that amount against the public benefit they provide. Local agencies have carte blanche in deciding how many financial hurdles to put in the way of housing development, reducing overall production and driving up the cost of however many housing units do get constructed.

The range of regulations, policies, fees and processes that affect housing costs would fill an entire book – make that several books. They come from every level of government, from special taxing districts to cities, then regional agencies, state governments and finally, federal agencies, most notable the Environmental Protection Agency.

Regulations cover land use, density, the size of lots for detached homes, design standards, building materials, construction methods and much more. Everything any agency has to review or process comes with a price tag attached, both in fees and in time taken for processing.

Environmental mandates have expanded steadily since the 1970s, most recently to include energy efficiency and greenhouse gas emissions, recycling of building materials and other things. New federal regulations for dealing with stormwater management are among the latest areas of controversy that could result in still more housing cost inflation.

Land, costly land

On average, land costs account for approximately one-third of housing costs. Land prices are not determined by market forces alone, but also by government policy. Local governments increase the cost of land per unit of housing in many ways, but they all boil down to the same concept: Require as much land as possible for each unit of housing.

The key to affordability is "density," or the number of units of housing per acre of land. The higher the number of units that can be built in a building site, usually measured on a per acre basis, the less the cost per unit of housing, since the cost of land is spread among more units.

Developers generally want higher density. City planners and land use regulators outside of central cities generally fight for lower density.

In 1992, the Bush commission said zoning restrictions were being used to create communities dominated by single-family homes. Downs wrote that local zoning codes that exclude housing developments with moderate or high density were "one of the most widespread and serious regulatory barriers to housing affordability."

If the opposition to density was serious in 1992, it was out of control in 2014.

For single-family, detached homes, the main point of control is lot size. Most suburban areas have a minimum lot size per dwelling unit, which ensures homes will be fairly expensive.

For multifamily housing, zoning is the key point of control. In years past, a city would designate various zones where it was legally authorized to construct certain kinds of buildings for certain uses. These included zones for multifamily rental housing. As long as a proposed building met a town's basic building and design codes and was no bigger than the zoning allowed, the private property owner was within his or her rights to build it. There were debates about what areas should be zoned for higher density, but once a decision was made, developers had some security that buying a piece of land in a properly zoned area would allow them to build an appropriately-sized building.

That is called "as of right" construction, and it's slowly going the way of the dinosaur. It has already disappeared in many cities and is under attack in many others.

Increasingly, developers can no longer get a building permit just by following pre-established zoning criteria. Every single development requires a full review, up to and including a vote of one or more commissions—plus a vote of the entire city council—before the permit is granted and the project can move forward.

This can take years and may require enduring the uncertainty of elections for city council or mayor that give voters a chance to kill a project by voting against anyone who supports it. It is not unusual for developers to watch as officials who supported their development are voted out of office for their pro-housing positions.

Developers, whether profit-motivated or nonprofit, are left with a complete lack of certainty about how long it will take or how much it will cost to get a property built. They may as well consult a fortune-teller as read the zoning codes or city design standards, because all of that can be rendered irrelevant by politics.

Conditions vary from city to city. On one extreme, there is Houston, the one major city in America with no citywide zoning policy. On the other extreme is San Francisco, where any project along the waterfront above a certain size must be approved by a public vote, with all the cost of trying to persuade individual voters to give their approval.

Developers of housing for middle and upper-income people can afford teams of land-use lawyers and cope with long delays, so they have a good shot at overcoming all the obstacles. After all, courts do sometimes support private property rights, though it can take a great deal of time and money to achieve that result. These developers simply pass on the added costs to tenants and buyers.

But most developers of affordable housing have trouble with years of delay and millions of dollars in added costs just to gamble on winning permission to build. If they do roll the dice and win, it almost always results in higher costs to the government agencies subsidizing the project and/or a reduction in the number of units that can be built.

A recent study of housing development in Eastern Massachusetts found that excessive regulation is a key reason the region is second only to New York City in the rate of increase in housing prices.

"The greater Boston area's housing shortage is not the result of a shortage of land, but rather of restrictions on the existing land that make denser development difficult to impossible. While low densities have their virtues, they also ensure that housing will stay expensive and retard economic growth," according to "Regulation and the Rise of Housing Prices in Greater Boston," a 2006 study based on data from 187 communities in eastern Massachusetts. Harvard professor Edward L. Glaeser was the lead author.

"Regionally, housing prices might have been 23 to 36 percent lower if regulation had not greatly slowed new permitting since 1990," the report concluded.

The normal rule of economics is that as prices for an item rise, more people will supply it and as the supply increases, the prices will decline. This is not true in housing in the area, despite strong demand.

The researchers found steady declines in housing production. In the 1960s, there were 172,459 units permitted in the Boston metropolitan area; in the 1980s, 141,347. However, despite the sharp rise in prices in the 1990s, only 84,105 units were permitted in that decade.

The decline in permits has been particularly striking for units in multifamily buildings. In the 1960s, less than 50 percent of all permits in the Boston metropolitan area were for single-family homes. In the 1990s, over 80 percent of all permits were for single-family homes.

The affordability outlook could be improved in short order if local governments allowed more construction of smaller homes, manufactured homes, accessory dwelling units (ADUs) and small apartments also known as studio apartments.

ADUs or "granny flats" are small apartments built on lots that already have a single-family home on them and are often used for the landowner to house an aging parent or to rent out for extra income. However, most local governments have used zoning and building codes to prevent any widespread use of this strategy.

ADUs are a prime example of a solution that is economically feasible but completely lacking in local political support in most places.

If just 10 percent of houses built before 1975 had such accessory apartments, it would add 3.8 million units to the housing supply, according to Downs.

Cities like Boston and San Francisco are allowing more construction of so-called "micro" apartments. But most towns have yet to recognize the need for more flexibility on unit size.

Infrastructure Needs

The unglamorous task of constructing and maintaining infrastructure is another major contributor to the increased costs of housing. This includes sewer and water pipes, roads and traffic signals, drainage and flood control, sewage treatment, and more.

In the past, cities created these facilities and then levied taxes on all the properties in town to pay for them. But when taxpayers rebelled against increases in their taxes, cities could no longer easily finance expansion or maintenance of these facilities. In response, they shifted the burden of paying for them to new real estate developments.

The problem was that, instead of paying just for the share of infrastructure costs related to a proposed development, builders were required to pay for improvements that served entire neighborhoods or even towns.

These costs take the form of impact fees, which go to the public agencies that build and operate the facilities, or requirements that developers build the infrastructure at their sole expense.

In one community in an area dominated by the recreation industry and vacation homes, no apartments affordable to people working at area businesses had been constructed for decades. When developers came to town to propose construction to meet the need for housing, they ran into fierce opposition and governmental obstacles.

Finally, with business owners complaining about their inability to keep employees on the job due to the lack of housing, the regional redevelopment agency invited a developer to undertake construction. It took seven years, tremendous patience, creativity, luck, and millions of dollars in up-front costs, but the company successfully constructed the first ever deed restricted affordable apartments in the area in 2012.

The cost of satisfying the county, the regional planning organization, and other special districts with control over the project totaled more than $2 million. This included fees charged for building permits, inspections, and impact fees.

Then there was the cost of new infrastructure that local authorities required the developer to build. The developer installed major upgrades to all utilities serving each of the individual buildings comprising the project. The cost was about $3.5 million. This does not include infrastructure that was exclusively for the new housing, such as water pipes from the main feeder lines to the buildings.

It all adds up to $5.5 million for 77 apartments. That's $71,428 per housing unit. That does not include any construction costs, the costs to keep control of the land for five years, or the cost of interest on loans.

The list of requirements and fees goes on and on, but one example stands out. Just when it appeared that construction could finally start, one more special taxing district threatened to block issuance of a building permit if the developer did not put up a large sum to pay for acquisition of a new and very expensive vehicle to serve all the properties in the area.

The developer called it "legalized extortion," but could not say no to the demand. This developer did not wish to be named for fear of facing retaliation from the local governments in the area for having criticized their entitlement processes.

This developer had the patience and creativity to fight through obstacles and take huge risks. If the project had fallen through, all the up-front money and effort would have been wasted.

For many other, smaller builders, the difficulty and expense has gone over the top, and they have gone out of business. As a result, our capacity for housing development is shrinking, which only exacerbates the supply problem.

Buildings and designs

Homeowners who have dealt with their local zoning or building departments about an improvement or addition have received a miniscule taste of what developers go through.

The fees, detailed requirements, and delays multiply year by year, and local officials show little interest in helping to expedite or simplify the process.

City requirements for a minimum number of parking spaces are a frequently cited barrier for building affordable properties in already built-up areas. However, a number of cities are reexamining these requirements as part of the overall effort to encourage high-density development and the use of public transportation, walking and cycling.

Housing Runs the Gauntlet

The mechanics of how local regulations, land use policies, and infrastructure needs push up housing costs are complex and interconnected. That's part of the reason no one in high political office pays them any mind. But it is important to understand the system in broad brush.

In the past, mayors and city councils called most of the shots about what could be built in their communities, with input from a city planner, a zoning commission, a traffic or street department, and a planning commission which included a sub-committee for design reviews. That was complex enough.

Now, control over real estate development is a collective process. It includes myriad specialized agencies, most of which can block issuance of a building permit. There are government agencies for running the sewers and sewage treatment, water supplies, fire protection, open space maintenance, ambulance operations, storm sewer systems, and air quality monitoring—among other things.

On top of that, there are special districts with taxing power to help neighborhoods or regional collaborations, like business improvement districts or homeowner associations.

The problem is that every department, every agency, and every special district has its own purpose. Those purposes almost always include generating revenue from the people who develop real estate. They almost never include trying to make sure housing is affordable.

While there is usually one agency in each city or county that focuses on promoting housing affordability, there are many more that have power over housing development but no concern at all for affordability.

The housing agency rarely has any influence over any of those organizations. Does this mean that agencies of the same government work at cross purposes, one trying to subsidize housing affordability while others drive up the costs of doing so? Yes.

The biggest problem with building codes is how they deal with housing rehabilitation.

Older housing is less expensive than new construction, but it's often in poor shape and lacks energy efficiency. Rehab is often required and is inherently risky, since property owners can't know the extent of the problems that will need fixing until construction is underway.

Onerous building codes make the process even worse. Most cities require that a property owner that undertakes significant improvements or repairs must also comply with every change in the building code since the building was constructed. This is usually so expensive that owners simply avoid making improvements. This is a major contributing factor to the deterioration and, ultimately, the destruction of older apartment buildings.

The good news about building codes is that many localities now subscribe to uniform nationwide codes, eliminating wide variations from place to place. The bad news is that the model codes become more complex every year, and each new requirement usually results in an overall cost increase for complying with the code.

As codes have become more comprehensive, adding provisions on everything from seismic safety and water conservation to handling of construction waste, the incremental addition to construction costs has increased.

Green building requirements are the newest and most widespread addition to local building codes. States and cities seeking to reduce greenhouse gas emissions have adopted codes that require more energy-efficient construction. In California, for example, all new residential construction is supposed to be "zero carbon" by 2020, meaning that they must be extremely efficient and use alternative energy sources, such as wind and solar.

Higher energy-efficiency standards can save money in the long run, because they reduce operating costs. However, they are another example of the many ways that costs are being driven upward without any regard to the impact on consumers of housing, that is, everyone in America.

A few localities have implemented innovative ways to help property owners pay for energy improvements, or stretch out the effective dates of requirements for improvements. They understand that more thought needs to be given to how to balance environmental and housing affordability goals.

The New Environmentalism

In general, affordable housing developers have done an excellent job of accommodating environmental concerns. However, the impact of a new development on the natural world is by far the most likely point of attack for groups that simply want to prevent construction of housing by any means possible.

Legitimate environmental concerns are aired thoroughly in most land use discussions. However, for groups opposed to density and affordability, environmental concerns can be like the improvised explosive devices of the entitlement process: Anyone can place them, and they can be very effective in frightening politicians and disrupting a fair and expeditious process of reviewing proposed developments.

In many land use debates, it has become impossible to distinguish between legitimate concerns about negative environmental impacts and trumped up objections that are intended to prevent affordable housing development, not to protect the environment.

A handful of citizens can kill a project just by voicing their concern that it might have some future negative impact on a park or a stream—or even that it will obstruct the view of a scenic vista. No hard evidence is required to convince politicians that they should not take a chance by approving a building permit.

If opponents to housing development cannot get their way with politicians, they can bring down the legal heat. In California, that means the California Environmental Quality Act, known as CEQA. There doesn't even have to be a probable serious environmental problem; The process of litigation itself would be so costly and time-consuming, it would kill most projects.

What drives developers crazy is that there is no standard procedure for whether such a suit can be filed or not. It doesn't matter if the proposed development was approved by all the relevant local and regional governments and agencies. Almost anyone can file a CEQA suit anytime right up until the start of construction, completely removing any degree of confidence that money invested up front could ever be recouped.

The question of whether environmental protection has gone too far was being debated vigorously in California under the governorship of Jerry Brown. The Democratic governor had become critical of CEQA, which has held up projects of all description, from affordable housing to high-speed rail transportation.

In the view of housing developers and other critics, including

Brown, the law is so broad and so vague, it is often used to block projects that have little or no negative impact on the environment or that, in the long run, will benefit the environment, like high-speed rail or infill housing development.

New York State's Environmental Quality Review (SEQR) law has faced similar criticism for creating delays and uncertainty in housing production. Ways to streamline it were under discussion in 2013.

"Much of New York, especially upstate, is suffering from what could be described as a severe development deficit," said one of the organizations arguing for change, The Empire Center for Public Policy, Inc., an independent, non-partisan, non-profit think tank based in Albany, N.Y.

The organization's proposed changes make sense for a balanced approach to environmental protection for any state, whether involving the executive or judicial branches of government:

- Reduce the potential for undue delays by imposing hard deadlines and incentives to ensure the process can be completed within a year.
- Mandate "scoping" of environmental impacts at the first stage in the SEQR review process, but also more tightly restrict the introduction of new issues by lead agencies later in the process.
- Eliminate the law's reference to "community and neighborhood character" as an aspect of the broadly defined environment potentially affected by projects, since the concept already is defined by local planning and zoning laws.

Looking ahead

U.S. government housing commissions since the 1960s have warned about the danger of letting local governments drive up the cost of housing through building codes, zoning, and other regulations.

There's little chance that local governments will stop driving up housing costs on their own accord, according to Downs. He opined that many of them wanted costs to rise because it increased property values for existing homeowners, and this, in turn, helped the local government collect higher property taxes.

"The major purpose of zoning ordinances and even of local government itself in some suburban communities is to restrict the type of households who can live there," Downs wrote. Many such towns were incorporated initially for the main purpose of maintaining their exclusivity, meaning high housing costs, he concluded.

The conflict between local interest in regulating housing and the national interest in having affordable housing has been on a low simmer ever since Downs published his article. It is likely to intensify as more and more cities find they have few sites that are suitable for housing development.

Many people would say that complying with codes and paying impact fees are the real estate developers' problem. But it is not true. If a government subsidy is involved, most of the costs that get added on to a housing development are borne by taxpayers. This reduces the amount of housing that a given amount of government spending can produce.

For market-rate housing, the added costs are passed on to tenants and homebuyers.

Housing developers and advocates do not suggest that local governments should not regulate housing or that the EPA should not protect the environment. On the contrary, developers accept and even embrace a certain amount of regulation.

After all, a well-planned community with consistent, high-quality design of its buildings, access to natural areas, clean water and reasonable traffic is great for real estate values and quality of life.

The question is how to make sure that the perfect housing development –which pays for infrastructure, preserves nature, and saves energy (among other things), but costs a fortune – is not the enemy of the merely good development – the one that can be built at a cost that regular people can afford.

Government officials need to balance each regulation and fee against the need to slow down the rate of increases in the cost of housing, and to make sure there are residential options for people of all incomes.

Changing the web of inflationary regulations and fees won't be easy, but there is widespread awareness of the need to do so.

"Demand for regulatory change has traditionally come from builders and developers, and affordable housing advocates have not been engaged in this discussion," according to Jessica LeVeen Farr, regional community development manager in the Nashville Branch of the Atlanta Federal Reserve Bank.

To bring change, a new approach is needed, she wrote. "Builders, developers, and housing advocates must join together with local businesses, real estate professionals, and banks to establish broad coalitions. Working together, (they) can make a stronger case for affordable housing and have greater leverage to encourage states and local jurisdictions to adopt regulatory changes that will increase housing opportunities."

CHAPTER EIGHTEEN

Why We Hate Housing

Andrew J. Spano faced a difficult decision in 2009. As the chief executive of Westchester County, N.Y., he could comply with a federal order to build affordable housing in his county or spend millions of dollars to fight it. He agreed to expedite development of 750 units of affordable housing in predominantly white communities in the county of nearly 1 million people and to market the housing to minority households.

That may not sound like a big deal—new affordable apartments for less than one-tenth of 1 percent of the county's population. But it was wildly unpopular.

Rob Astorino, a Republican, defeated Spano, a three-term incumbent Democrat, for county executive in 2009, largely because of his opposition to affordable housing development. He continued to argue against the housing settlement, and many local officials and citizens followed his lead. Four years later, only 124 units had been built.

In 2014, with his political prospects soaring, Astorino announced his candidacy for governor of New York.

Polls show that most Americans think affordable housing is important to the health and longevity of communities, not to mention their own children's futures. But as the Westchester situation shows, government efforts to persuade localities to allow affordable housing construction often meet resistance, and that resistance appears to be growing.

When it comes to a development planned in their own community, affordable housing is about as welcome as a nuclear waste dump. Nobody wants it to be built near them.

Anti-housing arguments range from the fear of increased crime and traffic to reduced property values and increased tax burdens. But scratch the surface, and the reasons often reveal incorrect assumptions, inaccurate or deceptive information, and entrenched cultural biases.

If you've ever been personally involved in a community-level battle over a proposed housing development, you know about the name-calling and hostility it involves. Anyone who speaks against a proposed development is labeled a NIMBY, which is short for "not in my backyard." The term has become shorthand for all kinds of opposition to affordable housing development.

Those who speak for a new development are said to be in the pocket of developers who are always described as greedy, even if they are nonprofit organizations. Government officials are often accused, with absolutely no evidence, of taking bribes to allow housing construction. Neighbors turn against neighbors, and charges and countercharges fly. It is not unusual for arguments to drag on for years and for lawsuits to be filed on both sides.

The problem is that the opposition to affordable rental housing development has been growing more powerful and more pervasive for years, even as the need for that housing has increased dramatically.

"NIMBY sentiment [is] frequently widespread and deeply ingrained. [It] is so powerful because it is easily translatable into government action, given the existing system for regulating land use and development. Current residents and organized neighborhood groups can exert great influence over local electoral and land-development processes, to the exclusion of nonresidents, prospective residents, or, for that matter, all outsiders. Restrictions on affordable housing [development] are the result."

That is not the opinion of a housing trade association or a liberal think tank. It is from the Advisory Commission on Regulatory Barriers to Affordable Housing appointed by President George H.W. Bush. The commission's report, issued in 1991, said that neutralizing the power of NIMBY to block housing development was critical to meeting our nation's affordable housing needs.

With the winds of opposition to affordable housing howling, it's no wonder that cities often use their regulatory and fee-charging powers to drive up the cost and delay or prevent construction of affordable housing.

Single-family homes at high price points may meet environmental objections, but the main force of opposition is reserved for any proposed developments with attached units and more than two stories.

The main mechanism of control is zoning, which determines how many housing units can be built on a given piece of land. The higher the number of units per acre, the less the cost per unit, since the cost of land is spread among more units.

This opposition often results in a reduction in the number of units allowed, which drives up the eventual rent or sales price per unit—or makes the proposed development financially infeasible and kills it altogether.

Anti-housing activists know they have time on their side. Most affordable housing built today is financed with federal low-income housing tax credits. Each state housing finance agency that uses the credit to finance development sets very strict construction start deadlines. If opponents can delay a project long enough, it will lose its tax credits and die on the vine.

• • •

Another political hurdle for housing is its place in municipal finances. Retail and office development generate more jobs and more tax revenue than housing, so every city pursues that kind of development. Housing generally requires more services and generates less tax revenue, weighing the balance against it.

The traditional urban development model of apartments situated over storefronts still exists in old "main street" districts and in very limited cases of new development. But as a rule, there is no system for ensuring that job-creating real estate provides the housing that workers taking those jobs need.

Municipal fees, regulatory requirements, and fiscal concerns play right into the hands of anti-housing groups that simply don't want rental housing built anywhere near them.

Taken together, anti-housing attitudes and onerous regulatory policies have a snowball effect. The more difficult anti-housing groups make it to build, the fewer organizations try to undertake the long, expensive process of development, with all the risk it entails. A number of small nonprofit housing developers, including faith-based groups, have simply gone out of business. Small, for-profit builders are not doing much better.

No one says that property owners don't have a right to question their elected officials about land-use decisions or to voice their views. Public participation is built into the processes cities use to plan development over the long term and to regulate individual projects in the short term. One development of less than 100 units planned for a California town was the subject of over 100 public meetings and hearings over five years. And that's not unusual.

But housing advocates from coast to coast say they are no longer seeing reasonable debate that is based on facts and conducted in reference to local codes and long-standing land-use plans.

Opposition to affordable housing has become automatic, increasingly strident, and less and less connected to the long-range plans most cities adopt. It has gotten stronger and more pervasive.

> *"Good suburban neighborhoods with good schools where jobs are being created are like exclusive private clubs."*
> *—Bart Harvey, former CEO of nonprofit Enterprise Community Partners.*

The power of the opposition has become so great that in certain regions of the country, apartments cannot be built as a matter of right. Now, in many places, every project must be approved by the zoning department, the planning commission, and, ultimately, the city council. This gives housing opponents tremendous power.

Housing developments aimed at families face the strongest opposition, largely because of questions about how schools will be impacted by new students. But, the opposition often targets properties intended for the elderly, as well. NIMBY even has affected housing for our military veterans.

Volunteers of America (VOA), a national faith-based nonprofit organization that builds affordable housing nationwide, proposed building low-rent apartments adjacent to the veterans' hospital in Omaha, Neb. It was a great deal for vets, who'd have affordable apartments very close to their medical services.

But VOA's vision clashed with that of some of the wealthiest, most powerful people in the city. The hospital sits adjacent to the Field Club, a high-end country club, and the homes adjoining its fairways. Neighbors and club members sued to ensure that the veterans' housing would not be built at that location. VOA won the case and the appeal. The opponents went to the Nebraska Supreme Court and obtained a ruling blocking the project.

All of these costs incurred to fight NIMBY are passed on to tenants and buyers, reducing any development's intended degree of "affordability." If a government subsidy is involved, taxpayers end up paying far more per unit of housing, which means far fewer units for the original given sum.

Joining the "resistance"

The latest tactic among anti-housing activists is to portray affordable housing as part of an internationalist plot against America.

The supposed basis for this is something called Agenda 21, a nonbinding, voluntary set of guidelines the United Nations issued in 1992 to encourage sustainable development, including higher-density real estate development adjacent to public transportation.

Municipal governments in many regions are collaborating on plans that link housing and real estate development with planning for transit and infrastructure. A key component of these plans is to zone land near public transportation lines for higher-density affordable and mixed-income housing. Oftentimes, there is also an overall goal of reducing greenhouse gas emissions.

This has triggered a wave of opposition from anti-housing activists. They contend that because of Agenda 21, their cities and counties are being forced by faceless U.N. bureaucrats to build unwanted high-density housing.

Members of this movement, inspired by people like author Glenn Beck, are calling on their fellow citizens to "join the resistance" against planning and affordable housing. Beck and his fans are doing their best to characterize the regional planning processes as Soviet-style central planning.

One critic of the San Francisco Bay Area's long-term land use plan likened it to an attack on individual freedom. "I am a private citizen but a former [U.S. Air Force] officer," she wrote online. "I took an oath to support and defend the Constitution of the United States, and it is being trampled on and shredded by this type of planning. It is critical that average citizens start speaking up." The writer called for people to "join the resistance and help restore America."

Governments at all levels have applied huge amounts of money over the past 50 years to encourage millions of Americans to leave cities and move to single-family homes spread out along vast stretches of freeway. Billions of dollars in spending on freeway construction, mortgage lending programs for suburban homes, and tax breaks for home buyers have had a powerful impact.

So, why would a much smaller-scale regional planning effort to support higher-density housing be so frightening to people like Beck's followers?

The answer is simple: Anti-housing activists know that density is absolutely essential to making housing affordable, and that affordability is the key to giving poor and minority households mobility. If increased levels of housing density can be branded as a U.N. plot to take away our freedom, then affordable housing development can be opposed on ostensibly patriotic grounds.

This motivates the anti-housing movement by playing to people's fears. It also gives politically moderate homeowners a politically correct rationale for opposing provision of housing for lower-income people.

The merger of anti-planning, anti-U.N., and anti-housing motivations has the potential to take root and grow, especially as more regions take on the task of planning housing and transportation so as to reduce greenhouse gas emissions.

Housing's bad rap

In 1989, the CBS news program "48 Hours" broadcast a story about the appalling conditions of certain public housing projects in Chicago. Dan Rather reported from the notorious Cabrini-Green project on the North Side. It was a graphic depiction of the failure of high-rise projects that were badly designed and terribly managed.

It is true that some of the properties built under the public housing and Sec. 8 rental subsidy program were colossal failures. But today's affordable housing developments bear no resemblance to those failed Chicago projects in either design or management.

Cabrini-Green has since been replaced with mixed-income low-rise housing and a Target store, among other amenities. Most of the worst public housing high-rises also have been redeveloped in similar ways—not only in Chicago but nationwide.

None of the new government-assisted affordable housing that has been built in America since the mid-1980s has anything in common with the high-rise projects of previous decades. Failures of design and management are almost entirely a thing of the past.

New affordable housing is almost always owned by private investment groups, not by public agencies. It is well designed, making even higher density buildings attractive. It is often indistinguishable from middle-income garden apartments built without subsidy.

Public housing was originally built for working families, but, over time, many developments became 100 percent occupied by people with little or no income. That mistake is not being repeated.

The privately owned affordable housing being built today is mostly targeted to retail clerks, teachers, and others who earn 50 percent to 60 percent of the area median income. Over time, most residents see increases in their income, creating a healthy mix of incomes.

Most developments have a small percentage of units targeted to people who have little or no income. Where there is extremely low-income targeting, property owners usually incorporate social services like after-school programs into their management operations.

Still, the images from Rather's report on the Chicago projects have resonated for more than two decades, prompting fears that affordable apartment development will bring the problems of the inner city with it.

Those images, and the fear they generate, explain why debates about affordable housing are often only superficially about density, design, and the increased traffic that the new development will generate.

Many anti-housing activists hate affordable housing with an intensity that makes negotiation about project specifics largely irrelevant. It is not uncommon for developers to be threatened or shouted down by very angry people who pack hearing rooms and outnumber proponents by 50 or 100 to 1.

In Oldsmar, Fla., a small, mostly white town 16 miles from Tampa, The Wilson Co. proposed to build affordable rental housing for families. When local residents learned the apartments would be for people earning less than 60 percent of the area median income, they organized a fierce campaign to kill the project.

The company held informational meetings and tours of its other developments, but no one attended. "We tried to educate them about who lives in these communities and the quality of construction, but it all fell on deaf ears," said a company executive.

Sadly, it is only after a project is completed that opponents realize how little the new housing resembles the worst of the old high-rise housing projects.

Developers who build these properties report that, time after time, people who fought bitterly against an affordable housing development reverse their stance completely after it's built.

One developer described the grand opening of a property he had succeeded in building despite community objections. A woman attending the event, who had opposed the development, beheld the building with a look of astonishment. "This is not what I was picturing at all," she said. "This is very nice." In the next breath, she asked if there was a unit available for her daughter.

In Oldsmar, when the Westminster apartment community opened, the city officials who had fought against construction quickly embraced it.

It's no wonder. If they were picturing a depressing concrete highrise devoid of greenery and aesthetic details, they would have been in for quite a shock. With well-designed buildings spread out over a landscaped site with a lake, open spaces, and recreation and playground areas, the completed development was welcoming and beautiful.

"As soon as we started leasing up, people from town were calling us for units. Now people who opposed us have relatives and adult children living in Westminster," said a company executive.

False equivalency

It's normal for people to be concerned about traffic, school operations, and the overall future of the neighborhood where they own property and raise children. Property owners and citizens have a legitimate right to want to make sure that what's proposed for their area will be nicely designed and well managed.

The best way to address those concerns is to form a realistic understanding about the dynamics of real estate markets and separate facts from politically motivated propaganda.

This clears the way for a reasonable process of reviewing and modifying a development proposal to suit the area where it will be located.

It is not constructive to make gross generalizations that have no factual basis. For example, one northern California newspaper columnist wrote this to help foment opposition to a new affordable housing development:

"High-density development is a failed model that harms neighbors while destroying the lives of the folks they (sic) supposedly benefit."

Such a blanket condemnation of multifamily rental housing is ridiculous. There are thousands of apartment properties serving less affluent people throughout America that are safe and well maintained, with residents who make very good neighbors. But it reflects a very typical charge made by anti-housing groups nationwide.

Another common assertion is that a multifamily affordable development in an area of single-family homes will bring down property values. This has been proven false time and again in studies by many academic and policy research institutions.

Anti-housing activists also point to older apartment buildings that are not well maintained or managed when painting a picture of what a new, government-supported property would look like. While it's true that all new buildings age, one might say that new affordable housing "ages gracefully." That's because new properties have many regulatory and financial obligations to practice good management and maintenance—far more than privately financed buildings do.

The subtext of race & class

A young African-American boy with big brown eyes stares out from a full-page ad in *The Wall Street Journal*. The headline reads: "How can we tell him that the color of his skin is keeping his family from the home of its dreams?"

The ad goes on to say that victims of housing discrimination should call HUD. But the fact is, most of the children who cannot live in the home of their dreams will never know why that's the case, and they will never get help from HUD.

As President Lyndon Johnson knew when he campaigned for civil rights in the 1960s, it was one thing to say African-Americans should be allowed to vote, but quite another to say they should be allowed to live in the same neighborhoods as whites. American communities were rigidly segregated in those days. In many suburban, single-family developments, buyers signed covenants saying they would not sell their property to anyone of color.

It was only after Martin Luther King Jr. was assassinated on April 4, 1968, that Congress passed the Fair Housing Act. The law has worked well to help prevent landlords and property owners from denying the rental or sale of existing housing on account of color, religion, sex, national origin, or handicap and familial status.

But it is very ineffective when it comes to how local governments decide what kind of housing will be built in their communities.

Anti-housing activists generally couch their objections to a new development in terms of the physical characteristics of the buildings that would be erected, not the characteristics of the people who would live there.

In NIMBY debates in most places, there are no references to the racial composition of the households that might occupy a new apartment building.

However, there is a fair degree of candor in discussing social and economic class. It's not unusual to hear anti-housing activists say they don't want lower-income people to live in their neighborhood. "If they can't afford to buy a house here, they should not be able to live here," as one California housing opponent put it.

What is rarely discussed but is fairly apparent to anyone who

---

The Rosa Parks of Affordable Housing

Ethel R. Lawrence has been called the Rosa Parks of affordable housing.

She took her stand against racial discrimination, not in the South but in Mount Laurel, N.J., a town near Camden and Philadelphia that was becoming more and more suburban in the 1960s.

Mrs. Lawrence's children, along with other black households, could not find homes that were affordable and in sound condition. Mount Laurel officials suggested lower-income families move out of town, while encouraging the mostly new white residents to move into upper-scale housing unobtainable to most of the town's black residents, according to Peter O'Connor, of Fair Share Housing Development in New Jersey.

Mrs. Lawrence went to court. Joining in litigation brought by civil rights groups and others, Mrs. Lawrence was the lead individual plaintiff in the court case that led to two New Jersey Supreme Court decisions (Mount Laurel I and Mount Laurel II), which stopped towns from shutting out the poor through exclusionary zoning.

O'Connor, one of the attorneys for the plaintiffs in that landmark case, founded Fair Share Housing Development in 1986 to implement the settlement agreement in the Mount Laurel litigation and began to develop a plan for new affordable housing there.

Working with the plaintiffs in the lawsuit, O'Connor's organization pro-

understands America's demographics, is that these "exclusionary" policies and attitudes have a disproportionate impact on minorities, whether that is intentional or inadvertent.

If a community allows nothing but high-priced housing to be built, it has effectively prevented most minority households from living there. In 2012, the median U.S. income was $57,009 for white households, $33,321 for black households, and $39,005 for Hispanic households. In many metro areas, the income disparity is even greater.

Very few local politicians will publicly address the racial subtext of anti-housing campaigns. But the Advisory Commission on Regulatory Barriers to Affordable Housing was not afraid to discuss the issue. It said:

"The personal basis of NIMBY involves fear of change in either

---

posed to build 140 housing units on 62 acres in the same community. Despite the court's ruling, the local homeowners still tried to stop the development, citing fears of crime and declining property values.

The property was constructed and named the Ethel R. Lawrence Homes. Ten years after it was completed, Princeton University did an objective study to see if any of the feared impacts occurred. Not one of them had, according to the report.

"Local residents repeatedly expressed their fears of dire consequences that were sure to follow in the wake of the project's opening—that crime would increase, that tax burdens would rise, and that property values would decline ... When we carefully assessed trends in crime, taxes, and home prices in the township and surrounding neighborhoods, we found no evidence whatsoever that the project's opening had any direct effect on crime rates, tax burdens, or property values," the report said.

The Mount Laurel legal doctrine has had a powerful impact across the state of New Jersey. It has been used to get localities to open their land to affordable housing development. It has resulted in the development of 60,000 homes affordable to lower-income households.

Nonetheless, the Mount Laurel doctrine has come under new political and legal attacks. In 2013, Gov. Chris Christie called it and the affordable housing it helped to create "a failed social experiment." The Christie administration urged the Supreme Court to reverse its position on exclusionary zoning. The court refused to do so.

the physical environment or composition of a community. It can variously reflect concern about property values, service levels, fiscal impacts, community ambience, the environment, or public health and safety. Its more perverse manifestations reflect racial or ethnic prejudice masquerading under the guise of these other concerns."

Legislators and the courts have recognized that the Fair Housing Act was insufficient to keep the doors open to residential mobility among poor minorities. Massachusetts, New Jersey, and several other states have enacted laws that empower developers or state authorities to override local zoning to ensure that affordable housing is provided.

At the federal level, HUD uses its grant money to influence local decisions on affordable housing across the country. It requires, as a condition of its grants, recipients to proactively work to provide housing for people of all races in their community. HUD calls it "affirmatively furthering fair housing."

But all of these efforts face increasing political resistance. In Westchester, among other places, politicians know they can win political points by lashing out at "big government" for interfering in local decisions about land use.

They play on fear and bias to gain votes, and use affordable housing as their straw man. Very few local officials are willing to stick their political necks out by actively supporting affordable housing. As Andrew Spano found out, even acquiescing to HUD's legally justifiable demands to build new affordable housing can be political suicide.

Advocates for affordable housing say the overall impact of NIMBY is to deny minority households the chance to move up economically and socially.

"Good suburban neighborhoods with good schools where jobs are being created are like exclusive private clubs. Most poor minorities have no chance of gaining admission thanks in large part to the lack of affordable housing," said Bart Harvey, former CEO of nonprofit Enterprise Community Partners, a national financier and developer of affordable housing.

Affluent communities have largely succeeded at blocking affordable housing in significant amounts. They choose to issue building permits for shopping centers but refuse to build housing for the workers in those shops.

They import their workers from other towns, which are often

located many miles away, where housing is more affordable, forcing workers to commute long distances.

State housing agencies and developers take the path of least resistance and build their developments in lower-income areas of major cities or in towns with lower income levels, where there is already a good supply of low-cost housing.

These patterns are contributing to the increasing concentrations of poverty in American communities, a trend that has the potential to perpetuate intergenerational poverty, according to many social scientists. It also explains why segregation by race is now holding steady after several decades of decline.

In 1980, 12 percent of American communities had majorities of their populations that were poor. In 2010, the proportion of mostly poor communities had increased to 18 percent, an increase of one-third, according to the Pew Research Center.

It is easy to see how the racial subtext of the local battles over affordable housing could intensify in coming years.

Minority households will account for seven out of 10 new households formed between 2013 and 2023, according to "The State of the Nation's Housing 2013" from Harvard's Joint Center for Housing Studies. That's 8.7 million entirely new households in 10 years, with many of them needing already scarce affordable housing.

Put another way, minorities will increase from 37 percent of the U.S. population in 2010 to 57 percent of the population in 2060. Some of those people will be prosperous enough to find housing in relatively affluent areas, but most of them will not.

By reducing affordable housing availability, NIMBYs erect an invisible barrier. It says to every young person from a lower-income or minority family that, no matter how personally virtuous they are, it doesn't matter: They cannot live in places with decent employment and educational opportunities—unless, of course, they happen to get rich enough to buy a single-family home.

In the Clinton's backyard

The success or failure of HUD's settlement with Westchester revolves around places like Chappaqua, a small town in Westchester County, about 90 minutes north of New York City.

The affluent area is home to some very prominent Democratic political leaders, including Bill and Hillary Clinton as well as Andrew

Cuomo, former secretary of HUD and governor of New York State.

After the HUD settlement supporting inclusionary housing poli-cies, a real estate developer responded to a request from the town leadership to build affordable housing within a short walk of the center of town, near a station on the Metro-North Railroad com-muter rail line, which runs to Grand Central Station in Manhattan.

As the development was being planned, opposition to the con-struction began to mount. The town council repeatedly debated the location of the property, its size, and its design. A change in the council's composition brought outright attempts to kill the project. It has added costs by delaying permit issuance and letting everyone in town air every possible objection to the project in a long succes-sion of public hearings.

As of mid-2014, the debate over the proposal had dragged on for four years and there was no telling when or how it would end – settlement or no settlement. Newspaper accounts are replete with townspeople acknowledging the need for housing, but saying this particular property and location were not "good enough" for lower-income folks.

Bill Clinton was asked about the proposed housing and said he had no opinion. Hillary Clinton did the honors of swearing in the new council member who is fighting to block development.

At last report, the plans had been altered to call for a reduced number of just 28 new apartments. As of mid-2014, the developer had spent at least $1.5 million to satisfy every request and require-ment the townspeople had raised. That comes out to $53,000 per unit—and even then, there was no certainty that the town council would allow construction.

That $53,000 in added costs for one of the new apartments would have been enough to buy the median-priced new home in America in 1978. Even today in New York State, it would be enough to buy a manufactured home. But instead, that money was spent simply trying to get permission to build.

CHAPTER NINETEEN

Slamming the Door on America's Dream

Politicians used to get misty-eyed talking about homeownership as the essence of the American dream of upward mobility. They described it in patriotic terms and saw it as the bedrock of our economy. Increasing the rate of homeownership was the closest thing to a housing policy we had as the 21st century opened.

Today, in the wake of the foreclosure crisis, the federal government has more power than ever over the mortgage financing that makes ownership possible. But it has struggled for years without setting clear goals for how to reshape the mortgage lending business, including the all-important issue of how to help lower-income people reap the benefits of ownership.

Banks and profit-motivated lenders are no longer interested in making mortgage loans to lower-income families, and are not so sure about middle-class, working people either.

The old policy of encouraging homeowership for almost anyone had an obvious downside. But the new approach of lender caution, regulatory indecision, and conflicting political goals may be worse in some ways, especially for communities hit hard by foreclosures.

It was, to some degree, an understandable dilemma. Policymakers wanted to balance the need to get mortgage credit flowing again and help lower-income folks buy homes against the need to prevent another surge in loans that might end up in default or foreclosure.

The inability to strike the right balance had gone on for six years as this book went to press. Considering that housing is the most powerful engine of economic growth and that having a home is fundamental to the success of our families and communities, that lack of clarity and certainty was not good.

This period of conservatism and regulatory uncertainty prevented many people and communities from taking advantage of the moderate housing prices and historically low interest rates that followed the foreclosure crunch and recession.

In 2012, mortgage payments on the typically priced home had been more affordable than at any time in the last four decades, Harvard's Joint Center for Housing Studies (JCHS) reported in 2013.

The homeownership rate began to fall in 2008 and continued to decline into the first quarter of 2014, dropping to 64.8 percent. Vacant and abandoned properties continued to increase in many lower-income neighborhoods. This was partly because mortgage financing was difficult for many people to get and more expensive than it should have been when it was available.

After allowing mortgage loans to be made to almost anyone with a pulse, the government and the banks reversed course drastically, slamming the door on homeownership for young families, low-income people, and minority households.

"It seems likely that the pendulum has swung too far the other way, and that overly tight lending standards may now be preventing creditworthy borrowers from buying homes, thereby slowing the revival in housing and impeding the economic recovery," said former Federal Reserve Chair Ben Bernanke in 2012.

In 2014, all indications were that the pendulum would stay on the side of conservative lending well into the third decade of the new century.

"Homeowners with excellent credit scores are not getting access to properties to buy," a coalition of 60 housing advocacy groups wrote to Federal Reserve Chair Janet Yellen and other financial regulators. "This appears to represent an ongoing reluctance of the industry as a whole to make reasonably priced mortgage loans to qualified households," the letter said.

The problem was not just a temporary increase in conservative loan underwriting. It was a systemic failure, with government at its center. After the mass production of profitable but risky loans brought us the foreclosure disaster, the U.S. government stepped in to clean up the mess and took an unprecedented degree of control over the home mortgage market.

The issues confronting federal policymakers were complex, but, to simplify, they revolved around two major issues. The first is how private lenders should have to do their business and how much of the risk of each loan they originate they should be able to pass off to investors in the form of securities backed by the mortgages. The second is how much the federal government should do to provide financial support for the mortgage market, including helping ensure liquidity for all mortgages and providing special assistance to lower-income and minority borrowers.

This debate started in 2008, and it was still in full swing in 2014; despite many millions of dollars spent on lobbying and lawyering, it had barely inched forward. Three things, however, were very clear:

- Mortgages were harder to get and more expensive, putting homeownership out of reach for many more people, especially lower-income and minority borrowers;
- Banks were in no hurry to help troubled homeowners or would-be homebuyers and faced very little government pressure to do so, despite having been bailed out by taxpayers during the financial crisis; and
- Regulatory uncertainties were expected to persist for years, and legal battles over new regulations could last much longer, all of which means continued constriction of lending activity.

Battle for the future

The foreclosure crisis was a kind of Rorschach test for Americans. Looking at the same disturbing statistics, people saw two remarkably different things.

One group saw liberal Democrats like James Johnson, who ran Fannie Mae from 1991 to 1998, and President Bill Clinton pushing too hard to increase mortgage lending to lower-income and minority homebuyers who, the critics say, were not creditworthy.

The other group blamed Wall Street investment bankers and slick mortgage brokers like Angelo R. Mozilo for pressuring unsophisticated borrowers into taking very high-risk mortgage loans in a rush to earn loan origination fees, regardless of the borrower's ability to repay. Mozilo headed Countrywide Financial until it collapsed under the burden of too many bad loans.

• • •

Those widely divergent views were not an academic debate about the history of the mortgage crisis. They were pushed aggressively by legions of lobbyists and hundreds of op-ed pieces in a high-stakes battle over how Washington should reshape the mortgage market.

This struggle involved lobbyists for financial services firms, home builders, real estate brokers, and investment banks worried about their business plans and profits. It also pitted political conservatives who wanted less government involvement in mortgage lending against social liberals and housing advocates who sought more government intervention to help minority and lower-income borrowers buy homes.

Nothing illustrates the opposing views on how to rebuild our broken mortgage lending system more than the fight over the future of Fannie Mae and Freddie Mac, the two companies that bought hundreds of billions of dollars worth of mortgages from lenders all over the country each year.

To housing advocates, they are essential to providing affordable housing and building healthy communities. To conservatives, they are evil empires with a liberal bent that use government backing to make money.

Fannie and Freddie, known as GSEs (short for government-sponsored enterprises), were created by Congress to make sure there was plenty of money available for local lenders to make home mortgage loans. They had the advantage over private companies of having access to the U.S. government to back up their credit in the global capital markets.

Beginning in the early 1990s, Fannie and Freddie were required by law to make sure that a certain percentage of the loans they purchased were made to lower-income and minority borrowers or were for homes located in distressed areas. These goals made a huge difference in credit availability, helping to increase the homeownership rate among black households from 42 percent in 1993 to 49 percent in 2006.

That commitment to affordable housing as well as the very existence of the two companies came into question after the foreclosure crisis.

On Sept. 6, 2008, the U.S. government bailed out the two companies, as it had done with many private financial institutions at that time. It put them in conservatorship.

Their goals for making loans available to low-income and minority households were suspended.

Congress debated the future of Fannie and Freddie from 2008 on, and only in 2014 did the first outline emerge of what mortgage finance might look like in the post-foreclosure era. Legislation began moving in the Senate which would replace Fannie Mae and Freddie Mac with a new private system of providing credit support for mortgage securitization. The proposal drew fire from many housing advocates because it would not continue the affordable housing lending goals that had been in place for Fannie and Freddie since 1992.

The proposed Senate legislation would drive up the cost of mortgages and fail to ensure that all communities had equal access to mortgage credit, said Marc H. Morial, president and CEO of the National Urban League.

"(The proposal) speaks volumes to the dwindling middle class in America...it tells them that homeownership will be reserved for the fortunate few and all others can become renters," he wrote.

"In these times of wage stagnation, declining numbers of good paying jobs and increasing debt costs for education, shifting the risk and burden of housing finance onto regular working and middle class families is a bad idea," Morial concluded.

While the debate over that bill moved slowly toward resolution, to reduce the very large role that Fannie and Freddie played in the mortgage market, the government began raising the fees they charged for their services as the conduit for securitizing loans.

The battle over the future of Fannie and Freddie raged fiercely for years after they were taken over by the government. Republicans argued that they should be abolished. Private financial services firms said the government had to provide some sort of credit support if mortgage loans were to be made again in high volumes through securitization. Finally, housing advocates wanted to see the two organizations get back into the business of helping lower-income folks and minorities buy homes.

Meanwhile, lenders and borrowers all over America were left in limbo, not knowing if they could plan ahead to rely on the two institutions or not.

The Federal Housing Administration (FHA) is the other federal government agency that plays a key role in mortgage finance. Unlike Fannie Mae and Freddie Mac, it has always been part of the federal government. It was created in 1934 to guarantee repayment of loans made by private lenders on modestly priced homes. A borrower's downpayment can be as low as 3.5 percent of the purchase price, and most closing costs and fees can be included in the loan.

When mortgage lenders that relied on mortgage securitization closed their doors or tightened underwriting after the foreclosure crisis, the FHA programs continued to insure loans and, as a result, saw volume increase. However, under pressure from Republicans in Congress, the Obama administration began reducing the volume of FHA activity.

The ultimate goal was to reduce federal credit support for mortgage lending and let private firms resume their historic role as the primary providers of loans. Housing advocates said that as of 2013, moves in that direction were already making government-backed loans unaffordable for moderate-income borrowers. "All but the most creditworthy borrowers face higher interest rates today than what is considered the prevailing rate," according to Harvard's JCHS. The only question was how high costs would go as the political movement to end federal support for mortgage lending continued.

Regulating private lenders

Former Sen. Chris Dodd of Connecticut and former Rep. Barney Frank of Massachusetts will long be remembered for mandating more government control of the mortgage business. They were the chairs of the committees on banking in the Senate and the House, respectively, when the foreclosure bomb blew up.

They pushed through the Dodd–Frank Wall Street Reform and Consumer Protection Act, a hugely complex law taking up 848 single-spaced pages. It gave the federal government vast new power over how and on what terms mortgage loans are provided to American homebuyers.

If the law works, they'll be heroes, and if it fails, they'll be goats. But we won't know for quite a while yet. The law was so complex, it required years of regulation writing, lobbying, and legal battles over the details.

Since the bill passed in August 2010, no less than nine federal agencies, including one entirely new bureaucracy, worked feverishly to write regulations to implement the law's provisions on mortgage lending.

Much of the process had to do with establishing what kinds of loans could be sold on the secondary market so that the originating lender retained no risk if the loan went bad. These were to be called "qualified mortgage loans."

The question became critical to the future of mortgage finance because in the run-up to the crisis, lenders retained little or no risk. They collected "origination fees" for making loans and then sold off the loans through securitization. With no liability for the loans on their books, they had no compelling reason to ensure proper underwriting or to spend time or money working with borrowers who had trouble making payments.

Another question was what percentage of the cost of a home

A Brief History of Deregulation

What is very rarely recounted in the postmortems on the foreclosure crisis is the deregulation that did so much to precipitate not just the most recent financial crisis, but the one before that, too.

Under President Reagan, deregulation was touted as critical to boosting our economy. In 1982, the President's Commission on Housing said thrift institutions, also known as savings and loans, would continue to play an important part in this system and would need "broader operating powers to function effectively in tomorrow's market environment."

Many of the panel's recommendations for freeing the thrift industry from government rules were enacted. The thrifts used their new freedom to go on a lending spree, making large numbers of real estate loans, many of which ended in default and caused many lenders to go bankrupt.

From 1986 to 1995, more than 1,000 out of the 3,234 savings and loan associations in the United States failed. This resulted in a huge cost to the U.S. government for payment of deposit insurance and a vast, multi-year effort to sell the real estate assets the government owned as a result of failed loans through the Resolution Trust Corp. Between 1989 and mid-1995, the Resolution Trust Corp. closed or otherwise resolved 747 thrifts with total assets of $394 billion.

Reagan's commission also called for a vast expansion of the use of mortgage-backed securities to increase availability of home loans. It advocated "removal of various tax, legal, and regulatory impediments to widespread private investment in mortgages and mortgage-backed securities." It said that new types of mortgage-related securities would help attract participants to housing finance and that this would "reduce the need for government programs in the residential mortgage markets."

The private market for mortgage-related securities was developed much as the panel wished, opening up fantastic profits for Wall Street. There was very little thought given to the need for safeguarding the system.

Roughly 25 years after the commission's recommendations were made, the mortgage-backed securities market overheated and precipitated the foreclosure crisis.

should a buyer be required to pay out of pocket as a downpayment for a "qualified" loan. At one point, federal regulators talked about requiring a 20 percent downpayment. This would have not only slammed the door on minority homeownership, it would have locked it and barricaded it with a chest of drawers.

There was no telling when the uncertainty about the federal rules governing mortgage lending would end. In the best-case scenario, the most extreme ideas of government lawyers for cracking down on lending would be rejected and a reasonable set of rules would be implemented. But the damage caused by years of delay would have been done.

While all that was happening, mortgage lending volume shrank dramatically.

Because of the uncertainty about their regulatory obligations, lenders continued to play it safe, setting strict requirements on the creditworthiness of home loan borrowers, including higher downpayments.

"The new mortgage rules do appear to be providing the industry another excuse for its failure to make credit available."
—Sign-on letter to federal financial regulators from housing and fair lending advocacy groups

---

Increased downpayment requirements are the biggest impediment to making homeownership possible for lower-income and minority borrowers. In 2010, median household wealth was just $2,100 for African-American renters, $4,500 for Hispanic renters, and $6,000 for white renters, according to Harvard's annual housing report. Cash savings account for less than $1,000 of the net worth for each group, leaving all these renters with virtually no cushion for emergencies, let alone funds for a downpayment, the Harvard report said.

Many experts do not believe that insisting on a high downpayment is necessary to increase the odds that loans will be repaid.

"I [do not] believe that a high downpayment is the best indicator of someone's suitability to assume a mortgage," said Ron Terwilliger, former chairman of Habitat for Humanity and founder of the ULI Terwilliger Center for Housing.

"We have seen millions of families become responsible home-owners after putting just a small amount down. The key remains proper underwriting, as well as counseling, to make sure low-wealth homeowners can meet their mortgage obligations," said Terwilliger.

Impact of rules

One new rule from the Dodd-Frank legislation that was finalized in 2013 puts federal bureaucrats in charge of telling mortgage lenders how to decide if a home loan borrower has the ability to repay their loan.

The 272-page rule from the Consumer Financial Protection Bureau requires that a mortgage borrower's debt of all kinds must not exceed 43 percent of their income. Many observers said this might put homeownership out of reach for families with higher levels of consumer debt as well as college grads carrying student loan balances.

In the atmosphere of uncertainty and caution among lenders, the new rule did not go over very well. Lenders were not sure how to comply or were unwilling to be the first to test out the new regulatory scheme, so they limited their lending to only extremely safe borrowers.

Anyone who might possibly be viewed as having trouble repaying a loan was rejected.

"The new mortgage rules do appear to be providing the industry another excuse for its failure to make credit available to qualified borrowers in low-income communities and communities of color," said the sign-on letter from housing advocacy groups.

This marathon regulatory process would end up lasting at least 10 years, including the time it would take lenders and their lawyers to figure out the rules once they were finalized—and even longer if there were major legal battles.

After years of legislative and regulatory debate in Washington, the reality was disturbing: Mortgage lending was still up in the air, and no one really knew if any of the new rules or proposed new market structures would succeed in preventing another foreclosure crisis while still maintaining the flow of credit needed to maintain healthy housing markets.

History does not provide much evidence to support the positive potential of new regulations on the process of how loans are made. There have been federal and state laws on the books for years to prevent deceptive credit practices and predatory lending. In the days of rapidly rising housing prices and increasing homeownership, those laws were not actively enforced.

What's more, there are always ways to circumvent regulations on lending, especially when home prices are rising rapidly, as they were in the early 2000s.

What comes next

There was no doubt that banks would continue serving middle- and upper-income borrowers—customers who yield the highest profit and lowest risk. What was uncertain was whether the U.S. government would continue to encourage them to lend to low-income and minority borrowers and neighborhoods.

In the 1970s, Congress recognized that the mortgage lending business was largely excluding minorities from homeownership. Banks were routinely taking savings deposits from lower-income

---

Where Have You Gone, George Bailey?

Older Americans may recall when mortgage lending was a local business with decisions made by a handful of prominent citizens like George Bailey, the owner of the "building and loan" in the movie, "It's a Wonderful Life."

In the movie, Jimmy Stewart played Bailey as a bit too big-hearted to be true. But there were people like Bailey in real life, and they did often make decisions on what was good for the long-term success of their communities and borrowers, as opposed to their own short-term gain.

Community lenders obtained capital from their local customers' savings accounts, used the funds to make home loans locally, and then held those loans in their portfolios of assets. If a borrower had a problem, lender and borrower could often work things out to everyone's satisfaction.

But our growing nation needed more credit, so we had to find a way for lenders like George Bailey to sell loans to bigger companies with access to more capital. This created a "secondary market" of investors to buy the loans, which provided more capital for new loans.

Fannie Mae was established in 1938 to create a liquid secondary mortgage market. Freddie Mac was created in 1970 to expand that market.

areas but refusing to make loans in those same areas—a practice called "redlining." As a result, those areas were starved for credit, which reduced property values and fueled urban decay.

Congress responded by passing the Community Reinvestment Act (CRA), which requires that banks meet the credit needs of all segments of the communities where they accept deposits. Federal banking regulators also enforce the Fair Housing Act's prohibition on racial discrimination in real estate lending (fair lending).

Thirty-some years later, opponents of those requirements seized the opportunity presented by the foreclosure crisis to attack the laws once again.

The American Enterprise Institute and other groups have blamed the foreclosure crisis on these regulations. They say strong enforcement of CRA under Presidents Carter and Clinton forced banks to make too many loans to low-income people, directly contributing to the mortgage meltdown.

In the 1980s, the secondary market took off after Wall Street investment banks got involved in a big way and deregulation made it easier to slice and dice the securities in increasingly creative ways that brought in larger and larger amounts of capital. This mortgage securitization effectively separated the process of making a loan from the process of collecting mortgage payments and dealing with borrowers if they were late or missed payments.

That meant that the people who decided whether or not to make a loan often had no liability if the loan failed. They were paid to originate the loan only, so the more loans they made, the more money they made.

The loans were part of pools, and the pools were owned indirectly by hundreds of investors in the mortgage bonds. Servicing was handled by contractors who kept costs very low, had no connection to the communities where the loans were made, and were unprepared for the wave of defaults in 2007 and later.

In 2014, there were still some community banks where people like Bailey made loans locally and continued to hold them and deal with borrowers personally. But in the competitive, globalized financial markets of the 21st century, they were an endangered species. The question for government regulators was whether they would allow them to become extinct.

"Lenders responded [to the enactment of the CRA] by loosening their underwriting standards and making increasingly shoddy loans. All this was justified as a means of increasing homeownership among minorities and the poor. Affirmative-action policies trumped sound business practices," wrote Jeff Jacoby, a columnist for *The Boston Globe*. It was an attack echoed over and over by right-wing media, including Fox News and *The Wall Street Journal*.

Housing advocacy groups and federal bank regulators refuted these claims very effectively. The CRA governs only banks and other institutions that take deposits. Most loans that went to foreclosure came from mortgage brokers, not depository institutions. Furthermore, CRA never required that banks change their underwriting standards solely to make more loans in low-income areas.

CRA is a very simple law. It requires only that lenders may not ignore the credit needs of borrowers in poor neighborhoods that are part of their regular market area for savings and checking accounts and other services.

The Federal Reserve Board has found no connection between CRA and the subprime mortgage problems. The Financial Crisis Inquiry Commission said CRA "was not a significant factor in subprime lending or the crisis."

Blaming fair lending rules is even more absurd, particularly the idea that loans must be made to minorities regardless of their financial status. Fair lending rules simply require that no one be denied credit on the basis of race, color, religion, national origin, sex, marital status, age, or whether they have received any public assistance. It does not say that any group should be treated more or less liberally during the loan underwriting process.

Furthermore, many fair lending advocacy groups fought against the marketing of high-risk loan types to low-income households.

The foreclosure crisis also gave financial industry groups a chance to renew their attacks on Fannie Mae and Freddie Mac and their federally-mandated goals for buying loans to low-income borrowers. The Federal Housing Finance Administration suspended those goals. The continued attacks were meant to ensure that the goals were not reinstituted in whatever new mortgage market structure Congress finally established.

But again, careful analyses have shown that those goals did not cause the crisis. "Based on the evidence and interviews with dozens of individuals involved in this subject area, we determined these goals only contributed marginally to Fannie's and Freddie's participation in subprime mortgages," the Financial Crisis Inquiry Commission stated.

What gets overlooked in the tug of war over the ashes of the foreclosure firestorm is that the CRA and the lending goals had a very positive long-term effect on making homeownership more widely available.

The untold story of the foreclosure crisis is that lending to lower-income people is perfectly safe when it is done prudently. There were far fewer problems with loans that were made to lower-income people through nonprofit, community-based credit providers than there were with loans by profit-motivated lenders.

Blaming lower-income borrowers and laws intended to help them for a crisis caused by the predatory lending of profit-motivated firms was a breathtaking twisting of facts.

It should not be allowed to obscure the truth about the value of homeownership for lower-income households, or the reality of how the foreclosure crisis came about.

Where We Go From Here

CHAPTER TWENTY

Where We Go From Here

When one looks at all the great things that have been done with federal and state funding, not to mention private philanthropy and local ingenuity, we are doing remarkably well in regard to housing and community development, considering the challenges. The proverbial glass is half full.

But the good things happening in America amount to a kind of holding action. The problems are simply too big to manage without more extensive help from federal and state governments, both in terms of public spending and in terms of intelligent policies.

The good things being done to provide housing are wonderful and inspiring, but they fall far short of the need.

At the federal level, the outlook for more resources and better policies is cloudy at best. A handful of politicos see the glass as half full and want to fill it. However, much stronger political forces seek to drain that glass. And in future elections, they could gain enough power to achieve their goals. Only a handful of state governments have shown any desire to be proactive on housing and urban policy.

Neither party shows any intention of tackling the thorniest long-term problems: how to reduce the inexorable increase in housing costs relative to incomes and how to balance inner-city decline with suburban expansion and sprawl.

It's not that the problems are hidden or unknowable, like the timing of earthquakes. They are obvious to anyone who spends time in major cities, steps around homeless people sleeping on our streets, or worries about how their children will afford to move out of the family home.

· · ·

The violent destruction of the Los Angeles riots in 1965 was just the beginning of a wave of unrest that shook our country to its core. More riots followed in Chicago, Detroit, and Newark, N.J., in 1966 and 1967.

Martin Luther King Jr. continued to stand for nonviolent social action. He argued against the aggressive tactics of the emerging Black Power movement, sticking to his long-held philosophy of peaceful protest. In the midst of the riots, he traveled to the Watts section of LA to plead with whites and blacks to calm things down.

On April 4, 1968, King was shot to death in Memphis, Tenn. Soon after his death, a new wave of violence swept over dozens of U.S. cities.

The fact was, no one knew if America was breaking apart. No one could predict if the race riots would become a race war. At one point, federal troops were called in to guard the White House and the U.S. Capitol as rioters rampaged just a few miles away.

There was no hesitation about the need to respond with new policies, not just police and military power. The presidentially appointed National Advisory Commission on Civil Disorders worked quickly to explain why our cities burned and what to do about it. Over 1.6 million Americans purchased the book containing the commission's report, and millions more read press coverage about it. By the end of 1968, Congress had enacted two landmark laws intended to revitalize cities, provide affordable housing, end segregation in housing, and break up concentrations of poverty.

Roughly half a century later, after the recession and foreclosure crisis and the shocking increase in homelessness, the social awareness and belief in our ability to address our problems that was a hallmark of the 1960s had disappeared.

In an earlier time, if we awoke to learn that 1.17 million children were suddenly homeless, we would have been shocked and jumped into action. It would have been considered an intolerable situation.

But when the U.S. Department of Education said that many schoolchildren were homeless during the 2011-2012 school year, hardly anyone noticed. That doesn't count children who are not in school. Plus, more recent data strongly suggests a continuing upward trend.

Millions more children live in horrible neighborhoods or deal with deprivation and overcrowding because their parents cannot afford good housing. Some parents watch in horror as random gunshots penetrate the walls of their children's bedrooms because they cannot afford to live in a better area.

But these horrifying realities have not inspired any meaningful national effort to fix broken housing markets and launch an all-out effort to end homelessness and extreme housing cost burdens.

As this book has shown, housing and community development programs funded by federal, state, and local governments have a tremendous record of achievement. Millions of people have been connected with good housing. Many have gained the opportunities to turn their lives around and work for better futures. Hundreds of neighborhoods have been revitalized.

We know how to create excellent new housing with supportive services that help families with children, the chronically homeless, and the elderly.

City governments, public housing agencies, and private developers can and do transform dangerous, desolate neighborhoods into communities of hope.

Bold experiments have shown us new ways to provide housing at low costs without subsidies.

All over the country, local governments have come together to work on making their regions more environmentally, socially, and economically sustainable.

The challenge now is to build on those successes and promising experiments. Our task is to rebuild the dream of America as a land of opportunity, where people of any background can move up economically and obtain a decent home, whether it's rented or owned.

But to fully realize the vision of America as a land of opportunity, we must also work toward realization of a day when "people will not be judged by the color of their skin, but by the content of their character," in King's words.

This is not going to just happen, not in today's climate of scarcity and fear. It will take dedicated, consistent work by all Americans. We must overcome divisive "us versus them" politics and rediscover the aspiration to equal opportunity that was the hallmark of the 1960s.

We must find ways to convince Congress that federal spending on housing and cities is not wasted money but an investment that has paid and will continue to pay very important dividends.

We must find ways to manage or reduce the constantly increasing gap between the cost of housing and what people can afford to pay for it.

The cost of addressing housing and urban issues is high. But the cost of ignoring them is much higher. There are many ways it costs our society and our taxpayers. However, the biggest cost is the least apparent or measurable.

You may have read news reports or books about the growing extent of income inequality in America. There are many macroeconomic causes and long-term solutions to that problem.

But what many analysts overlook is that neighborhoods of concentrated poverty are the factories of inequality in America.

Much can be achieved by investing in physical and social improvements to those areas. Housing and community development groups have been consistently turning neighborhoods of dysfunction and hopelessness into communities that offer new opportunity.

Some 50 years ago, President Lyndon Johnson knew we had to do exactly that kind of revitalization in such places or children living in them would grow up poor and stay poor.

Using the programs he convinced Congress to pass, and those pushed through by other presidents, thousands of organizations and local agencies work on using housing and community development to increase opportunity and upward mobility.

They know it's incredibly hard it to reverse decades of decay, isolation, and marginalization in the old public housing projects and in other districts with large percentages of poor people. They also know that it's worth every dollar and every ounce of energy they put into it.

The issue of race

On April 5, 1976, three months before the American bicentennial, a white man was photographed trying to stab a black man with a flagpole that was still flying the American flag. He was part of a protest against forced busing to achieve school integration in Boston.

The photo in *The Boston Globe* shocked the nation and marked the beginning of the end of busing. The federal courts had ordered cities, including Boston, to bus students from white to black areas and vice versa to integrate schools.

The courts had ruled that housing remained segregated, and, as a result, there had not been sufficient progress in desegregating schools. The Fair Housing Act had been on the books since 1968, but it had not reduced segregation in housing nearly as much as was once hoped.

Busing fell by the wayside soon after the Boston riot, but not because the pattern of segregation had changed. It was just too disruptive for children, too aggravating for parents, and too costly for cities.

The Fair Housing Act still has not ended housing segregation, or its impact on where children can attend school.

After the riots in 1965, 1966, and 1967, the National Advisory Commission on Civil Disorders issued a report saying, "Our nation is moving toward two societies, one black, one white—separate and unequal. Segregation and poverty have created in the racial ghetto a destructive environment totally unknown to most white Americans."

That report went a long way to get Americans to rethink their attitudes about race. But now, with increasing obstacles to the development of affordable housing in predominantly white areas, we need to admit that our progress is in jeopardy.

On the 40th anniversary of the report in 2008, just as the foreclosure crisis and recession were hitting with full force, Edward Brooke, the former Republican senator from Massachusetts and a member of the commission, described how little had changed for inner-city residents:

"The core conditions that the commission identified as key contributors to civil unrest are as prevalent, if not as virulent, today as they were 40 years ago. The lack of affordable, safe housing and the absence of jobs or hope for the future have confined even more of our citizens to an eerily familiar world that not so long ago gave rise to cities in flames," he stated.

Even as our population is becoming more diverse, our communities are becoming more segregated.

"Arrested progress in the fight against poverty and residential segregation has helped concentrate many African-Americans in some of the least desirable housing in some of the lowest-resourced communities in America," according to a 2013 report from the Economic Policy Institute (EPI).

In addition to much higher poverty rates, blacks suffer much more from concentrated poverty. Nearly half (45 percent) of poor black children live in neighborhoods with concentrated poverty, but only a little more than a tenth (12 percent) of poor white children live in similar neighborhoods, EPI said.

The situation is made worse by the continuing high rate of unemployment among blacks. The average unemployment rate from 1963 to 2012 was 11.6 percent for blacks and 5.1 percent for whites, EPI stated.

Today, the battle over equal opportunity in housing continues. Instead of outright discrimination against individuals who want to rent or buy in certain areas, there is a pervasive resistance to affordable housing in more affluent communities where housing is too expensive for low-income and minority households.

The vast majority of people who oppose creation of affordable housing in their neighborhood don't mention race and take umbrage if anyone suggests racism on their part. However, there is no doubt about the overall effect of that opposition on the degree to which housing is segregated.

The struggle over the issue of where to build affordable housing, with all the racial implications it carries, is likely to intensify, especially if the White House remains occupied by someone who supports strong enforcement of the Fair Housing Act, as was the case under the Obama administration.

But even if the government fully enforces the law, there is still a very long way to go to move beyond the very long history of racial discrimination in residential real estate.

For more details on the legacy of racial bias in housing, and how it has been repeatedly justified by its practitioners, see Appendix A for excerpts on the subject from "Where Do We Go from Here: Chaos or Community?" by King.

• • •

Every one of us makes our own choices about how to balance the greater good of society against our own perceived self-interests. But when it comes to communities and where people get to live in this country, it helps to reconsider some of our assumptions.

First, stories about the negative impact of newly built affordable housing are greatly exaggerated. Opponents regularly portray new affordable housing as potentially devastating, but it almost always turns out to be a positive addition to a community.

Second, it is often said housing subsidies are inherently unfair, because they reward poor people for not working. It is said they allow poor people to freeload off people who pay taxes. That overlooks the fact that affluent Americans who own homes receive much more subsidy than all the low-income renters in America. The subsidy comes in the form of tax breaks, like the deduction for home mortgage interest.

Less than 24 percent of Americans who have incomes low

enough to qualify for direct government housing subsidies (as opposed to tax breaks) actually receive rental housing subsidies. Poor
folks on the waiting list for assistance, the people who make just a
little too much for assistance, and everyone who rents unsubsidized
housing are the only ones who get no help at all.

Third, the trump card played in Congress over and over again is
that we can't afford to provide housing, maintain our government-
owned and assisted housing, or improve our cities. This too is dangerous, politically motivated nonsense.

The home mortgage interest deduction was projected to cost the
federal government $464 billion in lost revenue from 2011 to 2015,
an average of about $100 billion per year, according to the congres-
sional Joint Committee on Taxation. The deduction alone costs us
far more than all federal rental housing and urban programs put
together. So there's no question we can afford housing subsidies.
The only issue is who receives those subsidies.

· · ·

Many hundreds of billions of taxpayer dollars have been spent
on housing assistance and urban development, so it's fair to ask
what we got for the money. Since there are still problems, does that
mean the money was wasted?

The simple answer is that yes, some money has been squandered
under Republican and Democratic governments alike. There has
been waste and inefficiency. But that is not peculiar to housing and
development programs any more than it is to military procurement.
It does not negate the value of the programs at the Department of
Housing and Urban Development (HUD) any more than waste in
Pentagon spending invalidates the need for a strong military.

The real problem, and the most egregious source of unneces-
sary cost, is that we have had nothing resembling a comprehensive
national housing and urban policy for many years. Since President
Bill Clinton put forth a coordinated set of programs, there has been
no attempt at anything resembling a balanced, comprehensive set of
programs and policies.

To put it in context, imagine that we had started building the
interstate highway system without doing surveys or drawing up an
overall plan—and we just started clearing dirt. The results would be
horrible and expensive. Roads might not connect. They might take

Planning for regional growth that protects the environment and helps keep housing and transportation affordable has a high priority in Utah, as shown in this graphic from a planning guidebook published by Envision Utah, the nonprofit that is helping individual cities and areas master the art of forming consensus on the future. The book, "A Guide to Regional Visioning," is a very comprehensive, clear and useful handbook to help local officials engage citizens in discussions about future development.

drivers on needlessly circuitous routes. Construction would hit unknown obstacles. The whole process would be massively inefficient and needlessly expensive.

That's exactly what's happening in housing.

Just before the start of the 21st century, Congress initiated an effort to enact a new housing policy for the new millennium. When the commission it appointed issued its report, no one in Congress could be bothered to hold a hearing on it.

During the second term of President George W. Bush, the only objective on housing was to increase homeownership, no matter how much it cost. The Bush administration offered nothing new to help the millions of Americans who rent.

The consequences of that one-sided, politically expedient fig leaf of a housing policy are obvious for all to see.

The failure of Congress and the White House to agree on a housing policy and do the hard work of implementing that policy reflects an incredible lack of interest in such a fundamental part of our economic and social well-being.

The most fundamental problem is that federal, state and local governments keep adding costs to housing, with no constraints whatsoever.

Even within the federal government, some agencies issue rules that jack up the cost of housing while other agencies (usually HUD) pay higher and higher housing subsidy costs.

Under President George H.W. Bush, it was suggested that every federal agency be required by law to look at the impact its actions would have on the cost of housing. That proposal went nowhere.

Federal agencies are required to analyze the impact of every regulation they issue on the amount of "paperwork" they require, but they pay no attention to the impact on housing affordability.

This is not a minor problem. As environmental obstacles to housing development increase, state and federal government agencies will almost certainly layer on more and more costs.

As the economic slump has dragged on and personal incomes and savings have stagnated or declined, this failure is becoming more and more obvious.

The ripple effect is not immediately obvious, but it is powerful and dangerous. As moderate-income people use their resources to take possession of our limited supply of lower-cost housing units, lower-income people get pushed further and further into housing distress. Some become homeless.

It forces more and more people to look to government subsidies as their only chance for housing. At the same time, the government's cost to help a given number of people afford housing keeps going up.

For those lucky enough to win the lottery to get a housing subsidy, it encourages dependency on those subsidies. Even the most motivated tenant of subsidized housing finds it extremely hard to increase their income enough to move out and move up and free up their housing subsidy for someone else.

The prospect of getting a nice apartment in a good area, or buying a small house, is an incredibly attractive goal. When people realize that it's never going to happen for them, that they will never move up and out of their lousy neighborhood no matter how many hours they work at a low-wage job, it destroys the idea of upward mobility. It makes the promise of America, that anyone can succeed if they work hard enough, less and less credible to more and more people.

• • •

Very few people with political power want to discuss these issues—not because they are not important, but because they are incredibly complex and offer no clear political payoff in time for the next election.

The problems of the cities require multifaceted, long-term solutions—and billions of dollars in spending. Housing markets are even more challenging, caught as they are between public policy priorities to serve the common good and the narrow financial motives of city governments, financiers, property owners, and developers.

Since the people most affected by housing and urban problems, including all those homeless children, don't vote and don't
make political contributions, they don't matter to some members of
Congress. The challenges of continuing adequate levels of funding
for housing and urban programs are substantial.

That's not to say there's no hope. Hundreds of hardworking
people visit Capitol Hill every day of the week to make the case for
continued and increased appropriations and better policies. They
include the folks at the National Low Income Coalition, which bat-
tled for years to get Congress to create the National Housing Trust
Fund, and are now fighting to get a new source of dedicated funding
for that program. They know that success depends on persistence,
and they were encouraged by a preliminary vote in the Senate in
2014 for a mortgage finance bill that would include that funding.

But they need help, in Washington, and in state capitols, from
the rest of us, the Americans who do vote and do contribute to candidates and can meet with their congressmen or senators. They
need our help to make the case for the victims of the housing cost
explosion and the renewed decline of American cities.

We must look to our civic organizations, our local and state
leaders, the CEOs of our hometown corporations, the leaders of our
houses of worship, as well as ourselves. We must nurture the many
seeds of progress and beacons of hope detailed in this book, expand
them with our own resources, and make damned sure the people in
Washington know what's happening and what they need to do to
help keep the progress going.

In 1967, Martin Luther King Jr. called on the Chicago Housing
Authority (CHA) to improve living conditions for residents of the
city's high-rise public housing and reduce the concentration of poverty of the "projects." The Chicago Open Housing Movement, of
which he was a leader, called for replacing high-rise buildings with
smaller structures spread out in a wider area.

In 2000, the CHA and the city of Chicago finally started a large-
scale effort to achieve the kind of change King had suggested.

In the 33-year gap between advocacy and action, the high-rises
that troubled King became hellholes of crime, drug use, and violence. Thousands of children grew up in that time span. For many
of them, survival was the main objective, not school, not health, not
sobriety, not staying out of trouble with the law.

Politicians can win votes by talking about the need for personal responsibility, but those children, and many more like them in other distressed areas, had no choice about where they wanted to be raised.

The results of policy and budgetary decisions being made (and not made) today will not be obvious until 15 or 20 years from now. That's when all the children growing up in low-income areas battered by foreclosures and rundown public housing will come of age.

Will there be another wave of urban violence? No one knows. If it comes, will it be limited to the decaying inner cities, or will rioters invade more affluent residential areas? No one can predict.

However, it's absolutely certain that the more we let cities decay and the more we neglect housing costs and conditions, the harder

What You Can Do to Help

There are things every American can do to help with housing and urban issues. It doesn't require money, political connections or policy expertise. Anyone can start to make a difference simply by choosing not to give in to apathy or fatalism. For a few ideas about getting involved, see Appendix B.

and more expensive it will be to fix later.

It's highly likely that poverty in the suburbs, which increased rapidly in recent years, will continue to rise, along with the blight and disinvestment left behind by the foreclosure crisis.

Inequality will continue to be translated from an abstract concept into "facts on the ground" – the concrete, wood and brick of bad housing and worse neighborhoods – constant reminders to millions of people of their low social standing and nonexistent economic prospects. The cycle of decay and disinvestment will continue, punctuated by the occasional burst of economic exploitation whenever business interests see a chance to fleece the poor.

The more that affluent areas succeed in excluding lower-income folks and forcing them to gather in places of concentrated poverty, the more the gaps between groups will widen, with all the fear, distrust and anger that brings.

No one knows what the future will bring, but the warning signs are there for all to see, if they can be bothered to look.

There's a mythology in America that we can't solve big problems anymore. The basis for this is not in the real world, where mayors and city councils grapple with long-term problems of community every day. It's in the political fantasy world of Washington, where proactive, bipartisan work on long-term problems before they become crises offers more political risk than gain.

Don't let anyone tell you housing and urban problems are intractable, or that taxpayer money spent on them is wasted, or that some groups don't deserve help. Those are all lies. We can revitalize our cities and fix our broken housing markets. We can give every one of our citizens a chance at a better life. We are doing it, just not on a large enough scale and not with any consistency, and not with any assurance at all of continued federal support.

We can rebuild the dreams of millions of Americans to have decent homes in good neighborhoods—including homeownership for those ready for it.

King, Lyndon Johnson, Robert F. Kennedy, James Rouse, and others had to convince a deeply segregated nation that improving housing and making it available to all income and racial groups were critical to our national identity and even our survival. They changed hardened attitudes and unleashed a new wave of compassion and American ingenuity. Our task now is simply to continue what they started.

Housing & Race: The issue that won't go away

Most people remember Martin Luther King, Jr., for his work to advance voting rights and desegregation in the south. However, he also campaigned for fair housing, including very specific efforts to change patterns of segregation in Chicago. In the following excerpts from his book, Where Do We Go From Here: Chaos or Community? he discussed what it was like for blacks trying to find housing in the 1960s.

It has been over 45 years since he wrote the book, but his observations are relevant to the ongoing debate in American communities about where affordable housing is allowed to be developed and how government policymakers and regulators allowed predatory lenders to target minority areas for high-risk loans that lead to high rates of foreclosure.

The book was published by the Beacon Press in 1968, the year King was killed.

Reprinted by arrangement with the Heirs to the Estate of Martin Luther King Jr., c/o Writers House as agent for the proprietor New York, NY.

• • •

By Martin Luther King, Jr.

Nothing today more clearly indicates the residue of racism still lodging in our society than the responses of white America to integrated housing. Here the tides of prejudice, fear and irrationality rise to flood proportions. This is not a new backlash caused by the Black

Power movement; there had been no ominous riots in Watts when white Californians defeated a fair housing bill in 1964. The present resistance to open housing is based on the same premises that came into being to rationalize slavery. It is rooted in the fear that the alleged depravity or defective nature of the out-race will infiltrate the neighborhood of the in-race.

Just as the doctrine of white supremacy came into being to justify the profitable system of slavery, through shrewd and subtle ways some (real estate brokers) perpetrate the same racist doctrine to justify the profitable real estate business. Real estate brokers build up financial empires by keeping the housing market closed. Going into white neighborhoods where a few Negroes have moved in, they urge the whites to leave because their property values will depreciate. Thereupon, the real estate broker makes a huge profit from the whites that must be relocated and a doubly huge profit from the Negroes, who, in desperate search for better housing, often pay twice as much for a house as it is worth.

Many whites who oppose open housing would deny that they are racists. They turn to sociological arguments – the crime rate in the Negro community, the lagging cultural standards, the fear that their schools will become academically inferior, the fear that property values will depreciate – in order to find excuses for their opposition. They never stop to realize that criminal responses are environmental, not racial. To hem a people up in the prison walls of overcrowded ghettos and to confine them in rat-infested slums is to breed crime, whatever the racial group may be. It is a strange and twisted logic to use the tragic results of segregation as an argument for its continuation.

However much it is denied, however many excuses are made, the hard cold fact is that many white Americans oppose open housing because they unconsciously, and often consciously, feel that the Negro is innately inferior, impure, depraved and degenerate. It is a contemporary expression of America's long dalliance with racism and white supremacy.

Being a Negro in America means trying to smile when you want to cry. It means trying to hold on to physical life amid psychological death. It means the pain of watching your children grow up with clouds of inferiority in their mental skies. It means having your legs cut off, and then being condemned for being a cripple.

Being a Negro in America means listening to suburban politicians talk eloquently against open housing while arguing in the same breath that they are not racists.

The American housing industry is a disgrace to a society which can confidently plan to get to the moon. The costs of construction have risen more rapidly than most other items. Technological advances in housing construction are regularly heralded and seldom implemented. Banks and government policy have actively encouraged and even required segregated housing; federal mortgage policy has only recently changed to favor some integrated housing.

The end result is that the United States is today a more segregated country in many respects than it was twenty years ago. Problems of education, transportation to jobs, and decent living conditions are all made difficult because housing is so rigidly segregated. The expansion of suburbia and migration from the South have worsened big-city segregation. The suburbs are white nooses around the black necks of the cities. Housing deteriorates in central cities; urban renewal has been Negro removal and has benefited big merchants and real estate interest; and suburbs expand with little regard for what happens to the rest of America.

• • •

Additional suggested reading on race, residential real estate and government urban policy:

Stuck in Place: Urban Neighborhoods and the End of Progress toward Racial Equality, by Patrick Sharkey.

The 1960s-era belief that the civil rights movement would foster a new era of racial equality in America has been proven incorrect, according to this book. Four decades later, the degree of racial inequality has barely changed, it states. In this book, Patrick Sharkey, associate professor of sociology at New York University, describes how political decisions and social policies have led to severe disinvestment from black neighborhoods, persistent segregation, declining economic opportunities, and a growing link between African American communities and the criminal justice system, according to the publishers, University of Chicago press.

As a result, neighborhood inequality that existed in the 1970s has been passed down to the current generation of African Americans. Some of the most persistent forms of racial inequality, such as gaps in income and test scores, can only be explained by considering the neighborhoods in which black and white families have lived over multiple generations. This multigenerational nature of neighborhood inequality also means that a new kind of urban policy is necessary for our nation's cities.

Sharkey argues for urban policies that have the potential to create transformative and sustained changes in urban communities and the families that live within them, and he outlines a durable urban policy.

Family Properties: How the Struggle Over Race and Real Estate Transformed Chicago and Urban America, by Beryl Satter.

This book shows that "the decline of black neighborhoods into slums had nothing to do with the absence of African-American resources and everything to do with subjugation and greed," according to the publisher, Reed Business Information, a division of Reed Elsevier Inc. Focusing on the practice of "contract selling" of homes to black families in Chicago, the author draws on her father's records as a Chicago lawyer to piece together "a thoughtful and very personal account of the exploitation that kept blacks segregated and impoverished," according to the publisher. Satter is a professor at Rutgers University.

Our Town: Race, Housing, and the Soul of Suburbia, by David L. Kirp, John P. Dwyer, Larry A. Rosenthal

New Jersey has had a series of court cases on the issue of land use and affordable housing, as well as having had its share of racial conflict. That history is the focus for this book on race and the conflicts between suburbs and cities, by David L. Kirp, who is James D. Marver Professor of Public Policy at the University of California at Berkeley. Replete with details on the history of administrative and judicial decisions affecting land use, the book recounts the ways in which suburban political interests have eclipsed urban interests, including the impact on race relations and segregation of housing.

American Apartheid, by Douglas Massey and Nancy Denton

This book links persistent poverty among blacks in the United States to the unparalleled degree of deliberate segregation they experience in American cities. It shows how "the black ghetto was created by whites during the first half of the twentieth century in order to isolate growing urban black populations," according to the publisher, Harvard University Press.

It goes on to show that, despite the Fair Housing Act of 1968, "segregation is perpetuated today through an interlocking set of individual actions, institutional practices, and governmental policies."

"The authors demonstrate that this systematic segregation of African Americans leads inexorably to the creation of underclass communities during periods of economic downturn. Under conditions of extreme segregation, any increase in the overall rate of black poverty yields a marked increase in the geographic concentration of indigence and the deterioration of social and economic conditions in black communities."

A Citizen's Guide to Improving Housing & Communities

Americans concerned about housing and urban problems can help change public policy on these issues for the better. All it takes is a willingness to get involved and make your voice heard.

Some people have more political clout than others, including elected officials, business owners, bankers, real estate professionals, and heads of civic organizations. But anyone and everyone can help, including college students and recent graduates who have the most at stake in the health of cities and housing markets.

It helps to think like your grandparents or great-grandparents thought. Go to your local library or historical society and take a minute to look back in time. Chances are you'll find sepia-toned images of the folks gathered for a meeting of the "improvement society" for your area. Such groups were common a century ago, when people considered it part of their duty as citizens to work for the betterment of their communities. Generally, this did NOT include trying to keep newcomers from moving to their towns.

The most immediate way for you to make a difference is to work on increasing acceptance of affordable housing development among your fellow citizens. The key to success is to start doing the groundwork before a specific proposal is made.

Here are some key steps you can take, individually or preferably as part of a group or coalition:

- Make the public and policymakers more aware of the need for affordable housing, and the impact of the shortage on your community and region.
- A key step is to get the CEOs of corporations in your area

actively involved in supporting housing for working people. Housing affordability is making it hard to attract good workers and avoid upward pressure on wages. In California's Silicon Valley, for just one example, leaders of the high tech companies that dominate the region have been extremely effective in getting more government resources for housing and working to win community acceptance of individual developments.

- Demonstrate to the public and to policymakers that it is important as well as feasible to solve the problem. Work with owners of affordable housing properties in the area to get interested parties to visit those places, tour the facilities, and meet the tenants.
- Educate your neighbors and opinion leaders about today's affordable housing and how it has improved over the years, with good design and professional management. It's important to get this message out, whether you can reach out to a group or just speak one-on-one with a neighbor.
- Lend your political support to any candidates for local office who actively supports affordable housing.
- Challenge innuendo and outright lies that are intended to vilify affordable housing and the people who live in it (or would live in it if it was allowed to be built.)

Stand up for fairness and due process:

Once a proposal has been made for a particular housing development, the process focuses on the details of the number of units, who will live there, the design, the size, the location, and other characteristics. This becomes a process of negotiation between city officials, the developer of the proposed property, and local citizens and community groups.

People who had no experience with affordable housing before a development is proposed have many questions and hear many opinions expressed as facts. It's crucial to give people the facts about the current state-of-the-art affordable housing and dispel stereotypes that linger from the 1950s and 1960s.

This is where emotions often take over, as people act primarily out of fear of the unknown, and a strong desire to avoid change in the physical and social layout of their neighborhood. You can make a huge difference by simply standing up, proclaiming your open-mindedness, and urging folks to take a calm, rational approach to considering the plan.

It's not unusual for anti-housing activists to outnumber pro-housing speakers at public meetings by a margin of 100 to 1. If you support housing, or believe in giving a fair hearing to a development proposal, you can make a huge difference just by showing up at meetings of your local planning commission or city council considering the proposal. Don't be intimidated by ardent opponents. Stand up for fair play and free speech, and ask your neighbors to give the plan a fair hearing without pre-judging it.

Revitalizing neighborhoods

There's no question that government funding and tax breaks are critical for breathing new life into beaten-down neighborhoods. But individuals must start the process of revitalization. Oftentimes, even small steps can make a difference, like painting the facades of neglected or abandoned buildings or cleaning up trash in a neighborhood hit by foreclosures.

One small step leads to other steps. If a neighborhood starts to look like it's on the upswing, or even that its deterioration has stopped, people notice. They take better care of their property. They don't litter as much. Then maybe someone decides to invest in renovation. Then a developer may choose to construct a new building, or a business may open and create new jobs.

It may start with a church group or a block association, but if individuals take responsibility for their own roles in housing and community improvement, the political wheels will start to turn as well, and bigger things will become possible.

Something everyone can do is to use your own consumer spending to support positive outcomes for your city. If you stopped shopping at local downtown establishments because it was more convenient to do it online, go back to your Main Street merchants for routine purchases.

Build a coalition.

Chances are there is a housing advocacy group in your area already. If so, locate them and volunteer to help them with their work. If they have not already done so, work to build a broad coalition with other groups. There is power in numbers and in collaboration. It's important to join forces with other individuals, and for groups to collaborate.

Use your social networks and association memberships to reach out to other people who share your views. If you are part of a home-owner's association or civic group, you have a very logical place to start networking.

Enlist cooperation from all the existing interest groups that might be sources of support, networks and volunteers. These include labor unions, business owners, educators, faith communities, low-income housing advocates, local governments, and people directly affected by the housing shortage.

Seek collaboration with environmental groups. If they don't already recognize the advantages of multifamily housing development, explain it to them: A range of housing options can cut down on traffic and put housing closer to jobs and services, reduce pressure on open space, and reduce greenhouse gases.

Opponents of development often charge that it will cause environmental damage even though they have very little evidence to support their claim. Having environmental groups aligned with pro-housing groups is important to help fend off exaggerated claims.

If you feel more ambitious, find out if your city has a general plan that indicates where it's possible or appropriate to build low-rent apartments. If so, study it and use it as a starting point for encouraging public discussion about the big picture of housing needs and how to meet them.

Check out local zoning and building codes to see if they have lot size minimums and other provisions that discourage affordable housing from being built or if they impose exorbitant costs and delays on housing providers.

Let your local mayor and city council know you want them to set fair policies that strike the right balance between sound regulation and promoting housing affordability. It may be a long and slow process to get them to change their ways, but the more people who speak up, the more they will understand what's at stake.

Policy in brief: What's on the table

The specific policy issues facing state and federal legislators at any given time are subject to rapid change. However, there are some big-picture questions that keep coming up over and over again or will be crucial to housing and cities in the next 10 years.

1. Will the federal government maintain the flow of funding to help cities and their lower-income residents re-

cover from recession and foreclosures, or will it subject existing programs to the death of a thousand cuts?

By the time you read this, one can hope that the Budget Control Act will be a bad memory, and Congress can debate individual annual funding levels. However, if it remains in effect, federal spending on housing and urban programs is very likely to shrink dramatically.

Urban communities need a sustained commitment of funding from the federal government, and states, where that's possible. This is essential to maintain a consistent level of housing assistance, to let those receiving assistance retain that help, and to keep private owners participating in federal programs. It is also essential for the redevelopment and transformation of areas of concentrated poverty. The HOPE VI program showed the amazing potential of creating mixed-income communities where children could grow up in safety and with good social and educational opportunities. Continuation of adequate funding for the Community Development Block Grant and HOME programs is also very important, as well as instituting a new funding mechanism for the National Housing Trust Fund and expanding the Low-Income Housing Tax Credit program.

2. **Will the federal government ever exert meaningful influence over how localities regulate housing, including the practice of excluding high-density affordable rental housing and driving up its costs?**

The shortage of affordable housing could be relieved by a federal effort to counter the practice of exclusionary zoning in many American communities. The federal government enforces laws and regulations to require localities to proactively promote fair housing, but this adversarial approach is limited in scope and creates an enormous amount of resentment. The feds have to do more, using positive incentives to encourage inclusionary policies on a widespread basis.

The first step is to recognize the need for the federal government to play a role in local land use planning. Without some form of national leadership, it will continue to be a free-for-all in which some places allow affordable housing while many others exclude it, and the people who live in it, leading to ever increasing segregation by race and income.

3. **When tax "reform" finally comes to the top of the congressional agenda, will it help solve our housing problems or make them worse?**

At the federal level, the biggest ongoing issue is tax policy as it affects cities and housing. The most controversial and important tax question is whether to reduce the tax breaks available for homeowners.

There are powerful arguments for reducing the scope of the tax breaks, converting them to a tax credit useable by less affluent people, and redirecting some of the resulting increase in federal revenue to help preserve and build affordable rental housing.

4. **Will the federal government continue to support availability of safe, low-cost mortgage financing for low- and moderate-income borrowers and in predominantly minority areas?**

This issue relates to making homeownership possible for lower-income people. The question is whether Fannie Mae and Freddie Mac – or whatever agency succeeds them – will be required to promote mortgage lending to low-income and minority borrowers and provide a steady stream of funding for the National Housing Trust Fund. Housing advocates believe the answer to both questions is a resounding "yes."

5. **Will the state and federal governments consistently enforce laws against predatory lending targeting lower income and minority borrowers?**

In typical fashion, after the foreclosure crisis, Congress rushed to enact new laws governing mortgage finance. Massive amounts of money have been spent on the battle over how to implement those laws, and years have gone by. No one talked about the failure to enforce already existing laws intended to protect borrowers. No one was held accountable. To avoid that from happening again, citizens must remain vigilant and not let politicians get away with it the next time they are tempted to "look the other way" as lenders abuse their borrowers and, once again, sow the seeds of financial destruction for families and communities.

6. Local taxation for transportation and housing.

The financial bottom line is that local taxpayers will have to foot more of the bill for housing, transportation and community development. Even the voters of Southern California, land of the freeway, voted to pay more taxes to build mass transit and reduce traffic congestion. If you want to see progress in your area, you will need to help build political support for new taxes as part of well-thought plans for regional development.

Other policies that merit your consideration:

- More inclusionary zoning and less exclusionary land use
- Changes in local land use laws to allow smaller units, manufactured housing and accessory dwelling units.
- Enactment of local, state and national housing trust funds with dedicated sources of revenue so they are not subject to the legislative appropriations and budget process.
- Tax policy changes to encourage preservation of older housing
- Support for regional collaboration on land use policies intended to reduce sprawl, better link people and jobs, and provide housing for people of all incomes.

How to get more involved

If you want to get more involved, contact a housing advocacy organization near you and find out what's on their list of critical issues. Visit the websites of the following coalitions of local and state groups to find an organization near you:

- National Community Reinvestment Coalition, www.ncrc.org: Its members work on ensuring availability of credit for low-income people and neighborhoods.
- National Low Income Housing Coalition, www.nlihc.org: Its members advocate on behalf of low-income people in need of housing.
- National Rural Housing Coalition, www.ruralhousingcoalition.org: This organization represents local and regional groups that provide housing for farm workers and rural communities.
- National Housing Conference. The organization has good advice on how to make a difference at www.housingpolicy.org

Endnotes

CHAPTER ONE
Urban Decay Returns

"Although the Great Recession officially ended in June 2009, the fiscal impacts of the recession and the collapse of the housing market have lingered," according to an analysis of 2011 data by the Lincoln Institute of Land Policy.

"Newly Released Data Show Long-Lasting Impact of the Great Recession on Cities," Press release, Lincoln Institute of Land Policy, May 14, 2014.
http://www.lincolninst.edu/news-events/news-listing/article-type/articleview/articleid/2312/newly-released-data-show-long-lasting-impact-of-the-great-recession-on-cities.

In 2009 and 2010, over 85 percent of American cities reported that they were less able to meet their financial needs than in the prior year, according to the National League of Cities. The immediate outlook improved in 2011, 2012, and 2013, but not for every city. In 2013, a full 28 percent of cities were still less able to meet their financial needs than they had been in 2012. That's after several years of national economic recovery.

From the City Fiscal Conditions Survey, a national mail and online survey of finance officers in U.S. cities, as reported October 2013, National League of Cities.
http://www.nlc.org/Documents/Find%20City%20Solutions/Research%20Innovation/Finance/Final_CFC2013.pdf.

Between 2000 and 2010, the total U.S. population grew about 10 percent, from 281 million to 309 million. Over that same time, the exurban population grew by more than 60 percent, from about 16 million to almost 26 million people, according to an analysis by the Urban Institute.

"Population Growth in the Exurbs Before and Since the Great

Recession," by Todd Gardner and Matthew C. Marlay from The
Urban Institute.
    http://metrotrends.org/commentary/Exurban-Population-
Growth.cfm.

CHAPTER TWO
The New American slums

Impact of vacant properties

"How Can Municipalities Confront the Vacant Property
Challenge?"
    Business and Professional People for the Public Interest.
    http://www.bpichicago.org/documentsHowCanMunicipalities-
ConfronttheVacantPropertyChallenge_AnIntroductoryGuide-1.pdf.

*Property abandonment and neglect create a downward spiral
that is hard to stop. Even solvent homeowners think twice about
keeping up their property or paying their tax and mortgage payments if their neighborhood is going downhill. "On average, families affected by nearby foreclosures have already lost or will lose
$21,077 in household wealth, representing 7.2 percent of their home
value, by virtue of being in close proximity to foreclosures," according to the Center for Responsible Lending (CRL) in Durham.*
    "Collateral Damage: The Spillover Costs of Foreclosures,"
Debbie Gruenstein Bocian, Peter Smith and Wei Li, Center for
Responsible Lending, October 24, 2012.
    http://www.responsiblelending.org/mortgage-lending/research-
analysis/collateral-damage.pdf.

George W. Bush's statement on his homeownership plan:
    *"In order to change America and to make sure the great
American dream shines in every community, we must unleash the
compassion and kindness of the greatest nation on the face of the
earth," he said in 2002. To encourage homeownership, he said, "We
must use the mighty muscle of the federal government in combination with state and local governments."*

White House Press Release, Remarks by President George W. Bush, St. Paul AME Church, Atlanta, Georgia, June 17, 2002.

The Bush administration also worked to prevent state attorneys general from curtailing high-risk types of mortgage lending...

"Predatory Lenders' Partner in Crime," by Eliot Spitzer, The Washington Post, February 14, 2008.

http://www.washingtonpost.com/wp-dyn/content/article/2008/02/13/AR2008021302783.html.

The situation turned out to be a golden opportunity for others with large sums of capital. For example, rental housing investment companies had already bought 200,000 single-family homes by 2013, according to the Center for American Progress.

Invitation Homes, a branch of The Blackstone Group, spent $7.5 billion acquiring 40,000 houses from 2011 to 2013 to create the largest single-family rental business in the United States.

"When Wall Street Buys Main Street: The Implications of Single-Family Rental Bonds for Tenants and Housing Markets," By Sarah Edelman, with Julia Gordon and David Sanchez, Center for American Progress, 2014.

http://www.americanprogress.org/issues/housing/report/2014/02/27/84750/when-wall-street-buys-main-street-2/

"Nearly 50% Of All Home Sales Now Cash, As Institutional Investor Activity Hits New High," *Forbes* magazine, 10/24/2013.

Cost of foreclosures to California cities...

"Home Wreckers: How Wall Street Foreclosures Are Devastating Communities" by the Alliance of Californians for Community Empowerment, PICO California, California Reinvestment Coalition, and SEIU California

http://www.calorganize.org/sites/default/files/Home-Wreckers-Report-March-16-2011.pdf.

CHAPTER THREE
The Many Victims of Homelessness

*The most thorough tabulation of homeless families comes from the
U.S. Department of Education (DE). A total of 1,168,354 public
and charter school students were homeless during the 2011-2012
school year, according to the DE.*

"Education for Homeless Children and Youths Program; Data
Collection Summary, From the School Year 2011–12," by the
National Center for Homeless Education, March 2014.

---

*Comment on HUD's data on homeless veterans and information on
overall federal plan to address homelessness:*

"Opening Doors, Federal Strategic Plan to Prevent and
End Homelessness," United States Interagency Council on
Homelessness, 2010.
    http://usich.gov/opening_doors/.

---

*The cost of the public services in Los Angeles County for the chroni-
cally homeless.*

"Where We Sleep: Costs when Homeless and Housed in Los
Angeles," Economic Roundtable, 2009.

---

*"More than 1 million persons are served in HUD-supported emer-
gency, transitional and permanent housing programs each year.
The total number of persons who experience homelessness may be
twice as high." In other words, while HUD publicizes the 610,000
figure from its "point-in-time count" in all its public relations, it acknowledges in a much quieter way that as many as 2 million people
are homeless each year and that only about half of them receive
government assistance.*

HUD web site, under Program Offices > Community Planning and

Development > Homeless Assistance
    http://portal.hud.gov/hudportal/HUD?src=/program_offices/
comm_planning/homeless

CHAPTER FOUR
Struggling to Find Affordable Housing

An analysis of American Housing Survey data through 2010 found that 55 percent of children in poor families had moved within the previous 24 months, compared with only 31 percent of children in families above the poverty line.

"Should I Stay or Should I Go? Exploring the Effects of Housing Instability and Mobility on Children," Center for Housing Policy.
    http://www.nhc.org/media/files/HsgInstablityandMobility.pdf.

CHAPTER SIX
The High Cost of Neglect

Researchers at the Federal Reserve Bank of Boston said there is a direct impact of housing affordability problems on employment. "Overall, our empirical analyses—at both the California city and U.S. metropolitan-area and county levels—show that unaffordable housing negatively affects employment growth," the researchers said. In California, for one specific example, they said a one-unit increase in the housing-price-to-income ratio reduces city-level employment growth by 1.5–2.5 percentage points over two years.

"Unaffordable Housing and Local Employment Growth," (Working Paper 10-3, New England Public Policy Center at the Federal Reserve Bank of Boston, Boston, 2010), by Ritashree Chakrabarti and Junfu Zhang, www.bos.frb.org/economic/neppc/wp/2010/neppcwp103.pdf.

A study released by The Pew Charitable Trust found that the economic segregation of neighborhoods is linked to a person's prospects for moving up or down the economic ladder, or what is known as economic mobility. In an analysis of 96 U.S. metropolitan areas,

Pew found that those with distinct pockets of concentrated wealth and concentrated poverty have lower economic mobility than places where residents are more economically integrated.

"Mobility and the Metropolis: How Communities Factor Into Economic Mobility," Patrick Sharkey, associate professor of sociology at New York University, and Bryan Graham, associate professor of economics at the University of California, Berkeley.
    http://www.pewstates.org/research/reports/mobility-and-the-metropolis-85899523652.

The positive economic contribution of affordable housing development in New York State.

"Economic Impacts of Affordable Housing on New York State's Economy,"
    The New York State Association for Affordable Housing, May, 22, 2012.
    http://www.nysafah.org/cmsBuilder/uploads/HR%26A-Economic-Impact-Report.pdf.

Not long ago, school district officials in Glastonbury, Conn., a town with a median income of $80,660 near Hartford, kicked 48 students out of classes in their town. The children lived in nearby Hartford, and their parents lied about residency in order to get them into the high-quality schools in the affluent suburb.

David Fink, "Achievement Gap Tied to Affordable Housing," op-ed, *Hartford Courant*, April 11, 2014.
    http://articles.courant.com/2014-04-11/news/hc-op-fink-connecticut-education-gap-fair-housing--20140411_1_achievement-gap-open-choice-glastonbury.

"Housing at the Heart of Financial Crisis" (sidebar)
"The Financial Crisis Inquiry Report: Final report of the National Commission on the Causes of the financial and economic crisis in the U.S.," January 2011.

http://www.gpo.gov/fdsys/pkg/GPO-FCIC/pdf/GPO-FCIC.pdf.

CHAPTER ELEVEN
Restoring the Potential of Homeownership

In 2011, FHA reported that it lead the market in support for minority homeownership. While FHA insurance was used for 37 percent of all home-purchase borrowers, its share of minority borrowers was 46 percent.

HUD Web Site:
   http://portal.hud.gov/hudportal/documents/huddoc?id=FHAM MIFundAnnRptFY2011.pdf.

CHAPTER TWELVE
Toward a Strategic Vision

For most US banks, CRA regulatory considerations are a major force driving the execution of their community and economic development strategies. In 2011, US financial institutions made $209 billion in CRA-related loans including $47 billion of community development lending.

Federal Financial Institutions Examination Council website: www.ffiec.gov/craadweb/national.aspx.

CHAPTER THIRTEEN
The Not So Great Society

Lyndon Johnson recognized that areas with concentrated poverty were the factories of inequality in America. Sen. Robert Kennedy knew it. A long list of prominent Republicans also understood that dynamic, including George Romney, President Richard Nixon's housing secretary.

"George Romney, Richard Nixon, and the Fair Housing Act of 1968," by Florence Wagman Roisman, Poverty and Race Research

Action Council.

    http://www.prrac.org/pdf/RoismanHistoryExcerpt.pdf.

The Housing Act of 1949 declared it a national goal to provide "a decent home and a suitable living environment for every American family."

Additional quotation from the law:

    "The Congress declares that the general welfare and security of the Nation and the health and living standards of its people require housing production and related community development sufficient to remedy the serious housing shortage, the elimination of substandard and other inadequate housing through the clearance of slums and blighted areas, and the realization as soon as feasible of the goal of a decent home and a suitable living environment for every American family, thus contributing to the development and redevelopment of communities and to the advancement of the growth, wealth, and security of the Nation. The Congress further declares that such production is necessary to enable the housing industry to make its full contribution toward an economy of maximum employment, production, and purchasing power."

Commentary on the passage of the law:

    "A Study in Contradictions: The Origins and Legacy of the Housing Act of 1949," by Alexander von Hoffman, published in *Housing Policy Debate*, Volume 11, Issue 2 (2000).

    http://content.knowledgeplex.org/kp2/kp/text_document_summary/scholarly_article/relfiles/hpd_1102_hoffman.pdf.

CHAPTER FOURTEEN
Shrinking Housing Safety Net

"Overview of Federal Housing Assistance, Programs and Policy," by Maggie McCarty, Libby Perl, and Katie Jones, Congressional Research Service, April 15, 2014.

    "Decade of Neglect Has Weakened Federal Low-Income Housing Programs: New Resources Required to Meet Growing Needs," by Douglas Rice and Barbara Sard, Center for Budget

and Policy Priorities.
> http://www.cbpp.org/files/2-24-09hous.pdf.

Center for Budget and Policy Priorities website:
http://www.cbpp.org/research/index.cfm?fa=topic&id=33.

Home mortgage interest deduction, its cost and ideas for change:

"Mortgage Interest Deduction Is Ripe for Reform: Conversion to Tax Credit Could Raise Revenue and Make Subsidy More Effective and Fairer," by Will Fischer and Chye-Ching Huang, Center for Budget and Policy Priorities, June 25, 2013.
> http://www.cbpp.org/cms/?fa=view&id=3948.

CHAPTER FIFTEEN
Leaving Grandma out in the Cold

"A Quiet Crisis in America," Report to Congress of The Commission on Affordable Housing and Health Facility Needs for Seniors in the 21st Century.
> http://govinfo.library.unt.edu/seniorscommission/pages/final_report/sencomrep.html.

CHAPTER SEVENTEEN
The Anti-Affordability Conspiracy

"Not In My Backyard: Removing Barriers to Affordable Housing," Advisory Commission on Regulatory Barriers to Affordable Housing, by Thomas H. Kean and Thomas Ashley, July 1991.
> http://www.huduser.org/portal/taxonomy/term/2437.

"Streamlining SEQR: How to Reform New York's "Environmental" Planning Law," by E.J. McMahon & Michael Wright, December 16, 2013.
> http://empirecenter.intelliclient.com/publications/streamlining-seqr/#sthash.8wxStjrg.dpbs.

CHAPTER EIGHTEEN
Why We Hate Housing
Another common assertion is that a multifamily affordable develop-
ment in an area of single-family homes will bring down property
values. This has been proven false time and again in studies by
many academic and nonprofit institutions alike.

This is a partial list of such studies, provided by the National
Association of Realtors:
"Here comes the Neighborhood," (*New York Times*, Oct. 19,
2013). — Low-income housing's impact in Mount Laurel, NJ.
"Community Impact: The Effects of Assisted Rental Housing
in Delaware," (*Shelter for All*, Oct. 2012). The central findings of
the report are that the location of assisted multifamily rental housing is typically not associated with any subsequent changes in the
values of neighboring properties.
"Fear of Affordable Housing: Perception vs. Reality,"
(*Shelterforce*, Summer 2012). A study by Tufts University examines if any of the fears expressed for specific developments came to
pass once they were built. Housing prices show no impact.
"Affordable housing pays off for city," (*Crain's New York*, June
23, 2010).
"How Does Affordable Housing Affect Surrounding Property
Values?," (*Arizona State University's Stardust Center* for Affordable
Homes and the Family, 2008). This research synthesis is based on
a review and analysis of 21 recent studies measuring the impact of
various forms of affordable housing on property values.
"Spillovers and Subsidized Housing: The Impact of Subsidized
Rental Housing on Neighborhoods," by Ingrid Gould Ellen.
(*Harvard University—Joint Center for Housing Studies*, Mar.
2007). http://www.jchs.harvard.edu/sites/jchs.harvard.edu/files/
rr07-3_ellen.pdf
"Does Federally Subsidized Rental Housing Depress
Neighborhood Property Values?," (*NYU*, Law and Economics
Research Paper No. 05-04, Mar. 2005).

"Don't Put it Here," The Center for Housing Policy.
This succinct report includes findings from a survey of re-

search on the topic done by the Furman Center of New York University and funded by the John D. and Catherine T. MacArthur Foundation.

"Overall, the research suggests that neighbors should have little to fear from the type of attractive and modestly sized developments that constitute the bulk of newly produced affordable housing today." It found that sometimes, there can be a negative impact on property values when affordable housing was "highly concentrated, particularly when located in vulnerable neighborhoods that have high poverty rates and low home values." That does not describe the suburban locations where concern about the potential impact of development on their property values is often very strong. The report includes an extensive list of original research studies and literature reviews.

http://www.nhc.org/media/documents/Dontputithere.pdf

"What is the Mount Laurel Doctrine?"
    Web site article, Fair Share Housing Center
    http://fairsharehousing.org/mount-laurel-doctrine/

"Climbing Mount Laurel: The Struggle for Affordable Housing and Social Mobility in an American Suburb," by Douglas S. Massey, Len Albright, Rebecca Casciano, Elizabeth Derickson & David N. Kinsey
    Excerpt from the book:
    "Local residents repeatedly expressed their fears of dire consequences that were sure to follow in the wake of the project's opening—that crime would increase, that tax burdens would rise, and that property values would decline. ...When we carefully assessed trends in crime, taxes, and home prices in the township and surrounding neighborhoods, we found no evidence whatsoever that the project's opening had any direct effect on crime rates, tax burdens, or property values," the report said.

CHAPTER NINETEEN
Slamming The Door on America's Dream
The American Enterprise Institute and other groups have blamed the foreclosure crisis on these regulations. They say strong enforce-

ment of CRA under Presidents Carter and Clinton forced banks to make too many loans to low-income people, directly contributing to the mortgage meltdown.

"The Clinton-era roots of the financial crisis: Affordable-housing goals established in the 1990s led to a massive increase in risky, subprime mortgages," by Phil Gramm, Mike Solon, The Wall Street Journal, August 12, 2013.
http://www.aei.org/article/economics/the-clinton-era-roots-of-the-financial-crisis/.

"The Report of the President's Commission on Housing," by Carla Hills and William McKenna, 1982.
http://www.huduser.org/portal/publications/affhsg/presid_Comm_1982.htmla.

Bibliography

Advisory Commission on Regulatory Barriers to Affordable Housing.
"'Not in My Backyard': Removing Barriers to Affordable Housing."
Department of Housing and Urban Development, Washington, DC, 1991.

Apgar, William C., Mark Duda, and Rochelle Nawrocki Gorey. "The
Municipal Cost of Foreclosures: A Chicago Case Study." Housing
Finance Policy Research Paper No. 2005-01, Homeownership
Preservation Foundation, Minneapolis, MN, February 2005.

Apgar, William C., Christopher E. Herbert, and Priti Mathur. "Risk
or Race: An Assessment of Subprime Lending Patterns in Nine
Metropolitan Areas." Research report, Department of Housing and
Urban Development, Office of Policy Development and Research,
Washington, DC, August 2011.

Arik, Hulya. "A Housing Dollar Well-Spent: The Social and Economic
Impacts of Affordable Housing Development." Research report,
Tennessee Housing Development Agency, Nashville, TN, May 2010.

Arnold, Althea, Sheila Crowly, et al "Out of Reach 2014." National Low
Income Housing Coalition, Washington, DC, March 2014.

Arnquist, Sarah. "The Million Dollar (Homeless) Patient: Calculating the
Health Care Costs of Chronic Homelessness." Online report, Reporting
on Health, USC Annenberg School of Journalism, USC, n.d.

Bassuk, Ellen L., et al. "America's Youngest Outcasts 2010." The National
Center on Family Homelessness, Needham, MA, December 2011.

BeMiller, Haley, Courtney Jacquin, and Jakub Rudnik. "Finding Affordable
Housing in Chicago Lawn: One Renter's Story." Institute for Housing
Studies at DePaul University, blog entry, Chicago, IL, Dec. 20, 2013.

Bergen, Mark. "George Romney and the Last Gasps of Urban Policy."
Forbes, Feb. 28, 2012.

Bibby, Douglas M. "A New Housing Policy: Imagine the Possibilities."
PowerPoint presentation, National Multi Housing Council,
Washington, DC, April 2009.

Billingham, Chase, and Barry Bluestone. "The Greater Boston Housing
Report Card 2011: Housing's Role in the Ongoing Economic Crisis."
The Boston Foundation, Boston, MA, October 2011.

Bipartisan Policy Center, Economic Policy Program, Housing Commission.
"Housing America's Future: New Directions for National Policy."
Bipartisan Policy Center, Washington, DC, February 2013.

Bocian, Debbie Gruenstein, Wei Li, Carolina Reid, and Roberto G.
Quercia. "Lost Ground, 2011: Disparities in Mortgage Lending and
Foreclosures." Research report, Center for Responsible Lending,
Durham, NC, November 2011.

Bocian, Debbie Gruenstein, Wei Li, and Keith S. Ernst. "Foreclosures by
Race and Ethnicity: The Demographics of a Crisis." Research report,
Center for Responsible Lending, Durham, NC, June 2010).

Bocian, Debbie Gruenstein, Peter Smith, and Wei Li. "Collateral Damage: The Spillover Cost of Foreclosures." Research report, Center for Responsible Lending, Durham, NC, October 2012.

Bravve, Elina, Megan Bolton, Linda Couch, and Sheila Crowley. "Out of Reach 2012: America's Forgotten Housing Crisis." National Low Income Housing Coalition, Washington, DC, March 2012.

Brennan, Maya. "The Impacts of Affordable Housing on Education: A Research Summary." Research brief, Center for Housing Policy, May 2011.

Business and Professional People for the Public Interest. "How Can Municipalities Confront the Vacant Property Challenge?" Business and Professional People for the Public Interest, Chicago Metropolitan Agency for Planning, and Metropolitan Mayors Conference, March 2010.

California Reinvestment Coalition, Empire Justice Center, Massachusetts Affordable Housing Alliance, Neighborhood Economic Development Advocacy Project, Ohio Fair Lending Coalition, Reinvestment Partners, and Woodstock Institute. "Paying More for the American Dream VI: Racial Disparities in FHA/VA Financing." Research Report, California Reinvestment Coalition, Empire Justice Center, Massachusetts Affordable Housing Alliance, Neighborhood Economic Development Advocacy Project, Ohio Fair Lending Coalition, Reinvestment Partners, and Woodstock Institute, July 2012.

Campbell, John Y., Stefano Giglio, and Parag Pathak. "Forced Sales and House Prices." *American Economic Review* 101, no. 5: 2108—31, 2011.

Carey, Nick. "Cheap Detroit Houses Scooped up by Investors Can Be Costly for Communities, Bad News for Buyers." Reuters, July 3, 2013.

Carr, James H., Katrin B. Anacker, and Ines Hernandez. "State of Housing in Black America." National Association of Real Estate Brokers, Lanham, MD, August 2013.

Carter, Jimmy. "Housing and Community Development Act of 1977: Remarks on Signing H.R. 6655 Into Law." *The American Presidency Project, Oct. 12, 1977.*

Casey, Maura. "Book Review: 'A Fighting Chance' by Elizabeth Warren." *The Washington Post*, April 21, 2014.

Chakrabarti, Ritashree, and Junfu Zhang. "Unaffordable Housing and Local Employment Growth." Working Paper 10-3, New England Public Policy Center at the Federal Reserve Bank of Boston, Boston, 2010.

The Community Builders staff. "The Promise of Mixed-Income Communities." The Community Builders, Boston, MA, 2007.

Corkery, Michael. "Wall Street's New Housing Bonanza." Dealbook, *The New York Times*, Jan. 29, 2014.

Cortes, Alvaro, Meghan Henry, RJ de la Cruz, Scott Brown, Jill Khadduri, and Dennis P. Culhane. "The 2012 Point-in-Time Estimate of Homelessness: Volume I of the 2012 Annual Homelessness Assessment Report." The Selected Works of Dennis P. Culhane, 2012.

Crosby, Jackie. "UnitedHealth Invests $50 Million in Low-Income Rental

Housing." *Star Tribune*, Nov. 14, 2013.

Crouch, Elisa. "Normandy Chorale Heads to Carnegie Hall." *St. Louis Post-Dispatch*, March 7, 2014.

Culhane, Dennis P., Wayne D. Parker, Barbara Poppe, Kennen S. Gross, and Ezra Sykes. "Accountability, Cost-Effectiveness, and Program Performance: Progress Since 1998." University of Pennsylvania, School of Social Policy and Practice, January 2008.

Culhane, Dennis P., John Fantuzzo, Whitney LeBoeuf, and Chin-Chih Chen. "Alternative Approach: Assessing the Impact of HUD's Assisted Housing Programs on Educational Opportunity and Well-being." Research report, Department of Housing and Urban Development, Office of Policy Development and Research, Washington, DC, Aug. 11, 2011.

Culhane, Dennis P., and Stephen Metraux. "Rearranging the Deck Chairs or Reallocating the Lifeboats? Homelessness Assistance and Its Alternatives." *Journal of the American Planning Association*, 74, no. 1: 111—21, Feb. 8, 2008.

Culhane, Dennis P., Jung Min Park, and Stephen Metraux. "The Patterns and Costs of Services Use among Homeless Families." Journal of Community Psychology 39, no. 7: 815–25, September 2011.

Cuomo, Andrew. "Secretary Andrew Cuomo's Remarks at the Dedication Ceremony for the Robert C. Weaver Federal Building." HUD Archives, Washington, DC, July 11, 2000.

Dawsey, Darrell. "To CHP Officer Who Sparked Riots, It Was Just Another Arrest." *Los Angeles Times*, Aug. 19, 1991.

Department of Housing and Urban Development. "Affordable Housing Needs 2005: Report to Congress." Department of Housing and Urban Development, Office of Policy Development and Research, Washington, DC, 2007.

———. "Worst Case Housing Needs 2011: Report to Congress." Department of Housing and Urban Development, Washington, DC, 2011.

Downs, Anthony. "The Advisory Commission on Regulatory Barriers to Affordable Housing: Its Behavior and Accomplishments." *Housing Policy Debate* 2, no. 4: 1095–1137, 1991.

Dunford, James V., et al. "Impact of the San Diego Serial Inebriate Program on Use of Emergency Medical Resources." Annals of Emergency Medicine 47, no. 4: 328–336, April 2006.

Eisenhower, Dwight D. "Statement by the President upon Signing the Housing Amendments of 1955." *The American Presidency Project, Aug. 11, 1955.*

Fischer, Will. "Research Shows Housing Vouchers Reduce Hardship and Provide Platform for Long-Term Gains Among Children." Research report prepared for Center on Budget and Policy Priorities, Washington, DC, March 10, 2014.

Flaming, Daniel, Michael Matsunaga, and Patrick Burns. "Where We Sleep: The Costs of Housing and Homelessness in Los Angeles." Report prepared for the Los Angeles Homeless Services Authority, November 2009.

Fuller, Stephen S., "The Trillion Dollar Apartment Industry," National Apartment Association and the National Multi Housing Council, 2013

Gabriel, Stuart A., and Stuart S. Rosenthal. "The Boom, the Bust, and the Future of Homeownership (revised)." Working paper, Ziman Center for Real Estate, UCLA, Aug. 21, 2013.

Gallagher, Jim. "St. Louis Is Hot Spot for 'Underwater' Mortgages." *St. Louis Post-Dispatch*, May 9, 2014.

Gilbert, Ben W. "Ten Blocks from the White House: Anatomy of the Washington Riots of 1968." Praeger, 1968.

Gonzales, John. "Rebuilding Lives to Reduce ER Use." Report prepared for the California Health Care Foundation, Center for Health Reporting, April 5, 2012.

Goldsmith, Steve. "Milwaukee's Push to Turn Vacant Land into Urban Farms." *Governing*, April 16, 2014.

Governing staff. "Bankrupt Cities, Municipalities and Map." *Governing*.

Government Accountability Office staff. "Vacant Properties: Growing Number Increases Communities' Costs and Challenges." Report GAO-12-34, Government Accountability Office, Washington, DC, November 2011.

Habitat for Humanity. "Building Toward 1 Million and So Much More: Habitat for Humanity International Annual Report for FY2013." Habitat for Humanity, Atlanta, GA, 2013.

Han, Hye-Sung "The Impact of Abandoned Properties on Nearby Property Values." Housing Policy 24, no. 2: 311—34, 2014.

Hedberg, William, and John Krainer. "Credit Access Following a Mortgage Default," Economic Research, Federal Reserve Bank of San Francisco, Oct. 29, 2012.

Hickey, Robert, Jeffrey Lubell, Peter Haas, and Stephanie Morse. "Losing Ground: The Struggle of Moderate-Income Households to Afford the Rising Costs of Housing and Transportation." Research report prepared for the Center for Housing Policy, Washington, DC, and the Center for Neighborhood Technology, Chicago, October 2012.

Hoak, Amy. "How Foreclosure Backlogs Could Hurt Home Buyers: Slow Processing Could Keep Prices Down and Mortgage Rates Up." MarketWatch, Dec. 3, 2012.

Home Defenders League. "Foreclosure Horror Story: Bank of America Mortgage Modification Allegedly Goes Wrong." Huffington Post, March 12, 2013.

Home Defenders League. 100 Stories of What Wall Street Broke website.
———. "Victories." Home Defenders League

Home Wreckers. "How Wall Street Foreclosures Are Devastating Ohio Communities." Ohio Organizing Collaborative and Service Employees International Union, September 2011.

Home Wreckers. "How Wall Street Foreclosures Are Devastating Communities." Alliance of California for Community Empowerment, PICO California, CRC, Service Employees International Union California, March 16, 2011.

Housing and Economic Rights Advocates and California Reinvestment
Commission. "Need for immediate federal intervention to mitigate the
harmful impacts on local communities ..." Open letter to five leading
U.S. government officials from a group of 80 organizations, sent Feb.
22, 2014.

HR&A Advisors. "Economic Impacts of Affordable Housing on New York's
State Economy." Research report, New York State Association for
Affordable Housing, May 12, 2012.

Institute for Housing Studies at DePaul University. IHS Data Portal.

Immergluck, Dan. "Foreclosed: High-Risk Lending, Deregulation, and the
Undermining of America's Mortgage Market." Cornell University Press,
Ithaca, NY, 2009.

Immergluck, Dan, and Geoff Smith. "The External Costs of Foreclosure:
The Impact of Single-Family Mortgage Foreclosures on Property
Values." Housing Policy Debate 17, no. 1, 2006.

Johnson, Lyndon B. "Message to the Congress Transmitting First Annual
Report of the Department of Housing and Urban Development." The
American Presidency Project, April 17, 1967.

———. "Remarks at the Dedication of the Department of Housing and
Urban Development Building." The American Presidency Project,
Sept. 9, 1968.

———. "Remarks at the Swearing In of Robert C. Weaver and Robert
C. Wood as Secretary and Under Secretary of Housing and Urban
Development." The American Presidency Project,
Jan. 18, 1966.

———. "Remarks at the Signing of Bill Establishing a Department of
Housing and Urban Development." The American Presidency Project,
Sept. 9, 1965.

———. "Remarks upon Signing the Housing and Urban Development Act
of 1968." The American Presidency Project, Aug. 1, 1968.

———. "Statement by the President upon Nominating the Incorporators
of the National Housing Partnership." The American Presidency
Project, Sept. 9, 1968.

Joint Center for Housing Studies of Harvard University. "America's
Rental Housing: Meeting Challenges, Building on Opportunities."
Research report, Harvard University, Cambridge, MA, 2011.

———. "America's Rental Housing: Evolving Markets and Needs."
Research report, Harvard Joint Center for Housing Studies,
Cambridge, MA, Dec. 9, 2013.

———. "The State of the Nation's Housing 2013." Research report,
Harvard Joint Center for Housing Studies, Cambridge, MA, 2013.

———. "The State of the Nation's Housing 2014." Research report,
Harvard Joint Center for Housing Studies, Cambridge, MA, 2014.

———. "The State of the Nation's Housing 2011." Research report,
Harvard Joint Center for Housing Studies, Cambridge, MA, 2011.

Joint Economic Committee of Congress. "Foreclosure Predictions." April
2008.

———. "Subprime Mortgage Market Crisis Timeline." July 2008.

———. "Report Update: Sheltering Neighborhoods from the Subprime Foreclosure Storm." June 2007.

———. "Sheltering Neighborhoods from the Subprime Foreclosure Storm." April 2007.

———. "The Subprime Lending Crisis: The Economic Impact on Wealth, Property Values and Tax Revenues, and How We Got Here." Report and recommendations by the majority staff of the Joint Economic Committee, Sen. Charles E. Schumer, chairman, and Rep. Carolyn B. Maloney, vice chair, October 2007.

———. "Subprime Mortgage Market Crisis Timeline." July 2008.

Kaiser, Edgar F., et al. "The Report of the President's Committee on Urban Housing: A Decent Home." US Government Printing Office, Washington, DC, 1969.

Kingsley, G. Thomas, Robin Smith, and David Price. "The Impacts of Foreclosures on Families and Communities." The Urban Institute, Washington, DC, May 2009.

Kirp, David L. "Here Comes the Neighborhood." The New York Times, Oct. 19, 2013.

Kneebone, Elizabeth, and Alan Berube. "Suburban Poverty Profiles: Montgomery County, Maryland." The Avenue/Rethinking Metropolitan America blog, May 22, 2013.

———. "Confronting Suburban Poverty in America." Brookings Institution, Washington, DC, 2013.

Kneebone, Elizabeth, Carey Nadeau, and Alan Berube. "The Re-Emergence of Concentrated Poverty: Metropolitan Trends in the 2000s." Metropolitan Opportunity Series, No. 25, Brookings Institution, Washington, DC, November 2011.

Landis, John D., and Kirk McClure. "Rethinking Federal Housing Policy." Journal of the American Planning Association 76, no. 3: 319–348, 2010.

Larimer, Mary E., et al. "Health Care and Public Service Use and Costs Before and After Provision of Housing for Chronically Homeless Persons with Severe Alcohol Problems." The Journal of the American Medical Association, 301, no. 13: 1349–57, 2009.

Lauria, Mickey, and Erin Comstock. "The Effectiveness of Community Land Trusts." Working paper no. WP07ML2, Lincoln Institute of Land Policy, Cambridge, MA, December 2007.

Lewin Group. "Costs of Serving Homeless Individuals in Nine Cities." Chart book, prepared for the Partnership to End Long-Term Homelessness, November 2004.

Lewit, Meghan. "Homeless Cost Study." Research study for United Way of Greater Los Angeles, October 2009.

Mangano, Philip. "The Business Case for Ending Homelessness." PowerPoint presentation to Vancouver Board of Trade, The American Round Table to Abolish Homelessness, July 16, 2009.

Martinez, T.E. and M.R. Burt. "Impact of Permanent Supportive Housing on the Use of Acute Care Health Services by Homeless Adults."

Psychiatric Services 57, no. 7 (July 2006): 992—99.

Masnick, George S., Daniel McCue, and Eric S. Belsky. "Updated 2010–2020 Household and New Home Demand Projections." Joint Center for Housing Studies, Harvard University, Cambridge, MA, September 2010.

Massey, Douglas S. "Lessons from Suburbia." Pathways: 19–23, Spring 2013.

Massey, Douglas S., and Nancy A. Denton. "American Apartheid: Segregation and the Making of the Underclass." Harvard University Press, Cambridge, MA, 1993.

Millennial Housing Commission. "Meeting Our Nation's Housing Challenges." Report to Congress, Bipartisan Millennial Housing Commission, Washington, DC, May 2002.

Minnesota Community Land Trust Coalition.

Montgomery, Ann Elizabeth, Lindsay L. Hill, Vincent Kane, and Dennis P. Culhane. "Housing Chronically Homeless Veterans: Evaluating the Efficacy of a Housing First Approach to HUD-VASH." Journal of Community Psychology 41, no. 4: 505–14, 2013.

Mueller, Elizabeth J., and Alex Schwartz. "Reversing the Tide: Will State and Local Governments House the Poor as Federal Direct Subsidies Decline?" Journal of the American Planning Association, 74, no. 1: 122–35, 2008.

National Alliance to End Homelessness. "The State of Homelessness in 2013: An Examination of Homelessness, Economic, Housing, and Demographic Trends at the National and State Levels." Research report, Homelessness Research Institute, April 8, 2013.

National Community Land Trust Network.

National Center on Family Homelessness. "The Cost of Homelessness." Research brief prepared for Campaign to End Child Homelessness, National Center on Family Homelessness, December 2012.

National Housing Trust. "Housing Data." Website, www.nhtinc.org.

Nixon, Richard. "Remarks to Top Officials at the Department of Housing and Urban Development." The American Presidency Project, Feb. 3, 1969.

Pendall, Rolf, Lesley Freiman, Dowell Myers, and Selma Hepp. "Demographic Challenges and Opportunities for U.S. Housing Markets." Bipartisan Policy Center, Washington, DC, March 6, 2012.

Phillips-Fein, Kim. "Living for the City: Robert Clifton Weaver's Liberalism." The Nation, Jan. 12, 2009.

Reitman, Valerie, and Mitchell Landsberg, "Watts Riots, 40 Years Later." Los Angeles Times, Aug. 11, 2005.

Sauter, Michael B. "Cities with the Most Homes in Foreclosure." 24/7 Wall St., May 22, 2012.

Scally, Corianne Payton, and Richard Koenig. "Beyond NIMBY and Poverty Deconcentration: Reframing the Outcomes of Affordable Rental Housing Development." Ideas 22, no. 3: 435–61, February 2012.

Schildkraut, Jaclyn, and Elizabeth Erhardt Mustaine. "Movin', But Not

Up to the East Side: Foreclosures and Social Disorganization in Orange County, Florida." Housing Studies 29, no. 2: 177–97, 2013.

Schmit, Julie. "Report Estimates 8 Million Children Hurt by Foreclosures." USA Today, April 18, 2012.

Schor, Elana. "Washington's Black Community Remembers 1968 Riots." The Guardian, April 4, 2008.

Schuetz, Jenny, Rachel Meltzer, and Vicki Been. "Silver Bullet or Trojan Horse? The Effects of Inclusionary Zoning on Local Housing Markets in the United States." Urban Studies 48, no. 2: 297–329, February 2011.

Schwartz, Heather. "Can Housing Policy Be Good Education Policy?" Pathways, 2–27, spring 2013.

Sharkey, Patrick. "Stuck in Place: Urban Neighborhoods and the End of Progress Toward Racial Equality." University of Chicago Press, Chicago, 2013.

Shashaty, Andre F. "Help Us Shape Future of Federal Housing Policy." Affordable Housing Finance, 24–26, March 2008.

———. "Contracting Out of Control? Questions Persist about HUD Contracting as Congress Investigates Political Influence." Affordable Housing Finance: 36–50, March 2008.

Shin, Annys. "In Prince George's, Hundreds of Vacant Houses Plague Neighborhoods." The Washington Post, Jan. 13, 2013.

Shine, Conor. "Las Vegas Working on Way to Curb Blight of Foreclosure." Las Vegas Sun, Nov. 16, 2011.

Smith, Geoff, and Sarah Duda. "The State of Rental Housing in Cook County." Institute for Housing Studies, DePaul University, Chicago, 2013.

Sungu-Eryilmaz, Yesim, and Rosalind Greenstein. "A National Study of Community Land Trusts." Working paper no. WP07YS1, Lincoln Institute of Land Policy, 2007.

Sussingham, Robin. "Foreclosure Process Hammers Florida's Housing Market." NPR, Feb. 4, 2013.

Temkin, Kenneth Mark, Brett Theodos, and David Price. "Sharing Equity with Future Generations: An Evaluation of Long-Term Affordable Homeownership Programs in the USA." Housing Studies 28, no. 4 (2013): 553–78.

Thaden, Emily. "Outperforming the Market: Delinquency and Foreclosure Rates in Community Land Trusts." Working paper no. WP10ET1, Lincoln Institute of Land Policy, Cambridge, MA, October 2010.

———. "Stable Home Ownership in a Turbulent Economy: Delinquencies and Foreclosures Remain Low in Community Land Trusts." Working paper no. WP11ET1, Lincoln Institute of Land Policy, Cambridge, MA, July 2011.

Thaden, Emily, and Greg Rosenberg. "Outperforming the Market: Delinquency and Foreclosure Rates in Community Land Trusts." Land Lines, October 2010.

Turbov, Mindy, and Valerie Piper. "HOPE VI and Mixed-Finance Redevelopments: A Catalyst for Neighborhood Renewal—Atlanta

Case Study." Brookings Institution Metropolitan Policy Program, Washington, DC, 2005.

Urban Institute. "Expanding Housing Opportunities through Inclusionary Zoning: Lessons from Two Counties." Report prepared for the Department of Housing and Urban Development, Office of Policy Development and Research, Washington, DC, December 2012.

Urban Land Institute. "White Flint/Rockville Pike, Montgomery County, Maryland." In "Shifting Suburbs: Reinventing Infrastructure for Compact Development." Report prepared for the ULI, Washington, DC, 28–31, 2012.

U.S. Census Bureau. American Housing Survey for the United States: 2009. Current Housing Reports, Series H150/09, U.S. Government Printing Office, Washington, DC, 2011.

U.S. Conference of Mayors. "Hunger and Homelessness Survey: A Status Report on Hunger and Homelessness in America's Cities." Twenty-five-city survey, Washington, DC, December 2013.

Warren, Elizabeth. "Elizabeth Warren's 'A Fighting Chance': An Exclusive Excerpt on the Foreclosure Crisis." The Boston Globe, April 27, 2014.

Westlund, Richard. "Workforce Housing in the New Economy." BusinessMiami, Fall 2012.

Williams, Roger, Mark Weinheimer, and James Brooks. "Resilience in the Face of Foreclosures: Six Case Studies on Neighborhood Stabilization." National League of Cities, Center for Research & Innovation, 2011.

About the Author

Andre F. Shashaty is a writer, editor, and publisher with unique insight into America's housing markets and housing and urban policy. He has worked for publications in Cleveland, New York, San Francisco, and Washington, D.C., and has been published in The New York Times, The Washington Post, and many other national papers and periodicals.

Shashaty is president of the Partnership for Sustainable Communities, a nonprofit education and advocacy group that promotes new ideas for urban planning and housing development that contribute to social, economic, and environmental sustainability.

Previously, he was founder and owner of Affordable Housing Finance and Apartment Finance Today magazines and their related conferences, where he developed a nationwide following as a writer and commentator on housing issues. He was editor and publisher of these properties, in charge of editorial as well as marketing and sales. He sold them in 2006 and left the company in 2008.

Shashaty has won awards and national media recognition for his reporting on political corruption at the Department of Housing and Urban Development (HUD) under the administrations of Ronald Reagan and George W. Bush. In the 1980s, his exposé of influence peddling at HUD was widely quoted in the national media.

His series of articles about corruption and favoritism in contracting at HUD in 2007 won a Neal Award from American Business Media, among other awards. It was a finalist for the Grand Neal Award, the highest honor for business-to-business journalism in the United States.

He began writing about housing and community development in 1979 in Washington, D.C., covering Congress and the White House, and then spent six years in New York City, where he became editor-in-chief of a publication on commercial real estate.

Shashaty is an avowed urbanist and has enjoyed living in the central parts of Cleveland, Boston, Washington, D.C., and San Francisco as well as in Manhattan. He has traveled widely and is fascinated by the constant regeneration of culture, spirituality, and commerce found in the great cities of the world, including Barcelona, Istanbul, London, and Rome, to name a few.

About the Partnership for Sustainable Communities

The Partnership for Sustainable Communities (PSC) is a national 501(c)(3) nonprofit group that works at helping make American communities more economically, socially, and environmentally sustainable. PSC educates policymakers and opinion leaders about the critical role of affordable housing located near jobs and transportation to the sustainability of American communities. PSC also advocates for revitalization of existing neighborhoods, preservation of existing housing, and improved energy efficiency.

PSC provides information, news, research, and advocacy tools via its website (www.p4sc.org). PSC also produces a regular electronic newsletter for members.

If you care about housing affordability and urban revitalization, support PSC. It's only $45 to become a member for one year. For information, go to www.p4sc.org or call 415-453-2100 x 302. Donations are tax-deductible to the full extent allowed by law.

The Partnership for Sustainable Communities was founded in 2009, and is not affiliated with the federal government's interagency partnership of the same name. PSC is a private nonprofit that receives no government support.

Index

A

abandoned property, 7, 14, 16
Abramson, Jerry, 63, 83–84, 191
absentee landlords, 24–25
accessory dwelling units (ADUs), 94 134, 198–199
Advisory Commission on Regulatory Barriers to Affordable Housing, 194–196, 208, 217
Aetna Life & Casualty, 79
affordability gap, 42–43, 45, 54
Affordable Housing Land Trust Act, 129
African Americans, 16–18, 25, 43, 56, 215–217 228, 241
Agenda 21, 211
Alliance of Californians for Community Empowerment, 19
America's Rental Housing (Harvard), 45, 49
American Community Survey, 8, 47
American Dream Downpayment Program, 20, 157
American Enterprise Institute, 231
American Housing Survey (Census Bureau), 46, 181
American Public Transportation Association, 143
American Recovery and Reinvestment Act (2009), 159
Andrews, Nancy, 89, 121
anti-housing attitudes, 207–220
apartments, affordable, 85
Archives of Internal Medicine, 183
Arizona
    Phoenix, 59
assisted living, 182, 184
Astorino, Rob, 207
Atlanta Federal Reserve Bank, 205
Atlantic Richfield, 79
Augustin, Wilmina, 80

B

Bamford, Margret, 97
Bank of America, 13, 117–118
banks and banking, 223
    nononprofit
Barry, Tim, 126
Beck, Glenn, 211
Becker, Ralph, 35, 140
Benjamin, Stephen, 191
Bernanke, Ben, 222
Beyond Housing (nonprofit), 126–127

Bibby, Douglas, 50
Bidwell Training Center, 86
Bipartisan Policy Center, Housing Commission, 16, 62, 70–71, 92, 170, 195
blacks. See African Americans
Blackstone Group (firm), 24
blight, 6, 87
Bowen Homes, 106
BRIDGE Housing, 106
Broadcreek Renaissance (apartment complex), 80
Brooke, Edward, 241
Brookings Institution, 195
Brown, Eric, 189
Brown, Jerry, 172, 203–204
Budget Control Act (2011), 160, 163, 174
building codes, 134, 197, 202
building permits, 197–201
Bureau of Labor Statistics, 44
Bush, George H. W. (administration), 105, 156, 194–196, 208, 244–245
Bush, George W. (administration), 19–21, 39, 157, 168, 186, 244
Business and Professional People for the Public Interest, 15

C

California, 53, 60, 82, 119, 144–145, 172, 202–204, 210, 217
    Department of Transportation, 38
    Los Angeles, 143, 175, 188
    Los Angeles County, 38
    Northern, 41, 49, 213
    Ontario-Riverside area, 19
    Richmond, 18, 25
    Salinas, 60
    San Bernardino, 5, 19
    San Diego County, 39
    San Francisco, 49, 106, 165, 169, 197, 199, 211
    San Jose, 39, 58–59
    Silicon Valley
    Stockton, 3, 5, 19
California Environmental Quality Act (CEQA), 203
Calvert Foundation, 122
Carter, Jimmy (administration), 154–155, 189, 231
Carter, Michael, 98
Catholic Charities, 104
Census Bureau, 23
Censuses, 8
Centennial Place (housing development), 108–110
Center for American Progress, 24
Center for Budget and Policy Priorities, 61, 160
Center for Health Policy Research (UCLA), 60–61
Center for Responsible Lending, 14, 16, 17

chambers of commerce, 67
Charter School Financing Partnership, 119
Chicago Open Housing Movement, 246
children, 11, 29, 31–35, 43, 48, 64, 67–69, 71, 99–100, 238
Choice Neighborhoods program, 110–111, 114, 168
Cincotta, Gale, 115–117
Cisneros, Henry, 105
Clancy, Pat, 111–113
Clark Howell Homes (public housing development), 108
Clinton, Bill, 219–220
Clinton, Bill (administration), 105, 223, 231, 243
Clinton, Hillary, 219–220
Cohen, Rick, 187
Cohen-Esrey Real Estate Services, 51
college graduates, 58–59
Colorado, 33
    Denver, 109–113
    Denver Housing Authority, 103, 110–111
Commission on Affordable Housing and Health Facility Needs for Seniors in the
    21st C., 178, 184
Community Builders, The (nonprofit), 81, 111
community development, 80, 85–86, 103–104
Community Development Block Grants (CDBGs), 6, 83, 154, 156, 168, 185–190
community development financial institutions (CDFIs), 88–89, 115–116, 119–123, 131
Community for Creative Non-Violence, 37
Community Investment Note (Calvert Foundation), 122
community investments, 115–123
Community Preservation Development Corporation, 114
community redevelopment agencies, 172
Community Reinvestment Act (1977), 88, 116–118, 120, 123, 154, 230–232
Community Reinvestment Fund (firm), 119
community reinvestment movement, 115–123
commuter rail, 144
Confronting Suburban Poverty in America (Kneebone and Berube), 8
Congress, 6, 16, 30, 33, 36–37, 40, 224–226, 238–239
Community Development Block Grants, 186
Fair Housing Act (1968), 215
homeownership legislation, 159
housing policy, 68, 72
National Commission on Fiscal Responsibility and Reform, 190
Financial Crisis Inquiry Commission, 68
Joint Committee on Taxation, 166–167, 243
Joint Economic Committee, 68
Millennial Housing Commission, 65, 70, 156, 172
sequestration, 153–154, 160, 163–164
tax-credit legislation, 89, 92, 101
Connecticut, 22
    Glastonbury, 67–68
construction, 49, 51, 54, 66–67, 79, 82–84, 82–84, 92–96, 119, 141–145, 155,

155–169, 179–183, 194-203
Consumer Federation of America, 62
Consumer Financial Protection Bureau, 229
container homes, 135
Continental Illinois Bank, 79
CoreLogic, 21, 59
Cornett, Mick, 138
Countrywide Financial, 13, 157, 223
crime, 119
Cuomo, Andrew, 105, 219
Currier, Erin, 70

D

Delray Beach Community Land Trust, 128
Democrats, 113, 223
Department of Agriculture
Sec. 515 Rural Renting Housing program, 165
Department of Education, 11, 29–30, 238
Department of Health and Human Services, 37
Department of Housing and Urban Development (HUD), 30–32, 34–35, 88, 126, 146, 155, 164, 174, 187–188, 195, 215, 218–219, 243
Department of the Treasury, 88, 120, 129, 190
Department of Transportation, 146
Department of Veterans Affairs, 35, 98
deregulation, 227
Detroit-Hamtramck Assembly Plant (GM), 135
developers, 199–200, 205, 209, 213, 219–220
DHIC, Inc. (nonprofit), 85–86
disabled, 45, 87, 163, 178
disinvestment, 64, 185–191
DMA Development Co., 95–96
Dodd, Chris, 226
Dodd-Frank Wall Street Reform and Consumer Protection Act, 226, 228
Dolbeare, Cushing, 167
Dominium (firm), 93–94
Donovan, Shaun, 146–147
double bottom line, 88–89
Downs, Anthony, 64, 195–196, 204–205
DREAM Charter School, 98
Drew Charter School, 109, 112
Drug Abuse Foundation (Florida), 128
Duffield, Barbara, 34

E

E. M. Johnson (firm), 106
East Lake Foundation, 112
Economic Policy Institute, 56, 241

economic segregation, 70
education, 10–11, 34, 58, 67–68, 95–97, 99
educational facilities, 85–86
Egan, Conrad, 114
Eisenhower, Dwight (administration), 79
elderly, 45, 57, 87, 93, 177–184
Elderly Housing Development and Operations Corp., 180
Elizabeth Ann Seton, St., 95
Empire Center for Public Policy, Inc., 204
employment, 66–67
Energy Information Administration, 85
energy-efficiency, 41, 85, 202, 205
Enterprise Community Partners, 79–80, 105, 190, 218
Enterprise Foundation, 79
entitlements, 194
environmental impact studies, 194
environmental policy, 141–146
environmental pollution, 6
Environmental Protection Agency, 146, 196, 205
Environmental Quality Review (New York), 204
environmentalism, 145–146, 203–204
Envision Utah (nonprofit), 141, 148

F

Fair Housing Act (1968), 215, 218, 230, 240–242
Fair Share Housing Development (1986)
families, 29, 34–35, 213, 221–225
Fannie Mae, 20, 24, 52, 131, 133, 158–159, 168, 223–225, 230–232
Farr, Jessica LeVeen, 205–206
Federal Financial Institutions Examination Council, 117
Federal Home Loan Bank of Dallas, 97
Federal Housing Administration, 158
Federal Housing Administration (FHA), 129–132, 225–226
Federal Housing Finance Agency, 133, 168
Federal Reserve, 68
Federal Reserve Bank of Cleveland, 60
Federal Reserve Board, 115, 221–222, 232
Ferrer, Sarah, 127–129
Field Club (organization), 210
Field of Dreams (baseball fields; East Harlem, NY), 99
Financial Crisis Inquiry Commission, 232
financing, 96–97, 111, 116, 209
Fink, David, 67–68
Fischer, Greg, 84
flipping, 24–25
Florida, 172
    Delray Beach, 127–129
    Hialeah, 188
    Homestead, 15

Jacksonville, 164
Miami, 8, 47, 180
Oldsmar, 213–214
Ford Foundation, 79
foreclosures, 3, 5, 8–9, 13–15, 17, 22–23, 31, 59, 63–64, 68, 95, 132–133, 157, 221–233
foster care, 32, 35
Frank, Barney, 226
Freddie Mac, 20, 24, 52, 133, 158–159, 168, 224–225, 230–232
Free School, 95

G

Garcia, Rosalinda, 41
Garfield, Barbara, 27
General Motors, 135
Georgia
    Atlanta, 15, 25, 106, 109, 143–144
    Atlanta Housing Authority, 107
    Lawrenceville, 15
Glaeser, Edward L., 198
Glover, Renee, 107–108
Goldman Sachs, 118
Gorman & Co., Inc., 94–95
Government Accountability Office, 23
government housing assistance, 45
government regulations, 193–206, 209, 223, 226–227
government-sponsored enterprises (GSEs), 224
Great Recession, 4–5, 7, 55
green building requirements, 202
Green, Gordon, 43
greenhouse gas emissions, 85, 87, 211–212
Grove at Cary Park, The (housing development), 85
Guerrero, Ismael, 104, 110

H

Haas Institute for a Fair and Inclusive Society (UC Berkeley), 22
Habitat for Humanity, 52, 103, 136
Hambley, Steven, 7
Harlem RBI (educational services org.), 99
Harris, R. Lee, 51
Harvey, Bart, 218
Hawaii, 53
    Kona, 96
Hawaii Business magazine, 96
health care, 35, 71
Hear US (nonprofit), 31
Helbig, Deborah, 92
Heritage Park Senior Village, 179

high-rise buildings, 107, 148
Hill, Luther, 28
Hispanics, 16, 25, 43, 104, 217, 228
Holeywell, Ryan, 188
Hollier, Dennis, 96
Hollywood Community Housing Corp., 175
Home Affordable Modification Program (HAMP), 132–133
HOME funds, 97
HOME Investment Partnerships Program, 127, 156, 165, 168
Home Mortgage Disclosure Act (1975), 116–117
home prices, 8, 14, 59
homeless and emergency shelters, 28, 32, 34, 39–40
homelessness, 10–11, 71
     chronic, 35
     cost of to public, 38
     definition of, 32–33
     monitoring methods, 31
homeownership, 3, 57, 59–60, 125–134, 221
homeownership tax credit, 61
HOPE VI program, 81, 84, 103, 105–110, 113–114, 168–169
hospitalization, 71, 183
Housing Act (1959), 177
housing agencies, 201
Housing and Urban Development Act (1968), 154
housing assistance myth, 166–167
Housing Choice Voucher program, 82, 126, 163–164, 172–174
housing counseling, 127
housing density, 145, 196, 203
"housing first" approach, 40
housing innovation, 135–138
Housing Opportunities for People Everywhere (HOPE) program. *See* Hope
     VI program
Housing Partnership Network, 119, 133
Housing Partnership, Inc., 84
Housing Vacancy Survey (Census Bureau), 59
Hurricane Katrina, 21, 92

I

Illinois
     Chicago, 14, 25, 115
     Cook County, 13
     Naperville, 31
Illinois
     Cabrini-Green project, 212–213
     Carpentersville, 15
     Chicago, 212–213
     Chicago Housing Authority, 106, 246
inclusionary zoning, 136–138
incomes *vs.* transportation costs, 139

individual development accounts (IDAs), 127
infill development, 145
infrastructure, 191
infrastructure regulations, 199–200
innovation, 135–148
Insight Center for Community Economic Development, 60
Institute for Children, Poverty & Homelessness, 31
Integral of Atlanta (firm), 110
Interagency Council on Homelessness, 36
Internal Revenue Code, 166
Internal Revenue Service, 156
International Harvester, 79
investing in communities, 115–123
Invitation Homes, 24
It's a Wonderful Life (film), 230–231

J

Jacoby, Jeff, 231
job creation, 65–67, 95, 119
John Stewart Co., 106–113
Johnson, James, 223
Johnson, Lyndon (administration), 7, 88, 154, 160, 215, 240, 248
Joint Center for Housing Studies (Harvard), 8–9, 14, 17, 24, 42, 44–45, 47, 165, 170–174 219, 222, 226, 228
Jonathan Rose Cos., 99
Joseph, Laverne, 178, 182–183

K

Kaiser, Edgar, 70
Kansas
Overland Park, 51
Salina, 67
Keller, Robin, 181–182
Kemp, Jack, 126, 193, 195
Kennedy, Robert F., 248
Kentucky
    Frankfort, 83
    Jefferson County, 84
    Louisville, 63, 84, 126, 191
King, Martin Luther, Jr., 215, 238–239, 246, 248
Krehmeyer, Chris, 126

L

land use, 143–147, 196–197, 203, 210–211
Lauver, Dennis, 67
Lawrence, Ethel R., 216–217
lawsuits, 210

learning disabilities, 33–34
Levi Strauss & Co., 79
Lewis, Corinne, 163–164
Lincoln Institute of Land Policy, 129
Local Initiatives Support Corp., 79–80
Lokahi Apartments, 96
Los Angeles riots (1965), 238
Louisiana
    New Orleans, 188
Louisville Affordable Housing Trust Fund, Inc., 84
Louisville Housing Development Corp., 84
Low-Income Housing tax credits (LIHTCs), 79, 91–93, 166–167, 187

M

Maeva, Makani, 96
Manchester Craftsmen's Guild, 86
manufactured housing, 132–134
Manufactured Housing Institute, 134
Mariposa (apartment complex), 103–105, 113, 168
Marshside Village (apartment complex), 177
Martinez, Julianna, 27
Maryland, 53
Maryland, 22, 53
    Baltimore, 14
    Columbia, 79
    Montgomery County, 136–137
    Prince George's County, 15, 189
Massachusetts, 119, 131, 137–138, 218
    Boston, 10, 111, 47, 84, 138, 198–199, 240
    Boston (Innovation District), 58
    eastern, 198
    Fall River, 10
    Gateway cities, 10
    Dorchester, 142
    Smart Growth Zoning Overlay District Act, 137–138
MassHousing (finance agency), 131
Matkom, Ted, 94
McCormack Baron Salazar (firm), 110
McKenney-Vento Homeless Assistance Act, 37
McKinney, Stewart, 36–37
McLaughlin, Gayle, 18
Medicaid, 72, 183–184
Medicare, 72
Meeks, Gregory, 18
Meeting Our Nation's Housing Challenges (Bipartisan Millennial
    Housing Commission), 156
Menino, Thomas, 84, 142
Mercy Housing, 71
Michigan, 30, 92

Battle Creek, 97–98
Detroit, 5, 14, 135
Taylor, 178
Michigan State Housing Development Authority, 98
Michigan Urban Farming Initiative, 135
Millennial Housing Commission, 65, 70, 156
millennials, 55–62
Minnesota, 119
St. Paul, 93–94
Minnesota
Minneapolis-St. Paul, 93–94, 163
minorities, 16–20, 159, 228, 242
Missouri
St. Louis, 126
Mitchell, Silver,
mixed-income communities, 104–105, 108–114, 125, 137, 211–212
Model Cities program, 154
modular housing, 133–134
Morial, Mark H., 225
mortgage financing, 20, 24–25, 126–127, 220–231, 156–158, 246
Mortgage Resolution Fund, 133
mortgage revenue bonds (MRBs), 130–131
mortgages, 15–18, 22–25
Mozilo, Angelo R., 223
Murray, Liz Ryan, 17

N

National Advisory Commission on Civil Disorders, 238, 241
National Apartment Association, 50, 66, 158
National Association for the Education of Homeless Children and Youth, 34
National Association of Homebuilders, 66
National Association of Realtors, 129
National Center for Education Statistics, 59
National Center for Housing and Child Welfare, 30
National Center on Family Homelessness, 30, 33
National Church Residences, 179
National Commission on Fiscal Responsibility and Reform, 190
National Community Reinvestment Coalition, 118
National Community Stabilization Trust, 133
National Council of State Housing Agencies, 91–92, 130
National Housing Act (1949), 154
National Housing Conference, 139, 261
National Housing Institute, 71
National Housing Preservation Database, 171
National Housing Trust Fund, 168, 246
National League of Cities, 5, 186
National Low Income Housing Coalition, 53, 167, 261
National Multifamily Housing Council, 50, 66, 145, 158
National People's Action (organization), 17, 115–116

National Urban League, 225
Native Americans, 156
Natural Resources Defense Council, 145
Naughton, Carol R., 112
NCB Capital Impact (firm), 119
Neal, Richard, 120
Nebraska
    Omaha, 210
negative equity, 21
Neighborhood Stabilization Program (NSP), 16
NeighborWorks America, 125, 127
Nevada, 23
    Las Vegas, 3
New Hampshire
    Concord, 131–132
New Hampshire Community Loan Fund, 131–132
New Jersey, 22, 53, 119, 218
    Mount Laurel, 216–217
New Markets tax credits, 88, 120, 189–191
New York, 22, 67, 119, 183
    Albany, 204
    Chappaqua, 219–220
    East Harlem, 99
    New York City, 30, 198
    New York City Housing Authority, 107
    Westchester County, 207, 213, 218–219
Nicoson, Buddy, 62
Nilan, Diane, 31
NIMBY (Not in my back yard), 81–82, 85,208, 210, 215, 217
Nixon, Richard (administration), 154, 189
non-defense discretionary programs, 160, 173
Nonprofit Quarterly, 187
North Beach Place (housing complex), 106, 113
North Carolina
    2020 Affordable Housing Plan, 85
    Cary, 84
    Charlotte, 13
    Durham, 13, 140
    Raleigh, 147–148
Northcott Neighborhood House, 95
Northeast Ohio Sustainable Communities Consortium, 6
Northern California Community Loan Fund (NCCLF), 122
Northside Housing Initiative, 95
nursing care, 183

O

O'Malley, Sean, Cardinal, 142
O'Malley, Martin, 129
Obama, Barack (administration), 39, 116, 146, 153, 160, 226, 242

Ohio
    Akron, 188
    Cincinnati, 118–119
    Cincinnati Center City Development Corp.
    Cleveland, 14
    Columbus, 179
    Medina County, 7
    northeastern, 148
    Youngstown, 7, 47
Oklahoma
    Oklahoma City, 138–140
Olympic Games (Atlanta, 1996), 107–108
"opting out" (of housing programs)
Oregon
    Portland, 43
Oregon Office of Economic Analysis, 43

P

Pagett, Betty, 82–83
parents supporting adult children, 55, 59
Park Duvalle (housing development), 84
Partnership for Strong Communities, 67
Partnership for Sustainable Communities, 146
patient money grants, 89
Patrick, Deval, 137
Pawlowski, Ed, 185–186
Pay for Success (PFS) financing model, 116
Pennsylvania, 22
    Allentown, 185–186, 188
    Pittsburgh, 14, 86, 147–148
PLANPGH (planning approach), 147
Perry, Egbert L. J., 110
Pew Research Center, 70, 219
Plepler, Andrew, 117
Plusquellic, Donald L., 187–188
political participation, 143–145
population growth, 6–7
poverty, 7–8, 37, 43, 219
President's Committee on Urban Housing (Kaiser Commission), 70
private market housing, 171–173
Project 180 (Oklahoma City), 180, 139–140
property taxes, revenues from, 4
property values, 4, 17–18, 42, 83, 181
Protulis, Steve, 180
Prudential Insurance Co., 79
public housing agencies, 103–114, 164–165
public participation, 210
public services, 39
public transportation, 86, 139, 144, 148

public-private partnerships, 92
Purpose Built Communities, 112

Q

Quality Growth Strategy (Utah), 141

R

racial discrimination, 16–17, 215–219, 237–242, 249–253
RAND Corp., 69, 136
Rather, Dan, 212–213
Raza Development Fund (firm), 119
Re-Emergence of Concentrated Poverty (Brookings Institution), 7–8
Reagan, Ronald (administration), 28, 91, 155, 227
RealtyTrac, 15
Reconnecting Massachusetts Gateway Cities (Forman), 10
redlining, 230
Regulation and the Rise of Housing Prices in Greater Boston (Glaeser et al.), 198
Reinvestment Fund, The (firm), 119
Reinvestment Partners (advocacy group), 13
Rental Assistance Demonstration, 114
Republicans, 6, 113, 126, 155, 185–186
Residential Energy Consumption Survey, 85
Resolution Trust Corp., 227
Retirement Housing Foundation, 178
revenue sharing programs, 189
revitalization, 66–67, 79, 93–94, 104, 138–140, 189
revitalization of cities, 138–140
Richman Group, 105
Rodriguez, Marietta, 125
Rogier, Mary A., 122
Rohr, Debbie, 60
Rose, Jonathan, 99
Rouse, James, 77–78, 77–79, 89, 248
Rouse, Patty, 79
rural areas, 156

S

Samsung Austin Semiconductor (firm), 62
Sard, Barbara, 167
Sasha Bruce Youthwork, 34
Schmidt Artist Lofts (housing complex), 94
Schmidt, Elizabeth, 177, 180
schools (K-12), 29, 67–69, 108
Sec. 202 housing, 177–184
Sec. 202 program (new construction), 165, 167
Sec. 515 Rural Rental Housing program, 165
Sec. 8 housing, 101, 171, 174

Sec. 8 moderate-rehabilitation influence-peddling scandal, 155
Sec. 8 project-based rental assistance, 154–156, 179
Section 202 program
Section 811 housing, 178
securitization, 225–226, 231
segregation, 241
Sentier Research, 43
sequestration, 159–160, 163
Seton Home (housing development), 95–97
Shelterforce magazine, 71
Shore, Debby, 34
Sierra Club, 145
Silver Star Apartments, 98
Silver, Mitchell, 147–148
single mothers, 47, 81, 95–97
single parents, 45
single-room occupancy (SRO) hotels, 182
Skillern, Peter, 13
Slemmer, Thomas, 179, 182–183
Small Business Jobs Act (2010), 123
Smart Growth Zoning Overlay District Act (Mass.), 137–138
Snyder, Mitch, 37
Social Security, 177–178, 181
social services, 35
South Carolina
    Columbia, 191
South Lincoln Homes (housing development), 103, 113
Spano, Andrew J., 207, 218
Spitzer, Eliot, 20
sprawl, 6
St. Joseph's Academy, 95
State of the Nation's Housing (Harvard), 8–9, 22–23, 43, 170, 182
state-subsidized housing programs, 91–114, 129–131, 156, 164–165, 172, 209, 219
Stewart, John, 49, 113
Stone-Dino, Tracy, 85
Strickland, Bill, 86–87
Substance Abuse and Mental Health Services Administration
    Homelessness Resource Center, 37
suburbs, 72
Supportive Housing for Persons with Disabilities program (Sec. 811), 178
sustainable communities strategies (Calif.), 144–145
Sutton, Betty, 188

T

tax credit developments, 93–95, 100–101
tax credits, 166
tax incentives, 190
Tax Reform Act (1986), 156
Techwood Homes (public housing development), 108

teenage mothers, 95–97

Teixeira, Mark, 99–100

Terwilliger Center for Housing (ULI), 228

Terwilliger, Ron, 52, 228

Texas
    Austin, 3, 58, 62
    Dallas, 30
    El Paso, 47
    Houston, 5, 197
    Metro Dallas Homeless Alliance, 30
    San Antonio, 95–97

Trapp, Shel, 115–117

Trillion Dollar Apartment Industry (NMHC), 50, 66

Truman, Harry (administration), 154, 160

U

U.S. Administration on Aging, 181

U.S. Conference of Mayors, 3–5, 187, 191

U.S. Green Building Council, 145

U.S. Tax Code (1986), 91, 155

Underwater America (Haas Instiute), 22

unemployment, 5, 55–56, 95

United Nations, 211

Urban Development Action Grant (UDAG) program, 189

Urban Institute, 6, 169

Urban Land Institute, 145

Urban Renewal program, 154

Utah
    Salt Lake City, 35
    Wasatch Front, 140–142

V

Veltkamp, Marvin D., 98

veterans, 35–367 92, 97–99, 210–211

Villages of East Lake (apartment complex), 109, 112

violence, 33, 48

Virginia
    Alexandria, 179
    Arlington County, 143
    Richmond, 114
    Norfolk, 80

VitusGroup

Volcker, Paul, 115

Volunteers of America (organization), 178–179, 181, 210

W

Wal-Mart Stores, 43–44

Wallace, Steven P., 60
War on Poverty, 88
Warren, Greg, 86
Washington, 22
Washington Metropolitan Area Transit Authority, 143
Washington, D.C., 28–29, 34, 36–37, 53
Ways & Means program, 111
Wells Fargo Bank, 118
Where Do We Go from Here: Chaos or Community? (King), 242
White, Eleanor, 137
White, Ruth, 30
Williams, Lawrence, 165
Wilson Co., 213
Winn, Philip D., 155
Wisconson
    Milwaukee, 94
Woodstock Institute, 14
workforce housing, 62, 84, 87, 113, 167

Y

Yellen, Janet, 65, 222
Youth on Record (nonprofit), 104
youths, 111

Z

zero carbon policy, 202
Zigas, Barry, 62
Zillow Home Value Index, 8, 23
zombie properties, 13–14
zoning
    codes, 194, 196–197, 200
    commissions, 201
    exclusionary, 69
    inclusionary, 136–138
    policy, 134

Epilogue

"Urban decay? What are you talking about? American cities are doing great right now."

That's one of the comments I received in response to the advance publicity for this book. I can understand why that person was confused.

If you were to visit downtown San Francisco, you'd see construction happening on a large scale, including office buildings, high-rise condos, and much more. The social networking, gaming and other high-tech businesses are booming. The highly paid execs and software wonks are buying million-dollar condos and eating at steakhouses that charge $90 for four ounces of meat.

However, if you drive a few miles from the high tech precincts, you can visit Bayview-Hunters Point or Richmond, which is across the San Francisco Bay, and find a much different story. To put it mildly, they are not thriving.

A person who confines himself to the bustling parts of our cities could be excused for thinking everything is just peachy. But denying the existence of concentrated poverty, blight, and disinvestment in other areas is a form of ignorance that can be very dangerous.

The person who made the comment above may simply have a narrow world view. But I fear that some people actively wish to obscure the truth about the wide divergence of fortunes in our cities and now, increasingly, in our suburbs as well. That's a major part of my motivation for writing this book, even if the message is inconvenient to some.

The comment above moves me to repeat a quote from the National Advisory Commission on Civil Disorders, which examined the reasons for the riots in 1965, 1966, and 1967. It said:

"Our nation is moving toward two societies, one black, one white—separate and unequal. Segregation and poverty have created in the racial ghetto a destructive environment totally unknown to most white Americans."

It's been close to 50 years since that was written. Is it still true? It's very important that we all look beyond our own circle of people and places and ask ourselves that simple question.

Andre F. Shashaty,
August 1, 2014